INCIDENT IN ROME

The last shot of World War II had died, but it had not buried with it the bitterness and the deep feeling of revenge of two people whose lives had been cruelly changed by a single, bloody coup — the strange incident on the Belinoro Road.

Now, twelve years later, these two people, the beautiful Antonella and the famous ex-lieutenant Tom Linden met again at a sidewalk café in Rome —Doney's. And they were strangely pulled together by the memory of the night of the Belinoro disaster, of their abandoned passion, and of the vision to pay back a debt of life and death.

THE FLAGS AT DONEY by HARRIS GREENE combines the breathless excitement of underground adventure and the fury of romantic intrigue, set against the splendid majesty of modern Rome.

THE FLAGS
AT DONEY

HARRIS GREENE

▲
PYRAMID BOOKS • NEW YORK

To
TIM SELDES
Who Knew What He Wanted

THE FLAGS AT DONEY

A PYRAMID BOOK
Published by arrangement with Doubleday and Company, Inc.

PRINTING HISTORY
Doubleday edition published October, 1964
Pyramid edition published November, 1965

Library of Congress Catalog Card Number 64-19252

Printed in the United States of America

PYRAMID BOOKS are published by Pyramid Publications, Inc.
444 Madison Avenue, New York, New York 10022, U.S.A.

chapter one

AT THE EDGE of the darkened village where the pavement of the main street ended, a cluster of silent figures dispersed into two parallel columns, each following the verges of the wide dirt road. They moved slowly, almost painfully, as the raw wet wind slanted into their faces, and they leaned into it as if it could support them in their forward movement. Except for two men in the middle of each file, all were armed. A tall, lean man, face submerged in the hood of a parka, detached himself from the lead of one of the columns and stood in the middle of the road watching the bulkily clad figures moving past him. Some of them bore heavy rucksacks on their shoulders, and he made an occasional gesture to speed them on, such as a busy traffic policeman might do to a lagging motorist. His squinting eyes missed nothing; he noted with satisfaction the silence of the marchers—the minimum of clanking, jingling and other dangerous noises—and the good ten-foot interval between each of the figures. When the last had passed him, he waved briefly at two men moving cautiously behind the columns in the middle of the soggy road; there was a dull glint of their automatic weapons as each of them waved back. He then turned and loped down the road, his high-laced boots spattering through puddles as he passed through the files until he reached their head.

As the two lines of men reached a high, massive wall on their left which fronted the village cemetery, a solid figure in the lead held up one hand. Both files bumped to a halt behind him. Well ahead, two figures also obediently stopped and squatted where they were at the road's edges, cradling their weapons in their hands. The tall, hooded form moved quickly toward the man who had given the "halt" signal until he was virtually touching the face of the other in the wet blackness. Their eyes met in a glance that was both a familiarity and a challenge. The tall man spoke first, in an impatient, foreign-flavored Italian.

"Why do we stop here, Tonio? We have scarcely left Belinoro behind us."

The square old face relaxed briefly in a wry, amused smile, but the round dark eyes above a bushy gray mustache were alert with concern.

"I want to check with each of my people at this point, dear Major: the rear guard and then each of the men; the weapons, their boots, their instructions. Here I check everything, to make sure that each understands his assignment. It is one thing for them to prattle by heart the instructions while still around the warm cellar table, and quite another thing to remember them now out here in a howling night like this. It will take but five minutes."

His words were reassuring, but the expression on his face belied them. The tall figure said nothing and squatted in his place as Tonio turned and moved heavily but quickly away to the rear. A chilling mist twisted across the road from the darkened fields, and by the time Tonio had clumped a dozen yards, he was swallowed up in the blackness. He shortly re-emerged, shuttling from one side of the road to the other. He then moved with deliberate steps ahead to the two figures in their scout positions. Finally he returned to hunker down beside the major in the slanting rain.

"Everyone understands his job," he growled. "Their weapons are protected against the rain. Those in the center carrying the explosives complain that their loads will be very difficult to carry since the road is becoming a quagmire, and so I have redistributed their grenades to the others."

"Good," grunted the tall man, flexing his already cold fingers inside the knitted gloves. "Let's start for the railroad, then. We have seven kilometers to march, three of them on the road, four on the path from Arpegno, and we should be there within two hours . . ."

He stopped, sensing that the older man had something further to say.

"Fausto is uneasy," Tonio said slowly, nodding his head at one of the advance scouts squatting almost invisible ahead of them. "He knows these hills and fields since birth, and he has the nose of a hunting dog. He says that there is movement somewhere off to the left of the road. What it is he does not know. Possibly a lost animal or a shepherd or even perhaps a wolf or two. He asked permission to leave Tullio, who is with him, on the road and to take a quick look alone." The calm eyes of the old man looked into the tense face so close to him, and he took in the pulsing jaw and the stubborn line of the

6

younger man's lips, knowing the reason for the agitation.

"I told him to do so. The fields rise on both sides of the road ahead, and, you remember, we have been warned that German anti-partisan patrols are in this region."

Fausto, only a dim square shape through the rain-driven mist, rose from the road ahead, moved to the left into the fields, and disappeared.

"Tonio," the major said, an edge of exasperation in his voice, "Fausto and his friend looked over this route not three hours ago, is that not so? They scouted the road and verges as far as the little cluster of houses of Arpegno halfway to the railroad line and found nothing. Is that not also so?"

"True, dear Major," Tonio answered, looking at the protruding butt of the major's pistol in its shoulder holster, "but much can happen in three hours."

"As for the warning, Tonio, you know well that we have received such warnings before. There are always those who howl calamity. The Germans come and go, but hardly in such weather."

His voice rose to a thin, steely pitch, and in a nervous gesture the major peered at the luminous dial of his watch. "We are already half an hour behind schedule, and in this storm it will be damned difficult to reach the bridge, set the charges, and come away before dawn even without delays. Now we are delaying some more."

The tough old face stared impassively back at him.

"When Fausto is uneasy, Major, I am uneasy," Tonio rejoined. His frosted breath plumed as he spoke, and the rain now pelted down in doubled fury. Tonio glanced pityingly at the huddled figures on the road behind them, and the major, biting his lips under the parka hood, also turned to stare at them.

"Look at them, Tonio, they'll all be waterlogged and exhausted before we even reach Arpegno and the mountain path."

Tonio looked away in the direction Fausto had vanished, and he nodded his head under the tight black beret in agreement.

"Yes, I know."

"That bridge," the other spoke through gritted teeth, "must be blown."

Tonio smiled at the grim intensity of the other.

"The bridge; must it be blown tonight?"

The other nodded vigorously under his wet parka hood.

"Tonight. The battles to the south depend on it. German

reinforcements and supplies are flowing south by railroad to the front. We have got to help stop that flow. It will take them days to repair, given its location. There is a great battle raging near the Monte Cassino abbey, Tonio, and the Germans are holding there."

Tonio nodded, blunt mustache glistening in the downpour. "Ah yes, Monte Cassino; I visited there once. The Benedictines have a lovely abbey there on the very crest of the mountain. What a magnificent view of the Liri Valley!"

The American major shook his head with vexation. Here they stood in a bog of a country road at midnight in the hills of German-occupied North Central Italy, and old Tonio reminisced about Monte Cassino. Good Lord, there was a time and a place for everything! But he bit his tongue and was silent because the old man was touchy—a tough, loyal old Italian with deep pride and vanity. How could he explain to this little oak of a man that defeatism, like rot, was turning the entire mission into a washout. Nothing but failures and mishaps since they arrived. Dammit, no one was going to bring his show to the ground, ever! If this railroad bridge blew, and they did the job well, a principal German line of communication from Bologna south to Rome and to the Gothic Line would be cut and, in this kind of weather, stay cut for days. The Brindisi base, and Allied Forces Headquarters, would then realize what he could do by himself, with only an old ex-Bersagliere and eleven local partisans to help him. But to do this job he would have to end Tonio's musings about the Benedictines and his qualms about unidentified movements in the fields and orchards beyond, and push on across two hills to where the railroad winds south from Bologna through the valleys of the Central Apennines. God, what a job it was to convince these local bennies to get along with something vital, something that might shorten the war!

He pointed down the road which disappeared into the blackness ahead of them.

"*Avanti*, Tonio? Shall we put another nail in Mussolini's coffin?"

Tonio listened to the wind sighing through the silence and finally nodded slowly.

"*Va bene, avanti!* But you must kill the devil before you nail him in his coffin. *'M beh*, one thing at a time; first, your precious bridge. You Americans! Such monomaniacs!"

Tonio splashed slowly to the center of the road, raised his hand and pointed forward. Like two sluggish earthworms, the twin knots of men re-formed, and the two lines moved ahead again, with Tonio and the major leading the column on the left. The rain now became a torrent and beat down on them with a fury that slowed their pace and hunched their shoulders. Tonio's face had no protection from the downpour, but his great black cape covered him almost to his knees, and his sturdy mountain boots below the corduroy knickers slogged through the mud in the effortless motion of a native of the hills. The remaining scout had again disappeared from sight although he was but fifty feet ahead.

The road leveled and entered a deepening defile so that only a tall man walking through could see over the sides into the fields in either direction. Tonio suddenly reached for the major's arm, and they stopped abruptly. As the major opened his mouth to ask, Tonio's gloved hand came up to his lips. On the other side of the road, the man at the head of the parallel file also halted, gave a signal, and both columns again sank to their haunches without a sound.

A silence, broken only by the soughing of the tormented wind, settled on the band, and then a dry chirping sound, faint but distinct, cut through the inky night ahead of them.

"Fausto," Tonio breathed in the major's ear. "Two cicada chirps. Warning signal."

They crouched, sodden and chilled, for a long minute. Then a sound of steps pounding from ahead reached them. Both the major and Tonio drew their pistols and aimed them at the empty road ahead. Alongside and behind them, there was a metallic snickering or rifle and sten-gun bolts, as a single figure lurched toward them.

"Don't shoot! It's me, Tullio!" The advance scout shouted hoarsely as he rocked up out of the mist to them.

"What in the name of God are you doing, Tullio?" Tonio rapped, bunching his fingers at the man in a furious interrogation.

A young, thin-faced peasant clad in the ruins of an Italian uniform with his old, wide-brimmed slouch hat well over his eyes pulled up in front of Tonio, carrying his sten gun at his side like a valise.

"*Dottore!* There is a dead man in the middle of the road ahead! A dead German soldier! He is lying face up in the road!"

Before Tonio could answer, a half-dozen men had broken ranks to cluster around him asking urgent questions and descriptions.

"Get back to your places, you idiots!" Tonio hissed at them.

"What are you, a bunch of sheep gathering around a clump of grass? Get back there in your files!"

The major looked inquiringly at him as his men reluctantly slouched back to their places.

"This is bad business," Tonio told him. "If a German soldier has been killed up here, the SS will raze Belinoro to the ground and shoot its inhabitants. This they have done elsewhere in this zone all winter long. We must bury him immediately in a shallow grave in a secluded place off the road, difficult for the Germans to find. Then we can come back and dig a deeper grave tomorrow, or else bury him quietly in the cemetery."

The major again looked at his watch.

"No. No time. We are already half an hour behind and we are losing time as we stand here. Let's move ahead to the place where the body lies, and a couple of your men can carry it into the fields. We can cover it with grass and a bit of earth, and return tomorrow. No time now to dig at all." He turned to Tullio.

"You are certain that he is dead?"

Tullio's thin, stubbled face creased in a lopsided grin.

"Oh, he is dead all right, signore. Come and see for yourself."

Tonio gave the advance signal and the whole band surged forward again, their previous orderly double file now disintegrated into a single loose mass filling the entire width of the road. The major looked behind him at the broken ranks with dismay, but he said nothing, hurrying behind Tullio until they reached the center of the defile where sloping grass walls hemmed in the road completely.

"Here!" Tullio pointed proudly at a long, narrow, mud-splashed mound in the center of the road. A white face, eyes closed and lolling slightly to one side, glowed obscenely up out of the mud at them, a *landser* cap still rammed on the head. On the soaked collars of the uniformed dead German they made out the dread, runic SS. Each one of the band, except for the two of the rear guard who halted a few yards away, came up to have a brief look at the dead German. One, observing the SS insignia, spat on the sodden body. In little circles, they murmured to each other.

"A corporal of the SS. This means that the anti-partisan patrols are up and about here," Tonio said, looking at the dead face with its mouth agape.

The major answered with barely suppressed fury:

"And now, perhaps, we shall hold a vigil for him, complete

with candles? Call the priest? Measure him for a coffin? In the name of God, Tonio, are we going to turn around and go back to our beds because someone has killed a German SS man? Do we want to finish this war and get rid of Fascism, or not?"

"Yes, to your last question. But I told you this dead German can mean disaster to my entire village, if we let him lie here and the Germans or the Fascists discover him. It would be stupid to try to reach the bridge and blow it, if their mad dogs come up here and wipe us out with all our families. We are patriots, Major, but we are also men with families and homes here. And so we must bury this one carefully in the fields before we move." He spoke in a manner that brooked no further argument, but the major grasped his wet cape at the arm.

"Tonio, I plead with you: let's move on to destroy the bridge. We can dispose of this body later when . . ."

"Pick him up!" Tonio told the two men nearest him, as if he had not heard the major. "Wrap his head and carry him in his greatcoat. We return to the cemetery immediately!" His deep voice crackled at the mass of men now standing in a disorganized circle around him as a crowd stands around a street-corner orator. He looked around at the officer, and in laborious English, so that the others would not understand, he said to him, "I am sorry. The mission is aborted. Your bridge will not be blown by us tonight. There are too many things wrong: The warnings, this rain which will make the paths treacherous and the blowing of the bridge almost impossible, the noises in the fields, and now this dead German. I am sorry for our lack of success once again, Major, but we must go back. All of these men are my friends. Two are members of my own family. I do not intend to risk them tonight. We will try again another time soon."

"Tonio . . ." the Major began ominously, but the square little man shook his head and grasped the sleeve of the major at the bicep.

"No, dear Major, I have decided. Your battle at Monte Cassino will have to be won without the destruction of the bridge beyond Arpegno. We are returning to Belinoro." The round brown eyes reflected stern sympathy.

"I know what a disappointment we have been to you, dear Major. I appreciate your zeal in striking blows at the Germans and the Fascists and your support of my group as against the other partisans of this zone." He paused, watching his men wrap the head of the dead German in a wet scarf and their preparations to carry the corpse on a rough stretcher using two rifles.

"Perhaps we are the wrong group to be helping," Tonio continued, not flinching from the hot stare of the other. "Perhaps the Communists, the *Garibaldini*, would be more eager to blow your bridge. Those of them in this zone have no families or children to think about. They come from distant places: Bologna, Rimini, Florence. But we must live here, Major, and while I do not care for myself, the others are young and full of strength, and I do not want to see them die because of my mistakes in destroying your bridge. *Capito?*"

The major stared at him, his eyes filled with reproach and anger. Then he turned to the half-circle of soaked, laden men gathered around them, and he pulled back the hood of his parka so they could see his soft overseas hat with its gold-leaf insignia and his face and eyes.

"Re-form in your positions," he told them. "We advance to the bridge as planned." Tonio immediately stepped in front of the tall American, and even in the blackness the men could sense his rage.

"We do *not* advance to the bridge," he shouted at them. "Re-form, and we return to Belinoro cemetery bearing the dead German with us. *I* command here. Quickly, now! Face about and return! Ettore and Lullo, pick up this dead man and carry him. Give the others your rifles!"

The clustered figures clung together in stunned surprise for a moment, unwilling to understand that they had heard two contradictory commands within a matter of seconds. The major whirled Tonio around and grasped him roughly at the elbows in a half-intimidating embrace. Tonio freed himself, and his right hand touched his revolver butt in its open holster menacingly.

"You, who are a military man, must live by your own rules! Who are you to usurp my control over my men? How dare you give orders here! If you were not my friend . . ."

But the tall major with the deep eyes pounded a fist into his open palm no more than a few inches from the other's bluff face, and his words were choked with frustration.

"That bridge, Tonio, must be blown! You and your group have done nothing, nothing, nothing, since we came here! You told me when I arrived that you would make any sacrifice to strike at the Fascists! Well, tonight we strike, and tonight you've got to make good on your willingness to make sacrifices!"

The old Italian stared at him, and the corners of his mouth twitched as if he were going to laugh out loud. Instead, he turned on his heel and splashed over to Tullio who stood at the edge of the slowly re-forming group looking out at the darkness ahead.

"Where is Fausto?" Tonio asked the gaunt lookout.

"He's still out there, Dottore," Tullio muttered. "He told me to warn you of the body, and then he moved out to the left of the road. I hope he hasn't fallen in some damned hole in this rain and dark."

"If there are holes out there, Fausto knows where they are," Tonio told him. "Move out there and give him your signal."

"We go back?" Tullio asked hopefully. "We return to Belinoro?"

"Yes, my lion-hearted one, we go back to Belinoro. Now go out ahead and get him back. We move in three minutes."

Order had now returned to the road. The crude litter for the dead German was almost ready, and the rough twin files silently waited, headed now in the direction from which they had come. The faces of the partisans reflected mingled emotions: irritation and frustration at having ventured into the chill, biting rain for yet another abortive raid, relief that soon they would be home and dry without the dangers and the tense exertions of the mission originally planned and rehearsed. The tall major stood alone. He seemed oblivious to them, and he stared into the darkness with one hand on the butt of his shoulder holster strapped outside his parka, as if he were no longer part of the band.

They waited. The men shuffled nervously as they looked at their leader standing motionless, head slightly turned to where Tullio had disappeared in the darkness. Only the whistle of the wind through the naked, dripping trees and bushes high above them on either side of the road intruded on the uneasy silence.

Then from above them a hoarse voice shouted, "Friends! Attention! Ambush!"

A dry shot rang out, and the body of Fausto hurtled in a tumbling heap from the steep sloping embankment above them. No one on the road had time to fire a single shot, as the slopes on both sides of the road erupted in a downward hammer-fire of sub-machine guns on the trapped men. Two men of the rear guard turned to flee, but hand grenades arched down on either side of them and exploded with almost comic bangs to cut them down. One of the slugs from above hit the man behind Tonio, who was carrying a small sack of grenades, and he dissolved into a mass of riddled flesh. For a few moments, the air was filled with the madness of screams and curses. Tullio pounded out of the dark; he paused, and uttering a soundless howl, he fired his sten gun wildly at the slopes above until he crumpled sideways, still firing as he went down.

Tonio had only time to whisper, "Forgive, forgive," as he rolled over heavily, his beret-covered head lying on the fallen major's knees.

The terrible stuttering slaughter in the wet black night lasted only minutes. Then a great void of silence drifted over the road. Two figures stiffly detached themselves from the ambush positions almost directly above the road now filled with huddled bodies, and clambered slowly down to the road. One of them picked up the sten guns and other automatic weapons from the fallen. The other moved methodically from body to body and occasionally, leaning over almost lovingly, pressed his German automatic pistol to a head. The dry crack of the explosion would cut for a moment through the rain. He paused last of all at the body of Fausto, and he stepped back in a recoil of alarm as two muddy, dying hands reached tiredly for his ankles. He took careful aim and fired straight down at Fausto, once, twice. Then he walked deliberately away, sheathing his weapon and signaling the others now filing off from their ambush positions to follow him. In a few moments the road was empty and still, covered with the bodies of one German, one American, and twelve Italians in the slanting midnight rain.

chapter two

Two LITTLE BELLS on the pharmacy door jangled mournfully as the old priest stepped across the threshold and peered into the half-gloom of the submerged shop. He turned and squinted back into the bright siesta sunshine as if fearful that it would follow him inside. Then, with a dour smile, he picked up his cassock skirt to ensure safety as he clomped down the stone stairs into the *farmacia*.

An acrid, antiseptic smell struck his nostrils, a pungent re-
minder of the decades during which this room had served as
medical center, dental clinic, and political forum for those of
Belinoro and the entire countryside. Even though he now
rarely visited this pharmacy, the old priest could, if he wished,
walk unerringly to the precise shelf of the crowded wall
cabinets and pluck out the aspirins, liniment bottles, corn
plasters, and all of the other palliatives which, alas, he now
needed in continuing supply in these years of old age and
bodily decline.

From behind the high marble-topped counter, a soft, round,
woman's face barely looked up from her newspaper at the
dark form outlined against the doorframe.

"*Mi dispiace,* but we are still closed for the siesta. We re-
open at three-thirty."

She peered up more intently as the old figure in black continued to move into the room, and, in a tone of greater respect
mingled with a startled diffidence, she acknowledged her
recogniton.

"Ah, Don Tiberio, it is you! Well, good day to you! We are
officially closed but for God's Messenger we are ready to serve
at any time." She folded the newspaper as she spoke and
ran a plump hand down the front of her white pharmacist's
jacket.

"What may we do for you, *Reverendo?*" she asked, looking
straight into the old square-jawed face as if he were a passing
stranger instead of one of the most familiar figures in her life.

Don Tiberio pulled off his black beret, produced a handkerchief from the dusty folds of his cassock, and wiped his eyes.

"*Perbacco,* what a knife of a March wind still in these hills!"
he exclaimed, leaning directly before her on the counter.
"Even with this old body dressed warmly, I was almost frozen
as my bicycle rolled down from the clinic at Altomonte." He
smiled broadly. "God punishes me, knowing how this ancient
carcass of mine yearns for the warm sunshine."

She stood erect before him and folded her soft if work-worn
hands across her chest, the starched smock crackling lightly
and pleasantly with her slightest move. He peered at her,
holding her gaze in his alert gray eyes, and he nodded slowly.

"And thank you for your description, dear Dottoressa Antonella, mayoress of Belinoro. I am, as you say, indeed God's
Messenger and as you well know, in this region it takes much
courage to believe in God, much less to be his errand boy."
He tapped one finger on the masthead of the Communist
paper lying before her on the smooth marble counter.

15

"You did not bicycle through this bitter wind and cold from Altomonte to catechize me, did you?" she asked him with a smile as mocking as her tone. "Padre, we have been through this business again and again, and you are well aware that my soul is my own."

He cocked his grizzled head to one side as if she had said something unclearly, and he rubbed a large mole beside his nose.

"Ah, your soul is your own, Antonella? It does not, perhaps, belong to those out there across the piazza?" He waved one thumb over his narrow shoulder. "There with the large sign of the hammer and sickle over the door?" He smiled and again tapped the newspaper. "Or those scoundrels in Rome? Would *they* like to hear you talk so freely of your soul being your own? I had learned that those out there shared everything; 'to each according to his need . . .'"

She extended a hand to him in a gesture of impatience.

"Dear Don Tiberio, let's leave the matter of my soul to me, please. I understand your anguish as the priest who baptized me . . ."

". . . and who officiated at your first communion, and who married you, and who"—and the old eyes shone with compassion—"who buried your husband, along with your father and brother, may their souls rest in peace."

He cut the air with a tiny sign of the cross.

"For forty-seven years, I have been friend, confessor, virtually a member of the Passaglia family. I am the bosom friend of your late father. I have seen or heard you virtually every day of your life in Belinoro since you were born. Dear Antonella . . ."

"*Basta,* Don Tiberio! You know me and my life as perhaps no other man. But you do not recognize that the world has changed! And I changed with it, long ago. You refuse to understand why I changed, and why I am today the Communist mayoress of Belinoro, and why Karl Marx has supplied many more of the answers to my questions than ever did you, or the nuns who taught me the catechism at school, or your Pope who sits in Rome." He stared at her as if she had slapped him.

"And now," she continued, voice modulated to a professional coolness, "what do you want of the Farmacia Passaglia? Medicaments, pills? Speak or give me the prescription, and I'll find it for you in a jiffy."

But he had recovered as quickly, and he was clearly in no hurry to turn to pharmaceutical matters. Arms folded, he looked over her head above the high-tiered shelves to a row of five framed diplomas, all of them from a Bologna school of pharmacy, some dating back well into the previous century. He pointed to a gap between two of the diplomas which had been recently patched and whitewashed in contrast to the aging gray of the rest of the wall's surface.

"Until a month ago," he said in his quavering voice, "there was a statue of the Madonna in that spot with a little votive electric bulb burning beneath her in her honor. Why is the Madonna gone?"

"It is my right to remove her," she answered, and her face mirrored the stubborn Romagnole strength of all the Passaglias, including Gianfranco Passaglia whose bearded bust with Bersagliere feathered hat stood out there in the little square, and who, with his comrades, had rammed through the ruins of the Porta Pia into papal Rome to create the new Italy. But even Gianfranco had affixed the Madonna with her little light to the pharmacy wall, and while it was true that he had damned the Vatican as would any good Monarchist, he had come, devoutly, to the church and to the altar all of his life at all of the necessary times. And so had all of the other Passaglia who followed him.

Don Tiberio held out his hands in a gesture of truce, wagging his head as if ceding the round. Antonella, remembering warily the honed cunning of this time-seared parish priest, waited. With Don Tiberio, it was ever a mistake to sense victory. His arrivals at any home or place were never coincidental or haphazard, having always at least one solid if initially obscure purpose. She feared and loathed his rare appearances in her pharmacy, and she knew with an ache that the fear and loathing stemmed from her own irrepressible guilt at the pain she caused him. But she faced him with the certain knowledge that nothing would swerve her sense of identity with her Party comrades, nor the comradeship molded in fire and blood, nor the sense of purpose and dedication to which they had pledged themselves. The smoldering kettle of popular resentment and subjugation, contained by the heavy lid of Fascist police, had exploded with the war, and nothing would ever again be the same. And here, with his trembling old fingers extended to her, was the Enemy, or one of them. Those hands had sprinkled holy water on her at birth, and she had looked into those small gray eyes, the hard square jaw, and that flaring nose a thousand times, receiving communion, repeating after him the marriage vows, standing at his side as three coffins disappeared slowly from view in the tomb of the Passaglia family. From behind the mysterious wall of the confessional, his throaty voice had granted absolution along with the petty sentences of prayer and Ave Marias. Belinoro did not know a day when the plump sagging little figure, crouched on his bicycle and beret snugly capping his head, did not cross or crisscross the narrow cobbled little streets. He stood before her, the personification of that God in whom she could no longer believe; not if she were to be true to the Party's ideals to which she had pledged herself. She hated him for spotting immediately the removal of the Madonna; that had not really been her idea but that of Gelasio Mintone, the new Party section secretary for Belinoro whose nickname, "Leninello," Little Lenin, was well earned. But to give Don Tiberio any explanations was asking for disaster. She decided on an immediate offensive riposte.

"And how are the church properties in Altomonte these days, Padre? The Belinoro village council is waiting patiently for an answer to our request for sale of the land below the monastery so that we may build the road giving the farmers a short cut to their holdings instead of the eight kilometers they must now walk each day of their lives."

He lowered his hands and his head and gave her a reproachful smile.

"You will excuse me, Dottoressa Antonella, but I simply cannot accustom myself to dealing with you as mayoress of this village. You are the first woman of this locality to be so honored, I know, and your father would be most proud, but it—it does not seem right."

"You priests who live in another age, another world, will have to accommodate yourselves to the unfortunate fact that women are human beings and can become mayors in Italy instead of vessels for human reproduction and serfs of the home! If you had your way, we would all spend our lives beating a path between your church altar and the kitchens of every hut in Romagna. This, too, has changed—and we still would like to buy the strip of land to build the road."

He dusted his beret reflectively and she watched him closely.

"You may rest assured, Signora Sindaco, that my bishop in Forlì has the matter under active consideration." Looking around him in the cool dimness, he found three wooden chairs near the entrance steps and he beckoned her to join him. It was a gesture that simply could not be refused. After a moment's hesitation, Antonella walked quickly to the counter's end and emerged from behind the monumental old cash register into the store front. Father Tiberio had already settled himself in the most solid of the three rush-bottomed chairs and pointed imperiously to the one nearest him.

"As you can well guess, my dear Antonella, I did not bicycle through this brutal wind and cold to curse you because the Madonna is missing from that wall, although it grieves my heart deeply to see it gone. Nor did I come to discuss the matter of the road through church property, although I appreciate your zeal as village representative in seeing the matter through." His veined, twisted hands were folded precisely over the top of the little paunch which swelled through his dusty black cassock, and he did not look at her but fixed his gaze on the white spot where the Madonna had been. Then he leaned over toward her and said very quietly to her, "Peppino Deruta is dead of the cancer. He died up in the Altomonte clinic about an hour ago, virtually unconscious and without great pain since he had received a massive dose of morphine shortly before the end. He was confessed, was given Extreme Unction, and died in the arms of Christ." Don Tiberio slowly crossed himself. "May his soul rest in peace."

Antonella's mobile mouth was devoid of reaction although her great eyes glittered with the impact of the news.

"And why do you come here to tell me of this with such haste, Reverendo? The news would have arrived in the village in an hour or two. Or did you come to gloat that you had saved a poor Godless ex-Communist from your place called hell? Really, Don Tiberio, you are acting like a child in such matters!"

For once, the weary smile of Don Tiberio did not respond.

"You placed around him the wall of silence, for almost a year. None of you would talk to him, none of you even recognized that he existed. He was, for you and your comrades, a walking ghost. He suffered much, my dear Mayoress, in the last year. Between your silence and his cancer, this was a brutal end to a man's life."

Although her heart weighed as a stone in her, she answered, "Peppino was a traitor to the Party and to the Party's cause. He betrayed us to the Germans; this much we learned only last year when the Party by chance uncovered the betrayal in captured German documents which had been lying in the Resistenza archives."

Into her sorrow dripped the venom of indignation. Her eyes flashed as she leaned toward the prelate who, gripping one raised black-draped knee, listened to her with his head slightly canted as though to hear her better. His hearing was phenomenally good for his age, and he did not miss the tremor in her voice when she spoke of Peppino Deruta.

"And just what did the Resistenza files reveal after this grudging silence of a dozen years?" His voice sank to a hoarse whisper, and one hand wandered to play with the heavy crucifix dangling on his chest. "What great sin had Peppino committed that you should expel him from the ranks of the true and only patriots of Italy, namely yourselves, and commit him to a world of frozen silence and hostility?"

The clang of his words was directed straight at her: Peppino Deruta had been the sustenance of her postwar days, a devoted friend of the young bride made widow and orphan in one blast of gunfire. Practically a member of her family and almost daily at her dinner board, Peppino had for most of a decade nurtured the bruised, grieving soul of Antonella Passaglia, married name Cipriani, whose husband Fausto lay beside her father and her child-brother Antonino. Peppino, the village Socialist since the Great War of 1915-18, first to raise the red flag of revolt and defiance on that day in 1943, now so long slipped into the quicksands of time, when the Piedmont peasant accents of old Marshal Badoglio over the radio had announced that Mussolini was ousted, and that Italy had left the war and signed an armistice with the Allies. Peppino, standing on a chair steadied by a friend, exhorting the excited townspeople in the little windswept square: "Fellow Belinoresi, Romagnoli! At last, twenty-two years of Fascist infamy and shame are swept away! Now we fight for freedom: workers, farmers, day laborers, students, earners of your daily bread by honest sweat and labor! Now we shall rise and sweep them out, the Nazis, the Fascisti, and their kind: the grubbing priests, the usurers who lend for the price of blood, the arrogant landlords who pay a crust of bread and a hundred insults a day! Now is our day! *Evviva la libertà! Evviva il socialismo! Evviva l'Italia nuova e felice!*"

The Fascist militia from Forlì had appeared in Belinoro within the day, after the *maresciallo* of the local carabinieri had refused to take the slighest action against Peppino. They had rolled into the square in their trucks, screaming with anger and vengence, almost fifty of them, but Peppino had long since been spirited away. The only person they met was Don Tiberio on the steps of the parish church who icily told them to go back to Forlì. And when their black-shirted ranks had wavered, and a catcall of "Dirty Protector of Reds" had cut through the din, he held up one hand and told them that he had telephoned his old friend, the commander of the

Fascist Militia in Bologna, who ordered them immediately back to their barracks, and who was still on the village public telephone. Their leader had suspiciously picked up the earphone, stiffened at the fierce sound at the other end, and the four trucks had decamped with nothing worse for Belinoro than a few windows broken, a few bottles missing from Eugenio's Bar in the piazza, and a few village girls pinched and otherwise roughly fondled. It had been quite a day.

Don Tiberio looked sidewise into her eyes and she knew she had been silently baring her thoughts.

"A real man, our Peppino, eh?" he commented quietly. "He lived like a man, and he died like one, without the shrieks which the cancer usually brings to the lips of the strongest. A bag of bones he was when he died, scarcely forty kilos, and his eyes were sunken in his head as blue stones in deep water. I should hate him of course, since he fed his godless Marxist nonsense to you for years like a mother giving pap to her young. You drank it all, every word of it, and you believe it, and it was through him that we lost you and your soul and your friendship to your God; but he died like a true repentant Christian, his cracked white lips pressed against the cross—*this* cross." And he held up the black, brass-trimmed crucifix.

His anger, stirred with sorrow, stung her nearly into tears. "It was . . . cowardice! It was the trick of a scoundrel! Peppino's will had been sapped by his illness. You black ones always prey around the sick like vultures hoping to tear the soul out of brave ones when they can no longer resist. You are always there to make the last cheap conquest. Hateful, Don Tiberio, it's hateful of you!"

The tears did come, and she hid her burning eyes for a moment in her hands, digging to wipe the wetness away.

The old man toyed with his crucifix and regarded her with tenderness and compassion. He had lived entirely too long and had seen too much. This soft womanly thing spitting insults, defiance, and rage at him was, after all, the only daughter of his great friend and childhood companion, and the destiny that led him to this chair beside her had sorely tried his own faith and conviction. He had prayed to a mercurial God again and again on the subject of Antonella Passaglia, widow of Cipriani, and until this day God had given no light, no indication that the purely personal prayers of a seventy-year-old Romagnole parish priest had ever been heard. But today he was sure. Today God had spoken through the dying lips of Peppino Deruta and he knew, humbly and deeply moved on his knees at the bedside of that terribly

21

emaciated man, that God not only existed, not only moved in His own ways, but that He delighted in making His prescience known through the most obscure and surprising channels.

And as Antonella struggled to recompose herself, Don Tiberio grasped his crucifix and silently begged God to give him strength equal to that of the handsome, fiercely principled woman sitting next to him. It was going to be hard, achingly hard, but God had spoken.

His face was in complete shadow and he studied hers by the mulled gold of late sunshine streaming through the tiny display windows on either side of the frosted glass pharmacy door.

"You have not answered my earlier question, Antonella. What crime could Peppino have committed which would result not only in instant dismissal from your Party, but complete ostracism as well as the economic boycott of his garage business that reduced him to poverty?"

She answered as if the subject involved a disgusting family scandal.

"The Party headquarters, the Central Control Commission, sent us documents clearly proving he was in the pay of the Fascist police at the same time he was the trusted liaison man among the patriotic forces of the Resistance."

"The documents proved all this?"

"Yes, we studied them personally: Comrades Gelasio, Primo Sartelli, Nino Cardone, and Lullio Tremontini, and myself. There were photos of Peppino, his biography, and identity cards linking him with the Fascist police and as a trusted collaborator of the Germans in the Romagna zone. All were apparently found in the enemy files at the end of the war."

"And so, according to these famous captured files, your Peppino, the Number One Red of Belinoro after the war, who had during the Fascist era twice been beaten by their *squadristi* and once compelled by them to drink a *quartino* of castor oil out in that square long ago, before you were born, such a man was a craven spy against you? This does not speak well for your new religion, Antonella, if the best among you can do this."

She compressed her lips.

"Man is human and weak. Peppino had two brothers in Ravenna who were being held by the Germans there. It appears he betrayed us to save their lives. For *their* lives *my*

22

family had to pay with theirs!" The soft full face darkened like the passing of a cloud.

"You are certain of your documentation?" His voice had lost its old man's quaver and took on a firm aggressiveness.

"Of course!" she snapped. "It was unmistakable. And it was accompanied by the Party's statement that the evidence was irrefutable and the Central Committee recommendation for dismissal and shame for the man. It was signed by Comrade Spartaco Tamburri himself, chief of our Resistance veterans." She looked at him fiercely, and his hands trembled to see the visage of Tonio Passaglia in the face of this woman. "What devilment have you got up your sleeve, Don Tiberio?" she asked him peremptorily, and that too was a line Tonio had used a thousand times. Another time Don Tiberio would have slapped his thigh and chuckled. Now he only returned the fierce challenge of the glance.

"Devilment, as you so badly put it, is not my province, young lady, but rather that of your comrades. I am not one of those priests who can be accused of practicing my profession to the detriment of your precious patriots. This you and your fellows well know." And there was no reply. Don Tiberio had not only been decorated with the Silver Medal for valor in the Resistance, but there were at least ten men (four of them Communists) of Belinoro itself who owed their lives to his sanctuary. A small shoebox among his meager possessions contained letters in five languages from escaped American, British, French, and other prisoners of war to whom he had given succor, as well as to Italian Jews and others who were hunted as animals; these people had skulked into his domain like ghosts emerging from heavy morning mists and after being rested, fed, and provisioned had departed in the same manner.

"As I told you," Don Tiberio said calmly, "Peppino confessed himself to me. He told me everything, everything he knew. He talked, poor dying soul, for three long hours." And again, Don Tiberio crossed himself in the recollection of Peppino's final agonies, then fixed his eyes on the high-molded face of Antonella Passaglia, now the color of dark gold in the rays of a lowering sun. He licked his lips, suddenly dry and hesitant, but it was only a moment in which to gather the will to continue.

"What you say about Peppino's collaboration with the Germans and the Fascists in 1943 through 1945 is probably true," he told her, speaking slowly and carefully. "Peppino confessed this to me himself. But it was not to save his brothers in Ravenna. In any regard, he could have done little for them since they were slaughtered by the SS two months before the English troops liberated the city."

She snatched his black sleeve with both hands and imprisoned his bony wrist.

"What are you talking about? Quick, tell me!" The large eyes under the straight heavy brows, the Passaglia eyes, flickered in a spasm of incomprehension and intuitive dread.

He paused and reached into the ancient brief case at his feet with an involuntary grunt of exertion. Then he straightened slowly in his chair and handed her two tissue-wrapped objects; one was fairly large, the other tiny—a box, she could feel it, no larger than the kind a jeweler supplies with a purchased ring. She tore the paper off the larger object, and she sat back, her lips open with surprise.

"Yes," Don Tiberio said, "a pistol holster. Don't be afraid of it. It's empty."

She turned it over in her hands, and the priest noted the tremble of her fingers. He finally said dryly, "I suggest you open the flap and look inside."

She fumbled for an interminable second with the flap. Then it clicked open, and she bent the old brown leather back and read what was printed there in square black inked letters. Her face paled to a degree that alarmed the old cleric. He moved forward in his chair toward her and watched as she took a deep breath as one does after stepping out-of-doors from a fetid room. She carefully unwrapped the smaller package and opened the little cardboard box, holding it up without removing its contents. It contained only one small object, a badly tarnished little metal gold leaf—shaped more like a sea shell than like anything arboreal.

"These objects," the priest told her in the flat, severe tone that priests and physicians use to hide their feelings, "were handed to me by Peppino Deruta early this morning before he went into what turned out to be his final coma. *He* wanted you to have them."

The expression on her face startled him. It was the look of a sleepwalker dreaming a nightmare from which she was striving to wake.

"What else did Peppino have to say?" She finally spoke, the wavering of her voice betraying her great struggle to keep it at a normal pitch.

Don Tiberio shrugged. "Much of what he said stays in here," he tapped one large wrinkled ear, "as a secret of the confessional. But he told me to tell you that he was innocent of any betrayal, and that he loved you, loved you as your dead family did"—and he reached out unexpectedly and gently touched her hands clutched around the worn holster —"and as I love you, Antonella."

He thought, and hoped for a moment, that she would cry aloud and the liquid film that again gathered in the huge eyes brimmed, but she dabbed it back rapidly with the knuckle of her forefinger.

"Why did he send me these things?" she asked, and then remembrance of the origin of the objects filled her to overflowing. Jumping to her feet, she threw them on the floor, and with a brutal gesture she tore at his cassock as he rose with her.

"Priest, what kind of an insane joke are you playing on me?" she screamed at him. "What do you mean, telling me of Peppino's innocence? How do you dare bring these objects to me to torture me with the horrors of a dozen years ago? You must be mad, priest, in your dotage, to play such games!"

"The truth, my dear child," he told her as she clung to his cassock shaking his old frame with her violence. "I bring the truth from the poor shrunken lips of a dying man who loved you perhaps only a little less than I. He said he was innocent of betrayal with the knowledge that his minutes were numbered. When he gave me these objects, he could barely breathe the words 'For Antonella.' " He took her fists clutching his robe and firmly disengaged them.

"As for playing games, I play none in the presence of death, never! Even you, Communist paragon that you have become, know this about me."

She stooped and carefully retrieved the holster and the box. The little metal insignia had rolled on the floor, and this she picked up and examined carefully in the palm of her hand.

"I apologize, Don Tiberio. These objects evoke memories so terrible that I feel the same great loss that I felt when . . . the tragedy occurred. Forgive me."

He smiled.

"I cannot forgive you, Antonella, but God can. You are in need of God, and God needs you, child."

But he knew that this was not the proper moment for sanctimony, and she answered his words in an abruptly cold impersonal tone.

"Yes, I rather supposed you would eventually try to proselytize me. But God can wait."

He had one more thing to say, and while he hesitated, momentarily shocked by her blasphemy, he knew that it would be a long time, if ever, before he could talk to her on this matter again. And so it had to be said.

"Peppino muttered incoherencies at the end, as I performed the rite of Extreme Unction. He said three or four times, 'The American, ask the poor American . . .' Does this mean anything to you?"

A smile as wily as that of a she-wolf scenting the trap lifted one corner of her wide mouth.

"I have met only two Americans in my life, Padre. You know that. The dead one and the other whom you helped to escape."

"First the dead one, the major," he said.

"What can one say? He brought disaster with him for all of us in Belinoro, especially to myself. And yet he died with the others. The tears I wept for my family at the mass funeral were tears for him also."

The priest nodded.

"A fine man he was, although a Protestant, and his death caused me much anguish. I pray for his soul along with those of your family and the others, every day." He held her in a mild but steady stare. "Do *you* still mourn him?"

She looked at him. This old priest had to be watched with great care.

"As much as I mourn all the others who died," she said at last. "I wish that the other one, the lieutenant, had died instead."

"That is a hateful, inhuman thought! What kind of monstrous talk is that from a Christian mouth, no matter what the provocation for it?"

"You know very well, Padre, why I said it," she answered, eyes boldly holding his and tossing her head in challenge. "And you forget I am *not* a Christian, not any more."

"You were born one, and baptized one. You cannot become an animal simply because you will it. You are still a Christian, if a rather bad one."

"Let's argue the point another time, Padre. I must prepare to open my pharmacy."

"The American lieutenant lives," he flung at her.

She shrugged her shoulders as she moved with short, clacking steps to the end of the counter and made her way behind it to reach the door to the living quarters in the rear.

"He is in Italy; in Rome," Don Tiberio said softly.

She stopped and turned to look at him with the patent

26

medicine displays and advertisements almost obscuring her face.

"How do you know?"

"He sent me an Easter card; here it is, with the words *'Evviva Cristo Re'* on it. Lamentably poor taste, but the postmark on the card indicates he lives in Rome." He laid the cracked card, with a glossy photograph of St. Peter's, on the pharmacy counter.

She remained absolutely still. He shuffled toward a familiar glass case and asked, "Do you mind if I take my usual: some aspirins, some cough syrup, and the rubbing liniment? I shall leave the money here."

Out of the stillness behind the counter she asked, as one asks a traveler how the weather was during his journey, "What were Peppino's last words, Padre?"

"He was weak at the end, very weak. I held up his head and wet his lips, and then I administered Extreme Unction. He said, 'God forgive me.' Then he said, 'Mamma.' That was all."

As he turned back to the patent medicine case, the old priest lifted up his eyes and begged to be forgiven himself, for that had not been all. Cradling the hollow-eyed head in his arms he had whispered with the furious urgency of one who must outrun a fleet-footed assassin, "Listen to me, Peppino! You must give me permission to tell all of this to Antonella! I cannot tell of this confession unless you release me from my vow of silence. I have saved one soul this day. Let me save another! I beg of you, Peppino, do this last deed of penitence. Let me tell her the entire truth, that you were not guilty of betrayal, that you were innocent, and that it was the Party that betrayed you."

The suffering, deep-holed eyes flickered up at him with a ghost of Peppino's humor in them.

"As a favor to you, Don Tiberio? I would die with you in my debt?" the tired, cracked lips barely moved.

"As a favor for Antonella. She must understand that you were right and her godless ones are wrong. I will pray for you every day of my life for it."

At last the head in his arms barely vibrated, and he bent close to the lips to hear.

"No. Tell her only that I did not betray my friends or my comrades. Tell her this gently and carefully, but nothing else. Give her the *mementi,* but I forbid you to tell her how they came into my possession . . ."

"I promise. Thank you, Peppino. Now sleep." And he tenderly laid the head on the pillow, its eyes already closed for the last time.

He had hated to squeeze, in effect, the soul of a dying man, but there was still Antonella's soul to be saved. Peppino had come to him *in extremis* but Antonella was young and full of health. She was also a woman, and he beseeched God to quicken her sense of curiosity because of her love for Peppino.

It was not to be countenanced that the Madonna had vanished from that far wall. After all, he, Don Tiberio Vantuzzi, was a Romagnole himself and his head was as hard as any Passaglia's. He turned his eyes to the blighted spot where the Madonna had been and he crossed himself twice and his dry old lips twitched in silent prayer for the outrage. As Antonella disappeared through the rear door of the pharmacy, he slowly pushed open the glass casing and reached for the aspirins and the liniment and the cough syrup. It would be a slow, brutal effort in the cold wind to pedal up the sloping road again to Altomonte to arrange for the funeral of Peppino, but he would take great care that the procession stopped directly in front of the Party's headquarters in the piazza for a moment or two before the hearse swayed on to the cemetery of Belinoro.

chapter three

SPRING SUNSHINE LEAPED from the near-jungle of the roof terrace and vaulted dazzlingly into the high-ceilinged studio room as if bent on annihilating by merciless exposure the ancient and shabby furnishings. A pair of Siamese cats, male and female, bearing identical crooked and truncated tails as incestuous indicators, looked warily at each other on sun-warmed patches of marble floor and solemnly blinked under the brightness that filtered through the trellised, thick-leaved terrace vines.

It was past midmorning, and the sun had already warmed

an incomparable Rome sky to an intense blue flame, but the solitary figure on the wide pallet bed did not stir. It lay face down and from a tanned male torso uncovered to the waist, a naked brown arm sprawled straight past the dark head as if a commander had been cut down in the moment of waving his troops forward. Clothing lay carelessly on a square ugly chair, and it was apparent that he had gone to bed nude and in haste.

Beside him, a slight depression in the lumpy mattress indicated that another body had lain there recently. In fact, the outflung right arm, almost as if by its own uncoordinated volition, slowly and cautiously moved in that direction. Not encountering anything, the hand relaxed, and the fingers went limp with a certain relieved gratitude.

One complete wall of the large room facing the terrace consisted of French doors leading to the vibrant vegetation outside, two of them slightly ajar. Tucked in a far corner and as yet untouched by the probing shafts of sunshine, a Neanderthal refrigerator squatted—a monster with a grilled head of a motor perched on top and a once gleaming white surface chipped and rusted with a quarter-century of abuse and exhausting existence. A circular table of heavy black mahogany, *dernier cri* at the turn of the century but now sunk to new depths as part-time gambling table and ironing board, hulked close by the refrigerator. It was flanked by four chairs, each a worn relic of its species: a battered but authentic rococo with trembling insecure arm rests, a Renaissance chair looking for all the world like a large X with a rubber cushion above its intersecting crotch, a rickety beach chair with bottom and back of faded striped canvas, and a painfully modern womb chair with a bright yellow molded plastic seat and the word "Hers" painted bright red in old script at its top.

Wedged against the wall between the French doors stood another table, about five feet square, of obscure origins, with each of its legs ending in a claw clutching a ball. It was covered with piles of paper, cigar boxes, ping-pong equipment, and dominated by a large typewriter which had been on duty since the Roaring Twenties and whose loose ribbon mutely indicated that it was still in fitful use, although on one of its black metallic surfaces someone had delicately drawn a heart in the unmolested dust.

High levels of unpainted shelves covered one entire wall beside the bed, crammed with books, pamphlets, paper-backed Official Gazettes, and ragged piles of yellowing newspapers. Here and there under one of the shelves, a neat inscription was printed on a small rectangle of paper: "Resistance in Piedmont," "CLN Milano," "G.A.P. Formations in the Vencto 1943-1945." The largest section of all read "Resistance in Romagna." The material on the shelves had been repeatedly sifted, absorbed, and reexamined. But dust lay on it all, time's epitaph to a labor abandoned.

Two magnificently decrepit stuffed brown leather chairs mourned in a corner, flanking a square coffee table whose tortured surface bore so many cigarette burns and beer-glass stains as to create an abstract effect which visiting artist friends insisted was exciting. One of these had wanted to buy the table, martyrize its surface with a few more strategic cigarette burns and gouges, and exhibit it, mounted, as "Laocoon #9." ("Anybody, but anybody, will pay fifty thousand lire for it! All you have to do is mumble about its Mystique, and a clutch of snobs will rush up to form a line with their American Express checkbooks unbuttoned!")

One half of a large and once highly polished double door with a permanent dart board attached at eye level, its vcneer now outraged by hundreds of pocks from earnest but inaccurate dart throwers, opened. A mass of exuberant, glossy black-and-gray hair appeared, crowning a flat, square face so swarthy and hirsute as to make the division between hair and features difficult at first glance. Small, probing black eyes with an instinctive suspicion stamped in them above the straight sharp nose peered first at the recumbent form and then at the cats who returned her unpleased look with reciprocal malevolence. It was a silent but deadly exchange between mortal enemies who for convenience's sake must for the moment have a truce.

The dark head inserted itself further through the opened door and swiveled accusingly at the refrigerator. Not a tremor of life vibrated from the box. The wide, curving lips clamped in a straight line and a vertical crease like a thundercloud dissected the heavy eyebrows which had grown together as one.

"*Brutta maledetta cosa!*" she softly cursed the inert box and opened the door wider. Her entire figure then shuffled into the room on straw slippers: short, plumply solid neck merging immediately into a heavy chunky body and sagging bosom and terminating with solid, utilitarian, black-haired legs straight as poles, into the square ankles and wide, splayed feet. Once, not too many years ago, a surprisingly slim waist had flowed inward from deep rich peasant breasts, below which earth-mother hips and amply protruding but-tocks had ballooned out again. But cumulative tons of *pasta*, casks of red wine, gobbled sweets, and years of hard and unremitting work had stiffened the once supple frame and coarsened the body into a solid rectangle of flesh falling from the square shoulders to the wide flanks.

Her blue cotton blouse under the soiled apron was already stained with huge dark blotches of perspiration extending under her arms, evidence of early morning industry; and the faded tweed skirt inherited from some previous employer's generosity appeared to be utilized as a large duster, especially the portion covering the ample bottom.

She stopped just inside the threshhold of the sun-filled room and looked toward the bed; the vertical forehead crease vanished as if wiped away, and the swarthy face reflected a tenderness and affection which would have surprised anyone who knew her, including the occupant of the bed. It was the sadly tolerant, deeply affectionate expression of a mother regarding her slumbering infant in his cradle. That look of love would have cost her dearly in terms of unending jeers and a thousand malicious epithets, but no one saw it except the Siamese cats, who had the delicacy to look away.

The look of love was a fleeting one, however. It concen-trated its brief and intensive warmth on the back of the male head and upper torso emerging above the white sheet. But as the black beady eyes regarded the long, grooved im-pression on the now empty side of the bed, her expression matched those which had been bestowed earlier on the silent Siamese and the unresponding refrigerator. There was more: in the bright almost fathomless jet eyes the word "jealousy" was clearly writ.

She had told herself many times that his women were his own affair, and she was secretly rather proud of the impres-sive number of women—most of them young and many of those shapely and well-groomed, decked with costly clothing, jewelry, and perfumes—whom he had brought home and laid on that well-grooved mattress. These women were not at all abashed to find themselves there the following morning and usually shouted *"Cameriera!"* in a voice well accustomed to scurrying discreet servants. Maria had served many a cup of *espresso* to these tousle-haired, soft-bodied women, and they had sat propped up by pillows in the low bed, careless of revealed expanses of bosom and shoulders with their frilly undergarments indiscreetly visible, sipping the tiny necessary cups of *caffè nero* and stretching (the whores!) in the irresistible Rome sunshine like so many sleek cats.

The one last night had been different in that she was a *straniera,* a foreigner, which few of them were. And she had not stayed the night; she had departed at dawn, almost knocking down The Maria, who was lumbering sleepily across the foyer toward the kitchen. This foreign woman last night was also not one of the kind Dottor Tommaso preferred; she was not one of those ample-flanked, brassière-straining soft ones with a wedding ring almost as large as their bold eyes. No, this one was a slender thing, young, no wedding ring, with little meat on her bones, tumbling chestnut hair, and she fled still wearing the glossy black cocktail dress in which she had entered the apartment only three or four hours before. Without a word or gesture to The Maria, she had taken down the Dottore's cheap blue plastic raincoat from its peg in the dim hallway, flung it around her shoulders, and clicked swiftly down the endless flights of stairs in her elegant high-heeled shoes.

The Maria shook her head covered by the black work bandanna, shrugged her shoulders at the recollection, and sighed. All *stranieri* were crazy, and this one was perhaps even crazier than the others she had seen or had heard described. This signore, this American lying calmly on his side, almost penniless and with an economic future as promising as an illiterate orphan in her poverty-haunted native Sardinia, could nevertheless sleep long into the day as if he were an ambassador to the Vaticano or a Parioli black market millionaire. They were all truly crazy, these foreigners, and no one in her mountain village in central Sardinia (although they heard her out with all the silent respect due her) believed a word of her narrations whenever she sought to describe the *stranieri;* how they lived, acted, reacted in Rome. She knew this one was a real *studioso.* On ever rarer occasions he would sift through his books and scribble his notes with the concentration of a Jesuit, which in itself was crazy; why did he want to live like this, in a far off land? And what an ugly theme he dwelt on: La Resistenza with its brutality, counter-brutality and, always, death. Like children they all were, these foreigners, odd and eccentric and at times quite irresponsible children, especially this one. Look at him: had he not had her, Maria Seddu, as a *tuttofare* he would undoubtedly have long since gone to jail or starved.

A purely feminine, fiercely maternal fire kindled in her plump, sweaty throat and chest consuming all of the other feelings. This one and Paolo: for these two she saved this smouldering affection, and Paolo was almost beyond the grace of God. He was *buono,* this sleeping *Americano,* if indolent and spoiled and increasingly addicted to *viski.* With this one, it was the only time in her life that she, a servant born of servants and knowing nothing else than the miniscule triumphs and defeats of a house servant, had been considered as a genuine human being by an employer, nay, a family member of the household, an auntie. None of this could be communicated or even implied to the vast and interrelated network of Sardinian servants in Rome who among them knew more private and state secrets of the capital than did the entire Rome police force. This would have to remain her own secret. And besides, The Maria of Nuoro had a hard, flinty reputation to uphold among her own.

This American would never know the endless sly innuendoes and silent eyeball rolling she had endured from her fellow Sardinians in Rome. Any house servant who worked for a single male *padrone,* and a robustly notorious one at that, was presumed beyond any doubt to be sleeping with her employer. He had told her bluntly, that first day when she arrived for the interview, that five women, including one vain old girl of almost sixty ("*Scusi,* signore, but my husband would be very jealous if I came to work for you!") had turned down the job, pleasant as it was to keep house in such a small airy apartment for one other person, because they all feared for their reputations. But she, The Maria, looked around her deliberately, and then stared for a long moment into the somehow pleading eyes of the young-old American and said, "I'll try it for two weeks, as the law permits. If I like it, *va bene.* If not, I leave." That had been almost two years ago.

She cast another glance at the mattress hollow where the female figure, the interloper in the house, had been. Jealousy and pride: she admitted them in this still, sun-filled moment. That was the way it was, and in a deep sense she was content: after all, despite the *viski* and the laziness, her signore was a real man, not one of those thin-faced, thin-lipped, thin-hipped creatures with lilting voices and *senza coglioni* who sometimes came to visit this house. And if he had to take his pleasure, best that the creature be cleared out with the morning sun, sometimes never to return or be seen again.

But for a variety of reasons, two or three of them quite urgent, the Dottore would have to be awakened. She shuffled to the refrigerator, and standing next to this obsolete glory, again cocked her head. Not a sound. In all probability the butter and milk and meat within were spoiling rapidly. She uttered a powerful Sardinian curse, picked up a broom handle propped in the corner, and brought it up to shoulder level in a stance of a baseball batter. There would be two awakenings with one blow. Swinging around in an arc, she thwacked the vented top first on the right and then the left, the bang of wood against metal clanging like shouts of alarm.

The tortured refrigerator emitted a groan like that of a prodded bull. Maria Seddu returned the scarred broom handle to its place and turned to regard the body which had pulled to a crouch at the din and then rolled over on its back facing her, eyes half open.

"*Buon giorno*, Dottor Tommaso!" she called cheerily in a voice ranging between a fog buoy and a deep bass gong. "You slept well? Good! Caffè is ready in two seconds!" The man slowly propped himself up, hands straight behind him supporting the exposed torso, and shook his head gently as if incredulous that it was still on his shoulders.

"*Buon giorno* thyself, Zia Maria, but is it necessary to break into the slumber at such an early hour and in such a manner?" he asked in a weary and fluent Italian. "This is not a farm in Sardinia. This is not a factory in Milano. This is the city, this is Roma," he continued, his grievance gaining momentum. "And my head is filled with the fumes of *viski* to the bursting point." He reached gingerly to his forehead as if his own quiet words had deafened him.

"*Ai*, it is the city, Signor Tommaso, and not the country. And it is also the eleven of the morning, and thou art already more than two hours late for work." It was delicious to use the intimate *tu* with her employer, her friend, to whom she was *zia*, auntie, but The Maria had to speak sternly; it was expected of her.

He snatched his right hand from its supporting position behind him and held the wrist watch close to his puffed eyes.

"Damn!" he muttered in English. "And today of all days! With a head that could be used in a shot-put contest."

He was about to hurl himself from the low bed and recalled only at the last moment that he was utterly naked.

"Get the coffee, Maria, immediately!" he called to her and she shook her head with grim satisfaction and slopped heavily from the room. She had often surreptitiously glimpsed the still youthfully lean body of this man exactly as God had made it, and had in fact coveted it briefly in her early months here. But that was again one of the things never to be even hinted to the swarm of Sardinian house servants in her lengthy daily telephonic communications, or in her participation as conciliator and judge at the animated roundtable conferences at the Stazione Termini on the free Thursday and Sunday afternoons. Apart from the confession booth at Saint Eugenio's, it would never do that The Maria Seddu, *doyenne* of an incredible throng of kinfolk composing much of the Rome servant force, should degrade her exalted status to discuss the warm brown body of her employer. She knew what the others already thought of her behind that sea of intent and inscrutable black eyes; that The Maria, in taking such a position with the notorious American expatriate, was feeling her age, that the middle life she felt herself entering with such difficulty and reluctance had unhinged her mind! After all, she, The Maria, had been senior maid to a series of Fascist Excellencies, to a postwar Secretary of the Parliament, once to a Knight of Malta, even a brief and godly period in the household of an Eminence, a small and feeble old cardinal. Many of these jobs she'd had before most of these country bumpkins had even known there was a Continent and a Rome across the stormy channel from the cragged and medieval Sardinian coast.

Tom Linden gently turned his head to the thin-curtained wall of light and his puffed eyes picked out the Siamese, both watching him inscrutably and, he was certain, contemptuously.

"Look," he told them in a low voice, "if either of you had played stud poker with the Embassy Marine guards and drunk the amount of good commissary scotch and come home with . . ."

His cheeks felt suddenly drained of blood and his lower lip involuntarily quivered as he slowly tried to unravel the chronology of the events of the night before. He had come home with . . . ?

The Maria, in an effortless shuffle which kept the upper body in a proud vertical line that could balance a bucket of water on her head without rippling its surface, re-entered carrying a brass tray laden with a small brass espresso maker, cup, saucer, sugar, and two sweet rolls. She leaned her head in the direction of the now groaning refrigerator engine.

"Listen to that, Signor Tommaso! Like a mule: you give it a couple of good blows and it goes about its business, eh?" She smiled the triumphant smile of the fledgling engineering student who has learned to good effect the great precept concerning the Machine: if it doesn't work, the first thing you do is kick it.

He drank the syrupy, scalding coffee, his weary face reflecting a torrent of concern. The fumes of the night before gradually loosened their grip but were immediately replaced by far more tumultuous churnings and preoccupations.

The Maria fixed his drooping features with a warning glance.

"There is the small matter of the residence permit. An *agente* of the Questura dropped by this morning to talk to that pig of a *portiere*. The *agente* says you must report immediately to the Questura to ask for a renewal; you have been in Italy now for months with an expired residence permit."

"And why do they trouble me now?"

"*La burocrazia.*" She shrugged again. "We Italians are unfortunate ones, Dottore. But if we did not have the bureaucracy, many thousands would starve." She paused almost delicately, and sighed.

"Ah, if I could but salvage this *cretino* of a nephew of mine with a steady job in the bureaucracy, with the pension, a young sweet wife with some meat on her bones." The deep husky voice had sunk to a funereal whisper.

"Instead, he stands in the *galleria* reading *L'Unità* and waits for Fortune to walk up and kiss him. And he has thrown in his lot with Them, the Godless Ones." She spat vigorously through the opened doors onto the terrace, and her face was a mask of suffering.

He blinked his sleep-swollen eyes open. He had his own rather energetic ideas on how to handle Paolo, none of them keyed to tender, loving care, but there was always the strong possibility that Paolo in one way or another would take care of himself, possibly assisted by the long hairy arm of the law.

"Maria, would you like me to speak to your nephew?" he asked her, impelled by the stoic despair on the impassive and unconquerable face.

She shuffled deliberately to remove the small tray with empty coffee cup and crumbs from the brioche, and shook her head slowly with a small, rare smile.

"*No ringrazio*, Signor Tommaso. Paolo is my problem, and I will have to find a solution for him in my way. The way will appear." She spoke with the authority of sunset announcing that night will fall.

"Maria," he said uncertainly, "did a young . . . ?"

She gave him a slow, worldly nod of the head, the black eyes carefully neutral.

"The foreign one, thin and young with the reddish hair? She departed at dawn without a word."

Her strong olive face registered a resigned tolerant half-smile.

"She also took your raincoat to cover her. Thou art truly a *mascalzone*, a rascal, Signor Tommaso."

He slumped back on the lumpy pallet and passed a hand over his eyes.

The Maria transferred the tray to the clutter of the table top.

"There have been telephone calls this morning, Dottore," she boomed. He looked up at her quizzically.

"Phone calls?"

"A half-dozen! And three within the last hour from the Embassy! Your friend, the Dottore Brenta, is very angry with you. Very!" She continued to stand, arms akimbo, and she shook her head in remembrance of the angry words.

"Signor Tommaso." Her voice was a soothing, whining rumble now, and he picked out in it the familiar signal of household want. He pointed to his careless pile of clothing.

"Do not reproach me, Zia Maria," he told her, chewing hungrily on the remainder of the sweet roll. "In my jacket pocket thou wilt find sixty-two thousand lire. This amount I won over a long evening from five young marines who have much to learn about poker. Pay the rent and keep something for thyself."

"*Ringrazio*, signore!" she bowed exaggerately. "I must pay fifty thousand lire already owed on the rent. And what shall we use to buy pasta, bread, olive oil, greens, gorgonz—?"

He held up a confident hand although he had actually reached a point in his waking processes where his chest tightened with an unaccountable near-panic.

"Have no fear, Maria, Queen of all the Central Sards, adviser to governments and to Roman Eminences. As you know, today I work. Today I take up again my job as escort and interpreter through the military depots of the Rome area for our distinguished Embassy. By this weekend I shall have earned forty thousand lire and we shall eat like . . . like Knights of Malta."

"And between today and this weekend, what shall we eat?"

He looked up at her massive, black-browed form, the heavy black down above the full lips, and he smiled. When he smiled like that, she knew why she stayed in this impossible job.

"Until weekend, we eat with the ten thousand lire remaining after you pay the rent. This weekend thou will receive all thy salary plus enough to go to the bar of the Stazione Termini on Sunday and accept the homage due thee while buying espressos for all thy subjects."

He reached into the careless pile of clothing in the chair beside his bed and came up with six blanket-size notes.

"There's sixty thousand lire, Sardinian dream of love. I keep only two thousand for myself."

She did not move to approach and take the paper notes in his hand.

"The Dottore Brenta at the Embassy . . ." she began again, now in a rumble strangely soft and gentle for her. He sat straight up; this was her bad news voice.

"What did Dottore Brentwood say?"

"The last time he called, he said to tell you that if and when you ever reached his office, you should come prepared to lose some skin. He also said to tell you he deeply regrets the evil day he ever met you."

Only the feverish rattle of the refrigerator filled the momentary silence.

"What did thou tell the consul?"

"I told him that anyone who spoke such evil of Professor Tommaso was ignorant, a cretin born of a contented cuckold, a standing turd." Her glittering Sard eyes smiled triumphantly as she rolled the string of recalled invective into the room like sputtering Chinese firecrackers.

"Thou spoke harshly, Maria," he told her gravely, conjuring up the thunder-struck features of Second Secretary and Consul T. Vincennes Brentwood III in the calm of his little office listening to the hoarse baritone curses scraping out of the telephone.

She stood, a pillar of repentant flesh, looking at him as an erring hunting dog looks at his master for forgiveness from some incomprehensible wrong doing.

"*Vai, vai, vattene!*" he waved his hand at her in the sought-for gesture. "Depart and let me put on my clothes."

She turned to go with a grunt of acquiescence but wheeled back suddenly in recollection.

"Dost thou know a Signora Passaglia? One such called from the *stazione* at an early hour and wanted to speak with thee. Imagine, at seven in the morning! A northerner she was, I could tell by that singing accent they have."

The effect of her words was startling, confident as she felt herself in her knowledge of this man and his ways. His hands replaced the empty espresso cup on the tray with an erratic series of tiny uncontrollable clinks. He tugged at the white sheet as if to pull it higher on his torso against an indefinable chill eddying into the room. An expression of a wild fawn suddenly facing a mountain lion stared out of his eyes and his mouth twitched with a half-dozen shattered unspoken words. This meant but one thing to her: her Tommaso was in considerable trouble with this woman who had phoned. For The Maria, this sufficed as a clarion announcing a new problem and she looked at him with quickened interest.

He managed a tentative smile and asked, "What did she want?"

"Only to say that she had come to the capital and she wanted to talk with you. I told her you were not in and that she could reach you at the Embassy. She said nothing further and rang off. What rudeness!"

She watched him with concern now, because all of the days and nights of dissipation with the women and the alcohol seemed to ooze suddenly into his face, this face that bore the agonized suffering of those sinners, the damned, whom she had seen on the ceiling of the Sistine Chapel, mute imploration from their open mouths and the stamp of doom on them as they fell, arms clawing the air and beseeching help, into the Inferno. Only once before had she seen a similar expression on Dottore Tommaso's face and that was immediately after the brief visit of the widow of the American major who had been killed in the war; after she had gone he had pulled out a full bottle of that terrible *viski* and had swigged it as a day laborer swigs his cheap wine in the noonday rest; he had gulped until he toppled off his chair with a crash and had snored in drunken sleep for almost a full day afterward.

"*Mica male* that she did not ask to be put up here." The Maria grunted, looking at the littered room. "This is hardly the Albergo Excelsior."

He closed his eyes and he leaned his close-cropped head back until it struck the wall with a thump.

"The Signora Passaglia," he muttered, as if trying to recall a dream.

"There is much evil to undo this day, Signor Tommaso, between the Questura and the Dottore Brenta of the Embassy. Much evil," she told him briskly, sensing she had brought in something dark and foreboding and seeking to dispel it as best she could.

But the eyes remained closed and his cheek and jaw muscles sagged in a soundless groan. She knew he would not speak and that he wanted only solitude, so she shrugged despairingly as she shuffled to the door, and wished she had not told him of this call. As the door latch clicked behind her, she heard the refrigerator subside from its frantic throbbing with a final pathetic whistle and a thump.

He opened his haggard eyes and stared across the room. Fragmented images of a thousand faces and scenes whirled at him as dry leaves in an autumn wind and finally there remained the image of a young, achingly desirable girl named Antonella weeping next to him over the coffins. Then, almost as if he were leaning against the far wall, the figure of a long-faced, severe man, dignity undiminished by a soiled and wrinkled combat jacket, one hand impatiently and soundlessly snapping fingers emerged with deep alert eyes. The dry leaves rustled again and the same intense face looked up from the coffin at him, the eyes now shut as if concentrating on a very knotty problem. And always somewhere beyond them came the wail of weeping, a whole town weeping.

There had been years of this, the startled waking and the reappearance of the fragmented images, the coffins, the closed eyes, and the weeping. He had hoped it would start to fade and blur, but now the winds of memory blew clearly and sharply again and the catharsis of the rotgut and complaisant women would not help at all. If only Henning's eyes would open, if only the sound of weeping would stop! If only . . . his dry lips repeated again and again, if only Henning Dixon would look up!

chapter four

TWO YOUNG MEN sat without speaking on the rear seat of a ramshackle *corriera* as an overload of peasants, working girls, and a handful of bronzed, sandal-clad, and straggle-bearded German youths in *lederhosen* and sweat-rimmed checkered shirts swarmed noisily to the bus exit. Suspended in the wake of the animated chaffing, departing passengers was a concentrated distillation of odors that crinkled the nostrils of the two men. Diesel fumes, peasant sweat, unwashed hair and bodies, and the reek of garlic and onions which had escaped from a dozen sandwich hampers were enriched by the brine and the tang of the sea and the scent of the barnyard. Two crates of freshly caught fish, held aloft by strong hairy arms, bumped out of the bus door, followed by a slatted cage containing three chickens and a large honking goose who had ridden protestingly since Ardea on the floor beside the driver. Fish, fowl, and the chattering throng of country folk forcefully pushed through the narrow door to disperse into the huge Piazza dei Cinquecento, whose mastodontic railroad station, Stazione Termini, sprawled white and majestic in the early afternoon sun.

Once the aisle had emptied, the two men struggled to their feet in the narrow space. Each carefully lifted a cheap suitcase, and they made their way down the center, foreheads sweating from the heat of the vehicle's interior and the exertion of steering the heavy loads between the scarred seats.

The smiling bus driver, his visored cap shoved rakishly back, regarded their cautious passage to the door through his rear-view mirror.

"And what have we in there, *ragazzi?*" he chivvied as they gingerly stepped down holding their suitcases before them. "A load of eggs to sell to the rich of Parioli, perhaps?" He leaned conspiratorially toward the taller of them and whispered, eyes roguish with innuendo, "Or maybe a nice set of chinaware freshly filched from Anzio villa, eh? A few Etruscan vases out of some illegal tomb?"

Franco Furbo turned his perspiring face with its huge moose nose to the driver and sang out in slurred Roman dialect, "No such thing. The only thing we carry in here is bombs to blow up the Quirinal."

"Ah, very good, very good," the driver chuckled hoarsely. "That's what we need to stir up this *governo ladro:* a few bombs in the right place, a few less thieves."

"Including one right there," muttered the slim one, eyeing the other blackly and swinging his knee to catch his full-bottomed companion in the rear.

"Aoh, Paolo!" protested Franco as he turned at the bottom step. "You want to blow up the *corriera?* Watch that pushing."

The driver was vastly amused. "Happy bombing," he called to them in the street. Then, leaning toward them and giving them a broad wink, he added, "And if there is really anything left unsold in there by the end of the day, come back here to me, Giuseppino Russo, bus number 403. I have a few

41

clients in some nearby houses"—another wink—"who will buy all sorts of pretty things and pay the best prices. Or"—again a wink—"you can take it out in trade."

"*Grazie*, Giuseppino *bello*, blondes accepted in exchange!" Franco called as they staggered away to the shade of the nearby colonnade.

"You idiot!" hissed Paolo, as they carefully set down their burdens and wiped their faces with handkerchiefs. "Telling him you had bombs in there! Are you out of your mind?"

The moose nose turned toward him condescendingly.

"On the contrary," Franco Furbo answered him, "it was the most innocent thing I could have said. You may be a good proletarian idealist, Paolo, but you have a lot to learn about human psychology."

Paolo pinked and with nerves still vibrating from the strain of the afternoon's work, flashed at him, "And you may know a lot about human psychology but no one would accuse you of a willingness to do your proletarian share of the work. You made me sweat like a horse back here at the ordnance depot while you played your little game of 'lookout.' It was *I* who carried this damned load out of the shed and across a compound swarming with soldiers while you sat in the rear of the truck safely hidden behind a tarpaulin. It was *I* who unloaded these things from their crates and repacked them into these suitcases. It was *I* who carried both suitcases on foot for more than a kilometer in the blazing sun while you tripped lightly ahead to buy the *corriera* tickets from Ardea to Rome." He paused at the recollection of his recent experiences and was suddenly aware that his hands and knees were trembling as if he had been struck by fever.

Franco Furbo fished in his pocket and came up with a battered pack of Nazionali. He offered one to Paolo who could not entirely conceal his hand's tremor.

"Courage," Franco said soothingly, holding up a lighted match for Paolo's cigarette. "What you have just said proves my point. If I did not have my knowledge of human psychology, *I* would have had to do all of the strenuous things you mentioned. Aoh!" And he held out his thumb touching his fingers in a gesture of outrage that such labors might have been inflicted on him. "As it is, my dear Paolo, we have arrived here safely with the stuff, and it will be soon known to our great comrade, Il Duro, that both of us did the job and did it well."

The huge beak of a nose rose in a gesture of conscious nobility of achievement.

"And now, dear Paolo, *ciao* until tomorrow," he added in a friendly tone, running a small comb hastily through his greased locks and cupping his hand upward in a farewell gesture.

"What do you mean *ciao*? Do you expect me to lug more than thirty kilos to my room alone?"

Franco Furbo regarded his shabbily attired, perspiring friend from behind his silvered, opaque sun glasses, glanced down at his own ragged attire with distaste, and finally waved a half-apologetic hand.

"My dear *compagno*," he finally said with a martyred sigh, "of course I'll give you a hand. But couldn't we take a cab? After all, we cut a terribly poor figure in these tattered disguises. What if someone sees me, Dottore Franco Furbo, Communist Youth section leader of Torpignatara, in an outfit like this?"

Paolo shot him a look of disdain.

"No fear. No one who knows the well-dressed commissar will ever spot you in that getup. No cabs! Comrade Renzo specifically warned us that too many of them are police informants."

Franco held out nervous, impatient hands.

"All right, all right. Where is your room?"

"Only a few hundred meters away. *Andiamo!*"

"*Andiamo?*" Franco echoed with a groan. "Only a few hundred meters away indeed! These suitcases weigh a damned ton!"

"How would you know? *I've* been doing all of the carrying so far." Paolo pointed to the scuffed cheap imitation leather suitcases, and the day's strain tightened in him. "Now, my good Section Secretary of the Italian Communist Youth of Roma-Torpignatara, pick one up and let's be on our way!"

They stared at each other under the cool colonnade, and loungers eddied past looking curiously at them and their suitcases, as Italian loungers will look curiously at anyone and anything. Then Franco smiled a slow, sliding smile that lifted one corner of his face and said into the taut face of his accomplice, "Very well, my good Sardinian comrade, you *did* do most of the work today. And you've got lots of *fegato*, lots of courage. Worthy of a better cause." The voice was syrupy but filled with quivering innuendoes, none of them complimentary.

"What 'better cause?'" Paolo bristled. Really, this Franco was going to catch it from the Disciplinary Committee some fine day. Dogging this nerve-wracking chore all day long and now this needling.

"No offense, a phrase only," Franco protested hastily. "I only meant that your courage would have been better used in a *positive* sense, such as bringing about a great act of social justice for the masses, instead of stealing this sort of stuff for the Party."

"Everything we do for the Party is potentially an act of social justice for the masses," Paolo replied.

Franco ducked his head quickly in assent, eyes closed against any damning gleam, and he touched one of the suitcase handles with distaste.

"Certainly, certainly, Comrade Paolo. And now let's lug these two loads of social justice to your place." He ignored a fierce, contemptuous glance from Paolo, threw down his cigarette, and picked up one of the suitcases.

"Lead the way, comrade," he beckoned unctuously to Paolo, who lifted his burden and waited.

"We won't exactly walk together, eh, Paolo?" Franco continued. "Draws less attention to us, and, who knows, if one of us gets hit by a car, the other one can report to Il Duro."

"Coward!" Paolo answered with a bleak smile and trudged ahead.

Twice during the ten-minute, slow walk, Paolo turned to note the whereabouts of his colleague, and on both occasions caught him ten yards to the rear in the moment of making an outrageous comment or gesture to a blowsy bag-swinging streetwalker. The zone swarmed with the hardened railroad station whores whose asking price was twelve hundred lire, price discussible, for ten fast minutes of *amore*. Catching Paolo's eye, Franco waved cheerfully and crooked his free arm in an unmistakable implication. Paolo thought to himself: if all Party youth leaders were like this one, we'd be running a brothel, not a political revolutionary movement. But Comrade Franco had been detailed with him for this job, and he was stuck with him until the job was over. And it was almost over, thank God. But then, he caught himself again, we Communists can't go around thanking God.

Only after they had put down their suitcases at the huge cool open doorway to Paolo's shabby apartment a block away from Santa Maria Maggiore did the two speak again. Franco lowered his burden with a sigh and, moving his head close to Paolo's left ear, breathed, with heaving chest, "I think it would not be good that we are both seen entering your

44

apartment. You know that old witch ⌐
the suitcases up in the elevator by yourse⌐
in order." He smiled and his roguish black ey⌐
what he was about to say.

"And don't be angry with me, *caro*, but *you* are t⌐
who has been carrying the valise with the explosives. *I* ha⌐
been lugging the one filled with fuses and detonators. But
then you are the one with *fegato*, with much courage, eh?"

Paolo said nothing, heart and lungs pounding heavily from
the uphill climb with his thirty-pound burden.

"Remember, Paolo mio," Franco told him in a tone used
by an elder reproving brother, "if this thing is well regarded
by the Big Boys in the Botteghe Oscure, I was with you on
it, eh? You'll remember to mention that?"

"Yes."

"And if anything goes wrong with it, compagno Paolo, *you*
were in charge. You won't forget that, eh? Again, my friend,
ciao." And with a pumping of Paolo's unresponding hand,
Franco moved off, his large flat feet rocking him from side to
side like a moving pendulum. He disappeared in a matter
of seconds.

Paolo, his shoulders slumped with weariness, took a tentative step towards the elevator hulked darkly in its meshed
cage. But a large square of white cardboard was affixed to
the cage and bore on it a word that struck despair to his
being, a familiar word which he loathed as he did the word
"death" itself: "*Guasto*," it read, "Out of Order."

It meant that he would be straining more than sixty pounds
of explosives and detonator caps up five flights of darkened
stairs one step at a time. He thought again with painful
bitterness of Franco Furbo who had blithely dropped this
burden at his feet; those shifting beady eyes had quickly
discerned the *guasto* sign in the gloom, he was certain,
and Franco had fled rather than assist him in the climb to
his shabby rented room. What a creature! And yet Comrade
Franco Furbo was the apple of the Party youth movement
eye in Rome, the ex-Fascist youth leader who had been
wooed across the great chasm of political extremity to Marxism, and who filled a glittering role as a prize exhibit of Party
proselytization and conversion efforts. The Party had un-
ceremoniously dropped a good plodding young chap out at
Torpignatara and given his job to Franco to prove how it
rewarded those who saw the true light, even ex-juvenile
fanatics for Mussolini with all of their black-shirted nonsense.

Truly, Comrade Franco had been a bitter cup of tea. He

spection Group." Then, underneath, in severe hierarchical order according to date of rank were the names: Colonel Estland, Colonel Jamieson, Colonel Futtolo, Lieutenant Colonel Remoni, Lieutenant Colonel Phillips, Major Sallistis, Lieutenant Viles, Mr. Brentwood." He regarded the order-of-battle sadly for a moment. Poor Vinny should at least have been placed above the good lieutenant, but that was inflexible military precedent: first there's all of Us and then come Them.

Miss Brumacher, fading reddish hair almost the same color as her upswept sequined spectacles, looked up pleasantly enough from her typewriter and shorthand notes. Was there a glitter of warning in the thin smile?

"Morning, Mr. Linden. Go right in, please. Mr. Brentwood is in there. Waiting." The last word was definitely a flashing red light.

Inexplicably he found himself unable to toss back the usual spry rejoinder, merely nodding as he turned in the center of the high-ceilinged room to an inner door on his right. He knocked twice and pushed the door open.

"*Buon giorno, Excellenza!* he called, standing on the threshold of the quiet little room. He brought his right arm up in an exaggerated, quivering British military salute, forcing the smile and the bland wave, and aware of a dryness in his throat.

"Oh, it's you, finally. Come in here, Tom, and sit down, please."

He looked into Vinny Brentwood's pale eyes and immediately realized he was in for it: long ago they had learned to read each other's faces as sailors read the clouds and wind and sea. Vinny's expression was squalls and thunderstorms.

"Where do you find your inspiration in clothes?" Vinny grumbled after a quick appraising glance. "You look like a male model at a rummage sale."

Tom gave a controlled gesture of don't-give-a-damn.

"The jacket is a survivor of eight seasons of constant wear, Excellency. The pants are vestiges of a suit, half cast iron and half wool, that Omar the Tentmaker over in Prati produced for me during Holy Year. Said it was good until the next Holy Year, which is 1975, if memory serves. Shirt is clean if a little on the mottled side. My Maria unfortunately washed it with one of her pullovers which ran like blood, but it's not too bad with my coat on." He perched on the padded arm of a leather chair.

T. (for the unfortunate and never spoken surname,

47

Tristan) Vincennes Brentwood folded into an old swivel chair and lifted his long legs over a desk corner revealing hand-made pointed Italian pumps and clocked silk socks. His blond and now jowling features struggled to mirror and reaffirm a friendship extending back into their childhood but the pained smile and involuntary gnawing of his cultivated mustache betrayed the forced bonhomie. Tom well remembered that worried gnawing on the lip: it had signaled the end of whatever boyish lark or adventure they had begun, the point at which Vinny had to go home. It was always Vinny who quit first, but that was probably due to the fact that Vinny had a home to which he really liked to return.

"Perhaps you can talk me into switching to Brioni's?" he joshed. But Vinny was clearly not in the joshable mood. He leaned back moodily, his light eyes beneath the sandy eyebrows moving slowly from Tom's frayed collar tabs to the near-ruin of his jacket which mourned one button missing from one sleeve, two from the other. The orderly and coldly bureaucratic desk between them was a deep, narrow chasm which one could speak across, but not bridge.

Vinny reached for a half-consumed cigarette, inhaled deeply, and permitted the soundless smoke to curl out of his nose and lips. He's trying to figure out the impossible, Tom knew: he's trying to find where to put the knife in and yet not make it hurt too much.

Vinny brought his feet down, leaned forward, and reaching into a desk drawer threw a small blue square, neatly tied, at Tom.

"This yours?"

Tom reached slowly for it, unfolded it and poked his finger tentatively through a small tear near the collar. He nodded.

"Mine all right. Thought the Siamese had made off with it, or snitched by one of my maid's Sardinian charity cases she brings home," he lied. But an elevator within him started to descend.

Vinny said, struggling to keep his tone neutral, and succeeding only in sounding like a Foreign Office *démarche*, "It is returned to you herewith by Miss Nancy Hamill, courtesy of her father, who is, as you know, a senior officer of this Embassy." His careful officiousness began to waver, and suddenly cracked.

"Just what the hell were you doing with Miss Nancy Hamill last night?" he asked in a tight angry voice.

Tom's startled eyes were those of a boxer who has been

48

doing very well when he is suddenly slugged by the referee. He shook his head unbelievingly and stared at Vinny's heavy-jawed reproving features. Vinny had the good grace to look down at the cheap plastic raincoat on the desk and held out a pack of long American cigarettes. Tom helped himself to one, accepted Vinny's light, and curtly nodded thanks.

"I could say: none of your goddamned business. Nancy Hamill is well over twenty-one years of age. It being you, my childhood chum, I will merely tell you the unvarnished. I met Miss Hamill at the marine guards party last night. She was not precisely sober and a tall, very young marine corporal appeared to be entwined around her most of the night. I spent the evening at the poker table, which was why I went there in the first place, and managed at the end to win a fifty-thousand-lire pot even with the marines pouring good scotch into me like water, hoping I'd blur out of my luck. I remembered toasting my good fortune with them when suddenly she was next to me. She pulled me away from the card table into a fast rock and roll dance, we missed a beat and both crashed to the floor, good for the best laugh of evening. Next think I knew she was sitting on top of me pouring scotch straight from a bottle into my mouth. Another big laugh for all. Then she said to me, 'I can't stand these animals. Let's go to your place.' This was fine with me since otherwise I'd have to walk or hitch a ride with somebody. She had her little Fiat downstairs and on her way to my apartment she told me she heard I had quite a reputation as a lady-killer. I told her I was rather drunk and while I was somewhat interested in keeping my reputation, I wanted even more to get home safely which was highly chancy the way she was driving. She seemed rather agitated and finally told me that the tall marine corporal had tried to make love to her in a back bedroom without much preliminaries and she had to give him the knee and run. Apparently I entered the scene after that."

Tom's eyes drooped and he flicked the ash from his cigarette with slow deliberation into the ashtray. He added tiredly, "I remember her staring at me in the dark elevator going up to my flat, with an expression like a trapped rabbit. That's all."

Vinny's eyes were on him, hard and searching.

"So that's the plea: it all went black, your honor."

Tom stared back, mouth tight with irritation.

"I wouldn't expect her father to believe that story, perhaps. But it happens to be true. I have seen Miss Hamill only twice

before in my life: once last summer in a bikini at Castelfu-
sano; slender but not bad. Then again at the Embassy Fourth
of July party when I was pressed into service as a translator
for some of the official Italian brass. I'd never even really
talked to the girl until last night."

Tom shook his head in mock indignation.

"Imagine! We weren't even properly introduced!"

"Stop talking like that!" Vinny told him loudly. "She's not
one of your Italian whores!"

Tom's lip curled.

"Half right, Vin. She's *not* Italian." He studied the elegant
figure across the desk from him with growing curiosity.

"And now would you mind telling me, please, why Miss
Hamill has become so important in *your* life?"

The polished shoes and severe black socks balanced on the
desk corner disappeared and Vinny Brentwood was standing,
leaning on tight knuckles across the frontier of his desk, his
bland, plumpish face suddenly contorted with an unfeigned
fury. It was, Tom realized with surprise, one of the few
times he had seen Vinny goaded to such naked anger; he
had rarely dared to reveal irritation with his boyhood leader.

"I'll tell you exactly why she has become so important in
my life!" Vinny told him through gritted teeth, careful to
keep his voice discreetly low and unheard by Miss Brumacher. "I was supposed to escort her at that marine party last
night, and it was only because we have this congressional
VIP on whom I had to dance attendance down at the Grand
Hotel that I couldn't make it. Is that a good enough reason?"

He glared down at Tom, and banged both of his knuckles
on his glass-topped desk, his pale eyes dilated as if in surprise at his own vehemence. A moment of silence succeeded
his subdued outburst and then Tom, in a voice he had not
used in a long time, said, "Sit down."

Vinny blinked at the crackle of command and, as a klieg
light slowly dims, the fire in his eyes extinguished and he sank
into his armchair, his hands knotted into impotent fists.

Tom drew deeply on the cigarette and cocked his head in
the familiar gesture of alertness before he spoke.

"Vinny, I'm sorry," he said evenly. "I don't happen to have
the same proprietary interest in the conduct of *my* girl friends
that you have, but then *I'm* hardly a standard-bearer of Western morals. I repeat to you: this girl was kind of drunk and,
while on the make, a little pathetic. I certainly didn't lift a
finger to encourage her. If I had known she was your date,
I'd have left her at the marines, stoned as I was. There's an

50

awful lot of stuff lying around in Roma for the having; I certainly don't need any that belongs to someone else, least of all to an old friend."

He watched Vinny closely now, intrigued at the differences and the samenesses in the man who was once that fat, timid Brentwood kid, the cowardly little kid who had about everything except the respect of his neighborhood contemporaries. Vinny had followed Tom, the boyhood leader, all right, displaying a desperate courage to retain the prized status as one of Tom's Gang, a status he was constantly on the brink of losing only to regain it with a trembling complicity in breaking hothouse windows or painting the Civil War cannon in the Common a bright red. Now here he was behind his embassy desk, the well-turned-out FSO, face a bit pudgy as always but given dignity by the close-trimmed mustache and carefully groomed hair. Only the light eyes of Vinny, the plump, scared kid, were recognizable: they were the eyes of the kid, now the man, worried but on the make.

Tom smiled at the complete irony of their reversed positions. He crossed and uncrossed his legs with a glance at his ruined Italian loafers, and took a final drag of his cigarette before he crushed it out. From his expression, it was quite apparent that Second Secretary Brentwood was taking it hard.

"Look, you casual, free-living bastard," Vinny finally said in the same heavy officiousness he had used in his first words, "it is unfortunately known around this Embassy that you are a home-town friend, a childhood buddy. I showed up here four months ago, found you high and dry on the local beach, down to your last five hundred lire . . ."

". . . I have been down to my last five hundred lire a dozen times since the war," Tom interrupted him stiffly, "and will probably be another dozen times yet. Don't over-dramatize."

'Stow it. I found you employed as a lousy local interpreter for the Embassy and so I got you a better deal here with the field inspection teams of the Military Aid Group to whom I happen to be detached; so what do you do? First you damned near kill off the team . . .'

"The colonel wanted to see the old Gothic Line. How in the name of Sam did I know the area was still thick with land mines? And besides we only lost a jeep wheel."

"Don't interrupt. Then you deliberately gave that Italian general the idea that we were going to rebuild his ordnance garage despite the fact that we were recommending that he close the awful place down."

Tom folded his arms, head again cocked as Vinny remembered he did when the barb was digging deep.

"I did not 'deliberately' give him that idea," Tom answered, biting off each of his words. "The Italian general simply paid no attention to me. He thought that his prisoner-of-war English, which he learned in India, was so good that when Colonel Futtolo used two negatives in one sentence and in a pretty mushy Mississippi drawl to boot, the general thought it meant an okay. They were both convinced I was mistranslating until it was too late." He placed his hands on the arm rests of his chair and pushed himself to his feet.

"Vinny," he said gently, "I don't know what you're trying to tell me but do it nice and quick, please, and stop nibbling around the edges. We don't have to play games with each other." He paused, balancing in his hand the flat square parcel that was his raincoat.

"All right." Vinny's voice was strained and tight. "You're in the soup up to here and not only with me. Just before you got here, I was dismantled by my boss, a gentleman you know well, named Addison Hamill, who found out that his daughter spent the night, or most of it, at your place. Mr. Hamill is almost pathologically concerned with his daughter's welfare since she has no mother, and he acted as though you had taken advantage of . . ."

"Now just a damn minute," Tom broke in. "I gave it to you straight, Vinny. Last night, Nancy Hamill was acting like someone who wanted a quick roll in the hay. I can't honestly recall but as far as I am concerned, she is in exactly whatever virginal status she owned when I took her home, or rather the other way around, last night. Now just come off it, Vinny, right now!"

They exchanged hard measuring glances, and Vinny finally bobbed his head miserably.

"O.K., I believe you, although I can tell you old Hamill sure doesn't. When she showed up at home at five A.M., her father was waiting for her. He asked her where she had been and she said she was with you. He gave her unshirted hell and she simply went into her room, locked herself in, and has been there since. So . . ."

". . . so, he took it out of your innocent hide," Tom grinned in involuntary sympathy, his own anger fading. "I repeat, I'm terribly sorry, Vinny, that you got the dirty end of the stick."

It had always been this way. Just when you got peeved and maddened at the fat pompous little Brentwood kid staggering along, slowing everybody else down after a raid on an apple orchard, he'd wind up getting caught and absorbing a couple of swift kicks in the bottom, and you couldn't help feeling sorry as he sat there, a half-chewed apple in his hand, tears of pain and suffering streaming down the ten-year-old cheeks.

Vinny wandered to the half-window in his narrow office and in his slow, slouching walk Tom sensed the unspoken reprimand, the why-do-you-always-do-this-to-me. Tom raised a hand to his aching head and was surprised to find the fingers trembling. The knot he had tied on last night must have been a monster! He turned to follow Vinny's meanderings and found a right forefinger cocked at him not two yards away.

"And as if all this weren't enough, Colonel Jameison sent one of his field-grade flunkies in here about an hour ago to give me both barrels because you were supposed to be on tap at nine-thirty A.M. sharp to accompany my VIP, Congressman Briscoe, on an inspection of an Italian army unit down near Anzio. The Congressman happens to be a very large wheel on the House Appropriations Committee. You didn't show."

Vinny held up a large and complicated watch and tapped its dial.

"It's exactly eleven-forty A.M. They went off without you an hour ago, mad as hell."

"No excuses, sir. I hope this doesn't undo the Marshall Plan."

T. Vincennes Brentwood turned eyes on him which contained the pathos of an old beagle who has just heard he is being replaced by a Chihuahua.

"How could you fail me today of all days, Tom? You know damned well I've been here such a short time and that I'm trying, really trying, to show my stuff after a couple of rotten-luck things in Norway and Pakistan that I won't even try to explain to you."

He looked away, staring moodily at the vaguely disapproving features of the Secretary of State, whose photograph dominated one entire wall.

"When Vinny Brentwood's name is mentioned around here," he explained to the photograph, "it now registers as: ah, yes, the boyhood chum of that sad-ass expatriate, Tom Linden."

They were standing close together now in the quiet room.

53

Tom asked him evenly, "And how do *you* feel about that sad-ass expatriate?"

Vinny grasped Tom's shoulders with both his hands.

"You know damned well that I really don't care what these bastards think! But Tom, you sometimes make it awfully tough for me with these raunchy ways of yours. In this one morning, you've gotten both our tits in a wringer. You behave like a man who simply doesn't care!"

Tom said, "The Embassy pays me twenty-five thousand lire a week salary as interpreter when I'm working; that's equivalent to a little more than a dollar an hour. They need me, and I need them for the moment because jobs are hard to find. Also, when the Embassy uses me, I have a good excuse for the Foreigners' Office down at the Questura when I go to get a renewal of my residence permit, which is at the moment long expired. How much am I expected to care? But I'm sorry as hell, Vinny, that I got you into a double jam this morning."

Vinny stared at the cropped dark poll of Tom's head. He had something painful to say and, finally, out it came like a geyser of steam.

"One more thing. Just why the hell are you hanging around here in Italy like this, looking like somebody in the soup kitchen line at the Salvation Army? The first time I met you here last January, you told me you've been here since the war. Why don't you go home?" He pushed the reluctant words out one behind the other.

"It'll cost you one more super-long filter cigarette, *tipo americano*, to hear what is known as the Linden Rapid Autobiographical Line, Excellency, a story to fit all occasions and carefully tailored to please and impress the questioner of the moment." The corners of Tom's full lips were turned down in dark humor. "You've been dying to pop that one since we met last January, haven't you?"

He accepted the cigarette and the light, and perched on a padded arm of the chair. Vinny said, "You don't have to tell me a damned thing. You know that. Just say 'No go' and that's it."

Tom surveyed the ill-disguised curiosity of the other.

"No, Vinny, I don't mind giving you a quick fill-in. You know the part that came before the war. I'll make the rest short and snappy."

Vinny stepped back and leaned against the cold metal solidity of the three-drawer file cabinet. He inspected the hastily shaven chin and the dissipation-darkened pouches beneath the eyes with a sadness stronger than he cared to probe. This was once a crackling, devil-eyed slim youth, that Linden boy ("that damned Linden kid" to Vinny's father), idol and despair for ten years of Vinny's boyhood. This was Tom who was only two years older but who could jump higher, dive deeper, skate faster, go unwashed longer; later he could drink cheap hooch and kiss girls quicker than any boy around. And Vinny had been supremely content to be permitted to tag along, following the lazy, tilted head, the crooked smile, the Tarzan howl of triumph. So here the Linden kid sat, somehow shrunken and drawn, with a bony hand that trembled as it held the cigarette stub. The world was not only small that it should fling them together again in this great Roman *palazzo* of an Embassy after fifteen years; it was also mean and ugly. Although this moment perversely satisfied him after all these years, he honestly wished they had never met again.

"Well," Tom smiled, and the half-cock of the head was almost as depressing as the coquettish smirk of an old woman who has forgotten she is no longer young, "we never held back on each other, did we?"

"No, we never did."

"We achieve our successes in a variety of ways. You as a latter-day Talleyrand, I as a present-day bum."

"Now look . . ."

"Oh, come on now, Vin. It's true, about me anyway. Addison Hamill is right and so are the rest of your goddamned impossible Embassy friends, no matter what you'd like to believe."

He studied the heavy gold cuff links glinting discreetly from Vinny's crisp sleeves. Out in the Rome sunshine, his own clothing needed only to be clean. Here, standing before Vinny, he felt almost blasphemous. They had both come a long way.

And now he would have to do the thing he hated most. Tom had fought recall as a healthy body fights disease, instinctively and unfailing. Each time it twinged him, he got up and ran, into the arms of a wench or the obliterator that was alcohol. Now—with those pitying dog-friendly eyes on him, waiting for Tom the Leader to shinny up to the swaying top of a tree or to drop a paper bag filled with water from a high window, or to ask for five admissions at the ticket window of a Boston burlesque house as gruffly as a fourteen-year-old could—now he had to narrate. There was, for this moment at least, no escape.

"Short and snappy," Vinny prompted him, sensing the barrier.

"A war story, daddy?"

"The war to start with," Vinny echoed. "Make it easy on yourself."

"The war, my friend, poured us into different molds. Like cement, we've hardened in those molds, and all that remains of Tommy Linden and Vinny Brentwood of West Waterstow, Massachusetts, are a bunch of screwy idiotic experiences we had as kids together. Some of them pretty silly in retrospect but we didn't know any better, I guess."

"I don't know about you," Vinny said, eyes remembering some of the screwy idiotic things, "but a lot of them scared the hell out of me; I really got the strap sometimes for doing them."

"Yeah, but that was it: your parents gave a good damn about you, how late you were out, whether you got fed or not."

"Oh come on, Tom boy, your dad and sister did what they could."

"Correct, they did what they could—when my sister wasn't having a nervous breakdown from her latest bad marriage and when the old man was sober enough to go down to his law office and handle a few clients to keep us in groceries. Let's not pretend with each other, *amico mio*. Vinny Brentwood may have had a pretty stuffy D.A.R.-Masonic family life, but you got what you needed: clean sheets, a big hug every now and again, and somebody worrying about you. 'That Linden kid' was free as air and was out in it all the time because he didn't want to go home to a pretty sour old drunk of a father and a pathetic misfit of a sister." He shook his head with self-contempt.

"My God, I sound like one of those whiners on radio who used to ask Mr. Anthony whether she should drown her kids or her mother-in-law."

"All right," Vinny said, grinning uncertainly. "The war came and you went out first. I read a couple of tremendous letters you sent your sister from that infantry camp in the South, and then nothing. What happened to Tom Linden, the guy who would try anything once?"

"He died. Somebody else named Tom Linden survived infantry basic, used some body English to get into OCS, and, three months after becoming an officer and a gentleman, was on a Liberator heading for Tunis. Nine weeks later, after being pushed out an airplane door five times in four days

56

over the desert to qualify for paratroop wings, he jumped as one of a three-man team behind German lines in the mountains south of the Po Valley. Special operations."

"Jesus!" exclaimed Vinny, eyes shining, "you're not making this up?"

"I could always make you believe some real whoppers, Vinny. But just for laughs, let's say I'm telling the truth. Well, there's not much after that. It was one of those liaison-with-partisan teams. End of the war found me happy as hell in the out-patient ward of the Army General Hospital in Leghorn. Got my discharge in Caserta."

He cocked an eye at Vinny. "Lots of laughs after the war here. More Italian poontang than you could imagine, and then after a language-school course in Perugia, I settled down in Rome. Picked up a bit of cash doing all sorts of things: writing publicity blurbs for airlines, translating Italian movie scripts into English, steering American tourists to the right restaurants and stores. Made a small pack on that last bit during Holy Year . . ."

He caught the expression of mingled disgust and disillusionment on Vinny's face and stopped in mid-sentence with a mirthless grin.

"Getting a little weak in the stomach, Excellency? It's all right. I was just about through." He waved an indifferent hand.

"Picking up a bit of cash by out-sharking some nineteen-year-old marines at draw poker on their payday. Is that part of your odd jobs 'career'? Like last night's hundred-dollar pot?"

Tom rendered a classic Italian shrug.

"Last night I was lucky. When I'm very, very drunk as I was last night, sometimes I can't lose even if I want to. And I need this money, Vinny boy, I really need it, above and beyond the sad little peanuts I make working with your olive-drab friends in the next room." He threw his stub on the terrazzo floor and ground it out with his heel.

Vinny shook his head. "Look, Tom, I'm not as stupid as you might think. *I* can see flies in the ointment as well as the next man. Now you tell *me* why a goddamned bright guy with three years of Harvard behind him never goes back after the war to finish up, never goes home to see his family and home town, and winds up in Rome twelve years later, snagging card money from a bunch of fuzz-cheeked marine guards, playing Romeo to a sad bunch of local Juliets, and reduced to a string of cheap jobs and errands."

"I'm sure Nancy Hamill must have some of the answers. Why don't you ask her?" Outside, a cacophony of exasperated Roman motorists caught in a traffic jam blared up faintly, and Tom waved a hand toward the window.

"It was a low blow, Vinny, and I'm sorry," he grinned apologetically. "But in answer to your question, blame the fatal allure of the Eternal City. Too much sunshine and outdoor cafés. Lots of foreign devils get stuck here and live out lives of noisy desperation. If you're an American Negro here, you can almost forget you're black. If you're a homely American, there's always a local girl who thinks you're Barrymore. Here I can almost forget I'm Tom Linden. My Maria and my whole neighborhood call me Dottore, mostly to be polite and because I own more than fifty books; just Dottore. Tom Linden is a name for files: the Rome police records for foreigners, the embassy records on my passport which also expired a couple of months ago. I'm just another damned *straniero* here and I like it, I like it a lot. And we won't go into anymore 'whys' on that."

He rose from the chair arm and rubbed his hands with synthetic briskness.

"And now, Excellency, a big favor. Perhaps you can trot across the way and square things with the inspection tour officer, Light Colonel Phillips. I really need the job right now, and the only reason I was late is directly the fault of the marines who plied me with enough scotch last night to drown in." He held out a beseeching hand. "Tell him I'll take that Congressman on a special conducted city tour tonight that will add half a billion dollars to your military aid appropriation."

"What about Addison Hamill?"

"I'm ready to talk to him *and* his daughter any time they say. I've got enough black marks against me without getting one for free." Then he smiled one of his rare do-this-for-old-Tom smiles. "How about a go at Phillips?"

Vinny rubbed his chin. Staying out of trouble here was work enough without sticking out his neck. Even if he succeeded with Colonel Phillips, that didn't clear him with Hamill at all. And not one word to Addison Hamill, oh indeed no! He wondered whether Hamill would get wind of this little situation; he knew deep down he eventually would. Addison Hamill was a bit like God: he found out everything and he *never* forgot any of the bad things . . .

The telephone on his desk burred shrilly four times, the

inter-office signal for him, controlled by Miss Brumacher outside. He reached it in a bound.

"Brentwood here."

He stiffened to a more alert stance and said, "Why, yes, sir . . . yes, sir, he's here."

Vinny looked up at Tom and his face compressed into an angry knot.

"No, sir, I do *not* understand why. Effective immediately? But can't we discuss this a bit further, sir . . .?"

Tom secured the little square that was his plastic raincoat and fingered the tear in its collar as he moved slowly to the door. Vinny held up his hand to hold him.

". . . very well, sir, but I must say . . ." There was a long silence and Vinny finally said in a metallic tone, "Right, sir," before he placed his finger on the cradle to cut off the speaker at the earliest second.

"That was hardly how they brought the good news from Aix to Ghent, now was it?" Tom asked softly.

Vinny breathed deeply twice before he answered in a half-strangled voice.

"That was Mr. Hamill. Colonel Estland has been in to see him, complaining how embarrassed he was when you didn't arrive to meet the Congressman this morning to take him to Anzio. Hamill's furious. He won't hear of any continuation of your services. You're to report to the Embassy finance officer and arrange to have him send you whatever we owe you.

"Tom, I'm sorry, sorrier than I can say." His eyes pleaded forgiveness as he stood with one hand still resting on the offending phone.

Tom opened the door. "So long, Excellency, and thanks for the cigarettes. I filched a couple for later.

"And never mind what happened in those other countries." He pointed to the stern photo on the wall. "Give your all for dear old Foster Dulles. Somebody's got to put old Waterstow on the map." He paused. "When you next see Addison Hamill tell him to keep Nancy away from marine guard parties. Lots of booze, bad language, and temptations there." He waved. "Don't move. I'll find my way out." He looked around the room. "Pretty large for a cell."

As the door closed behind him, Vinny pressed the inter-office button.

"Miss Brumacher, get me Mr. Hamill's office, please."

And when that authoritative, nasal voice answered, Vinny, summoning a shaky courage to respond, said, "He's gone. And

I told him he was fired although I really hated to do it. Now what else did you want to talk to me about?"

"I am reading the results of a routine check we made of Linden through the military attaché following his employment by us here as a local," Hamill told him crisply. "The Pentagon check has just come in. A very strange story. He was a junior officer in some kind of wartime mission behind enemy lines up north of here."

"I already know that, sir," Vinny said, pleased that he could sound fully cognizant and prescient.

"Indeed!" responded Hamill, a vein of irony lacing through his precise voice. "Then perhaps you also know what happened up there on that mission."

"No, sir, I don't."

"Well, then, Mr. Brentwood," Addison Hamill said coolly, "why don't you get on your little bicycle and come on down to see me. Takes too long for the phone. But I *can* tell you that it's a very strange story, very strange, indeed."

"I'm coming down, sir, I'm coming right down."

chapter six

TWO MEN STOOD shoulder to shoulder looking through the high narrow window down into the traffic-choked thoroughfare called the Street of the Dark Shops. Across the way, chatting animatedly in a close-knotted group, lounged three uniformed Pubblica Sicurezza agents in dark blue tunics and lighter blue trousers with red facings and ridiculously tiny pistols in little leather holsters at their belts. A short block away to the left, the men in the window could see two carabinieri standing silently aloof, side by side like a pair of identical kewpie dolls with their gleaming white belts ranging over one shoulder and sagging at their hips under the weight of the traditional black leather cartridge box with its brass-bomb insignia, their somber navy blue uniforms slashed by a broad red stripe down their pants legs. Without craning their heads, the men in the third-floor window knew that immediately below in the dark, medieval streets, there were at least another half-dozen uniformed policemen plus an indeterminate number of stubble-cheeked plainclothesmen lounging with all of the labored and convincing innocence of the wolf outside the house of the three little pigs.

"We seem to be occupying the full-time capacities of at least a platoon of the finest Forces of Order, as usual," Comrade Giorgio said heavily. "I wonder what they find to talk about for so many hours?"

"They are Italians: soccer and women, in that order," his companion replied crisply, his rapid Milanese accent contrasting sharply with the soft, slurred Neapolitan speech of his questioner.

"As do most of our Party rank and file, for that matter," Comrade Giorgio commented, with mixed asperity and resigned tolerance. "I can understand the late Duce's despair at attempting to make militants out of Italians. Look at them!" he growled disgustedly, watching two of the uniformed policemen cup furtive cigarettes in their hands despite their on-duty status.

Comrade Piero half turned to look up at the hard gray eyes and the contemptuous frown.

"It gives us status," he said. "Everyone knows the Party is here and in business. They're afraid of us."

Comrade Giorgio turned on his heel and marched heavily back to his desk, Piero on his heels. They faced each other, Giorgio taller and much bulkier, with a slouch that added an insolence to his bearing and a close-cropped Prussian haircut which harshened his large and somewhat loose features. He looked appraisingly down for a moment at the steel spring of a man before him.

"And so, it's confirmed," he said finally. "This young ruffian of a Comrade Franco is a police spy." He nodded his great head slowly. "Very shrewd of you to find out so quickly." Piero slightly bowed his gleaming, close-groomed head in silent acknowledgement. From Comrade Giorgio, this was unstinted praise.

"I exclude," Giorgio went on, "for the moment the other one." The sentence was almost a question mark.

"Yes," Comrade Piero assured him, "I also exclude Comrade Seddu. True, his political indoctrination is still rather mediocre; he has no command of Marxist philosophy or orientation, a sort of starry-eyed idealist with some romantic bourgeois concepts, but basically very well motivated, good

61

material. No, it was Franco Furbo, that miserable Fascist opportunist!"

Comrade Giorgio stared through his own cigarette smoke as if carried away in thought, although Piero knew full well that the barb had firmly anchored: it was, after all, Comrade Giorgio who had enthusiastically supported the idea of seducing a few key neo-Fascist leaders into the Party as evidence of its irresistible lure. And he had found a minor district position for Furbo (at the expense of a now embittered Party youth leader) solely to make the bait more attractive. Comrade Piero's voice took on a staccato arrogance.

"Our suspicions had been aroused when one of my men saw Furbo by chance during one afternoon at siesta sitting along the Bernini colonnade in Saint Peter's Square with one of those *questurini;* you know, the kind with the flat-footed walk and a slouch hat. You can spot them instantly. And now the trap is sprung. He flew to them like a pigeon the moment he returned from the Ardea job today."

Comrade Giorgio reached for a long pale box of cigarettes with Russian lettering on it and picked one out, lit it and smoked it in the Russian manner, with thumb and forefinger. He had had many years in Moscow to learn such habits, before and during the war.

"How does our . . . er . . . representative at the Questura come to learn so quickly of such things?" he asked the little man. "After all, the explosives were pinched from Ardea only this morning."

The chisel-faced man smiled self-deprecatingly and leaned towards Comrade Giorgio in a conspiratorial confidence.

"Franco reported in to them immediately. His police contact came back to the Questura and reported to the vice-questor who immediately telephoned the Ministry of Interior." Piero grinned a lean smile of a wolf regarding a stray sheep far from the shepherd's eye. "One of our comrades is on the Questura switchboard, and he simply listened to everything the vice-questor related." He looked up into the hard eyes of his superior. "Do you know: they intend to give Franco a bonus of fifty thousand lire?"

Comrade Giorgio held his interlocutor in a steely gaze and then his large meaty hand came down on the other's shoulder.

"Bravo, Piero, well done." Giorgio took another puff on his long-stemmed cigarette and tightened his massive jaw. "Franco will also get a bonus from us. One that may require fifty thousand lire in medical bills."

Piero nodded and made a mental note of the instruction.

"Should we tell Comrade Spartaco?" he asked, suddenly reminded of a seamed, battered face darkened in anger. "He was most unhappy at your selection of Furbo and Seddu for special assignment when, as he told me, he had a hundred partisan veterans in the Party ranks of Rome alone who could steal entire artillery pieces out of depots, if he gave the word. Now he will noisily claim that he was right and that we don't know what we are doing here at headquarters."

"We were wrong even in telling him of the matter! I wanted him to be in on it only so that he would not raise a new outcry that we had again circumvented him in his post as Party *responsible* for the para-military apparatus."

He glared moodily at the heavy window draperies. "Yes," he grunted finally. "You had better tell him. As for myself, I have an outcry: I am getting damned sick and tired of our Comrade Spartaco."

He trudged behind the large cluttered table that served as his desk, and eyed Comrade Piero from under shaggy brows as if weighing whether he should continue in this vein.

"He is a Party hero, from the Party's beginnings; a man who served with Comrades Togliatti and Gramsci even before Mussolini's March on Rome," intoned Piero in the flat voice of one who has long memorized his lessons.

Comrade Giorgio, facing him directly now, suddenly grinned widely, displaying unnaturally even, white artificial teeth and nodded vehemently.

"Just so, Piero," he grunted in leaden irony, "he is Il Duro, faithful comrade from the Party's beginnings in Italy, survivor of Fascist truncheons, Spanish Falangist air bombings, and pride of the Resistenza. But it will come as no secret to you, Comrade Piero, since we have reached a point of complete understanding with each other"—and he lowered his voice—"that even a Party hero must heed the Party's discipline and its new directions faithfully, fully. Otherwise he plays the role, willingly or not, of traitor to his own cause."

The quick dark eyes of Piero formed an unspoken query. Comrade Giorgio reached forward heavily in his comfortably upholstered desk chair for a thick brown folder on the mounds of documents and files piled high on his table desk. He beckoned Piero into an adjoining chair and addressed himself to the folder which he had opened. "The Party, the Movement, always needs heroes. We can never have too many of them, just as the Mother Church needs saints and martyrs. Believe me, we have damned few left who actually know what our great Comrade Gramsci looked like. Up to now we have needed Il Duro just as our lungs need air. He is a symbol of our militant past. The majority of our present cadres have poured in since the end of the war. The old cadre lies buried in prisons and battlegrounds in Italy, Spain, Germany"—and after a pause—"Russia." He lifted his head slowly. "And when did you enter the Party, Comrade Piero?"

Piero, understanding full well that his questioner already knew the answer, replied shortly, "Nineteen hundred and forty-three."

"Ah, yes," Giorgio acknowledged with feigned surprise, "I remember now. You joined in Milan where you began the work you are doing now: guarding the Party against traitors from within."

He kept his voice completely level, free from the slightest intonation, but there was no mistaking his tone: you are the watchdog, but remember for whom you watch. It is for *me* you watch, for me and the tiny group who guide this Party, but first of all for *me*, very much indeed.

"Yes," Piero answered. "Just as now, there was much to watch out for during the war. Apart from vigilance over German and Fascist spies attempting to penetrate the Party's Resistance ranks, we had to worry about the clandestine printing presses, to move our headquarters from one point to another, dodge Allied air raids, and to keep an eye on the so-called Resistance activities of the reactionary groups. We were quite busy, I assure you."

"And it was there that you met our Comrade Spartaco, Il Duro, our Party hero?" The soft southern speech was smooth, mellifluous, courteous. Comrade Giorgio continued to shuffle the papers in the folder. Piero, watching him attentively, himself quite conversant with the contents of the folder, saw only the bulky nose and stubborn, slightly receding chin.

"Yes. I would meet him from time to time either in his area of operations in Emilia-Romagna or, infrequently, when he would arrive clandestinely in Milan for assistance or Party conferences. As chief of the *Gappisti*, he rarely left the Valley of the Po."

"You perceive whose portrait hangs on that wall beside that of Comrade Togliatti?" Comrade Giorgio held out a surprisingly delicate hand at the high wall at his left.

"Of course," the other answered dryly, "Comrade Khrushchev." He studied the portrait's features for a moment and added cautiously, "An excellent likeness."

"Quite true. Now let me tax your memory, my dear comrade. Whose portrait was hanging in that very space, let's say, a year ago?"

"That of Stalin."

"Excellent memory, Piero. And I trust that *your* office has made the same . . . er . . . interior decoration changes?"

The sharp little face tightened with annoyance.

"Comrade Giorgio, enough of these little games, please! I am as aware as you are of the speech of Comrade Khrushchev at the Twentieth Congress in Moscow last year and the full consequences of his revelations. The errors of Stalin are now recognized in their full magnitude despite his great leadership, and the new leadership of Comrade Khrushchev will provide guidance for us in Italy to correct those errors. I trust you did not request me to break off my inspection trip of the cadres in Puglia to give me a lesson in basic Party indoctrination."

Comrade Giorgio appeared not to have heard the outburst. He looked at the end of his long-stemmed Russian cigarette, methodically crushed it in a huge half-filled bowl of an ash tray, reached for another, and lit it reflectively.

"I smoke too many of these things but it's an old Moscow habit when you're working under strain," he commented blandly, looking at his yellowed thumb and forefinger. "Fortunately the Soviet Embassy seems to have an unlimited supply."

Then, as if recalling Piero's words he leaned back in his chair.

"No, I am convinced of your depth of indoctrination, my dear comrade, be assured of that. I will not play baroque games with you. You were recalled from Bari primarily to discuss Comrade Spartaco with me. I will tell you bluntly that the Party leadership is quite concerned about his refusal to accept the new Party ideological theses. Specifically, his recent negative remarks in the Central Committee session concerning the reappraisal of Stalin, the new peaceful aspects of coexistence with capitalism, and the non-inevitability of war were savage and disruptive."

Piero said, "The man has spent twenty years in the Party struggle. It is hard for him to comprehend in a short space of time that Stalin made the errors and committed the excesses now attributed to him. Besides, I trust I am not indiscreet when I say that he occupies no real position of power within the Party."

Comrade Giorgio struck his table desk with a heavy fist, jarring the untidy piles of paper.

"That may be! But as a Party hero, he has refused to change his ways! He still delivers that same damned 'barricades' speech to the youth cadres and partisan groups he has been giving for the past ten years, the one about marching on the Quirinal Palace, street fighting, elimination of the priests and the reactionaries. That may have been good stuff in 1946 but it is not today. And he won't stop!"

Piero stared at the red-draped portraits of the scholarly Togliatti and the tough Ukrainian peasant, and said slowly, "It is true. He told me personally that the new Moscow direction was soft-bellied and mistaken, and he felt that someone had been advising both Comrade Khrushchev and Comrade Palmiro badly."

Comrade Giorgio continued to regard him obliquely, and the message finally registered in Piero's nimble brain.

"If what you say is true, Comrade Giorgio," he started up in a new and enthusiastic tone, "then Il Duro truly represents a grave danger to Party unity. He dominates the ex-partisan organizations of the Romanga and Emilia, and it is quite clear that if he continues in this undisciplined Stalinist line, great confusion will prevail in the cadres of those areas and nationally."

Comrade Giorgio smiled broadly like a teacher expressing pleasure at the swift solution of a complicated mathematical problem by his favorite pupil.

"Precisely. And since an old dog rarely learns new tricks, the Party must be prepared to take swift and thorough action in Comrade Spartaco's case to protect himself and its unity." He patted the bulky folder lying open before him.

"This, comrade, is the personal Party file on Comrade Spartaco Tamburri, clandestinely known as Il Duro. It goes back over thirty-five years. I am sure you probably know most of its contents. It is a very complete file," he emphasized heavily.

Piero looked at the file with the professional hunger of a bird looking at a fat but inaccessible worm.

"Our Party hero is not a squeamish man," Giorgio said, eyes moving across a document in the file. "In Spain, while with the International Brigade, he served with Andre Marty in the liquidation of traitors and cowards. In the battle of Guadalajara, he summarily executed, with bullets in the back of the head, a squad of Blackshirts who had already surrendered to our Garibaldi Battalion. And in the last days of the Resistance activity in Bologna, he personally ordered the elimination of well over two hundred Fascists, collaborators, and Black Brigadiers who fell into the hands of his formations."

Giorgio turned a page and his eyes continued to flicker across the typed lines. "Yes," he mused, "quite a bloodthirsty animal."

He closed the folder with a decisive gesture.

"Your work is cut out for you, comrade," Giorgio said, rising and jabbing his finger at Piero. "I can tell you in full sincerity that the Party Secretariat wants nothing, no incidents, in Italy which will reflect unfavorably on us. We have already lost more than three hundred thousand faint-hearted members who refused to renew their Party cards this year because of the recent Hungarian affair. The intellectuals" (and the word was spat out like a sour grape) "all talk about our bloodstained hands. *Capito?*"

"*Hó capito bene,*" Piero said looking at his watch. "Rest assured, my men and I will follow this matter closely."

His narrow forehead creased in a frown.

"Too bad Spartaco did not realize that many of those killings at the end of the war were really unnecessary. But then, none of us has superhuman foresight."

Comrade Giorgio looked up at him.

"The Party has foresight—and hindsight. The mistakes of individuals may be faulty and incur punishment, but the Party itself is intact, pure in its aims and its eventual goal despite the means used to achieve those ends. Let neither of us forget this. It was not the Party which killed unnecessarily; it was the human error of Comrade Spartaco. He may in time be called to atone for his errors but the Party goes on and progresses to its golden ideals unsullied."

"I couldn't have expressed it better myself," said Comrade Piero, with his hard little face devoid of any emotion. He had all too often heard Giorgio speak eloquently, on the theme of Party purity, and it had become an abrasive platitude. But the Party was offering him, Piero, big game and the scent of it filled his nostrils with pleasure and anticipation. It offered him, the watchdog of the movement, a new opportunity to to prove his usefulness, his ferocious thoroughness, in rooting out the errors of a Party pioneer and hero. It was all so marvelously simple: Comrade Spartaco Tamburri dared to question the rightness of the Party's new opposition as laid down in Moscow and endorsed by Comrade Palmiro and Comrade Giorgio and the rest of the leadership. Comrade Giorgio was the new power in the Party and he, Piero, had coldly weighed the strength of this new rising star.

Comrade Giorgio quashed yet another *papiros* and automatically reached for the opened box. "Remember, I want a complete account of the activities of our hero with emphasis on his failure to follow Party orders."

"The Party's partisan bands unfortunately settled many personal scores with the Fascists during the war and immediately afterward with few eventual repercussions," Piero said. "Comrade Spartaco could not now be brought to court for any offenses of that period with the official amnesties long since in effect."

Giorgio looked up at Piero with undisguised irritation.

"I am not talking of any court action, *cretino*," he said insultingly. "I am speaking of the publicity that the neo-Fascist and Church-controlled press would spill out, if they ever learned the details. The smell of the garbage would drive away those trembling members we have recruited from the bourgeoisie for whom the Party is only a socially progressive group fighting for reforms by parliamentary means. And, I repeat, at this moment, barely six months from the Hungarian counterrevolution, we must be doubly careful." The little head nodded.

"We will handle Spartaco and his Stalinist indiscipline within the Party, within the Secretariat, Comrade Piero, understand?"

Piero opened his tight little mouth.

"Are you also aware, compagno, that Spartaco is a pederast?"

Giorgio made a sound halfway between a wheeze and a chuckle.

"Old history, Piero, for the past twenty years." He held up a warning hand. "And don't use that fact at all vigorously in any findings you make to the Control Commission; *that* stone can break many Party windows." He rose agilely, and shook Piero's hand briefly.

"Cancel the remainder of your Puglia inspection trip for the time being. This matter is of much greater priority. And now that we have identified the spy in our midst, let's wind up the affair of the explosives as soon as possible. Who has them now?"

"Comrade Seddu, of course. He was instructed to secure the explosives and to report to Spartaco immediately."

"And where is Comrade Seddu now?" Comrade Giorgio's voice could become soft as a child's.

Comrade Piero consulted his watch.

"As of half an hour ago, still in his apartment room, exhausted from the mission and two valises with explosives in the room with him. Once he rests up, I am certain that he will take immediate steps to inform Comrade Spartaco of the success of his mission."

"I would relieve him of his burden as soon as possible," Giorgio said, the command as mild as a chance greeting. "If the police should get to him first, arrest him with the valises, and force from him the story of who sent him on such a mission, it could be most painful and embarrassing for everyone."

The cold gray eyes looked up from under his eyebrows with a piercing glance.

"And do *not* telephone any news. You know why. Simply phone me to make an appointment, and we shall see each other as soon as possible." Piero's eyes blinked once in assent.

"I can see that we will be of great mutual benefit to each other as long as we continue to understand each other." The loose lips parted and the unnatural teeth appeared in a smile of dismissal.

Piero raised his hand in a proletarian fist of farewell. This was definitely his man, he said to himself as he closed the great office door behind him. This was the Party tiger, softspoken and deadly, and he had not made a mistake in seeking him out and offering the tacit alliance. He glanced at the names he had jotted carefully one below the other: "Spartaco," "Furba," and finally, "Paolo Seddu." He had his day's work cut out for him. With genuine verve, he strode out past the fortress-like Party building with its studded heavy gates, past the knots of lounging policemen into the sundrenched expanse of the Piazza Venezia. Hard by the Column of Trajan, a tiny Fiat with its motor already running, waited for him. Without a word of greeting, Comrade Piero slid in and looked at his two subordinates.

"We are going to call on a certain Comrade Seddu," he told them, and the little bug of a car moved slowly into the Street of the Imperial Forums, its occupants impervious to five civilizations lying in bleached ruins all around them.

chapter seven

Tom sat alone at a Doney table facing the surging traffic of the street, with the warm sun of early afternoon creeping across his face and soon to leave him in shadow. The second negroni followed the first coldly and satisfyingly down his throat. A bit too much Campari soda in that one, and the first one had contained just a fraction too much Carpano. But his luck would be running well if a third negroni ran too high with gin and this would give him three beautifully proportioned negronis inside him, all united and harmonious for the sole purpose of bringing out the best in the day.

Already the strollers seemed to be happier, more cheerful; the legs of the little shopgirls clacking by were a bit less hairy and squat, the men's shoes less pointy, their hair less oily, their jackets longer, and their smiles more sincere. Another drink and he would be seeing nothing but Greek Gods and incarnated Botticellis everywhere, and all of them wreathed in laughter. It was good to sit there, well dug into the wicker chair at Doney, the cold drink clinking in his hand.

He reached tentatively toward the little flag limp on its thin black staff and, with a slight refocusing, identified it: It was, bless his soul, a Union Jack and he muttered "Gorblimegorblimegorblime" in a ritual incantation to keep away evil spirits. As if to test the power of his magic, a slenderly erect gentleman of middle years sauntered slowly past, unmistakably English, wearing a light blue jacket with brass buttons and a darling ascot scarf beneath his trim jaw. He raised an inquiring eyebrow at Tom and slowed briefly to a mincing inviting gait. Bemused, Tom smiled but shook his head and waggled "no" with one hand. The blue-jacketed spirit shrugged ever so slightly and regretfully, lengthened his stride and resumed his search further up the Veneto. Perhaps one of the *bulli* in need of a bit of spare cash standing on the corner of Doney will take him up, Tom mused. Seemed like such a nice old chap; probably an ex-Royal Navy bloke. He would have done much better at Taormina or Capri or Ravello; swarms of them there. Royal Navy queer as spotted minks, he'd heard from more than one. Too much time at sea, perhaps. "Frigging in the rigging, there's naught all else to do . . ."—that was their salty song.

None of this, however, was extricating him from his chair on the Veneto. He would rise, he hoped, without attracting attention, beckon a cab and whirl back to his flat. Hopefully, the elevator would be in order and let's see, this is Tuesday, The Maria should be home accepting the first of the Sardinian telephonic communiqués and bulletins from all quarters of Rome and although she did not expect him home, she was always ready to drop some fresh pasta in the pot to give it that precise chewy consistency, *al dente*. Meanwhile he would sit out on the edge of the jungle of his terrace staring across to the green crown of the Pincio on one of the less fragile chairs until *"A tavola!"* was bellowed. Yes, that is what he would do, and the Count and perhaps the Countess would deign to hop heavily and malevolently into his lap and purr there noisily for the Big Scratch. But first one more negroni, just one more, and soon Vinny Brentwood and Addison Hamill or Hamilton Adler, or whatever his name was, would fade into wraiths, and if he closed his eyes he could begin to unravel slowly and carefully the sleeve of time starting from this place on a now deserted sidewalk of Rome back through the sunlit days and the warm embracing nights until he reached some point of safety, some bleak little piece of recognizable high-ground and there take stock. Certainly, he was as irretrievably lost sitting here staring at this little British flag as he might be in the trackless Gobi desert.

The white-jacketed waiter, a little twist of gold braid on one shoulder, glided up silently and deferentially and anchored the bill for the second negroni under the flag on top of the first one. The two negroni chits together totaled twelve hundred lire, exactly two hundred lire more than he possessed. He smiled warmly at the waiter who, quick to please, smiled back.

"A day for the countryside, fit for the Little Easter," he told the waiter in a near-perfect Roman accent. It amused him that alcohol invariably improved his Italian pronunciation.

"Magari," answered the waiter clasping both hands as if in prayer and supplication, "would to God one could take a picnic, but with five *bambini* and a sixth in the belly, who can go to the countryside? Only the signori with this"—and

he rubbed his thumb against his two front fingers—"can go."

"Pasquale, you are right," Tom said with male understanding, "for those who have five little ones and a sixth one almost made, there remains only the consolation of achievement. *Auguri* to number six, eh? *E tutti figli maschi.*"

The waiter cocked his head in a slight, stiff bow of acknowledgment.

"*Grazie,* signore. And my name is Aldo, not Pasquale. Unfortunately there are three girls, three dowries to raise."

"Aldo, I salute you and your fruitful signora," he told him, holding the emptied glass up to the waiter. "Now, one more negroni and this time with much emphasis on the gin."

He closed his eyes slowly, feeling the redness of the sun through the covering lids, and shook the newly arrived third negroni slowly in his hand, listening to the gentle melodic collisions of the ice cubes before replacing it on its tray. There was much to mull and to reorganize on this day which had started so badly and would not become any better as long as he sat there drinking the third hair of the dog that bit him the night before. But the cool languor of the Roman spring sun and the gin massaged the necessity to leave, act, move. He had been long aware of the sapping effect of this insidious Rome air which filled the outdoor café tables with clients who should be moving mountains elsewhere, a breath from the ruins which slowed the pace of living. After fighting it fiercely in his first months in the city, he had arrived at an uneasy truce with it, surrendering to the small nap after lunch and arriving at all appointments just a little bit late. But with negronis at noon on an empty stomach, one not only embraced languor: one started to manufacture it.

In the gleaming surface of the tray, a twisted face that was almost his and yet hideously not his, stared up at him, nose and mouth distorted but with the eyes intact, the puff-rimmed eyes and the dark forehead meeting the poll of his head. He stared at the caricature in the metallic tray and he tiredly asked himself the inevitable question: What the hell are you doing here? Vinny had asked it. Others had also asked it over the years, some contemptuously, some in soft puzzlement, and he did not recall a day in the past ten years when he had not asked himself the same question, jeeringly, despairingly, in the darkness of a cinema, in the drained empty seconds after the act of love. What in hell are you doing here?

And what had he been doing here these endless years which were half dream, half jail sentence? Well, he couldn't remember all of the jobs, some of them so fleeting that they had lasted but a day. A hasty translation of a business document into English. A week with a divorcee from Keokuk who ostensibly had wanted a guide to Sicily but had insisted on the second night in Siracusa that he stay with her because she was "frightened" of all those Mafia men outside," an exhausting protective vigil which lasted for two entire days and nights. A month, a wonderful month, driving alone in a tiny Fiat to the shipyards of a hundred cluttered little Italian ports, contacting the boat builders and fishermen for an American bilge-pump outfit, and he remembered the sharp briny fish smells of the sea with undiminished pleasure. One endless year teaching three little sons-of-bitch scions of a Roman *arrivista* millionaire the fundamentals of English speech and grammar and suffering their kicks and tantrums for the need of money. So many jobs, all of them in willful violation of the Italian work-permit laws. And until this morning, he had been for some weeks interpreter for a bunch of monolinguistic American military sachems seeking to give away an enormous pile of obsolescent military hardware to an Italian Army as hapless as the tired equipment they were getting.

Well, he told his mutilated image in the tray surface, some things we did not do and, please God, we will not do. We have never gone with men and this we can never bring ourselves to do. We have not yet killed or maimed, nor stolen from the poor. Sins? He wouldn't even try to itemize them and they all pointed wearily to that cursed, early developed sin of accommodation. And he had accommodated himself all right, these twelve Rome years of fat and lean, mostly lean, moving on, forgetting, moving on again.

But one thing there was no forgetting and that was why he was still here. Tom's face darkened as if the sun had left the sky, and he clutched the negroni glass tightly. The momentary lifting of the protective shield of forgetfulness brought on the Memory like a blow on the head with a heavy hammer. He slowly lifted his gaze from the crumpled face on the tray to the cheerful handful of siesta strollers and to the roar of traffic. Well, at least if he had to drink and suffer yet another aching round of why-are-you-here, he was doing it here in the sun with the clack of high-heeled shoes and the cheerfully flapping tiny flags on the tables at Doney's instead of in the dark and littered New England study that his father had sat in and slowly died from the brain on down for those many years at Waterstow, the half-empty bottle a symbol of residence.

The logicality of his mind automatically clicked on through the encroaching fuzziness of the negronis. Immediate problems: paying an eighteen-hundred-lire bill for three negronis, plus at least two hundred lire for Aldo and his five-and-a-fraction children, out of total funds of one thousand lire. Now, if he had not this morning "loaned" the other one thousand lire with such gallantry to a proud pointy-shoed scrounger of a friend in front of this very café, he could settle this ridiculous matter. With the other thousand, he could have risked the pangs of conscience by cutting the tip to 175 lire for Aldo and using the twenty-five lire to catch the *circolare* tram to the Lungotevere and to his penthouse kennel to face The Maria.

The Maria! He had almost forgotten what it meant to confront that square, impassive face, the pitying, half-contemptuous hands on hips when he stumbled in and announced that he had been fired, sacked, and that he had no money, no ability to pay her salary. Of all the people in this vast city, he hated most of all to make a *brutta figura* with The Maria. And yet, she was the only person to whom he could turn. O.K., Dottore, try accommodating yourself to this one!

He had without being aware of it, held up his hands to his face to peer into the blackness and despair. Someone eased into the neighboring chair and he took his hands away to look at the interloper, hoping it wasn't another foreign fairy.

It was a pleasantly attractive young woman dressed in a nubby spring coat with short stylishly curly hair and a large leather handbag. There was something very familiar and un-Roman about her as he focused dully on her rather round features, the mildly cleft soft chin and high smooth cheeks, and the huge slightly staring eyes . . . he half rose and the woman caught his negroni glass as it tipped with the convulsive gesture.

"Antonella!" he choked and the past became the present.

She nodded and the wide familiar lips formed a rueful half-smile.

"The *Tenente* Linden remembers after a dozen years," in a voice whose familiar singsong lilt was as Romagnole as the flat little villages of the Po. "Congratulations." She indicated the negroni glass with a little plump-fingered hand. "I trust I do not disturb. Do you expect someone?"

"On the contrary. May I offer you . . . ?"

"No thank you. I had caffé and brioche at the Termini station. I have just arrived from Milano. I rode all night and

74

have napped and washed at an *albergo diurno* near the station this morning. Did you get my telephone call?"

He simply stared at her, not understanding her, numbed by her presence, looking into the past in the clear brown eyes of this woman, now suddenly and unwantedly here.

"I went to your Embassy a few moments ago," she continued after a moment. "Your maid said on the telephone that you worked there. But after much confusion and telephoning, they said you were no longer employed there. Is that true?"

He bobbed his head in wretched assent.

"Fully true. Three hours ago, they would have answered you differently but now they are right. I am no longer there. A great career has come to an end."

She looked at him as most women look at most inebriates: pity mingled with contempt. The look cut through and piqued him, and he attempted to pull himself into complete erect alertness but it was as if he were in deep water, and fighting his way to the surface.

"Do you live in Milano now?" he asked stupidly, rallying his tired brain.

"No, I am still of Belinoro. Compared to Milano and all this"—with a wave at the thickening traffic, the mass of buildings opposite, and the great Roman wall beyond—"Belinoro isn't much, but it *is* my home, the place my family has lived for some hundreds of years, and I work and feel useful there, despite the terrible things that happened."

He gripped his cold wet glass to stem the welling sensation within him.

"Welcome to Rome," Tom said, fighting to keep his speech steady and unblurred. "Will you be in the city long?"

The huge eyes moved from his face to the ratty tie, to the frayed collar tabs, the overworn jacket, and the near-ruined loafers, and for the second time that morning he suffered the irritation and shame of being weighed and found badly wanting.

"It depends," Antonella said. "I actually came here to look for you among other things. And here I find you sitting at a café within an hour. This is really a smaller city than one would imagine."

"You looked for me? Why?" He took a deep gulp on the negroni and savored the strong bitterness of the drink draining down. "I thought everything between us had been over since the war."

Into her low clear voice sprang an antipathy that cut like a sword.

"You incredible egotist! You think I would come chasing after you down here after a dozen years to seek out your affections? You?"

She leaned toward him and he could barely endure the close-range scrutiny of those eyes. The chin and soft face were those of the girl of wartime Belinoro but the expression in the eyes was that of a woman for whom love is a heap of dead ashes in a dark hearth. He looked at the lips, briefly crushed by his in an unendurable hour of loss, mourning, passion, and disaster. They were straight and unyielding.

He shook his head, now light and a bit giddy. "No, I didn't really think you had come here for reasons of affection. It was a jest, my usual hilarious humor." And, half sensing, he asked her, "Why *are* you here?"

"I want to talk with you. It is an important matter for me." She took his arm.

"Please let us go elsewhere where we can speak more freely. We cannot speak of the things that concern me"—she waved her hand at the serried rows of sidewalk chairs and tables—"out here in this place."

He wagged an admonitory finger at her, realizing what a sodden fool he was making of himself but too loose with the alcohol to care.

"Sorry. Can't go with you, Antonella."

"Why not?"

He reached for the three little chits, waved them at her like a summons and whispered to her, "I am waiting for many important events to occur here. If you sit here long enough, they happen before your eyes. The Popes depart, Garibaldi arrives, the Fascists come, Mussolini goes, the Americans arrive!" He felt her great eyes burn with disgust and he knew he could not pursue the ridiculous role. "Go," he told her softly but bitterly, "go elsewhere and spare me the shame. I can't pay the bill."

She dropped her glance into a cavernous handbag, came up with two thousand-lire notes and flung them on the table. He felt a surprisingly strong arm pulling him to his feet.

"Where shall we go?" she asked, her hand still grasping him firmly at the elbow. But she sensed his wretchedness and her eyes glittered for a moment as she looked at the short gray-flecked hair. He felt her pity sting through the looseness of his groins like a needle touching a nerve. He hated having to be held erect, his drinks paid for by this woman whose lips curled with contempt and who had sprung from the outer darkness of his past in which there was mainly a sound of weeping.

He realized as he swayed against her in the sun before the crowded tables at Doney's that he was now momentarily a part of the "important events" that happened here all the time, as the murderous whispers of *"povero disgraziato,"* *"straniero ubriaco,"* and worse, hissed softly up from the tables around him. Bastards! He shouted within himself, bastards! You grovel and belly up to the man on top but when a hapless body falls, there are ten pairs of pointed and highly shined shoes suddenly appearing to kick the inert form. Ah, I know you well, you goddamned lizards sitting there in the sun waiting for a fly to fall.

He found himself walking slowly down the Veneto, and realized that Antonella had him completely in tow, past the slowly turning idly curious heads and flashing whispers. An ageless Lancia taxi was waiting at the Hotel Excelsior stand and he somehow stepped into its capacious interior.

"Where is a good outdoor *trattoria?*" he heard the low, controlled voice of Antonella ask the driver.

"On such a day, the Appia Antica," the man answered without hesitation, mentioning the most distant fare he could hope to gain. "There are several fine *trattorie* there far from the city noises, with the Roman ruins everywhere."

"He is a hopeless scoundrel," Tom broke in. "It is a ride of several kilometers and he will retire a rich man from such a fare."

"Avanti!" Antonella ordered without hesitation. "To the Via Appia."

"No!" Tom countermanded. "To the Lungotevere delle Armi." He turned to her with a twisted smile. "I have visited your home many times, and now you must visit mine."

He looked back at Doney as the cab groaned away from the curb and made out his table with the little Union Jack now fluttering alone among the glasses. He desperately wanted to be back at that table, just sitting there on the broad sidewalk, watching the drift and flow of humanity and mulling his present which was a fuzzy ruin and his future which was worse. But the cab rolled away from Doney, past the empty tables and chairs of the siesta hour, and its antique motor protested the upward slope of the Veneto toward the Pincian Gate.

Antonella sat beside him, a huge handbag separating them on the old leather seat, and looked straight ahead. The cab lumbered through the open gate in the massive Aurelian Wall and coasted slowly downhill through the Borghese Park now awakening in the first green moments of spring.

He broke the silence like a shattering of a glass pane.

"What do you want from me, Antonella?" he asked her, studying the handsome profile with involuntary admiration. She reached into the bag beside her, and pulled out a brown empty pistol holster, cracked with age. She bent the flap back and handed the holster over to him in that position.

"I don't know what I want of you, Tommaso," she said, surprising him by using the intimate "*tu*," "but tell me if this is actually what it appears to be. And if it is, how did it happen to come into the hands of Peppino Deruta?"

He hunched over it, seeking to hold it steady in the lurching cab, and he read aloud, "Major H. Dixon, U. S. Army, 0-35732." He looked up, the holster still in his hands. "It's his, all right. It's the shoulder holster of the pistol the major carried." He handed it back as if it were fragile enough to crumble in his hand. "I don't know how Peppino Deruta got it." His voice was flat, almost rude in its finality.

She returned it to the depths of the bag, brought out a photograph still in its thin silver frame and protected by glass. He recognized it immediately. He had his own copy, cracked and yellowing, somewhere in his desk at the apartment. It was a group photograph of five men and a girl, all clad in the heavy winter clothing of the hills. The girl, broadly smiling, vibrant and full-bosomed under a heavy knitted sweater, was Antonella, and the hand around her waist belonged to her husband, Fausto, the massive chunk of a man on her left. Beside Fausto a slim serious youth, proudly brandished a sten gun. That was Antonino, her younger brother. Close by him, Dottore Antonio Passaglia a short, dignified, heavy mustached man with the tight-fitting beret of the region on his head, regarded his children with stern but unmistakable paternal pride. Flanking Antonella on the other side of this family group stood himself, hatless and in open-throat Army ODs, eyes and face reflecting the sun and the clear tingling air in that moment long ago on a Romagna hillside. At his elbow a tall man, even taller with his overseas hat on, in officer ODs and a white army winter parka, stared unsmiling and alert into the camera lens as if it were a potential booby trap. Strapped over one shoulder and smuggled under his arm, a holster and gun butt protruded. This was the last photo ever taken of Major Henning Dixon. Only two persons in this snapshot were still alive—Antonella and himself.

Tom curtly nodded his recognition of the photo.

"Now what do you want?" He instinctively knew the reply, but before it came one of her hands reached out to grasp his wrist with a surprisingly cruel strength, her nails cutting into his flesh.

"The answer to why this holster was in possession of Peppino Deruta to be handed to me in his dying hour," she told him, hurting him in the vise of her nails. Sensing her anguish, he did not move to withdraw his wrist from the pain. The old cab rolled with a steady rumble past the mossy fountains of the Borghese, and she leaned toward him, eyes fixed on the square black head of the driver.

"If I am wrong, Tommaso, and Peppino was a traitor and sent me this memento only as a final reproach, I must go back to my Party comrades of Belinoro and offer my deepest apologies."

The vibrating claw on his wrist released its grip slowly, and her fingers brushed his bruised flesh like a caress.

"But if I am right, there was a deep motive for Peppino's act," she whispered, biting each syllable, "and I want revenge!"

chapter eight

ONCE THE LITTLE apartment was clean and dusted, the terrace swept, a hose turned onto the thirsty jungle roots, and a few intimate garments of both herself and Dottor Tommaso washed and flapping dry on the rim of the vine-choked terrace, The Maria lowered her tired bulk into a camp chair in the cool corridor next to the telephone and waited. It was at this hour—just after the serving of lunch, and with their employers taking their little siesta snooze—that the tightly interlocking society of those of Nuoro province now transplanted to Rome paused in their daily labors in a variety of deluxe apartments, villas, and governmental offices all over the city and made ritualistic telephone contact with each other. And at the center of this daily surge of communication among the Central Sardinians in Rome sat The Maria. She rarely called anyone save in emergency; *they* called her, the dozens who were beholden to her by tangled skeins of blood and family relationships, by calculated respect for her knowledge and her calm omniscience over the years, and not least of all, for services rendered.

The Maria had not been elevated to her preeminent position among the hard-working Sards in Rome by virtue of inheritance, beauty, or by early acclaim. She had won it the hard way, after years of toil and assistance to a thousand of her island kinfolk in a thousand ways. Did a swarthy little housemaid barely six months out of her natal Barbagia Ollolai need a heavy hand of pressure to legitimize a most untimely result of over-frisky comportment with her *fidanzato?* The Maria, and sometimes a priest, appeared as whirling black clouds of conscience until a solid promise to marry was extracted from the guilty impregnator. Did a little Sard tailor need five character witnesses, quickly, to swear in a lawsuit that they had known him for five years or more and that he was of impeccable character? The Maria saved the hapless one the harrowing necessity of negotiating with and paying off of five strangers to perjure themselves by conjuring five cheerful and willing perjurers from her following at a huge saving in "fees." Did a jobless, fresh-faced girl, two days off the island boat from Olbia, need a place to sleep without falling into the clutches of an oil-voiced panderer? She slept temporarily in The Maria's room until a job was found for her, and the employer of The Maria knew nothing or simply preferred not to notice the "guest." When Maria uttered those words, "*Ci penso io,* [leave it to me]," it *could* be left to her and she moved mountains with but a telephone for a fulcrum.

The only days in which the siesta hour calls did not come winging to her were those of the traditonal free afternoons off for the servant class of the great city: Thursdays and Sundays. On those days, The Maria, in her best walking-out dress, emerged from the pompous ugly Fascist-era apartment building, gave a stare of hostility at the stubble-faced *portiere* and proceeded slowly but erectly to the circolare stop. At the Stazione Termini she would descend, often to find a small knot of dancing-eyed servant girls already standing on the platform to greet her, gaudily dressed, wearing clumsy white shoes, wiry black hair piled in a variety of imitations of the latest Italian screen vamps, peasant tongues and lips flashing around white small teeth, glad as darting little swallows to be free of the homes, kitchens, nurseries, toilet floors. For most of that day and evening she sat adjudicating squabbles, affairs of heart and property, a Sardinian Deborah whose decision rarely was challenged.

Whether they phoned her or spoke to her over the tables of the little bars flanking the railroad station, the tongue was one which no foreigner could ever understand, nor could any mainland Italian unless he too by chance was born or raised in central Sardinia: it was a swift-streamed dialect of Spanish clang, a language and a way of life in itself, full of *u*'s and clashing chopped consonants and occasional gutturals of Arabic intonations.

She had learned much from these telephone calls of recent years, a world of submarginal information which bubbled from the lips of her friends and kin as the underground rivers of southern Italy rush along a hundred feet below the surface. Much of the information, like the waters of these rivers, was fresh and sparkling with human interest but useless to her. However, the shrewd brain beneath the graying shock of hair sifted and sorted whatever she heard, as a lone sourdough patiently pans river sand and gravel: every now and again, she strained out a tiny shining nugget of information or corroboration. This she filed away behind the forbidding brow with a thousand similar items, occasionally offering a counter-fact as a *quid pro quo*, most of the time muttering only, "*Molto interessante!*" And even this last was high praise for those who eagerly babbled the tidbit in her ear; usually she already knew.

Within fifteen minutes the phone had rung four times. The first call was titillating but basically useless: the *direttore generale* of a government ministry was having it out with his wife and each had lost his wits in the desire to sting and had bragged that each had many times cuckolded the other. How they were screaming at each other, their fat little cook breathed excitely into The Maria's attentive ear. But the latter shrugged her solid shoulders and had answered, "'M beh? He is a born *cornuto*, a cuckold, and she has always been *poco seria*, very lightweight. As long as they stop yelling when their children come in from school, *va bene.*"

The second call was little better, a long machine-gun staccato delivered by a distant kinswoman of hers who worked as a quasi-permanent seamstress in one of those fancy ultra-modern villas on the Monte Mario. Apparently the young daughter of the house had taken advantage of the absence of her chronically traveling parents and had opened a sort of floating teen-age orgy, complete with dice throws to select bed partners of the opposite sex, lots of loud mad jazz music, and very hard American liquor. The Maria crossed herself as she listened grimly and patiently to the clinical account of the goings-on, and wondered if those of that Monte Mario set called in a ferret-faced local abortionist to interrupt embarrassing complications as she recalled they did in her youth. Probably not; *that* kind now always had private clinics in Switzerland to which they repaired as if it were part of a holiday.

But the third call, coming within seconds after the second had ended, brought her massive perspiring body leaning forward with agitation and concern. It came from one of her cronies in the camp of an upstart who was blatantly trying to usurp the place of The Maria.

"You know," the building doorman's wife intoned, a strong asthmatic wheeze giving evidence of years in a tiny damp apartment below the street level, "I met The Pinetta yesterday . . ."

"I know no one who is called *The* Pinetta," interrupted The Maria in a voice at least an octave below the other's. "I know several Pinettas, most of whom are of little importance."

"You know which one I mean," insisted the *portiere's* wife without heat. "The one with the two silver eye-teeth who now works for a rich *americano* diplomat near the Villa Torlonia. She is achieving considerable prominence with the cigarettes and commissary supplies she hands out to Our People, stolen from her master."

"I know this Pinetta to which you refer," The Maria admitted grudgingly, more to pull out the information than to cede a point. "She is hardly a Sard, you know. She is fruit of a liaison between a carabiniere *maresciallo* from the Po Plain who was assigned to duty at Cagliari, and a local girl of the town. And as one of Nuoro, you know full well how false and treacherous are those Sards of the south."

"The mother and the father subsequently were married and besides, not all of Cagliari are false despite the Arab in them," corrected the *portiere's* wife, a stickler for precision and fair play. "However, as you know, I do not like her: this stealing from her employer to make a *bella figura* with Our People in the city is disgusting.

"It is for this that I tell you what she mentioned to me when we met by chance yesterday at the Piazza Vittorio market. When I mentioned to her that her gifts were indeed welcomed and looked for, she tossed her head and said, 'My American diplomat will do anything to assist me. He is powerful and is very rich. Certainly I can do more than the old Seddu of Nuoro with her starving, jobless Dottore!' "

The Maria glanced through the open door of Tom Linden's bedroom-study and her hot black eyes under the beetled brows picked out the two Siamese sitting on the terrace floor under the mottled pattern of sunshine. As she watched, the bull-necked male, Il Conte, reached out with his paw and slapped his slender-faced mate, La Contessa. *Porco,* like all men, she exclaimed to herself almost automatically.

The *portiere's* wife assumed this to be a muttered imprecation against the offending Pinetta and went on.

"I told her that she would have to go some to match The Maria in the esteem and respect of Our People here, that it mattered little to us whether her employer is rich or not. What matters to us is the heart and the wisdom of our own people, and in these virtues you are esteemed. I told her of a few of the things which you have done for others, Maria, including the medical treatment you managed to obtain for my man when he fell from his motor scooter. This Pinetta sniffed and said, 'Apart from his poverty, anyone who would work for a coward and a scoundrel such as her American Dottore must be in her dotage. Do not provoke me or I shall tell of it.' "

She felt a pain in her chest and throat as if her heart were stopping. The smooth plastic surface of the telephone suddenly went slippery in her hand.

"Why did you not ask her to speak of the sins of my employer?"

"I asked her harshly to tell me of such things and she only laughed and said, 'There is time, the right time.' I told her that we of Nuoro have dangerous punishments for bearers of false tales but she curled her lip and moved off."

"My thanks, dear Elena. Until Thursday."

"Ciao. Until Thursday."

She sat in the canvas-bottomed chair, body rigid with emotion. What could that silver-toothed thief know of her Dottore Tommaso? It was true that she knew little enough about him and his past, but of one thing she was unshakingly certain, from a knowledge of men extending back to her fourteenth year: Tommaso was *not* a scoundrel. A red-blooded philanderer, yes; a strange, brooding type, turning to tortured bouts with alcohol, certainly. But no thief, no rascal in any moral sense.

She made a mental note, cool and dispassionate now. The Pinetta, whom she had ignored for months, this one she must seek out now and nail her statements to the wall of truth. Such scratches of blackmail could not be permitted to fester. Perhaps this adder-tongued Pinetta felt she could hold up to ridicule The Maria and employer, purchasing the affections and smiles of those little Sard geese with American cigarettes, canned goods and clothing, but not even the geese could forget the Code of the Island or their ties and vows of eternal kinship and allegiance.

Completely absorbed by the plans and stratagems for spinning invisible webs around her rival, she did not hear the insistent telephone until it had pealed three long rings, by which time both cats had turned their heads in irritation.

"Ah, you sleek, lazy beasts, you shiftless, indolent, curse-tailed fiends," she burst out at them. "If you were not under the protection of Dottore Tommaso, I would dump you in the ruins around the Pantheon and let you fight it out for spa-ghetti scraps with the others!" They regarded her calmly, aware that she was railing futiley against their entrenched status, and when she had finished, both casually rose and stalked off one behind the other, jagged tails high and con-temptuous.

It was a male voice. She immediately recognized it, al-though he gave no identification, as that of a sober policeman once assigned to patrol the area outside the house of the old cardinal for whom she had worked. Once the short lean policeman had half-proposed a "friendship" and had taken the rebuff with a smile. He was now assigned to the central Questura, promoted to a *brigadiere*. Through the years an instinctive mutual sympathy had developed between them, especially after she had learned that his grandfather had been an islander, from Sassari, and she occasionally sat with him on the Via Nazionale hard by his grim police office, and took a caffè with him. She had frankly discussed Paolo and his fall from grace to Communism with him and he had been gruffly kind and understanding.

"I must tell you something in all confidence, Maria," his low voice now came through the receiver after their brief exchange of greetings. "Excuse my way of speaking but I am using the public telephone in the bar downstairs in the Questura and I do not want the others to hear. Your nephew Paolo is up to something. What, I do not know. I heard the merest fragment of a conversation between a plainclothes *maresciallo* from the Ufficio Politico and the vice-questor of that office. Paolo is carrying out some sort of illegal business for his comrades, the Red ones. I suggest that you get hold of him as soon as possible, talk to him and tell him to get out of that business or he will yet find himself in a damp little 'room' on the lower levels of the Regina Coeli."

At the mention of the name of that historically notorious Rome prison, The Maria crossed herself twice and her lips twitched a prayer to Mary, Mother of God. "I thank you with all my heart but how can I do this? I do not even know where Paolo now lives. I have heard that he has a small room somewhere in the area of Santa Maria Maggiore but from the moment he threw in his lot completely with Them, I have not talked to him nor seen him for these many months."

The brigadiere hesitated for a moment, and replied, "*M beh,* why don't you try a few of your famous contacts in that area. Start with the doorman at the San Giorgio Hotel. He is from Dorgali of your Nuoro province and he knows many."

"I know the man of Dorgali. Thank you and I shall mention you in my prayers," The Maria told him with deep conviction, "together with the Cardinal, bless his memory."

"Put in a word with God while you're at it to soften my superior's heart. I have been waiting for my promotion for four years now." And he rang off without another word.

She rose slowly, took the telephone off its hook and lay it carefully in the table; she wanted no more calls this day. Pacing distractedly into Tom's study, she mounted the two short steps to the terrace level and stepped out into a slurry of green and blue and gold, a cool afternoon wind overhead. This she had expected deep within her for some time, that Paolo, her Paolo, would eventually come to grief. One always did with Them, the Godless Ones, who laughed at the religious festivals, sneered at the priests, damned the hierarchy, blasphemed the Pope himself. Perhaps the priests had done their job badly with Paolo. Had he not many times told her, his determined little child face in a set straight scowl, "Zia, I spend three hours of the day on my knees on the stone floor of the chapel in the *collegio.* Must my knees always hurt to worship God?" Then, the answer had been easy: yes, your knees must hurt and you must suffer a little, as a tiny sample of how Christ suffered. Did not her own creaking knees ache from kneeling for these many years on cold marble church floors or on the hard wooden confessional steps?

Oh, my Paolo, why did you leave me, deny me the pleasure of your presence, the satisfaction of seeing your dark head bent over a plate of food prepared by my own hands, the joy of running my hand along the angle of your jaw in a passing, lasting caress? It was in such moments as these, rare and excruciatingly unendurable, that she wished herself dead, struck down on the spot.

But she was not The Maria for nothing. The mind that had created and executed a thousand microscopic stratagems had already begun to film over the place of hurt and pain, and the shrewd, hard-rock peasant pragmatism began to sift and probe and ponder the avenues of exit. There would be barely enough time to stop at Saint Eugenio's and to recite the rosary for Paolo, the cardinal, for Dottore Tommaso, and for her *brigadiere* at police headquarters, as well as for her parents who were now in the mists of her memory.

And then, since Dottore Tommaso had told her he would not be back for lunch this day, she would sally out into the city although it was only Tuesday, and she would find this Pinetta. Then, after she had confronted this foul-minded rival, she had to hunt down Paolo, her Paolo. Mmmm, there were at least three Sards much beholden to her who lived in or around the cobblestone hubbub that was the Piazza Vittorio market place, and with these and the man from Dorgali, she would commence her search for Paolo. She *had* to find him! She paused. No, first The Pinetta and then Paolo. She longed to reverse the order but first The Pinetta.

The air was smitten with a wave of clanging church bells close by; two o'clock, announced the bells of Saint Eugenio across the Tiber, and there was much to do. She straightened, whirled about, and headed for his room. This was a signal occasion and she would do only what she did on her afternoons off—take a bath, and attire herself in her walking-out dress.

As she passed the rustling hulk of the refrigerator, she stopped short. The beast had stopped again. She picked up the broom handle and swung a familiar lethal blow heavily against the slotted metal head. Nothing. She took emergency action: she opened the refrigerator door and slammed it shut with all her might. With a tiny, almost human scream, the ancient motor turned over, the scream rose in intensity and pitch, reached a climax, and subsided into a series of deep choking gurgle and rumbles. That was better! And to think how many thousands of lire Dottor Tommaso had spent in a futile effort to make this monster work automatically! *Brutta bestia!*

Then she remembered the cats. She flung open the refrigerator door again, pulled out two lumpy and hastily wrapped bundles covered by newspapers. With them in her hands she shuffled quickly to the terrace edge, lay them on the pavement, and opened them. Both contained a mixture of pasta and meat scraps prepared the night before. She turned and left without a backward glance. The Count and the Countess were there, watching her from among the tangled roots of the great round cement pots, she knew, but they would not touch the food while she was in sight. After all, everyone had his pride.

chapter nine

THE LITTLE MAN behind the huge mahogany desk sat quietly, hands in a praying position under his nose, until Vinny Brentwood had finished reading the flimsy carbon pages. He simply stared neutrally back when Vinny's head came slowly up with round-eyed surprise.

"Good God!" Vinny groaned. "He was booted out! A dishonorable discharge! For insubordination, no less!"

He carefully laid the typewritten pages on the desk and ran a hand over his carefully brushed dark blond hair.

"I . . . I'm terribly sorry, Mr. Hammil, for making that fuss over the phone about Tom. For a minute I thought he had gotten a rough deal; he needed the money, and all. But now with this . . ."

Mr. Hamill took his precise hands away from his mouth and he said in a voice that cracked like a lion tamer's whip, "Now just a second, Vinny. I happen to be one of those people who doesn't shout 'Unclean' and throw stones simply because a man happened to get a dishonorable discharge from the armed forces. As you are already very much aware, I don't happen to like this Linden fellow, and the Embassy of course could not have a man with that kind of record working for it, but I'm sure that as a close childhood friend of his . . ."

Vinny held up a courteous hand to interrupt.

"Hardly a 'friend,' sir, if you don't mind. We *did* come from the same home town in Massachusetts but I'd describe him simply as one of the neighborhood kids I knew. Came from good family but they went to seed, all of them. Drink, bad marriages." He shrugged. "I guess old Tom ended up the same way."

Addison Hamill studied him with an air of a man who sniffs an undefinable but definitely unpleasant odor.

"We don't have to make a pincushion out of him, Vinny. His goose is cooked with the Embassy but I can't help feeling a bit sorry for the poor devil, even if he . . ."

He straightened in his impressive high-backed leather chair, remembering.

"Vinny, what about our VIP, the Congressman? Is everything squared away? Who took Linden's place this morning on the Anzio inspection?"

Vinny put on his broadest all-is-well smile.

"Our Congressman is already in Anzio, sir. We tried a new wrinkle: we sent along a good-looking female receptionist, bilingual in Italian and English, to accompany him and he went off in the Embassy car with the chauffeur and Major Edwards happy as a clam. We scheduled half an hour for the inspection of the Italian installation near Nettuno, a leisurely lunch by the sea, the rest of the day visiting the military cemetery, and a slow scenic run through Castel Gandolfo and the hill towns. He should be back by nightfall pretty pooped, with a lot of good photos. He's loaded with counterpart lire and we even supplied him with color film from the commissary."

Addison Hamill said with only, for him, faint irony, "You're a real Elsa Maxwell, Vinny. Keep 'em busy and moving and tuck them in tired but safe and sound, eh? Well, that sounds splendid and takes care of today. But please remember: tomorrow's the big day and I want you to be absolutely sure to be on deck at nine A.M. when we go off with Chief MAAG to accompany the Congressman on the visit to the Minister of Defense." He paused and his eyes seemed even more veiled than usual.

"No fluffs tomorrow, like this tardiness by Linden today. It's got to go like cream tomorrow."

Vinny bobbed his head twice in agreement and promise.

"There won't be any slips, sir, you can bet on that," he said, sensing in his superior's preoccupied toying with a pencil that the interview was over. "And Mr. Hamill, about this . . ." and he tapped the sheets of the report lying before him.

"It's not your funeral," Hamill told him shortly. "It's Linden's." There was a delicate hiatus and the compact little man coughed once. "About . . . uh . . . Nancy, I'm really sorry I bit your ear earlier today, Vinny, but you understand how I felt."

Vinny, completely vindicated and rehabilitated now, waved the words away in a generous amnesty.

"Please, Mr. Hamill, forget it. I can imagine how you must have felt to have your daughter spend the night elsewhere with . . ."

But his voice trailed away under a renewed fixed stare from those hooded eyes.

"I was just called from the house, Vinny. She took her little car about an hour ago and left. The maid and butler don't know where she went."

He made a little arched roof with his hands.

"Be a good lad and see if you can find her," he commanded Vinny, eyes belying his surface calm. "Try both sides of the Veneto. She loves to sit there with a vermouth. If you spot her, use some stratagem to bring her here." He paused and said very deliberately, "If she won't come, at least phone me right away."

First Secretary Hamill bent over his papers in a gesture of dismissal and finally looked up with an irritated curiosity.

"Well, Vinny, be off and have a look, please."

"But sir . . ."

"You *do* care for her, don't you, Vinny? You are genuinely serious about her?"

"Well, yes, sir, I must say that I do, but . . ."

"But what?"

Vinny gnawed on his lower lip, a gesture as identifiable to his superior as it had been to his childhood chums.

"What if she has gone back to . . ."

"To Linden's place? Please go there, then, and bring her away with you."

But he abruptly folded his hands on top of the document he was reading which was stamped "Confidential," and the habitual controlled alertness fell away from his small features.

"Vinny, I'm sending Nancy back to her aunt and uncle in New Jersey. As soon as possible, by the first air reservation I can get. I'm not going to have any more repetitions of this disgraceful business of last night."

He was now a little middle-aged man without a wife and with a daughter who was a problem far beyond his solution.

He looked forlornly across the huge glossy desk at Vinny, sighed and continued in a new tone. "If you are at all serious about her, I want you to know what you're getting into, young man. I told you a white lie this morning when I implied she was a little Red Riding Hood among the wolves. Well, she's no such thing." Addison Hamill looked as if he had inadvertently bitten his tongue.

"I assume I can trust your discretion never to repeat to anyone what I tell you here."

Deliberately avoiding his superior's eyes, Vinny said self-consciously, "Of course, sir."

"Well," Hamill continued, turning slightly away from Vinny to study a bright little painting of Roman fountains, "Mrs. Hamill died when Nancy was eleven. I was stationed in the Near East, and with World War II at an end I sent her to Swiss private schools, although I am not a wealthy man. By the time she was sixteen, she had been asked to leave three successive schools for misconduct of one kind or another. Then I tried an English private school and she seemed to be doing well there. But when she was just past seventeen, I found her mixed up as corespondent in a very messy divorce suit with one of the school's instructors. Since that time she has stayed with me, at whatever posts I have been. It's been"—and he buried his face in his hands as if fending off a dazzling light—"a hell of a time. Up to now I have been spared the ultimate embarrassment of having her chase after my embassy colleagues. But enough is enough, and her behavior at the marine party last night was the last straw. I had already written to my sister and brother-in-law very frankly about this. They are prepared to take her in and look after her, as well as arranging for some psychiatric care."

Like an elastic band snapping back into shape, the professionally impassive diplomat's expression returned to his face. Addison Hamill said lightly, "It's lunch time, so take a little stroll on the Veneto, Vinny, and look around for her. I shall be very grateful to you."

Second Secretary Brentwood rose, straightened his faultless suit jacket, and tugged at the waistcoat. "I'll look for her," he said with a gesture of a Northwest Mountie assuring his captain. "I won't come back until I find her for you."

My God, he told himself as he closed the great paneled door behind him, smiled mechanically at Hamill's secretary and hurried through the outer office, Tom Linden was right as rain! He reproached himself as he hurried down the long corridor to the embassy elevators: Tom told the straight truth and I chewed him out for it.

It had seemed like such a natural match, Nancy Hamill and himself, and in recent weeks his thoughts and daydreams had crystallized to the point where he had almost memorized

90

the wedding announcement which would have appeared in the New York *Times* as well as the Boston papers. Under the headlines, DIPLOMAT MARRIES IN ROME, all of the impressive details would be dropped casually in: "The groom was graduated from Harvard University in 1947 after two wartime years in the U. S. Navy where he achieved the rank of lieutenant. He joined the Foreign Service in 1948 and is currently serving at the American Embassy in Rome with the rank of Second Secretary."

Then there would have been all of the protocol narration about Nancy, her father's career, the private English and Swiss schools, and a brief description of the church ceremony. He had decided that it would be much more fashionable to have the ceremony at the smaller Saint Andrew's in Rome rather than at the huge Episcopal Saint Paul's on the Via Nazionale.

God, God, he had even mentally invited the Ambassador, the entire embassy office staff and MAAG hierarchy, as well as selected Italian government and military brass with whom he had been dealing on behalf of his section. Maybe, he had often dreamed, Mrs. Ambassador would have been willing to stand in for the bride's deceased mother. Now, hurrying out the driveway of the Embassy and onto the broad sidewalk of the Veneto, a painful sense of loss swept over him. What a bride Nancy would have made, with that russet hair of hers, the slim, vibrant body, and the smooth skin enhanced rather than marred by a light spatter of nose freckles.

He shook his head to scatter the image and the sound of her voice, and he felt a rush of grudging gratitude toward Addison Hamill, that tough exacting little bastard, for leveling with him as he had. It took guts for a father to tell him of his daughter's tarnished virtue and, while he was amazed at himself that this in itself did not bother him, he knew very well what it could do to his career. Wives made you or broke you in this kind of life and having a wife around quite capable of putting the horns on him would only make him a laughing stock, a pathetic figure to be guffawed at behind his back by friends and, even worse, his superiors. And it was only by being respected and esteemed by your superiors that you got anywhere in life. He, Vinny Brentwood, both hated and loved this Foreign Service life, all of its marvelously precise protocol and its very clearly spelled out ground rules, and while his heart irrationally tugged at him to reconsider, his brain had already dismissed Nancy Hamill from his plans and his future. All that remained now was to find her and bring her back to her father who would be most grateful. Efficiency reports were almost due. . . .

"Hey you," the light familiar voice called to him, and he realized that he was walking blindly between the sidewalk chairs and tables at Doney's. He swiveled in his tracks at the greeting. Behind one of the tables with her back to the Doney window, face almost lost behind large black sun glasses, lounged his quarry.

"Yes, you, there, with the stuffed shirt!" she called beckoning with one slim finger. "You're such a diplomatic ball of fire: come over here for a minute and tell me what kind of a flag this is."

"Nan!" he exclaimed, triumphant that he had located her so quickly. "I'm so glad to see you . . ."

Her bright lips parted and she said, "Cut the crap, Vinny, you're not bellying up to some minister-counselor. And, besides, I'll bet that Addison Hamill, that distinguished American Foreign Service officer, has sent you off as his prize beagle to flush me out and bring me back in your mouth. You have that hunter look about you."

"Nan!" he remonstrated with her, looking quickly around to see whether anyone had overheard. "For God's sake, do you have to talk like that? You sound like a Dead End Kid."

"I am, sort of," she retorted, completely unabashed. "And you know what *you* sound like?"

He had to admit it; here at the sidewalk table, with the sun striking her face, she was marvelously alive and young. She wore a white trench coat buttoned up to the throat and the short russet hair sparkled with vitality in the fresh April wind.

"No, what do I sound like?"

"You sound like a priggish kid from the most priggish family in town who's been stuffed with elocution lessons, Sunday School honors, Boy Scouts and DeMolay. You've learned to say pretty-please almost as if you meant it. And I hate to say it after the dinners and drinks I've cost you but you are of a mold, Vinny, a tiresome type I have seen in every damned diplomatic post my dad has been in."

As recently as a day earlier, had she spoken to him like that, and she usually did, he would have bled profusely inside. But he had dropped her now; he had mentally discarded what his family would have said was "Not For You, Vinny," and her words, while they stung badly, did not wound him to the quick. He grinned with an effort at her, sat down opposite her and nodded in pseudo-cheerful agreement, moving the little flag to one side to see her better.

"You're dead right, Nan. I happen to be all of those things. And you? What sort of a mold do you fall into? The classic diplomat's daughter type? Teas, bridge, doing charity work for the local orphanages? Running off movies of Bangkok travels for the church bazaar? Yes, I can just imagine you doing all this, indeed I can."

She drained her vermouth glass and looked at him carefully. "You look like you've just eaten two canaries, whole, complete with feathers," she said at last, her cheerful insolence gone now. She made a snapping gesture of command with her fingers.

"Come on, Vin, out with it. You know who killed Cock Robin."

He offered her a cigarette, lit it for her and took one himself.

"I'm surprised to find you here on the Veneto rather than at Tom Linden's place," he told her malevolently. But if her words no longer hurt him, his seemed to bounce off her.

"I was just there, as a matter of fact. But no one was home." She nodded and the dark flame of her hair rippled with the gesture. "Aha, so you diplomats have been comparing notes again. Dad, that monster, has told you all."

"Why shouldn't he?" he protested. "He knew how interested I was in you and . . ."

"Did you say 'was', *Signor Diplomatico?*"

He flushed in spite of himself. Damn, how things slipped out.

"Yes, after last night, 'was.' I'm sorry, Nan."

"No questions, no taking of testimony; just stand me up there against the wall and ready-aim-fire, is that it, Vinny?"

"You're presupposing innocence," he said, uneasiness beginning to take him. She was at any time most disconcerting in her frankness and, while this had secretly appealed to him as something he had rarely ever heard from a woman, he knew how ravaging it could become. "Look, Nan, I'm not going to interrogate you or badger you. I heard a pretty good account of what went on last night during *and after* the Marine Ball, and that's enough for me."

It was hard to discern but he sensed that she was, incredibly enough, laughing at him behind those twin pools of black glass.

"We're finished, then? Our little tête-a-têtes, dinners, a couple of warm smooches and a little tentative feeling-around

on your part, some serious talk about getting engaged, a dis-
cussion of what places I'd like to see most in the world as a
second secretary's wife—that's all over?"

He nodded slowly, unable to say the word.

"And all because of last night?"

He nodded again, cleared his throat and said, "Last night
and all the other Last Nights."

She opened her mouth in mock dismay.

"You *are* a nasty one, Vinny."

"Did you or did you not go home with Tom Linden last
night?" he asked in a low tone.

She leaned across her coffee cup toward him so that their
noses almost met in the center of the little table.

"Yes, I did," she whispered, lips parting in an involuntary
smile whose irregular teeth added to its charm.

"Did you . . ."

She whipped off the glasses and glared at him as if he had
uttered a loathsome curse.

"No." She stared up at the sun now slipping behind the
top of a great gray building. "But I suppose I wanted to.
He was kind but he was out with drink."

"Did you know that he is a disgrace, that he was cashiered
out of the Army for disobeying a command while behind
enemy lines, that he was sent before a court-martial and . . ."

"Whoa, there, Vinny boy," she said almost sweetly. "Save
it. I heard the whole thing from the military attaché two days
ago, who passed the report to my dad. So you got to read
it, finally."

"Then you . . . you knew all about him before that marine
party and you . . . you went to his place with him after all
of that . . ."

She settled back in her chair and her features drooped with
fatigue or disappointment; it was hard to tell which.

"Vinny, what the hell difference does his war record mean?
If you must know, one of the reasons I went home with him
was precisely that. He was such a sad brave chunk of defeat
sitting in his threadbare clothes playing poker with the
marines to win. I knew he was playing because he *had* to
win; he needed the money. Something came over me. I felt
he needed love, warmth."

"And the others?" Vinny nipped at her. "The English school
instructor and all of the others since? They all needed love?"

"You bastard, Vinny," she hissed.

He leaned back, feeling both sick and triumphant.

"All right, I'm a bastard. And you're a . . ."

The chance passersby and those sitting inside Doney behind the plate glass windows which face the Via Veneto, idly monitoring the animated conversation between the elegantly dressed foreigner and the woman in the trench coat, stared as the woman reached across the table and slapped the foreigner hard, first on one cheek and then the other. Then she sprang to her feet and pushed his chair over backward. As he went sprawling on the sidewalk, clawing the air helplessly to break his fall, she threw down a five-hundred lire note on the little table and left, clicking swiftly away in high-heeled shoes around the corner and out of sight. Vinny lay on the sidewalk until the blue-jacketed *maître*, aghast at the position of his client, rushed up with two waiters to assist him.

They immediately hoisted him to his feet and began frantic brushing motions on his jacket and trousers muttering incomprehensible phrases of apology and embarrassment. Vinny pointed to the little banner on Nancy's table.

"Pakistan," he told them, pointing to it. *That* flag he knew very well.

The solicitous waiters exchanged meaningful eye-rolling glances as they brushed their client: that was a foreigner for you every time. Knock him off his feet, and he gets up to identify the table flag.

chapter ten

THEY FACED EACH other across the rickety table, the empty, sauce-stained pasta plates and a small bowl of fruit between them. The warming sun fingered through the terrace vines to touch them but they were oblivious to it. They eyed each other intently as do passengers in a train compartment after several hours of journey—familiar strangers imagining and seeking to probe the thoughts and the real nature of the person opposite. Despite the half-drained glass of red wine at his elbow, the past two hours with this woman had burned through the pulsating hangover of last night and the negronis of this noon. Antonella's appearance had shocked him into wary alertness.

His two Siamese paraded soundlessly up to Antonella and brushed her legs for attention.

"They rarely are friendly to anyone but me." Tom seized on their presence to break the strained silence. "They usually hide in the vines here and pounce on visitors to frighten them. For my maid, it's a constant state of war with them." He remembered with a frown that The Maria was still absent.

"I wonder what happened to *her*. It's not one of her days off." He shrugged. "She must have gone over to Saint Eugenio to pray for her nephew again."

Antonella reached down to scratch each of the soft heads in turn.

"Cats mean no harm to anyone," she said in a voice pitched to soothe the animals as she petted them. "They are the last free living things in Italy."

The large somber eyes looked up and locked with his again, cool and patient.

"As for your maid, say nothing evil. Her kitchen is spotless."

"Her spaghetti does not excel yours," he told her with a lame gallantry, studying the long straight nose, the firm Passaglia chin. The face had a strength that stopped short of beauty and he tried without success to relate it to the soft, open face of twelve years ago that had never stopped smiling.

His compliment on her cooking skill was gently parried.

"I simply boiled the water and threw the pasta in. I found the sauce in the icebox, a magnificent concoction I have never tasted before."

She was spinning out the minutes, waiting for him to utter the correct opening phrase, and he found himself wanting to delay indefinitely the inevitable confrontation with the past which he had spent so long banishing, repelling, evading. He deeply wished that the torpor waiting for him could suddenly drop over his consciousness and take him out of this chair, this tepid sunshine. With her sitting opposite, lightly resting on her elbows, this could not happen. She had come too far and her face told of too much suffering for that.

"The sauce is Sardinian. Everything here except for my books and clothing is Sardinian." He attempted a smile. "I live here with a tribal matriarch, not a maid."

He leaned back, dug in his shirt pocket for the two long cigarettes he had extracted from Vinny Brentwood's pack that morning, and offered her the least rumpled of the two. She declined, nodding her thanks as he lit the other.

"And now," he said, blowing a brief blue curtain between

them, aware that he was at last at bay and striving for insouciance, "you have fulfilled the American proverb that the way to a man's heart is through his stomach. Also, if it were not for you I would still be sitting at Doney with many chits for many unpaid negronis. I am saved from social disaster and my hunger is eased. What can I possibly do for you in return?"

She leaned toward him and said quietly, "Something you have already told me you cannot do: give me the answer to why Peppino would have kept the Major Dixon's holster all these years, to send it to me by Don Tiberio, the priest of Belinoro, in his dying hour."

"I told you in the taxi that I knew nothing about it except that it is definitely the major's holster," he told her testily. "As for my opinion, whatever it's worth, maybe it *was* Peppino's way of paying you a final bad joke for the way you and the Party treated him. Maybe this was his way of hurting you who had turned on him, by sending it along with Don Tiberio, the very person you probably least wanted to see at this time. And if what you told me is true, and Peppino was collaborating with the Germans, he probably got it from someone on their side who had participated in the ambush of your father's partisan band. Perhaps the holster passed through many hands before it reached his and he meant it only as a bitter souvenir."

"No," she said shortly, "Peppino would never keep such a grisly memento, no matter how much he collaborated with them. He would have burnt it or buried it. Not for anything would he send it on to me only to hurt me." Her voice faltered and her eyes glittered full for a moment. "I know Peppino. In Peppino there was only love."

Tom lowered his glance into the empty spaghetti plate as if looking for insight there.

"Agreed. From what little I saw of your Peppino he would not do such a thing."

He suddenly struck a fist savagely into his other hand.

"Damn your Peppino! *He* could have come down to Caserta and testified in my behalf. *He* was the man who warned me that the Germans were out that night. He could have helped me at the court-martial more than any of you. But he didn't come." His voice sank to an undertone. "None of you came."

She reached for the wine bottle and poured a half-glass for herself and the same for him, and as she handed him back his glass, her fingers touched his wrist.

"Forgive us, Tommaso," her voice thrummed with a deep sincerity. "The Party forbade us to come. And besides, Peppino felt that Communist testimony for you might have done more harm than good."

Tom reached for the wineglass and held it up to her, the Chianti like thick dark blood against the sun.

"Probably he was right," he said more calmly. "Well, then, I drink to the repose of your Peppino's soul, Communist, ex-Communist, traitor, or whatever he was. He was on all three of the missions I led, and he was a very brave man. Besides, I liked him."

He drank deeply, feeling the sour strength of the Chianti as it went down, until his glass was again empty. He was surprised to notice that she had done the same, and he looked curiously at this once coveted, still desirable woman.

"Peppino and your father were friends despite the political differences between them, isn't that so?"

"They were inseparable friends from their earliest years. He was almost a part of our household after his wife died. He was like an uncle to me."

"And yet you cut him completely out of your life because the Party had documents proving he was collaborating with the Germans at the same time he was a Communist member of the Resistance in Romagna. You told me you actually didn't speak a word with him for over a year, until he died last month. Why is this?"

The brown eyes flashed in exasperation.

"You sound just like Don Tiberio. I told you: since the war, Belinoro has been in the control of the Communists and Socialists. We control the area, we are by far the majority on the town council. In Belinoro, the only punishment for such a person who would betray his comrades is ostracism. The Party was not going to hand him over to the carabinieri and sully its own good name. So, we ignored him." Stung by the expression on his face, she added, "It was not my idea. The Party decreed it, and I am loyal and disciplined when the Party speaks."

He was very alert now, brain alive and keen for the first time in days and it was as if the sun and the wine in him kindled a fast-burning fuel.

"And you also obeyed them when I wrote and asked for your presence and the presence of the others in the summer of 1945 at the court of inquiry? You wanted to come, but the Party said no? Is that right?"

She nodded, and her unheeded tears asked silent forgiveness. He pushed back his chair after a long minute passed and the Siamese, sensing the heavy atmosphere, slunk away. Tom rose and nodded his head toward the open-doored studio.

"Very well. Everybody is telling the truth today. And now I'll help you in whatever way I can. Come with me. We'll clean up out here later."

He walked under the heavy vines and into the study beyond. She followed and stared at the crammed bookshelves covering one whole wall from floor to ceiling.

"This is probably one of the best private collections of partisan documents and unit histories of the Italian Resistance in existence," he told her. "I have been collecting them since the end of the war. I used to travel throughout the Resistance area from Piedmont to Venezia Giulia, mostly by *corriera* and motor scooter, after I became a civilian, visiting the ex-partisan clubs and societies of every political coloration and size you can imagine." He snorted in recall of some of the encounters. "Your Communists, those of the ex-Garibaldini formations, in some places treated me like a carrier of the cholera."

"You did not visit Belinoro," she said more as a factual statement than a reproach.

He ran his finger along the dusty edge of a shelf marked "Resistance in the Romagna." "No, I did not. I passed close by, several times, on the Via Emilia, and on one occasion I stopped at Forlimpopoli to talk with the *ex-partigiani* there, but I couldn't bring myself to turn off on the Belinoro road and go up there. I think you understand why."

Her eyes ran slowly along the cluttered shelves of pamphlets, booklets, and bound volumes, each spelling out its story of courage, resistance, torture, betrayal, repression, and death.

"Why did you do this? Why do you interest yourself in our struggle?"

He pushed a protruding volume back into line and he said, without looking at her, "To try to understand something I never knew about twelve years ago." He wheeled and his eyes were black fierce coals. "To understand something that has cost me my reputation and my peace of mind."

"We all paid, Tommaso," she answered quietly. "In one way or another, we all paid."

"Yes, we did; your family and the major with their lives; for you a life as a widow and an orphan. For me? This."

He suddenly grasped her shoulders, soft through the silky fabric of her chemise, with a fierceness that was painful.

"The difference between me and you and the dead ones

99

is this, Antonella: I was punished for something I still don't comprehend. *Capito?* I still do not understand what went wrong up there in Belinoro. So, I am looking and studying to try to find the answers."

Abruptly he released her and with an ironic bow he said in a completely altered tone, "Signora Passaglia, I beg your pardon. It was stupid of me to maul you and to harangue you in such a manner. Please forgive me."

She studied the haggard, haunted eyes glowering in the shadows of the room and finally said, "The Lieutenant Tommaso I knew was a bold laughing man who once climbed to the top of the highest roof in Belinoro to rescue a lost kitten of my little cousin. He was everything I had never seen before: full of gaiety and games, stories from another world, new dance steps, strange folk songs. He wanted to fight the Fascists and the Germans with his bare hands, to win the war all by himself."

"That man is dead. He died just after the war in an American military courtroom in Caserta. Before you stands another person who uses the same name and represents him on earth."

She looked up into his face, the top of her glistening coif barely at the level of his forehead, with the same derision and scorn as two hours before.

"Very dramatic. The young American officer who once lived among the partisans of Belinoro is now dead, and instead we have someone who sits and drinks negronis at Doney for which he cannot pay!"

"And what did you expect to find?" he asked gently. She had expected her taunt to move him to a shouting rage but instead he held her stare, taking the bite out of it with a weary tolerance. "Did you hope I had become ambassador, or a big American businessman, or a *pezzo grosso* in the cinema industry? Be happy you find me no worse than I am."

She stared at him, as if seeing him in full light for the first time and appalled at what she saw.

"That other person, that Lieutenant Tommaso of Belinoro," she said, her voice tearing with emotion. "With my martyred husband scarcely cold in his grave, I let him take me to bed, let him make love to me, returned his love like a person consumed with a wild burning fever!" She reached to grasp him in her agony of recall. "On that bed of love, I, the widow of Fausto Cipriana for but one day, I hated that Lieutenant Tommaso for making love to me in that terrible moment of sorrow. I hated myself even more for yielding to it. It was a blasphemy, a betrayal of the dead!"

He trapped her hands on his shirt, held them between his and said in a husky whisper, "It was not meant as betrayal at the time, Antonella, neither on your part nor mine. You know how I felt about those who fell in the ambush. What we did may sound brutal but it was life. From the day I parachuted into Belinoro, I coveted you during every waking hour. I think you felt the same toward me. It was a sin, yes, but after the disaster of the ambush, I knew I would have only once to show you how I felt before I had to flee myself. Just once . . ." His eyes lifted slowly and he asked her, "And what will be it now: love or hate?"

"Neither," she said, the fire and the hurt drained from her. "After I made love with the Lieutenant Tommaso, I confessed my sins, fool that I was, to my priest, Don Tiberio. He was infuriated with me and he made me cry and pray for a month. Now I understand things much better. Once you have been to the Party schools and have studied the Marxist-Leninist doctrine, these foolish ideas about individual guilt and sin disappear."

"You say such things bravely, like a small boy whistling to keep up his courage as he passes the cemetery at night," he told her. He took in the smooth soft curve of her chin, the surge of her bosom against the white chemise and the Antonella of the past suddenly whirled into his mind and his vision. He stepped forward deliberately and reached around her, bringing her close to him gently as if fearing to crush her, and his mouth moved down like a hawk's on hers. He kissed the wide, labile mouth but it remained firm and unresponding; slowly he relinquished his embrace.

"Thank you, Tommaso, for still caring, but I did not come to Rome for love. I came to find out about Peppino. We Passaglias are very strange people, and if we have done injustice to a friend, the ends of the world will not be far enough to seek repentance. Something in my heart tells me I wronged Peppino to his dying hour . . ."

The telephone in the hall jangled insistently, and Tom moved to the offending instrument, and lifted it.

"*Pronto,*" he said.

"Dottore Tommaso! Can you come at once to where I am now calling?" It was the voice of The Maria, loud enough to be heard across the room, and her blurted request was an entreaty.

"Why should I come? Where are you?"

"I am in the San Giovanni sector, just off the New Appian Way."

"Tell me, Maria," he repeated with exasperation, "why I should come? I have a visitor here."

"The Signora Passaglia," grunted The Maria. "The woman of Belinoro, perhaps, who telephoned this morning?"

It was eerie how this servant of his sensed or knew so much, he thought, feeling the hair on his body rise with astonishment.

"Yes," he managed to answer.

"Bring her, then," The Maria commanded. "This concerns her as well." She paused delicately. "You did not tell me of this affair of the war, and I did not care to ask, although I knew of your studies into the Resistance. But today I have learned of something that you must know."

"Why should you concern yourself in such things?" he scolded her, feeling the cool afternoon wind blowing in from the terrace.

He thought the connection had been severed, she took so long to reply.

"They have called you the worst kind of coward, Dottore Tommaso. Such a charge must either be proven or the insult erased in blood. I want you to come here and hear what has been said, and tell me if they are right."

"And if I do not choose to come?" he said incredulously.

"In that case," the booming voice replied, "I shall come back to the apartment long enough to pack—and to spit in your face."

He looked at his watch and sighed.

"Give me the address. I will be there within an hour."

"Will you please bring the Signora Passaglia?"

"Very well!" he agreed after a moment of blank surprise.

The Maria dictated the address and rang off without another word.

chapter eleven

THE TINY ELEVATOR with frosted glass windows rumbled
tremulously to a halt at the top floor, and as they flung open
its heavy grilled door, The Maria stood waiting for them, her
shock of peppered black hair tightly combed back in a bun,
heavy brows knitted in an expression of grim anxiety.

"Dottoressa Passaglia," Tom told her, with a small gesture
to Antonella. The Maria stepped forward, gave the tiniest
of bows and shook the extended hand once, studying Antonella with black unfathomable eyes.

"I regret to disturb you, Dottore," she addressed Tom
formally in a tone of complete non-regret, "but there have
been grave charges made here and I have insisted that you
confront those who made them."

She led the way through a small foyer and they were suddenly in a cramped little room filled with small dark people,
none of whom was taller than Tom's shoulder. In the center
of the room, under a small glass chandelier, a sunken-cheeked
little figure sat hunched in a wheel chair, close-cropped hair
white as a dove's, his huge mustachios yellowed with nicotine
at the mouth's edges. He was clad in wide-striped pajamas
and the lower part of his body was swathed in a cheap blanket of equally striped ticking. The old hands resting in his
lap trembled incessantly with a palsy, but fierce undimmed
eyes looked up from above a generous hawk nose when The
Maria led Tom and Antonella up to him.

"*Ecco*," The Maria loudly addressed the old man in the
chair and the room at large. "My *signore* has come to hear
your vile charges and to refute them. Now repeat what you
said into the face of my *padrone*."

Her voice had an immediate intimidating effect on the
short swarthy people, although she appeared to be directing
herself specifically to a chunky woman standing behind the

wheel chair, whose high cheekbones, nose, and expression matched those of the old man before her.

Tom and Antonella recognized the bent old man with the palsied hands simultaneously, but it was she who exclaimed first, "Maresciallo Vitale! You!"

The fierce old eyes looked up and straight into hers.

"Aha, thought I had been done in, eh?" His head wagged as if it dangled from a thin wire. "Not me! Not Maresciallo Maggiore Ezio Vitale of the Carabinieri Reali." Then the quavering old man's voice rose, and his eyes burned as he croaked, "Three cheers for the House of Savoy; *evviva! evviva! evv . . .*" The frail form half rose out of the chair. One of the trembling hands came up to a salute and he abruptly slumped into silence again.

A young solid girl with the wonderful ruddy olive complexion of the Sardinian peasant caught Tom's eye and tapped her forehead with an apologetic move of her lips. But the woman who looked so much like a younger version of the old carabiniere spoke in a biting voice, "How he has suffered! They dragged him away because he would not swear fealty to the Fascist Republic of Mussolini! They beat him and starved him! And yet he never yielded. He remained true to his oath to the King!"

The Maria gave her a calculating glance and explained quickly to Tom, her eyes flicking to Antonella from time to time, "This is the home of this woman, Pinetta Vitale, who is of"—it was clear that Maria was wrestling with properties here—"of Cagliari. These people are all her relatives on her mother's side; all are of Cagliari and have migrated to Rome. Their family name is Landru. The old man here is her father, who married her mother while he was assigned to carabinieri duty on the island."

The hawk-nosed woman with the two silver-eye-teeth which flashed whenever she spoke added derisively at Tom, "*He* knows my father. The American knows him full well."

Tom looked beyond them out a small uncurtained window where the Alban Hills pillowed up in the distance, and he tried to remember what the smell of this room connoted. It came to him: in the crowded cellar room of the Passaglia house just before a partisan mission, the room filled with the pungency of unwashed and fearful men. Here the smell was much the same, but now it was a smell of expectancy rather than of fear.

The old carabiniere at last lifted his head again and the room hushed as he gazed furiously at Tom.

"Yes," he said, and his head nodded almost uncontrollably. "I know him, Pinetta. It is the Lieutenant Tommaso, the American who floated out of the sky in his parachute with the two others. It is because of his cowardice that his commander is dead." The frail croak became stronger and more strident.

"Is that not so, American? Did you not remain behind to slink in your quarters while the others went to their death?"

The room was as still as if there were no one but the two of them alone in their dialogue. Tom looked straight down at the old hawk eyes, found something disconcerting there, and licked his lips with an embarrassed distaste.

"It is true. I remained behind, and the others went to die."

The room exploded with the excited cries and expostulations. The circle of dark, almost Arabic eyes was cruel and hostile now. "Coward" and "rascal" were repeated again and again. Tom held up his hand and since that did little to subdue the din, The Maria yelled *"Silenzio!"* in a voice that could shatter glass. Silence immediately returned to the room. Tom held the old eyes in his as he went on, "You know full well that I was ordered to remain behind in my quarters by my commander despite my efforts to go out with the band. You, as a *maresciallo* of the carabinieri, know that I was placed under house arrest."

Again the shriveled and shaking forefinger.

"You were placed under arrest because you did not want to take the group out on their mission," the old man shouted hoarsely. "You refused to let them go. That was why your commander had to replace you. You refused to go out."

"And he was right!" the voice of Antonella cut through the rising babble. "If his fool of a commander had listened to him they would all be alive today instead of dead! *Maresciallo,* this is an outrageous slander! How dare you accuse this man of such a thing!"

The old man's eyes and those of the others in the room turned to her. Maresciallo Vitale appeared about to tremble himself out of his chair.

"Eh, eh," he panted, turning the quavering forefinger on her. "Look at *this* shameless one, speaking up for the coward! She, daughter of the finest man of the village who now lies dead; she, married by the priest and today is a Communist! Not only that, a Communist mayoress, no less! Godless whore!"

He actually tried to step out of his wheel chair to strike her, and succeeded only in sprawling face down on the worn floor at her feet. The atmosphere exploded into a milling confusion during which the old man was lifted back into his chair, a pill and water were put into his sagging mouth, and Tom and Antonella were literally pushed into a corner, where they faced a semicircle of angry gesticulating hands and faces.

"*Basta!*" Antonella called out in despair, the soft coif of her head now drooping over her forehead and eyes in a straggling disarray. "Let me ask the old man one question—please! Only one question and let me go!"

A narrow human corridor opened between her and the shriveled old man in the wheel chair, and she approached him as a tigress stalks her meal.

"Now, Maresciallo Vitale; you who were in charge of the carabinieri for Belinoro-Altomonte during the war: where was Peppino Deruta at the time of the ambush of the band of my father? Do you know this? I beg of you, despite what you think of me and my politics, answer this question for me. I have traveled from Romagna to Rome to ask it: where was he at the time the Germans ambushed the Gruppo Passaglia?"

The old man appeared to be dozing, his head cocked sideways and a bit downcast, and the fierce eyes were closed. Then, across the pale, almost white lips under the great mustaches, an almost boyish smile appeared, and the sunken yet alert eyes tilted slyly up at her.

"Who said the Germans killed your father and his band?" he asked her, almost in a whisper.

"Who else then?" Antonella asked, the great eyes now staring at him as if he were a bloodstained apparition. "Who else but the Germans or the Fascists?"

"Who else?" he echoed with a ghost of a chuckle. "Why not your precious friends, those whose cause you serve so loyally?"

She would have flung herself on him had not The Maria physically restrained her. The Sardinian arms held Antonella in an iron grip.

"Prove that, Maresciallo!" Antonella panted, her eyes wet with fury, futilely struggling to free herself to get at the old invalid. "You know that's a filthy lie! Italian patriots don't kill each other! The partisan band led by my father died in a German ambush. You were there, know this! You bicycled down from Altomonte yourself that very night to investigate the slaughter!"

The sunken eyes of the old man stared beyond her into the past. Then they turned on her with the same childlike mischief written in them and the ancient carabiniere said quite clearly,

"They called you here to hear me say that this American, this Lieutenant Tommaso, was a coward. Very well, I say it again. Look, does he deny it?"

He turned to stare bleakly at Tom and they looked into each other's eyes in bitterness and understanding. Then, in the heavy silence, the invalid said,

"I want to speak no more of that terrible business. *Basta!*"

But Antonella tore herself out of The Maria's arms and knelt at the feet of the old rural policeman, hands clasped in supplication.

"Maresciallo, speak about me however you will, but in the name of all my dead ones, tell me: where was Peppino Deruta in all that happened during the ambush? I beg of you, tell me if you know. Peppino is dead now. Nothing can harm him. Tell me, please!" Every eye in the room fixed on her and the emaciated figure huddled under the blanket in the wheel chair.

Tom moved with compassion to her side. But the old man's eyes opened and a smile of incredulity edged itself onto his face.

"Peppino? Dead, you say? Of what did he die?"

"Of the cancer. He died a month ago, in Altomonte."

Her reply set off a nodding of his head that seemed destined never to stop.

"Of the cancer, you say?" he croaked. He snorted triumphantly.

"God exists!" he barked, turning to the close-huddled group. "Do you hear me? God exists and the punishment of Peppino the Athiest is hard!"

"Why do you say that?" Antonella whispered up at him. "Why do you blaspheme the dead?"

"Because my dear signora, because he sat above the Belinoro road with the others, on the steep slopes on both sides of the road, and he fired with the others. He was there. He killed his own friends, fellow patriots; he made eight women widows, he made fourteen children orphans . . ."

"Stop it! Stop it!" Antonella screamed. "You are like Don Tiberio; you're insane! You cannot say such things of a man who was like one of our own! It was the Germans! They and the Fascists did the crime! They left a German SS man lying in death behind them!"

"The SS man had been dead for almost two days," Maresciallo Vitale told her, his hands trembling on the arms of the wheel chair. "This was quite evident when we examined all the corpses the next day. The German had been stabbed in the back, but we found no knife, no instrument among the dead Passaglia partisans to indicate *they* had killed him. No, he had been killed earlier, by someone else. He was laid on the road as bait. And those who baited the trap were the same as those who killed the Gruppo Passaglia."

Except for a gasp of horrified surprise, there was not a sound from the circle of swarthy black-eyed Landrus. The Maria reached to pluck Antonella from her kneeling position at the old man's feet, but Antonella ignored her.

"How do you know that Peppino was there, Maresciallo?" she asked in a voice drained absolutely dry of emotion. "How do you know this thing?"

"Dear signora," the old man whispered. "You called me 'insane' before. Do you know where I have been for the past ten years?"

His hawk-nosed daughter with the silver teeth said bitterly, "Only three months ago we were able to gain his release from the insane asylum of Rieti. His sufferings in German captivity were so terrible that he lost his mind. Now he is better, so they permitted us to bring him here because of the palsy which has affected him. They let us take him home to care for him as long as he lives."

She reached down and stroked the ravaged old cheek of her father with a strong work-veined hand.

"There is a madman in the Rieti insane asylum," Maresciallo Vitale quavered, his eyes studying the mass of Antonella's shining tangled hair almost in his lap, "named Nando Martinuzzi. How he raves! The moment I saw him I remembered him immediately. He had been with the Communist Garibaldini during the Resistance, and he comes from the same town as my mother's relatives, Castel Bolognese. Poor *disgraziato* of a Communist, he had suffered too much. He has been confined since the end of the war and he spends days strapped in the jacket of confinement or in a cell with padded walls. How he howls!"

He looked down at Antonella.

"I have listened to his story over and over. He was with them that night; he was one of the ambushers. They had told him that they were lying in wait for a German anti-bandit patrol to come by. Instead, he was tricked into massacring other patriots. Over and over again he cries out, asking the dead men for forgiveness. Over and over."

The trembling hand descended at last on the soft mass of

Antonella's hair and she hung her head at his knees as if in prayer.

"Your Peppino was there, signora. Nando told me so. Your Peppino shot down your family and friends and the American major. Why? Who can tell? Perhaps the American coward here can say."

The glittering circle of eyes turned to Tom.

"I know nothing of this," he said slowly, "except that it was Peppino who told me that there was danger that night of ambush. I trusted him completely and begged my commander not to go out. He would not listen." Tom snorted in sardonic amusement. "You see, I should be grateful to Peppino; it is because of him that I am alive."

It was The Maria who said in a deep rumble of finality, "*Mo' basta*," and gently plucked Antonella to her feet. She marched the dazed younger woman to the door of the hot fetid room with Tom at her heels. On the threshold, she wheeled.

"Something does not go here," she informed the swarthy little people and the huddled figure in the wheel chair. "Something does not fit. I warn each of you: if I hear a single public word of this confrontation, it will go badly for all of you. This much I swear to you." She fixed Pinetta Vitale in her scrutiny. "Much remains to be explained and until more is known, do not insult Maria Seddu or these two who are her friends." The jet eyes swept the room regally, arrogantly and she spat out a "*Buona sera*" before closing the apartment door.

They walked slowly down the seven narrow flights into the noisy square reviving from the siesta, raw and dusty, its stone benches crowded with gabbing housewives and their toddling broods. A diesel bus rumbled up to the bus stop and The Maria walked rapidly toward it.

"I shall return to the house much later, Dottore. Please do not wait for me to return for supper. I have many things to do."

Tom, looking at the broad erect back marching away from him, realized with sorrow that she no longer spoke to him in the familiar *tu* but with *lei*, as servants speak to their masters or as strangers do to each other. He turned to Antonella as the heavy bus roared away toward the city's center and watched her pin her disheveled hair back into a rough, restraining bun. Only when her eyes met his did he realize the full extent of the ordeal she had just passed. He thought she was going to weep but she struggled it back, and they walked together arm in arm to the far side of the piazza where two old taxis hulked close together, their drivers patiently reading sports sheets behind their wheels.

"Where do you want to go, Antonella?" Tom asked gently.

She plucked a small notebook from the great handbag and examined it intently for a moment.

"A train leaves for the north within an hour, from Termini Station," she finally told him. "I'm going to catch it. My suitcase is in the baggage room at the terminal." Her voice was matter-of-fact but he could feel the thin edge of control along which she teetered, and he said nothing to her during the long lurching cab ride to the station. She passed him the cab fare with a fleeting smile of half-apology as they rolled up to the colossal white façade of the train terminal. Silently he followed her to the baggage room, and still without a word he lugged the heavy bag onto the train platform where a shoving if good-natured crowd jostled its way up into a somber line of passenger cars, each marked ROMA-RIETI-FIRENZE. With expert skill, Tom used the suitcase as a battering ram and plowed through the throng in the train corridor. He found a seat for her in one of the second-class compartments, stowed her suitcase on the overhead rack, and fought his way back onto the platform where she waited, sitting on one of the marble benches in complete composure. When he reached her, she smiled her thanks and uttered the first words since their arrival at the Termini.

"You know where I am going, caro?" Her voice was soft as velvet.

He nodded wearily, his eyes cast down.

"You're going to Rieti, to talk to Nando, the poor lunatic who knows about the ambush." Tom said, licking his lips as if to ease the passage of the difficult words. " You are torturing yourself, Antonella. The dead have been dead for thirteen years."

She stared at him in the gathering dusk as one looks at cheerful liars who emerge from the rooms of the very sick.

"Are they dead for you, Tommaso?"

The crowds crowded and pushed around them, and Tom finally answered,

"No. But I do not dig them up as you are doing. I leave them in peace."

"Then why do you seek and study the annals of the Resistance; what are you looking for?"

"Nothing any longer," he said, looking slightly down at her, noting that the stress of the day drooped her shoulders.

"The dead long lay in peace until the day Peppino died,"

she explained. "Now I cannot go back to Belinoro cemetery until I learn all there is to know."

A crowd of nuns like a dense flock of little black birds twittered past them to cram onto the already chock-full train. Something about the incongruity of their severe black garb and their lighthearted excitement at being out in the bustling world softened the eyes and lips of Antonella.

"I was going to be a nun once, when I was twelve, did my father ever tell you? I thought about it for a long time until I met Fausto who was . . ."

She dabbed her eyes with a small handkerchief. Tom moved with her to her train carriage, and she mounted the first high step, where she turned and held out her hand.

"And now?" Tom asked. "You found your answer concerning Peppino. You know that he was at the ambush and that he probably picked up the major's gun and holster, that he sent the priest to you as a confession of his guilt. Now what do you seek?"

The train master with his dispatching disc under one arm strolled authoritatively down the train platform and the exchanges of farewell became more frantic among the dense crowd. Antonella, looking down at him from the train step and smoothing her now badly wrinkled suit in an instinctive feminine gesture, arched her eyebrows in surprise.

"What do I seek? Were there not others in the ambushing group? Were there not men who fired and shot and slaughtered my own, my husband, my flesh and blood!"

She clenched one small fist and again Tom saw in the chin and the compressed lips the face of Old Tonio Passaglia.

"I seek their names, their identities," Antonella told him, brooding.

"Then?"

"Then? Remember what I am, Tommaso: first of all a Passaglia. Then I am a Romagnole. When I have their names, all that remains is—vendetta!"

The train dispatcher waved his disc in an oscillating signal and blew his shrill departure whistle. Tom brought the soft hand to his lips and held it there as if to blow warmth on it.

"Which is more important to you?" Tom asked, tilting his head to look up at her. The dispatcher's whistle again shrilled and the train stumbled for a moment and began to slide very slowly out of the station. "Which is stronger with you, love or hate?"

The hand he had held to his cheek squeezed his fingers.

"Love, of course," she replied above the rising rumble of

the train wheels. "But the truth is even more important than love."

He walked a few steps along with her, and then as the train gathered speed, he released her hand and stood unmoving among the others frantically waving white handkerchiefs and calling out the sad farewells. Her face on the train became a little dot of white and disappeared and he stared as the entire length of the northbound *direttissimo* clacked by. He could not take his eyes away from the expanse of track that lengthened between himself and the last car and when he turned with a start, he was alone on the platform and the darkness of night had slipped in around him.

chapter twelve

SOMEWHERE BEHIND one of the forbidding doors up the gloomy stone stairwell a housemaid's raw but irrepressible voice sang like a witless bird's:

> *"Quanto sei bella, Roma,*
> *Quanto sei bella, Roma, prima sera . . ."*

Paolo Seddu plodded slowly up stairs whose walls were grimed with plaster of a generation ago, very carefully grounding his acrid-smelling burden at each landing. He brooded on the cricket-cheerfulness of his Party accomplice of this morning. Just the sort of trash the Party was attracting these days; the cynical lazy ones like Franco Furbo, all making sure they had a foot in a potentially good thing, ready to run like rabbits at the first scent of police harassment or crackdown.

Then there was this entire preposterousness that came with being of Rome, as that *cretino* Franco bragged so disgustingly. "*So' Romano de Roma,*" Franco brayed time and again. But who in all Italy liked or even trusted a Roman? Certainly no revolutions were ever going to start here, despite the Party's reiterated call for action. No, revolutions and Renaissances all began someplace else, in Milano or Firenze, Siena, or Napoli, in a dozen hot-headed, proud little northern Italian cities but nothing new and stirring ever started in Rome. Everything always ended here; the debauched and rotten Roman Empire, the whimper that was the end to Vatican power, the dull thud of an ousted Mussolini and of a departing House of Savoia that had almost brilliantly managed never to do anything right. And now the strangling bureaucracy of the Christian Democrats with its priests and cronyism and the desperate inanities of the *dolce vita*.

The seductive sky and the somniferous splash of the fountains, the feeling that everything had happened before and everything would eventually turn to whitened skeletons like the Forum and the crumbling Imperial Baths—all this made Rome a bad, frustrating place to revolt, to cry for justice and morality. The sweet weed of Roman corruption crept in like wild ivy and entangled itself around an ideal, a value, a protest; softly, sweetly it smothered and strangled. What, the Romans would protest, hands aflutter, a revolution? With tomorrow Sunday or tomorrow a feast day or just before (or just after) Christmas, or New Year, or Epiphany, Easter, Ferragosto? Take over the Parliament at the height of the rush rour? Invade the Ministry of Interior during the siesta? Another time, another season, *per favore;* we'll make an appointment to have the revolution in Rome on a nice sunshiny day in midwinter, preferably in the middle of the week when it can be arranged without too much confusion to the public transport system or interfere with the big Sunday soccer game at the stadium between Lazio and Roma.

And Franco Furbo was Rome, touching his forefinger to his forehead and muttering "madman" at anyone suggesting the high hard road to progress. Franco, the shoulder-shrugging cynic whose motto was, *"M beh, pazienza,"* or maybe still the Fascist *"Me ne frego,"* whose mind worked like a dynamo to maneuver him out of the slightest physical exertion or honest labor. He, Paolo, was grimly glad he was not a Roman; being a Sard had no social ebullience, but it also connoted a serious man, a worker, one whose word was his bond and whose honor was closely cherished.

Lungs bursting, he reached the topmost landing, meeting only two silent, black-shawled crones pattering down with their market baskets who made no answer to his greeting, glancing enigmatically at each other. It was fortunate, he remembered, that this was the final hour of the siesta and that most of the city was stretched out in its *pisolino*, the needed midafternoon nap, prior to returning to the long afternoon and evening of work. He himself actually yearned to reach his drab little room with the grimy cheesecloth curtains and the ancient soot-colored furnishings, to take off his shoes and slump into the lumpy bed. He knew now that, despite his initial surge of excitement at the assignment, he was simply not cut out for stealing dynamite from Italian military installations. He would have to inform Il Duro sadly but decisively of this fact once the inevitable compliments for the success of his exploit had caressed his ears. He would talk with Comrade Spartaco about a more suitable Party task: a study program in one of the People's Republics, perhaps, followed by a challenging assignment in one of the poorer provincial headquarters of the Party in Sicily or Lucania, where the downtrodden masses would in time look up to him as their friend and savior. He stood breathing heavily before the door of the apartment in which he rented his bleak little room and his imagined Party career took higher wing: he would get a job on *L'Unità* and Paolo Seddu's name would crown the documented articles thundering against the clerical and absentee landlord exploitation and the misery of the poor of the Basilicata.

Dynamite was not his forte, not at all. Had it not been for his great reverence for Comrade Spartaco and the sure knowledge that the task was a necessary one, he would certainly have asked why the Party, growing stronger every day in Parliament and in popularity, should require enough explosives to blow up a large palazzo. He straightened his shoulders and held his head up: no, *he* had proletarian discipline even if that ruffian Franco Furbo did not. *They* had asked and he obeyed well. It all meant something: it would all be explained in good time, of that he was certain.

He fumbled with the key to the great black door. The old lock snapped loudly and gave its usual grudging squeak as he stepped into the constant twilight of the internal corridor of Signora Piccini's apartment. He cautiously bumped the suitcases, one after the other, into the dim foyer and closed the door, relieved that there was no challenging "*Chi è?*" from the Piccini kitchen.

A final effort with gasping lungs and leaden arms moved the suitcases down the end of the corridor where his room awaited him. He carefully put them down side by side, stood at the threshold of his room and listened. Snores and the reassuring grunts of siesta-takers were the only sounds detectable. He quietly closed the door to his room, bitterly regretting Signora Piccini's inability to supply a proper lock so that he could secure it behind him, and slumped to the narrow bed with its wafer-thin mattress. He lay down, careful not to set up a pinging of bed springs which would bring in the ever prying Signora Piccini, and said to himself as he stared up at the grimy ceiling: I will rest for a few moments, wash, change, go out for a bite, and get into contact with Comrade Franco Furbo, who will in turn find out where I must bring the suitcases . . . Within seconds, he was sound asleep.

A yielding wooden crackle from a cane-back chair by the window opened his eyes, and the sight of a large indistinct form in the chair brought him to his feet as if catapulted. The form slowly rose and standing before him, face in complete shadow, was The Maria.

"*Zia!*" he faltered, surprise choking him. "W-what are you doing here? How did you find me?"

Her square heavy figure was silhouetted against the window's muted light and Paolo saw with a pang that her shoulders drooped as those of an old woman.

"I have sat and watched you slumber for an hour. You do not embrace your aunt?" she asked him in her deep voice and held up her cheek to be kissed. He put his arms around her and pressed her to him, kissing her strongly on one cheek and then the other.

"*Zia . . .*" he said and the fierceness and resistance drained out of him as does the air from a punctured balloon. She took his arms from around her and pulled herself gently away from him.

"How did I find you!" she mocked. "You are a Sard, no? Your name is Seddu? You are young and handsome, living without family? I have combed this section of Rome moving from one of our people here to the other. The fourth Sard portiere I met knew of you from Signora Piccini, despite the fact that in this building no one knows you by name."

She tossed her head triumphantly.

"If you must hide, do not choose Rome. Here you cannot hide from me if I choose to find you."

"I do not hide from you," he said stiffly. "You sought me out. I live here as an honest citizen, under my own name, paying my rent. I lead my own life in my own manner." But he watched her lips tighten under the rebuke, and his heart beat like a piston with the instinctive guilt of a young child who has profaned the name of God.

"So," The Maria said with the finality of the day ending, "you lead your own life in your own manner. And what is it that you are doing with this life?" One hand suddenly extended toward the two suitcases sitting on the floor inside the doorframe. "Selling objects on the black market, perhaps? Dry goods from door to door?"

"I have bought up a lot of university books I need for my studies," he lied stiffly, thankful that the ferret mind of Franco Furbo had at least given him this ready-made alibi.

"Ah, books, university books," she nodded as if the words were holy ones. "*Bravo*, my Paolo, returning to his studies after his infatuation with the Godless Ones." She sniffed the air, scenting the odor from the suitcases.

"I should like to see your books, dear Paolo. I want to see with my old eyes these books that you again will embrace and whose words will burn into thy brain. They must be old books, filled with age indeed, to give off such a stench."

He stood rooted to the floor, cheeks tingling with the sting of her irony. From out of the darkness of her face, the black eyes hardened and flashed like steel striking steel.

"I wait, Paolo. I want to see the books. Open the suitcases."

His words came out from a mouth choked with sand.

"No, I will not show you."

"I must see the books."

"No, they are not of interest."

"I insist."

"You have no right to insist *Zia*. There are but books in there."

Suddenly she laughed and it was a crashing terrible sound.

"You stupid cretin! You mushy-brained ass! You poor chicken, bought and sold by Them, your head filled with their manure!" The harsh words rolled out and cuffed his ears.

"The books. I want to see them."

Paolo stepped back to the suitcases, opened hands held out in warning.

"No, *Zia*, I cannot."

"Ah, you *cannot*. That's better. Now, *nipotino mio*, close the door."

He obeyed dumbly. She walked up close to him, so close he could see a familiar wart below the short blunt nose. Her open hand lashed out without warning and struck him on his cheek with a mighty slap that knocked him to the floor.

"Why did you strike me?" he gasped at her, stumbling to his feet, holding his livid cheek, and he saw with even greater astonishment something he could not recall ever having seen there. The eyes of The Maria were brim-filled with tears.

"I struck you to save your soul, my Paolo," she answered and her deep voice took on a throaty waver. She took one step closer to him and spoke to him swiftly. "Now listen closely and well, my Paolo. You are in great trouble. I will explain only that the police know of your acquisition of explosives for"—she could not bear to say the name of the Party—"for Them.

"They will certainly come for thee and search this place. We must move these putrefying suitcases immediately to my house until we can decide what to do."

Paolo rose to his feet slowly, his cheek feeling fiery and swollen.

"I do not come with you, Aunt. I have my duty to my comrades to do what I must do. I am working for a greater cause than myself."

She looked at him intently with the implacable face of a stone image.

"I do not ask you to report yourself to the police," she told him coolly. "I ask only that you do not leave these . . . articles . . . here since I know full well that the police will come. I seek to save you from certain arrest and myself from shame."

He quickly deliberated her argument and could not find any rejoinder. He knew she spoke the truth and that she would never betray him.

"Very well, Aunt, you are right. I will take these suitcases to your house temporarily—until I can consign them to my comrades." His hand came up to his smarting cheek again.

"You have the strength of a man."

"I have a heart of a chicken. Striking you was like stabbing my own breast." She paused.

"I will not inform on you in any way, my Paolo, but I warn you: I am going to fight for thy soul."

"*Zia, Zia,* we have been over this matter so many times. There is too much injustice in Italy; too much hunger, too much grubbing and corruption and fattening by the industrialists and the Church and the landowners. The little people are suffering here. What can you do to convince me otherwise?"

"I will attempt to show you in any way I can," she said in a soft rumble, "that They are as bad, that They are worse than those They fight. I do not deny the hunger and the injustice but this can be fought in other ways. Those you serve

117

are evil, and when they no longer need you, they will abandon you in the gutter. They have no God."

Paolo smiled a half-grimace at the quiet passion of her words.

"The Communist movement has its God, *Zia*, and his name is Marx."

"This Marx, this God of Theirs, cannot win because he preaches hate. The real God preaches love. Love wins over hate. You will learn this, my Paolo." She reached out and her hand caressed him under his chin.

"And now we take our smelly burden down these stairs and away before the police come."

Tentatively she lifted one of the bulging suitcases and grunted,

"*Mannaggia*, your books must be made of stone."

Paolo warned her with an embarrassed frown.

"Be very careful with the suitcase, Zia; there are . . . uh . . . delicate materials inside."

As Paolo and his aunt emerged from his apartment building, a plump ferret of a man, wearing a slouched felt hat in an ancient police tradition, detached himself from a doorway across the street. He strolled along paralleling their slow progress to the nearby trolley stop, a toothpick in his mouth and a roll of newspapers under his arm.

Further down the street, Comrade Piero, cramped in the front seat of his tiny Fiat beside the driver, intently watched Paolo, his aunt, and the conspicuously furtive plainclothesman on the opposite sidewalk.

"*Porco mondo*," he growled bitterly. "Our visit with Comrade Paolo will have to wait until later. With that imbecile of a cop at their heels, we can only trail along behind."

Pointing to the dull green *circolare* onto which their quarry swung their suitcases, two paces ahead of the round little policeman who boarded at the last moment, Comrade Piero tried not to sound self-conscious as he barked a command to his driver which he had heard in a movie thriller the night before, "Follow that tram."

chapter thirteen

A POWERFUL BLACK police car, an unmarked Alfa-Romeo, rolled swiftly up the Avenue of the Imperial Forums among the shadows of the dying afternoon. Past the massive Roman ruins and wall maps of Imperial Rome vulgarly memorialized in marble, the vehicle squealed in a tight climbing turn around the huge traffic pylon that was the Colosseum, and slowed at the corner of one of the streets debouching into that immense navel of Rome. Franco Furbo, his sartorial elegance restored after the degrading costume and chore of the past day, slouched with studied nonchalance on the curb as the black car swung slowly by him and, as the door flung open, took two lightning steps, was inside, and had slammed the door as the Alfa gathered speed around the immense ruin.

He peered through his sun glasses at the unfamiliar figure sitting behind him and the sensitive moose nose quivered in silent alarm until the very familiar face in the front seat beside the impassive police driver said, turning around. "Don't be concerned. May I present my chief, Vice-Questor Fracassi of the Central Questura. You should feel complimented. He wanted to meet you."

Franco extended a reluctant hand to the other, a saturnine man in a brown sports outfit fully as meticulous as his own.

"Pleasure," the vice-questor said, taking his hand and shaking it without enthusiasm.

"He knows all about our . . . work, Franco," the man in the front seat assured him.

The vice-questor leaned forward.

"Drive out to Saint Paul's Outside-the-Walls and back, and slowly, please," he commanded. He sat back in the comfortable leather seat and offered Franco a pack of long filter cigarettes. Franco, studying the police official carefully from behind his black lenses, accepted one and the light that went with it.

"I know you from somewhere," Franco finally said to the vice-questor.

"Yes, I was *capo commissario* for the Flaminio district three years ago when we caught you and your two neo-Blackshirts out in Parioli in the act of painting 'Death To The Communists!' on the Party's section offices in the early hours of the morning. It was quite a job getting that black paint off the building's walls." He smiled bleakly. "Times have changed, it seems, politically."

Franco took off the black glasses and sniffed contemptuously at the taunt.

"Let us understand one thing very clearly, dear Mr. Vice-Questor. My political allegiance never changes: I am loyal to Franco Furbo, first, last and always. The *Missini* appealed to my sense of *Italianità*, true; but I am neither Fascist nor Communist: I am a Franco-Furbist." He jabbed his narrow chest. "I am for me, for Franco, and I work for anyone who can help Franco. Are we understood?"

"Perfectly," murmured the vice-questor, staring at the raw, white, boxlike buildings sprouting at the city's western edges and the sharp deep shadows everywhere. "You are, in the old Fascist terms, a *menefreghista*, a to-hell-with-it-er. Bravo! We certainly understand each other."

"Very well," Franco rejoined, cupping his hand, "fifty thousand lire, then, in bills of any dimension. I told your Maresciallo De Luca here the entire story of this morning. And now the money, please."

The vice-questor smiled at the brash cynicism.

"A few moments of patience, Franco, the fifty thousand are here." He reached in an inside jacket pocket and briefly tugged out a tight roll of bills before putting them back. "First, I want a few confirmatory facts."

He held out one large hand and ticked off the points on his fingers.

"You stole the dynamite from the military dump at Ardea."

"Yes."

"How much?"

"About twenty kilograms. The stuff comes from America and is marked 'Fifty pounds.' Plus detonator caps and time pencil fuses. Comrade Spartaco specifically stressed the time pencils. Our soldier comrade at the camp knew exactly where everything was."

The vice-questor clucked unbelievingly.

"Twenty kilos! That's enough to wreck a good-sized building. Did you have any trouble?"

Franco threw up a deprecating hand, as a racing driver would if asked if he knows how to steer.

"It was like stealing a handful of beans in the market place. We were picked up outside EUR on the Aprilia road early this morning by a Party comrade who was drafted into the Army and who is assigned as a driver at the dump. He was using a small, covered army truck with spare work uniforms in the rear. We put on the uniforms en route to the camp, drove through the front gate past the sentry to the area of the underground bunkers where the explosives are kept. I was the lookout (I have a delicate physical condition). The soldier-comrade and Paolo Seddu entered the bunker, picked out the dynamite packs, put them in suitcases, and we loaded them in the back of the truck. Back through the gates of the camp, out to the town of Ardea, while we changed back into our old civilian clothes in the truck. We hopped out with the suitcases as if we had just hitchhiked down the road on the military truck. Then we waited for the *corriera*, flagged it down, and rode into Rome. We dragged the suitcases off, lugged them to Paolo's place near the Piazza Vittorio and that was it."

The vice-questor plucked a handkerchief out of his jacket pocket, mopped his brow, and ran one hand nervously through very curly black hair.

"Pretty nervy," he muttered, "pretty nervy. And tell me, Franco, where is this precious load of dynamite now?"

The narrow cement-girdled bed of the Tiber appeared on either side of a new bridge as they approached the great basilica of Saint Paul in the thickening traffic of the Viale Marconi, and Franco stared straight ahead of them to where the great orange ball of an afternoon sun hung swelling in size as it neared the cloudless blue horizon.

"Bella Roma," he said, entranced. "I rented a room at Ostia overlooking the sea for two weekends last year, with a girl. Do you know what it is to make love at the precise moment that the sun drops into the sea? Hit it right on the nose two evenings in a row. That's living," said Franco Furbo.

"The dynamite," the vice-questor repeated tightly, in a voice that brought an inquiring glance from his subordinate in the front seat. "Where is it now, Franco?"

"At Paolo's, I told you. That's where I left him." He abruptly smiled in recollection. "Poor devil, the elevator was out of order. He had to lug those suitcases up five flights of stairs. Well, it serves the poor Communist *cretino* right. I did it for fifty thousand lire. *He* did it for nothing. He actually believes that ideological manure the Party shovels out, you know."

Maresciallo De Luca interjected, "Excuse, Dottore, but are you all right?"

"It's all right, Edo," the vice-questor replied, mopping his forehead again. "Probably something I ate.

"Listen to me, Franco," he said in a tone that brooked no levity. "I want you to listen to me closely. Go to Paolo Seddu and convince him of one thing and one thing only: not to move about with his precious suitcases but to stay where he is. We want to close in at his lodgings."

Franco's small eyes turned bewildered to Maresciallo De Luca, who was looking back at him.

"I don't understand, Marescia'," he complained to the plainclothesman. "*You* offer me fifty thousand lire for bringing the dynamite to the Party big shots so that you can arrest the responsible ones, including Il Duro, with the goods, and now your boss here says he is just going to arrest Paolo, who is only a poor idiot and a Party errand boy. What is with you police types? Don't you tell each other what you're going to do next?"

Maresciallo De Luca in turn shot his chief a stare of bewilderment. The other's face darkened with anger.

"You will do as I say! Now get back to Paolo Seddu immediately and tell him to lie low with his suitcases, that to leave his room is dangerous because the police are in the area. I want that dynamite to remain just where it is."

He smiled, but it was a strained effort.

"The dynamite will serve as cheese. If it does not come to Il Duro and the Party, perhaps they will come to it. *Capito?*"

This Franco understood quickly.

"*Capito.* I will do it."

The vice-questor's hand disappeared into the inner pocket, came out with the tight roll of bills, and handed them to Franco.

"And another big bonus if we make arrests of some fine Communist functionaries," the vice-questor promised. Franco Furbo's face opened in a grin of pure exhilaration as he pulled out a very ornate Florentine leather wallet and shoved the flattened bills inside.

"At your service, Signor Vice-Questor," he rejoined, bowing his head. "We will do what we can. Now, let me off to pay a call on my good Party comrade, Seddu."

The police car flew through the crowded boulevards now darkening in the first moments of early evening, the driver

122

expertly threading through a near chaos of traffic. No one spoke again until the Alfa pulled up at the great waterfall of steps of the Santa Maria Maggiore and Franco sprang out.

"Telephone me," De Luca told him, "you have my number. And if we must meet the place will be just inside of the door of the Central Post Office, agreed?"

"Agreed," Franco said. He shook his head as he leaned in the car door to bid farewell.

"That stuff we pinched has such a stink, I'm surprised we weren't thrown off the bus this morning. Next time, we'll steal something without a smell, like diamonds. *Ciao*." He strode away with the air of a banker who has completed a brilliant transaction and is en route to new triumphs, not once looking back as the police car rocketed off.

"Dottore," De Luca addressed his chief and his fingers bunched briefly. "For five months we have been busy building this trap for Il Duro and his comrades, paying this swine of a Franco Furbo thousands upon thousands of lire and listening to his cheeky talk. Now, on the brink of success, what happens? You suddenly change all of our plans. This morning we were completely agreed to permit the explosives to be taken anywhere by Furbo and Seddu to their Party leaders, under our close surveillance every moment, and then make the arrests *in flagrante delicto*. Now, you say, leave it in Seddu's flat! What makes you think the Party will go there to pick it up? They will certainly order Seddu to deliver it elsewhere. If Paolo refuses and passes on the word to the Party that the police are watching his flat, our game is at an end. Really, Dottore . . ."

The Alfa moved slowly in the mush of traffic past the Opera House and the vice-questor pointed to the billings.

"The answer is there in the title of tonight's performance, dear Edo," he told his subordinate with a slight preoccupied smile. "*Forza del Destino*. When we spoke about this business this morning, what did you tell me about the explosives?"

"Simply that it represents no real danger. The explosives are in one valise, the detonators and time pencils in the other. Seddu knows what he is carrying around and is exerting more than the normal amount of caution."

The vice-questor reached to turn on the dome light in the Alfa, and took a piece of paper from his pocket.

"Half an hour ago, Edo," he told his subordinate, "the carabinieri post at Ardea reported the theft of dynamite from the military dump near that locality. Apparently the depot authorities make a daily check and found it was gone, fifty

American pounds of it as Furbo said, in one hundred sticks. Here I hold a circular telegram sent out by the Central Carabinieri Command in Rome to all police and carabinieri units warning them to be on the lookout for it."

De Luca made an impatient gesture

"It was to be expected that they would discover its loss."

The normally composed face of the vice-questor betrayed an unusual agitation, and he leaned forward to lend emphasis to his words

"The dynamite which was stolen by our two young friends this morning, my dear fellow, was *old* dynamite condemned for any military use and was to have been destroyed tomorrow. Its present consistency is such that the slightest jar or movement could make it explode. At any movement, a stray kick or shove of those suitcases will detonate twenty kilograms of high explosive, enough to kill hundreds of innocents in the apartment building in the Piazza Vittorio area where Seddu is living." He mopped his brow again. "Do you begin to understand?"

The dark eyes of Maresciallo De Luca widened in surprise and apprehension and even the impassive slab of a police chauffeur, Folco, turned around briefly and pursed his lips

"*Santo cielo!* That explains that crack of Franco about the stink from the explosives." He stared at his superior who still studied the carabinieri teletype message, head down and shoulders hunched in preoccupation. The vice-questor looked up finally as the Alfa crawled slowly in the thick traffic of the Via Nazionale at a traffic signal, and shook his head as if he had been reading De Luca's thoughts.

"Do we inform the carabinieri and the explosives squad to rush in and confiscate the stolen dynamite? No, my dear Edo, not yet. We have been working too long on this bunch of Bolsheviks to stop now, and besides, the fact that there has been no explosion yet, miraculous as it seems to be, is all to the good. If we can keep it safely stored in Paolo Seddu's flat, we have time to decide when to call in the carabinieri and the army. For now, nothing. But you must have that building of Seddu's watched as it has never been watched before. Who is there now?"

De Luca consulted a small notebook.

"Maresciallo Bottoni is on duty. He is stationed across the street from Seddu's building, in a small bar."

The vice-questor groaned.

"For God's sake, Edo, couldn't you get anyone else? Bottoni hasn't been worth five lire since he was assigned to us. He's a favorite of one of the Ministers but he is such a notoriously stupid old *questurino* and a hopeless Fascist to boot, he should be writing out traffic violations on the Corso."

"We are most short-handed. And, besides, I was told he was a smart old wolf before the war."

His superior grunted, "That was twenty years ago, dear fellow." The Alfa turned sharply into the Questura driveway and crunched into the inner courtyard, where Folco expertly steered it into a reserved space, jumped out, and held the door open for the vice-questor. His commissario fell in beside him and the two men marched quickly into the doorway and, disdaining to wait for the elevator, climbed the narrow stairs.

"I don't care how short-handed we are," Fracassi told his subordinate. "I want another two men in a parked auto to join Bottoni on the surveillance of that building, in order to follow if any of the comrades arrives or departs in a vehicle."

But as they turned into the vice-questor's office, a slim young police functionary in the accepted police civilian garb of sweater, sports jacket, cuffless trousers, and pointed loafer shoes rushed through the door a moment behind them and announced, "A telephone call from Bottoni, Dottore! Seddu has flown the coop! He just left his building with the two suitcases and an old woman in black. Bottoni followed them onto a tram to Prati where they got off. They walked to a residence building along the Tiber and took an elevator to the top floor."

"Who lives on the top floor?" the vice-questor asked calmly enough, but his face betrayed great concern as he exchanged glances with De Luca.

"An American by the name of Linden, for years a resident here. We have a dossier on him. His residence permit has expired."

"An American!" Fracassi echoed, laying one finger by his nose in a gesture of astonishment. "What do you say to that, De Luca?"

"I would say, Dottore," De Luca answered self-consciously, but his black eyes glittering with conspiracy, "that the situation becomes somewhat obscure."

chapter fourteen

PAOLO SAT ON the hard wooden chair with increasing anxiety as the minutes dragged into a lost hour. The three Party functionaries sitting in bureaucratic disorder on the other side of the large bleak room eyed him with mounting distaste from time to time as they looked up from their desks covered with open pages of *Il Paese* and sports dailies. He had promised The Maria that he would be back within the hour with the excuse that he had to retrieve his shirts and laundry from a little *stireria* in Piazza Vittorio, and he hated lying to his aunt because he could never remember an occasion when he had done so and remained undiscovered in his lie. But he could not bear the pressure building up in him concerning the disposition of the explosives, now cached under The Maria's bed, and Comrade Spartaco had specifically told him never to telephone him on any matter of consequence. And so, he sat in the outer office of Comrade Spartaco's Veterans of the Resistance headquarters in a dark and depressing apartment in a dark and depressing building in the Largo Argentina, with dread for the lie which would certainly be uncovered by The Maria gaining on a sense of pride and anticipation for the interview ahead. Certainly, at the very least, he would get a firm slap on the shoulders, a good handshake, a ringing well done!—and the susurration from the admiring Party youths at future section and cell meetings as a real Bolshevik, a comrade who risked his skin for the Party ...

A small-eyed little monkey of an usher, with a broad black mourning stripe on his lapel just under the hammer-and-sickle button, poked his head through a far door and silently beckoned him. He led Paolo down a corridor whose dirty terrazzo floor was littered with half-inch cigarette butts. At the end, the usher knocked twice on a huge wooden door. Half of the door opened; another man, bigger and with a two-day stubble on his heavy chin, said, *"Va bene,"* and Paolo was suddenly in a large, well lit semicircular room with good Persian carpets. A handsome Venetian glass chandelier and a large, curtained double window hinted of the room's once aristocratic origins. A small sofa at one side with two armchairs around a coffee table seemed lost in the vastness of its dimensions. But the walls were covered with anything but aristocratic tokens: everywhere were mounted mementi of the Resistenza—partisan pennants like long tattered feathers, bold sketches of men and women caught in the act of fighting and dying. A terrifying photograph, blown up to yard-square dimensions, seemed to have been taken upside down until one recognized it as a cluster of men and one woman hanging by their heels: the one of the riddled Mussolini, his mistress, Claretta Petacci, and the Fascist hierarchies swinging in the Piazza Loreto gasoline station in Milan shortly after their summary executions by partisan machine-gunners. And flanking the window on either side were large framed colored photographs, the one on the left that of a benign and avuncular Stalin, the one on the right, that of a lean, hard Luigi Longo, hierarch of the Italian Resistance.

In the precise center of the room an enormous desk hulked, cluttered with more partisan souvenirs and with documents and periodicals, and behind this massive object Paolo saw only the sparsely gray head of a heavy old man bent over his work.

The head rose and before Paolo sat Spartaco Tamburri, secretary general of the Veterans of the Resistance, pioneer member of the *Partito Comunista Italiano* and member of the Central Committee. Until six months ago, he had been one of the handful holding Party power, the Secretariat itself. He was still Il Duro, the Hard One, a Party legend whose mashed-nose features dominated the front ranks of a hundred rowdy street demonstrations and a thousand noisy rallies. He looked up at Paolo who had never before seen him alone at such close range. As Paolo stared at the short plump man who now slowly stood up giving a limp clenched-fist Communist salute and looking more like a weary businessman at the end of a long day of haggling and bargaining, he felt a sudden shock of disappointment. Was this the same human being as the then bearded partisan chief with the ever present machine-pistol in hand who squinted into the lens of countless wartime photographers, alert as a mountain goat? Was this the impelling, air-stabbing figure on high Party rostrums with the grating voice urging his listeners to remember that this was a party of revolution, not evolution, that this was the party which would emulate the great Bolshevik Revolution and march on the Campidoglio, on the Quirinal Palace, yes, even against the Vatican walls themselves?

Paolo roused himself to recall why he had come here. He gave a ferocious clenched-fist greeting in return.

The hard little eyes above the crushed nose stared over the desk at him for a moment and Comrade Spartaco did not extend his hand to be shaken. Instead, his left hand came up cocked like a pistol at Paolo.

"*Cretino!* Imbecile that you are! What sort of madness brings you here?"

Paolo felt the earth sway around his ears.

"But I came to report that I have accomplished the mission for which you selected me and Comrade Furbo," he replied, voice quivering with indignation. "We risked our lives to steal the explosives at Ardea."

"You risked virtually nothing at Ardea. I know the place well; you could steal the boots off the officers' feet out there and they wouldn't know it. You were also told to wait until we got in touch with you, idiot. Don't you know the police are always around here?"

"I know I was to wait," Paolo answered apologetically, "but I had to tell you that I moved my residence and the suitcases containing the explosives from my own room to that of my aunt. It was a matter of security; my landlady became suspicious of the suitcases," he lied with what he hoped was ringing conviction, "and I was told never to telephone on matters of any consequence."

He looked helplessly at the third man, Pasquale, who lifted his unkempt head and nodded in support. "He's right, chief. Those were his orders from Renzo."

"Don't you realize that they're probably onto you, you cotton head, since your Comrade Furbo has gone to the police with the whole story, the Fascist turd!" Comrade Spartaco flailed on, ignoring Pasquale's interjection, pudgy hands on equally pudgy hips. "And you lead them right to me! If this were during the Resistance, I would have Pasquale here"—tossing his jowly head toward the unshaven one—"take you out and put a hole in the back of your head to ensure security." He folded his arms.

"Did you know that 'Comrade' Furbo was a police spy?"

Paolo frowned in his concentration to understand the precise meaning of his hero's words, but it was all a ceaselessly turning kaleidoscope.

"Comrade Furbo a police spy?" he asked weakly. "How do we know?"

Comrade Spartaco snorted.

"How do we know, indeed! This is a revolutionary movement, a party with vigilance, you fool! There is ample evidence, and I can tell you that the police now know of your little outing of this morning at Ardea. I can also tell you our late 'Comrade' Furbo will bitterly regret this day. But now that you're here, you understand that you must never, never reveal to anyone, no matter under how much torture, anything you know of the explosives, or of me, or of the Party, in the event they arrest you. In such an event, we, of course, must announce that both you and Furbo are provocateurs of the police acting with them to embarrass the Party's good name. We will have to denounce you openly in the Party press for such reasons. Do you understand?"

Paolo found himself dry-mouthed and unable to respond, his world in ruins around his feet.

"I . . . I don't understand, Comrade Spartaco. I have sacrificed the last two years of my life with the Party, I have suffered the agony of breaking with my loved ones for my beliefs. I believe in what the Party stands for. Surely . . ."

Comrade Spartaco's laugh was much worse than his bark. He sounded as though he was going to choke.

"You stand there and tell *me* about sacrifices, you soft-headed dolt! *Me*, Spartaco Tamburri! Why, I had this nose smashed in by the *squadristi* of Rimini thirty-three years ago! I was burned by Fascist OVRA cigarette butts all over my body before you ever saw the light of day! I lay on the ground near Brunete, north of Madrid, with a Falangist bullet in my hip almost freezing to death in the snow when your mouth was still sticky with your mother's milk. Don't use the word 'sacrifices' in my presence, you understand?"

He looked at Paolo's dazed expression and his sandpaper voice changed from a shout to growling complaint.

"I honestly don't know what the Party is taking in these days. Waves of women; soft bourgeois types like you; and Fascist scoundrels like that Furbo! Where are the workers, the peasants, men prepared to fight and die for the Party's ideals without a whimper? *You* broke from your loved ones! *My* loved ones had to drink castor oil because Spartaco was an anti-Fascist! *My* loved ones were under police vigilance for fifteen years because I was alive and fighting for the Party! The Party is not a *Dopolavoro* center; it is the instrument of bringing Communism to the peoples of the world. *Capito?*"

Paolo said, finding himself unexpectedly cool in the wake of a rush of distaste he suddenly felt for this man, "What shall I do with the explosives? They cannot remain with my aunt."

"Why did you take them to your aunt, of all persons? Is she a Party member or sympathizer? I thought you said you broke with her?"

"My aunt," Paolo told him slowly, hands at his sides, "hates the Party, but she is the only person in this world I really trust."

"More than you trust your comrades?"

"As much as I trust anyone. We Sards trust our kin," Paolo replied with deliberation, a deep flush of emotion mottling his cheeks.

"And where is this anti-Party aunt whom you trust so much?"

"She is a maid in the home of a foreigner."

"A foreigner? What kind of a foreigner?"

"An American."

Comrade Spartaco slapped his forehead with one hand in horror.

"An American? You brought the explosives to the home of an American?" His incredulous laugh sounded like the spluttering of a motor scooter with water in the gasoline.

"That's priceless! Our young Chekist here carries stolen explosives to the home of an American! Are you taking it all down, Pasquale?"

The unshaven one nodded without lifting his head from his rapid scrawling. "It would be a delightful climax to hear that this American is the American ambassador," Comrade Spartaco said.

"No, but he works in the Embassy. He knows nothing, however. The explosives are under the bed of my aunt. The American does not even know I am in the house. We brought in the valises while he was out."

"And the *portiere?* He, too, was out when you brought them in?"

"I didn't see him," Paolo answered truthfully.

There was a long silence, in which the muffled cacophony of the Largo Argentina was the only sound in the room. Comrade Spartaco stared down at his desk as if looking for something there and he shook his head twice as if banishing thoughts too terrible to contemplate. He looked up from heavy brows.

"Did you have any inkling that Furbo was working for the police?"

"No. Although I deplored giving an ex-Fascist youth leader any sort of Party status. He acted strangely at times."

"Aha, he acted strangely! Did you report his 'strange' activity?"

"No," Paolo admitted, "it was not quite that strange. He often said funny things, and I never knew whether he was jesting or not."

"And you reported nothing of these 'funny things' he told you? Aren't you aware of the need for constant vigilance by every member of the Party against possible enemy provocateurs and spies?"

"I am aware. I didn't connect anything he said with such activity," Paolo retorted stoutly.

Spartaco flailed out in a cutting-off gesture.

"*Basta!*" he shouted. "You had been selected to procure explosives for the Party at Ardea. In my opinion, you have botched your instructions in every way. I don't know what the Questura is doing but unless they're even worse than I think they are, they are somewhere in this vicinity, right on your tail. You were extremely stupid to come here in person; you could have sent me a note. Now you are in the soup and so are we. I want you to remember that we shall throw you to the wolves if this matter winds up in the hands of the police. We shall deny you, reject you, call you every sort of name to protect the Party. The Party must survive at all costs, to carry on its great mission, even if it must sacrifice its own to achieve that survival. Do you understand? Are you ready?"

Paolo asked him with a face of stone, "What do you want me to do with the explosives?"

Comrade Spartaco turned to the unshaven one, who stopped writing immediately and opened a little pocket address book through which he rapidly thumbed.

"At a quarter to midnight, the Campo de' Fiori," Pasquale said in a voice which sounded rusty with disuse. "In the doorway of number 11 in the Campo, leave the suitcases and walk away quickly. *Don't* look back."

"*Va bene.* And what then?"

"Nothing," Comrade Spartaco broke in. "For the next month, don't come to any Party meetings or offices. Lie low. Do you have a job?"

"I was working part-time in a notary's office. He is of Sardinian origin. I got the job through my aunt. Perhaps she will help me get it back."

"Again your precious aunt," said Comrade Spartaco. "'*M beh*, the Party will contact you when all of this blows over. I will generally inform Comrade Spezzi of the Prati section and he will understand your absence."

The cold eyes bore into Paolo's.

"And now, do you begin to understand what sort of guts you have to have to be a real Party man? Perhaps this episode will put a little hair on your chest. The Party needs *men*, not hangers-on. Come through this business, and we may yet make a good Chekist out of you. The enemy is all around, but they lack our drive, our purpose."

Paolo said, "I will deliver the suitcases to the Campo de' Fiori number 11 at quarter to midnight, as you instructed. Is there anything else?"

Comrade Spartaco stared at him and finally said, "No, that's all."

Paolo gave a last look at the battered head of Mussolini swinging by his heels in the terrible photograph, briefly bowed his head, and turned on his heel, ignoring the parting clenched-fist salute of Comrade Spartaco. When Paolo had closed the door behind him, Comrade Spartaco said to the unshaven one, "What do you think?"

"You went too far, chief. Admittedly he was a dolt to barge in here and tell you he had moved, but he acted out of honest motivation. And you drew blood when you talked of his aunt that way. One must be very careful with Sardinian comrades. Much Spanish and Arab blood, you know."

"Do you think he'll talk?"

"No," Pasquale assured him. "No, he won't talk because that would be unlike a Sard. But I think we may have lost ourselves a comrade."

Pasquale was a shrewd judge of character. Paolo blindly walked down the broad steps to the *piano nobile* of the once princely palazzo, and out of his whirling, confused thoughts, a great bitter howl of realization rang through his head. He had done all for his Party and yet in the moment of his accomplishment the Party had mocked him, swore at him, reviled him. They had spoken of his aunt, The Maria, in tones that nobody (no, nobody!) was permitted. For him the Party was finished. No more the endless, boring cell meetings, no more attendance at the enforced frantic public demonstrations, the tediously tortuous explanations of Hungary, Stalin and the Party line. No more the worn, artificial language of "fascist," "bourgeois-clerico reactionaries," the slavish reading of *L'Unità*, *Il Paese*, and the theoretical periodicals. They were swine: the Furbos, the Pasquales, the Spartaco Tamburris, like those they opposed. He would deliver the dynamite tonight, but that would be his final contribution. He would indeed lie low, as Spartaco had requested, but they would never see him in their Party premises again. Never!

He reached the street door and, with a feeling of liberation welling in him he looked at the outlines of the republican Forum stark against the evening sky. It was all ended and he would return to his aunt and try to build his bridges back to his own kind. With a sigh of relief, he was about to step onto the crowded sidewalk when two men moved in from behind him and took him smoothly under the arms from each side. "Please keep walking," one of them said in a firm if pleasant tone. "You are under arrest."

chapter fifteen

THIS TIME IT did not help at all, Tom knew as he strode wearily through the darkness. In the light of a shop window he glanced at his watch; he had been walking well over three hours since he had watched the last car of Antonella's train clack out of the station. It had never failed before, this long aimless stroll. Always it had given him the precise catharsis he desired: the feeling of anonymity, a pair of disembodied eyes in a vivacious city of great beauty and great age and complete strangeness. He had followed more or less the same route this time as always, although his starting point had been different. He had passed and paused and savored every time-revered ruin, every splashing fountain, every sudden vista and perspective, now and again coming up against the ubiquitous Wall of Aurelius with its gates and battlements. And all the other times, he had found the yearned-for nothingness in this melange of centuries.

But not this time. At the end of it all, footsore and hungry, moving along the river's embankment toward his flat, he was still Tom Linden, a man who had three times in this one day had his face slapped with a past he had been avoiding as the tongue attempts to avoid an aching tooth. Three times, by three people he had never dreamt at the dawn of this dying day would ever speak to him of the past, two of whom he had never expected to see again. He had lived in this great city far from home because here such things were never mentioned, because here one was simply the foreign dottore, and no questions asked. But suddenly, he was Tom Linden again, *the* Tom Linden, of West Waterstow, Massachusetts, singled out for contempt by a half-mad little carabinieri sergeant major and his Sardinian relatives, by The Maria, and by Antonella. Each successive arrow of scorn had hurt more than the previous one. And finally, of course, there was the Embassy, in the person of Vinny Brentwood, the fat scared snot of his childhood who had attempted literally to buy affection and friendship, and would now twist the knife in the wound.

Oh, this was a real day, he assured himself as he crossed the near-deserted Ponte Garibaldi and looked instinctively to his left at the great mass that was the Isola Tiberina dividing the narrow muddy river. This was a favorite view of his, but today it did not stop the remembering.

And now, a sore ankle slowing his stride to a limp, he stopped for a brief moment to study the last of his favorites: the Castel Sant' Angelo. It had never failed him before: Hadrian's Tomb, Tosca's downfall, Cellini's fortress. Its great barrel shape reared out of the night aided by skillful fingers of light at its base, and the sword-armed archangel soared over it all, but this time it did nothing. It was just another tourist *spettacolo*, and he was Tom Linden, the skillful evader who could evade no more.

The leg started to hurt, throbbing with each new step, and he remembered how he had broken it years ago in a stupid ski accident at Terminello. It was the bad cast they had put on it that had done more damage than the broken ankle bone. Despite his entreaties, the know-it-all physician at the resort, a real *sportivo* type himself, had made it too tight, and it was a year before he could walk on the leg without pain. He smiled involuntarily in the darkness of the night remembering what it did to his love life. Turning around in bed with the heavy cast became a chore, and some of his women had demonstrated black-and-blue marks along their flanks with indignation and protest, but they had all generally been kind to him as he clomped about for months with the damned thing. And now the pain returned and he wanted very much to rest the leg for a moment.

The night was heavy with foreboding and as he slowed his pace, a far-off mutter behind the Monte Mario signaled what was soon to come: one of those momentary blinding sheets of spring rain with the whole orchestration of thunder and lightning. Rather than risk a drenching, he pushed on.

Just beyond the Ministry of Justice a woman approached him in the darkness. She was unmistakably a whore by her exaggerated swagger, her huge bag swinging slowly and deliberately as she prepared for a large hello. He made out the huge pendulous breasts, the white sweater with cleavage almost to her navel and a tight shiny skirt that seemed to ripple as she walked. He recognized her immediately as one of the regulars in the area, a real chunk of woman still reasonably young, with a pretty face scarred by acne and by poor broken teeth. She was the one they called La Bambolona, Big Doll. She in turn spotted him as a familiar foreigner in the neighborhood and she came up to him in the middle of the sidewalk to block his passage unless he chose to step into the gutter to pass her.

"*Buona sera, Dotto,*" she greeted him in her rough husky voice with what apparently passed for an ingratiating smile. Her huge puffy breasts almost touched him, and the smell of cheap violet perfume struck him like a thick cloud. "How are we this evening?"

He had never patronized any of the street whores who clustered with each evening's darkness up and down the length of the Lungotevere peddling their weary wares both to pedestrians and to passing motorists in fifteen minute doses, but they all greeted him cheerfully nonetheless and never stopped trying. The Big Doll was no exception.

"Listen, Dotto'," she urged him, one hand resting on a protruding hip. "How about a little love this evening? I have a fine little furnished room just a hundred meters from here and for five thousand lire we can . . ."

He shook his head with a sincere enough smile.

"Thanks for the invitation, but not tonight. I have had a bad day and it is best it come to a peaceful end."

She chortled, a sound halfway between a shriek and a guffaw and prodded his chest with a knuckled hand.

"Ha, Dotto'! Come with La Bambolona, and she will show

you how to end a bad day A solid hour of love, Dottore, and you will be like new."

She appraised him calculatingly in the darkness, and then cocked her frizzled head in the direction of the insistent muttering of the approaching storm

"Listen," she told him in the tone of a fine-arts dealer who decides to offer an irresistible bargain to a wavering client, "you look like a real giovanotto, someone who can make a woman really feel she's been laid. What do you say, five thousand lire for the whole night! The storm's coming up and we both might as well get off the streets, eh? Come on, now, with the Bambolona and she'll teach you something about *amore* that you never heard of before Come on, now, quick! Last offer."

Tom, despite the aching ankle and the bitter taste of the day's defeat in his mouth, smiled his amused refusal

"I'm a fool for turning you down, signorina, but I'm sorry To be frank with you, I haven't got fifty lire even if I wanted to take you up on it."

She sauntered off immediately, one hand flung contemptuously in his direction.

"*Ma, vai!* If there's anything I hate it's a liar. A foreigner without five thousand lire! Why don't you tell the truth— you haven't got the balls for it." The darkness swallowed her, and he tramped slowly on. She was right in a real sense. Even if he had the lire, he knew that he could not lose himself in that particular oblivion of calculated and repeated passion, in the lassitude, the rousing again, the grinding and the agony of it again. Not this night. This night, there was no oblivion to be found, and he was going to have to taste the bitterness of remembering, like a burning acid in the throat, again and again.

He strode through the open doorway of his apartment building. Although it was not yet time to lock the great front door, the *portiere's* little glass booth was vacant and dark, and for that he was grateful, because, like The Maria, he could not stand that stubble-bearded pig who sat in fat slovenliness and did nothing for anyone unless his palm was crossed with silver. The elevator was not on the ground floor and although he turned the key in the retrieve position, nothing happened. Some idiot had probably left the elevator door open some floors above. Tom slouched slowly up the endless stairs cursing softly and rhythmically to himself all the way.

At the top floor where the staircase narrowed and spiraled

for the final climb up to the penthouse level, he heard a door open and he knew that The Maria was listening and had recognized his step. It was not going to be at all pleasant, and perhaps she was waiting only long enough to hand him back the house keys, maybe spit in his face as she had promised, and leave, but he was beyond caring. He reached the top of the stairs. There in the lighted doorway stood The Maria, and beside her a dark young Italian whom he recognized as Paolo, the no-good nephew.

The Maria bowed, almost formally.

"Good evening, Dottore," she greeted him in that incredible bass voice. He stood at the threshold, almost unwilling to enter.

"Good evening, Dottore," Paolo Seddu echoed, hesitantly. "Please excuse me, but my aunt . . ."

"I brought him here, Dottore."

"Why?" Tom asked. He was in no mood for amenities.

"Two things," The Maria answered, equally dryly. "First, he is my flesh and blood and he is in trouble. Secondly, I felt that the Dottore could help us in some way. It is a very delicate matter."

They studied each other before he entered, like two chance strangers. Then he realized that she was asking him for help, the first time in their two years together that she had ever done so. He looked at the face of her nephew. He had, actually, a good-looking Italian male face. If he weren't such a trial to everyone, he could easily be *simpatico*.

"Good evening, Paolo," he said, severely. "You have caused your aunt great sorrow, great unhappiness."

Paolo hung his head.

"I know, Dottore. I have behaved badly. I have been wrong about many things."

"Well, then," Tom said more cheerfully, happy that one lost black sheep had found its flock again, "do we have anything to eat? I'm famished."

The Maria looked at Tom's exhausted face, the dusty shoes and clothing, and turned to her nephew, standing half a head taller than she.

"Go draw a bath of water for the Dottore, immediately," she commanded. He nodded obediently and disappeared.

"First of all," The Maria addressed Tom in a low voice, watching the retreating back of her nephew, "there were many telephone calls for you. One from Signora Luisa who reminds you of the next weekend at Bracciano. And there have been three calls in the past hour from an American signorina named Nenzi." She paused for a long moment which permitted him to match the words "Nenzi" and "Nancy" in his mind.

Tom slowly removed his jacket and handed it to her.

"You said this morning that the devil had gotten up earlier than I. You didn't know how right you were."

The rush of running water and a louder rumble of the impending storm filled the little flat with sound, and he caught a glimpse of the two Siamese retreating in padded silence into his bedroom from the terrace outside.

"I know. When I returned, I read your note. I'm sorry that you lost your employment at the Embassy, Dottore. I trust it was not because of the evil names I called your employer on the telephone . . . "

He waved off the apology, although he noted that she was still addressing him in the polite form: the strain of performance this afternoon, when the old carabiniere accused him, was apparently still on her. He held up his hand to prevent her passage into the kitchen.

"Just a moment, Maria. Now what is this 'delicate matter' you spoke about? What kind of trouble is your Paolo mixed up in now?"

"My Paolo is being sought by the police," she said at last.

"Why?"

"Because he has stolen explosives, for Them, for these Communist criminals. They told him to steal and he did so. The police have learned of the matter, and I"—she looked around to see if Paolo was within earshot—"have found out that the police know."

"Explosives! What kind of explosives?"

"I know not, execpt that they fill two suitcases."

He almost hated to ask her, "And the suitcases are . . . ?"

"They are in my room under my bed, Dottore."

Tom held the back of one hand to his forehead as if testing for fever.

"My incredibly aching back," he said in English. Then he fixed her with a baleful stare.

"Why in God's name here? Why didn't you bring him to one of your fellow Sardinians in Rome?"

"I cannot expose my friends and compatriots to such a risk, Dottore. I told you it was a delicate matter. You as a foreigner and a wise man can do many things. Beh, if you won't help me, I shall . . ."

"Just a minute," he snapped. "I didn't say I wasn't going

to help. Give me time to think. We'll come up with something."

The forbidding face with the straight heavy eyebrows softened perceptibly and The Maria said in a smooth soft rumble, "I thank you, Dottore Tommaso, from the bottom of my heart. You are a good, kind man." But she still used the polite *lei* in addressing him.

"Bath is ready, Dottore!" Paolo called from the other end of the short corridor which led to the bathroom. The Maria again turned toward the kitchen.

"There will be *bistecca di vitello* in fifteen minutes, with a good salad and a *crema caramella*," she announced. The swarthy diffidence relaxed for a moment into what was almost a conspiratorial smile.

"I see that you and the Signora Passaglia ate my spaghetti and my sauce today. The Signora left two thousand lire on the kitchen table with a nice note, and with this I purchased the meat."

But Tom, unbuttoning his sweaty frayed shirt, said, '*Un momentino*, Maria. One last question. If the police know that your Paolo has stolen all these explosives, how long will it take before they find him here?"

"No fear of that," she grunted, moving evenly toward her kitchen with effortless peasant's gait. "They are already here. There is one below who is watching beside the newspaper stand and two more who sit in an automobile a block down the street. Not to mention three strange ones in a Topolino who have passed many times but who do not wait to watch."

Tom walked blindly to the bathroom, knowing now that no matter how badly his fortunes seemed to have gone thus far, his real troubles appeared to have only just begun.

A small plump man with graying temples, in a cheap blue raincoat and flop-brimmed hat waddled up to the newspaper kiosk, reached into his trouser pocket for a coin, and ordered, "One telephone slug and five blanks for the football pool."

"*Mannaggia*, how we make money on you!" rasped the kiosk keeper. "Won't you even buy a twenty-five-lire paper?"

"Shut up," said the little man, pocketing the football-pool forms and inserting the slotted *gettone* slug into the public telephone installed on the wall of the kiosk, "or I'll run you in for insulting the forces of public order."

"Ah," grunted the kiosk man with a grudging discretion in his voice, "*a poliziotto*. I might have known."

"*Maresciallo* to you, and no guff," bristled the little man.

He glanced briefly across the street where the gloom grudgingly yielded ground to a feeble street light. Carefully dialing his number, he could hear the rushing murmur of the Tiber in the blackness far below the parapet behind him. A metallic voice answered, "Pronto, who speaks?"

"Ah, *Eccellenza*, Maresciallo Bottoni here. On duty, as ordered, surveilling the American's apartment building."

"Well, well? What's the latest news? Who arrives and departs?"

"*Un momentino Eccellenza*," the plainclothesman murmured in a broad Neapolitan accent as he fished quickly into his pocket for his notes and a pair of round eyeglasses.

"Will you cut out that 'Eccellenza' business?" the other said with considerable irritation. "Either call me Vice-Questor Fracassi or Dottore Fracassi, or simply Dottore. 'Eccellenza' went out with Mussolini."

"Excuse, Excel . . . Vice-Questor," Bottoni stammered. Then, with lips close to the mouthpiece and sinking his voice to the lowest possible level, he held up a tiny notebook to the kiosk light and studied the inked scratchings carefully through the thick lenses.

"Let me see. At sixteen-fifty hours, as I previously phoned you, the housemaid of the Americano arrived with her nephew." He cleared his throat with pride. "This I can personally ascertain myself, Eccellenza, Vice-Questore Dottore, since I followed them on the tram from the Santa Maria Maggiore sector. The building *portiere* saw them and positively identifies the woman as the housemaid of the Americano, a formidable type named Maria Seddu. Do you know, this *portiere* was a centurion from my old Fascist outfit in Messina and is a grand invalid of war . . ."

"*Porco mondo!* Will you spare me the biography of your ex-Fascist friend and get on with the details?"

"Certainly, Dottore," responded Bottoni, struggling to keep the hurt out of his voice. These rude young police officials had no sense of detail or of *ambiente* these days. Everything rush-rush, quick-quick. A good policeman had to proceed carefully, thoroughly, deliberately.

"And what have you been doing since the woman arrived?" the vice-questor prompted helpfully? "Have you been dozing on a bench or working on your eternal football pool when you should have had your eyes frozen on the front entrance to that building?"

"Eccellenza, I will assume you are kidding me," the *maresciallo* responded, his voice breaking with indignation and one hand touching his jacket pocket to see if the football-pool forms were still there. "Even so, I scarcely think it is a funny matter. I have been wide-eyed on this case, watching like a hawk since the beginning of the siesta, Eccellenza, and I am weary with my great vigilance. It is seven hours now that I have been on the job and I . . ."

"*Va be', va be',*" barked the vice-questor impatiently. "I'm sorry, Bottoni. So you weren't snoozing. You will be relieved within the hour. Now what else did you find out from your Janus, the ex-centurion of the Fascist Militia?"

"He calls himself Aurelio, not Janus," Bottoni answered with perplexity. Really, the way these half-grown *dottori* down at *questura* referred to people they didn't even know!

"All right! His name is Aurelio," with a sigh.

Maresciallo Bottoni consulted the scratched notes with increasing desperation. The words swam together and it was only his personal recall that saved the moment.

"Aurelio was sitting in his little *portineria,* just inside the main door of the building at the beginning of the siesta," he began ponderously, not hearing the grinding teeth of his superior at the other end of the line. "And he saw the American himself arrive with a young attractive signora. The American arrives at home often with such *signore, beato lui,* but rarely in the middle of the day. My friend Aurelio says that he has never seen the woman before."

"Go on," the vice-questor said grimly. "Tell me everything."

"Well, they stayed at the American's penthouse flat for two hours, and emerged together again. They took a taxi at the Piazza della Libertà at, let me see here, at fourteen-fifty-five hours. I don't know where they went," the maresciallo added apologetically, "but the taxi headed off in the direction of the Vatican."

"*Very* shrewd, Bottoni," his superior said heavily.

"Thank you, Eccell . . . er . . . Dottore," the plump little policeman answered, brightening under the praise. "As I tell my Giovanna, 'Giovanna,' I tell her, 'I try. I watch. I am vigilant.' "

"Formidable philosophy. Anything else?" the dry voice of Fracassi attempted to contain itself. He heard paper rustling and Bottoni muttering, "*Accidente!* What a wind!"

Then finally, "The American returned alone on foot two hours ago at twenty-thirty-five hours. The signora who was with him at noon has not reappeared."

"Amazing. Now listen, my eagle: about the two Seddus.

Are they still in there? You followed them across the city in a tram to the house. Are you *sure* they're still in there?"

"I swear by the innocent head of my first-born!" shouted the little plainclothesman. "Now let me tell you what my informant, the ex-centurion Aurelio, tells me about this housemaid. She is no ordinary creature. She is apparently a key figure in a kind of Sardinian *Camorra* composed of servants and workers from the island, and she . . ."

"Look, I don't care about the Sardinian *Camorra*. We know all about the woman. We know about her nephew. Now, listen carefully; were they carrying anything when they went to the American's apartment?"

The *maresciallo* squinted his small dark eyes to focus through the spectacles on the notebook page. *Dio*, how the jottings swam before his vision in this wretched light. "Nothing."

"Nothing! Are you sure?"

Bottoni's lips hoved slowly across the words he had written. "Nothing, Eccellenza . . . oops, *scusi*, it slipped out again, Dottore."

"Nothing?" the voice at the other end rose angrily.

"Not a thing. Only the suitcases they brought with them from the nephew's residence. The nephew carried an old one and his aunt had one like it probably because the nephew was moving back in with his aunt. They were carrying nothing suspicious."

"Of course not," the vice-questor put his hand across the phone and looked across his desk at his colleague who listened on an extra earphone.

"The explosives in the swo suitcases are still in the American's flat. That young scoundrel Seddu wouldn't admit it this afternoon."

He returned to his dialogue.

"Anything else, my eagle?"

The *maresciallo* looked carefully around him in the warm evening darkness and whispered. "Dottore vice-questor, the nephew is a Communist, and he . . ."

"We know that. Who else of interest came in and out?"

Again the pudgy little policeman scanned his notes and wished his first-born, Ezio, were here to do his reading for him.

"There is an apartment of assignation on the second floor," he read triumphantly. "Three whores are in there doing a tremendous business. On the door it says, 'Esthetic Massages,' but I have counted at least eight happy customers arriving and departing, checking their flies, in the last hour . . ."

"Maresciallo!" the vice-questor entreated. "Enough of the prostitutes. What about the apartment of the American?"

"But this is *clandestine* prostitution! This is a contravention, Dottore!"

"I know, I know," sighed the vice-questor. "I shall immediately inform the Vice Squad. What else?"

"Well," Bottoni finally deciphered his own scrawl, "the nephew left the building at seventeen-fifteen hours and returned only at twenty-fifteen hours, a few minutes before the American returned. He left carrying nothing. He returned carrying nothing."

The vice-questor exchanged glances with the grinning *capo commissario* standing opposite him and shrugged his shoulders helplessly.

"And that is all?"

Bottoni said, "*Un minuto.*" Two long minutes passed and then he blurted into the receiver almost in a squeak, "A gray American car with diplomatic plates just drove up, Eccellenza. The driver has locked the car and gone into the building after ringing the bell and waking Aurelio. He is a tall, well-dressed foreigner, and, according to my friend, he pushed the elevator button and swore in English when told the elevator was out of order. He said he had to climb to the top floor. That makes him a visitor to the American's penthouse."

"The number of the vehicle! Did you happen to write it down?"

"Did I happen to write it down? You are asking this of Maresciallo Bottoni, one of the old wolves of the Questura? Eccellenza, again you insult my professionalism!"

The sigh at the other end was prolonged.

"A hundred pardons, Maresciallo. The license number, please; we are going to trace it this instant."

The policeman read off the number and the vice-questor ran his fingers quickly down a list before him.

"Second Secretary Brentwood of the American Embassy," he murmured aside to an authoritative beak-nosed man now hovering over him.

"Extremely interesting," the other mused in deep concentration. "First, the explosives are brought to the Linden house, now the diplomat arrives. Two Americans now involved, one a diplomat. We are onto something very murky, Fracassi. Tell Bottoni to keep the house under watch until his relief arrives. Tell him his questor personally commands!"

he vice-questor relayed the command to the little plain-thesman who jumped to attention at the phone and answered, "At your orders, Eccellenza." Then in an aggrieved tone, "And please tell your squad in the little Fiat Topolino to be a little more discreet. They parked down the street for hours this afternoon in the same place. Can't they drive around the block every now and again?"

"We have no Topolino in that area," the vice-questor answered in astonishment. "Move immediately to the car and ask everyone to identify himself."

"I can't," Bottoni said sadly. "They shoved off an hour ago." And his jowly round face tightened as he recalled that the occupants of the little car had given him that obscene greeting with the crooked arm slapped on the muscle by the other hand. He had thought it only a friendly joke by other policemen, but if they were only ordinary citizens insulting the forces of public order . . . his teeth ground in frustration and he said, "Eccellenza, if that Fiat comes by again, I'll stop it with gunfire."

He hung up, retreated to a nearby streetlight and leaned up against it. Out came the complicated football-pool forms and a cheap ballpoint pen. And as the ominous thunder of the spring storm freshened along the quiet street beside the Tiber, he commenced to calculate the intricate pros and cons of the Inter-Torino match and the other twelve contests of the Sunday ahead, looking up occasionally to focus on the dimly lighted doorway.

In the little park across the street, two of Comrade Piero's men sat in darkness on a bench, puffing their cigarettes, and alternately eyeing the threatening sky and the rotund figure in stony silence. The presence of the fat little policeman had delayed for hours their plan to recover the explosives, and they awaited the imminent return of Comrade Piero with something less than enthusiasm.

chapter sixteen

TOM LINDEN LOOKED past the despairing face of Paolo Seddu seated across the table in the plastic chair marked "Hers," his eyes wandering to the battered head of the ancient refrigerator and back to Paolo again. He finally shook his head disbelievingly.

"You mean to say that the police picked you up outside Spartaco's office, took you to the Questura, questioned you and then simply let you go?"

"They did not take me to the Central Questura but to a police office near the Campo Marzio. They questioned me for two hours concerning my activity in the Party, my knowledge of the activity of Comrade Spartaco and the other Party militants, and they finally offered to find me a good job, to give me all sorts of benefits and money if I would keep them informed about the Party. When I refused, they threatened me that they would throw me into Regina Coeli prison and let me rot there on charges of 'suspicious activity.' I told them I could not betray my friends, and if I had to go to prison . . ." Paolo shrugged his shoulders without finishing the sentence. "Then, the chief police interrogator, whom they called only Dottore, signalled for them to let me go."

He looked disconsolately at Tom who reached over to fill Paolo's empty wineglass with dark heavy Chianti.

"You did not tell them about the explosives then?"

"Of course not!" he exploded. "Tell the police anything?" His voice rose to a near-squeak of passion and he leaned one elbow on the table, careful not to disturb the supper dishes, his eyes riveted to Tom's.

"Listen, Dottore, I have already told you how unhappy I am with the Party, with Franco Furbo, with Comrade Spartaco. But surely you know enough about Sardinians to understand our code. With the police only this": and he held a finger to his lips. "The law of *omertà*, silence. We handle our own problems, we settle our own quarrels, but to tell the police *anything?*" And he drew the finger across his throat.

"Bravo, Paolo" his aunt complimented him as she shuffled into the room to remove the crockery. "Spoken like a true Sard." Paolo glanced at her affectionately, embarrassed at her point-blank refusal to accept Tom's request to sit and eat with them ("A servant simply does not eat with her master unless she is something else other than a servant") but pleased at her status as an outspoken equal in this strange and decrepit household of the American Dottore.

Tom, still tired but relaxed after the warm bath, a shave, and with Maria's first-rate *bistecca* and salad inside him, snorted derisively.

"Bravo, Paolo! Don't tell the police! Why, then, is the outside of this house crawling with *poliziotti?*"

The Maria paused in the act of stacking the soiled dishes on the table.

"Dottore, the police have been watching this building for weeks for other reasons. Below us on the third floor is a small brothel which, thanks to the greased hand of that pig of a *portiere* is running full blast. And on the fifth floor, I am almost certain that there is some kind of a gambling haven, a *bisca*, in operation. Perhaps the police are of the Buon Costume."

"Yes, and perhaps Paolo can sprout wings and leave this place with those two suitcases in your room. No matter who they're watching, we are also in this building. Did it ever occur to you that after what happened to Paolo this afternoon with the police, it is highly probable that they simply let him go in order to lead them straight to his comrades?"

Paolo and his aunt exchanged glances and The Maria's forehead was a thunderhead of concern.

"The Dottore may well be right," she admitted finally, "in which case we must think well before we remove the explosives."

Paolo said stubbornly, "Leave it to me, Aunt. I want no trouble for you and the kind Dottore. I shall deliver the suitcases tonight to"—and he swallowed hard—"my comrades as I promised, and wash my hands of the entire dirty business."

Tom, both amused and touched at the young man's heroics, asked, "What do you mean: 'deliver tonight as promised?' "

"This afternoon, before the police arrested me, Il Duro and his secretary gave me instructions. I am to deliver the explosives at a quarter before midnight tonight to a doorway in the

146

Campo de' Fiori, to leave them in the doorway and simply walk away. This I shall do." He nodded meaningfully at his aunt. "Then I shall walk away—much further than they realize."

Tom leaned back in his chair, the old Spanish one built in the shape of an X. He rummaged in vain in his shirt pocket for a loose cigarette and accepted a Nazionale from Paolo with a wry smile of thanks.

"You are absolutely crazy," he told the intent young man. "Do you really expect to deliver, all by yourself, over twenty kilos of explosives"—he glanced at his watch—"within two hours without alerting every policeman in this district?"

He looked reflectively at the dingy French-door curtains which billowed slowly in the rising evening wind. "It can't be done. The stuff will have to stay here for the time being."

Paolo, mouth very much like his aunt's, shook his head stubbornly. "I gave my word that I would deliver the explosives tonight, and I intend to keep my word," he told Tom slowly and clearly as if reasoning with a dull child.

"Even if you wind up serving several years *in galera* for possession of stolen explosives?" Tom shot at him.

"Even so. If all I have left is my sense of personal honor, so be it."

Tom sighed. "By Marxist criteria, Paolo, you are a sentimental bourgeois fool." He pushed back his chair and rose.

"All right, let's have a look at the stuff." He grinned suddenly, his face almost boyish. "I was a demolitions expert during the war, Paolo, while you were still playing *giro-girotondo*."

He crushed his cigarette out in a plate and motioned Paolo to do the same.

"At the *asilo*," Paolo said stiffly, if courteously, "only the girls played *giro-girotondo*."

The Maria had moved ahead and turned on the naked light bulb in her bleak and spotlessly clean room. The narrow bed was neatly covered with a white linen bedspread and the old *prie-dieu* Tom had bought her at the Porta Portuese flea market filled one corner, with a large, brightly colored framed image of the Madonna affixed to the bare wall above it. Her missal and rosary beads rested on its little stand. The room fairly bristled with piety: apart from a chest of drawers with two photos of Paolo on it, a *guardaroba* with empty valises on top, one painfully stiff-backed chair, there was nothing more except for a large crucifix over the bed and an oval hand-woven rug on the terrazzo floor. In the middle of the little room lay the two battered and scuffed suitcases, their cheap locks fortified by two canvas straps.

Tom knelt beside them, expertly undid the straps, and worked at the catches. As he snapped open the first one, a pungent smell filled the room and Tom stared up at Paolo unbelievingly.

"*Per la miseria!* You idiot, how long have you been carrying this stuff around?"

"Since this morning," Paolo answered, bridling at the insult.

Tom picked up a brown, stained package as gingerly as possible.

"Paolo," he said gently, "what were you ordered to steal at the munitions dump; can you remember that?"

"Plastic explosives. The comrade driving the military truck said that such explosives would be in one section of the underground room and so I picked up these sticks and put them in the suitcase." His eyes blinked under the stare of Tom still on his knees beside the suitcases. "It was dark, very dark, in there," he added defensively."

"Paolo," Tom said patiently, "have you ever seen plastic explosives before, or any kind of explosives?"

"No, Dottore. But I did not know there was any difference."

"There is enough difference at this moment to blow you, me, Maria, the Siamese cats *and* the brothel downstairs into little pieces. Paolo, my Bolshevik, you have not stolen plastic explosives but sticks of commercial dynamite, which is another matter completely. Further, this dynamite has been stored so long it has gone bad. Do you see these stains on the wrappings? Do you smell that smell? This is old, and old dynamite is very treacherous, very unpredictable dynamite, and could go off any time, any time!"

He pulled out a handkerchief and mopped his brow.

"You say you brought it in on the *corriera*, all the way from Ardea, on that bumpy road?"

Paolo nodded, gap-mouthed, and Tom shook his head, rolling his eyes upward in mock piety.

"God exists. That bus should be in tiny pieces this moment and its passengers in even smaller ones." He opened the other suitcase and carefully examined the familiar detonators and time pencils. Then he closed both valises gently, rose, and said, "We are not going to move the one with the dynamite at all," he told The Maria and her stunned nephew in a deliberate tone. "Not at all. It is a miracle, a wild miracle, that you brought these here from Ardea and then from your room to this house without being disintegrated in a loud bang. But now that it *is* here, it *stays* here until the police come and take it carefully away stick by stick"

"I must take it tonight. It is a matter . . ."

"*Basta* with your damned 'honor,'" The Maria boomed suddenly. "You will do what the Dottore says, do you hear me? We will call the police and you will suffer whatever punishment there will be, *capito?* If the Dottore says this material is dangerous, that's enough for me."

As she marched out of her room, the knocker on the apartment door vigorously thudded. Paolo's eyes opened in fear. Tom, five steps behind her, watched her move close to the door, make no attempt to open it, and cry, "*Chi è?*"

"Brentwood! *Amico* Signor Linden. *Americano. Diplomatico.*"

She worked the heavy latch chain and flung the door open after a swift glance at Tom's assenting nod.

It was Vinny all right, but a wild, unkempt Vinny, swaying slightly on his feet, gleaming pumps ruined by dust and scuff, suit rumpled and tie loosened and askew, badly in need of a shave and with a bleary light in his blue eyes that Tom had never seen before. Even his precise blond mustache was awry.

"O.K., Tom." Vinny grated, swaying uncertainly past The Maria toward him, "Where is she? I gotta take her back to her father. And no crap, Tom. I mean it."

"The Promotion Board should see you now," Tom told him calmly. "And who is 'she'?"

Vinny laughed harshly, humorlessly, and the alcoholic fumes enveloped Tom.

"That's rich! 'Who is she?' he asks. You know damned well who I mean, old Tom, old tomcat, old buddy. The same 'she' you had here last night, the same one who's been breaking her neck to get back up here and into the sack with you, that's who."

He reached for Tom's shirt but Tom stepped back, studying the drunken features with the distaste of a distant spectator watching a street argument among strangers.

"She isn't here, Vinny. She hasn't been here since last night."

"Ha, likely story! She told me herself she came here earlier today but nobody home."

"Maybe so, and she *did* phone. But no show, Vinny." He swept the little hallway with his hand. "Look anywhere you like: under beds, in the john, the terrace."

Vinny lunged by Tom into the studio-bedroom, out onto

the terrace where a crash and a curse marked his collision with one of the large cement pots. More crashes, more mumblings and he reappeared, face mottled with the effort and his anger, and a small welt rapidly rising over one eyebrow.

"Goddamned jungle out there, complete with tigers," he complained bitterly.

"Who is this person?" The Maria asked Tom in a swift Italian staccato of distaste. She had seen many reeling foreign drunks in this apartment but there was no law that said she had to like them.

Tom opened his mouth to answer, but Vinny, catching the tone if not the precise words, walked carefully up to her, shook his finger in her face, and replied with heat in American-accented Italian, "I am an American diplomat, the one with whom you talked on the telephone this morning. Are you the person who called me all those names?"

The Maria looked back at him stonily.

"I beg the Consul's pardon. I was sorely provoked by the Consul's attitude toward my employer, but I regret the words I used."

Vinny, only momentarily mollified, turned to Tom, his anguish shining out of pale, red-rimmed eyes.

"Tom, old friend," he begged, voice thickening, "where is she? I promised ol' man Hamill I'd bring 'er home. Almost had her on the Veneto at noon, but I flubbed it. Made the mistake of getting her sore at me. She took off and I can't find 'er. Been lookin' since, all over. Trastevere, Parioli, Affari Esteri Club, Bricktop's, everywhere. No dice. I can't go back to Hamill and say she can't be found."

"You seem to have picked up refreshments en route."

"I've been lookin' for hours 'n hours," Vinny said forlornly. "You know me, Tom. Never touch the stuff. But I was so damned discouraged a couple of hours ago that I drank two double scotches neat, at the Ambasciatori bar and, boy, you don't know what they can do to an empty stomach."

Tom smiled broadly for the first time since Vinny had arrived.

"Vinny, I know exactly what they can do." Then, more kindly, he took the other's arm.

"Come on out for a minute and relax on the terrace. If you can't find her by this hour, she's either in bed or *not* home and in bed someplace else. Either way, she's probably off the streets." He propelled the uncertain Vinny to the terrace and guided him past the large hedge boxes and cement pots from which sprang the vines that seemed to shut out the sky. In ten paces they had reached the terrace wall and below sparkled a million pins of light. Vinny had never seen the city at night from such a vantage point, with the Tiber glistening blackly, the flood-lighted Trinità de' Monti a horned mask behind its obelisk, and the silver necklaces of light strung along the heights of the Pincian Gardens.

Tom eased him on to an old swinging divan and himself slumped into a canvas sling chair, head lolling on one of its wings, stockinged feet sprawled before him. A liquid gleam flickered from his eyes as they turned to his visitor.

"Well, Console Brenta! Twice in one day! I know it's banal to say, but I was almost expecting you." He lit a cigarette and in its momentary glow, Vinny, focusing his eyes in the half-dark, glimpsed a strange face he had not seen before, fatigue and defeat etched in the sagging lines.

A cool wind, heavy with the impending rain, ruffled the mass of vines over their heads like distant applause. Vinny held his hand to his head and goggled at the city spread out in the glittering darkness as the sky suddenly lit up with the jagged fingers of a lightning bolt beyond the Pincio. Nancy and the whole futile day faded into momentary dimness. He felt as though he sat on a high throne.

Tom, watching him from the sling chair, sensed the mood. "Tremendous view, eh? Best time is sunset when every window on that damned hill—the Trinità, the Villa Medici, Casina Valadier—turns to fire. And it doesn't cost a dime unless you count the rent which is sometimes one of those things."

He turned his head and sang out in a clear cheerful voice, "Maria! Two cognacs, please."

The deep voice of The Maria responded from almost at his elbow, "*Subito!*" And she was standing there with the generously filled glasses.

"I don't know if I should," Vinny said as the solid bulk of The Maria bent over him with the metal tray. "My head already aches from those drinks I had a couple of hours ago." He gnawed his lip in the familiar gesture of uncertainty, but the heavy form before him had a silent insistence and he took the glass filled with amber liquid without further protest. Tom lifted his glass in turn and held it out in a silent toast to the Pincio.

"Chin-chin. It's all down there, Vinny, the far past, the near past, the just past and the present. Bella Roma; the city's there and it doesn't give a damn. Tom Linden can come, go, die; all the same. Maybe he would rate three lines on the

Cronaca di Roma page, small type. Nobody's hurt, nobody particularly cares, and this is fine, just the way he wants it. Anywhere else he's somebody. Here he's just another goddamn *straniero*, not particularly welcome when he's got only a little dough and nothing much else to add to local prosperity. But not unwelcome, either. The Romans have been taking in foreigners, visitors, invaders, floaters, for the last two millennia and they take them the way they take everything. Nobody particularly likes the Romans: they size you up, take whatever isn't nailed down, but then they leave you alone. Oh yes, kiddies, this is Tommy Linden's town."

A flash and a far-off clap of thunder punctuated his bitter words. Vinny drank deeply and the cognac's fiery descent down his throat gave him a reckless, bitter courage.

"So you live here like a blasted jellyfish, floating along and waiting for something to sting and eat?"

Tom grinned, "Pretty close, Signore Console, pretty close," He leaned toward Vinny in the half-darkness.

"You know, I like you better when you speak your mind. When we were kids, everything you said was calculated. You'd never say what you felt; you were always buttering us up, buying favors, trying flattery. But when it really came down to something risky, something nervy, you always found some reason to beat it home without admitting you were scared blue.

"You've done all right, Vinny, you finished college, you went on to the diplomatic corps, you wear nice clothes, you make a damned good appearance. You'll marry well, I'm sure. You've progressed.

"But you know something, Vinny?" he said softly. "I still think you're nothing but a horse's ass."

Vinny did not move but his eyes were like those of an infuriated lion at bay.

"Thanks for the compliment." Vinny's thin nasal voice was wiped clean of any alcoholic slur. "You used to call me names like that when we were kids and I would go home and cry my head off. That used to hurt, Tommy boy. After all, *you* were Number One. But now look at you—and look at me. I'm not much yet, but by God, I will make it, up to the very top. And where the hell are *you?* A lousy expatriate with a dishonorable discharge, living up here in a flea bag with a view."

A distant rumble, like a tentative roll on a tympani, announced the evening shower to come, and then there was only the squeaking of Vinny's swinging divan to mar the silence.

"So you finally got the court-martial story," Tom said, as if commenting on the delivery of late mail. "Well why not? To-day seems to be the day for everybody to throw it back at me. And I've got it coming."

Vinny, half appalled at his own venom, tilted his cognac glass again and braced himself as the fiery liquid coursed into him.

"Hamill told me," he blurted. "The military attaché's office came up with it after they checked the Pentagon records."

From within, there was a sound of windows being shut and two small shadowy figures stalked on silent pads toward the French doors: the Count and Countess were heading inside.

"It really rains in the Romagna," Tom said without moving. "Comes down in solid sheets up there in the hills."

Vinny's voice abruptly changed in timbre and temper.

"Do you want to talk about it?"

"To you *Signor Diplomatico*, here, now? Sorry. Some other time, some other place."

A great jagged flash of lightning lit up the whole night before them, and in the abrupt darkness and thunder crash which followed, the street lights along the Pincio suddenly winked out, wavered, winked again, and came on.

The great slab figure of The Maria loomed into the weak circle of light.

"It will rain, Dottore," she announced as if she were in charge of the storm. "Shall we go inside?"

"Two minutes. Perhaps a couple of *espressi* for the *Console* and myself?" She grunted acquiescence and moved away, plump arms propelling the silent graceful glide of her heavy body.

Vinny licked his lips and finally said what had been on his tongue.

"Did you chicken, Tom? Did you . . . did you really let somebody else take the rap as the court-martial says?"

The first big drops of rain plashed on the terrace floor, followed by others and others. The entire magnificent view startled out of the darkness in a huge flash of lightning, vanished, and they were shelled by a mighty crack of thunder almost directly overhead. The Maria appeared, her deep voice outshouting the thudding rumble.

"Dottore! Paolo has taken the suitcases and is carrying them down the stairs. He says he must deliver them. Dottore, they will catch him and my Paolo will go to prison for years!" Her husky baritone had a feminine wail in it he had never heard before.

As Tom dashed for the door, the two Siamese stared dispassionately up at him, curled in comfortable crouches on Tom's low lumpy bed. He remembered that they were the only calm beings in the suddenly agitated room. He clattered down the darkened six flights of stairs, a perplexed Vinny at his heels, and caught up with the heavily burdened Paolo just as he reached the great double door to the building, now closed and locked to the outside world.

"You stupid, crazy idiot!" Tom hissed at him, keeping his voice low not to arouse the *portiere* or any of his brood now nested for the night in their little apartment behind the glass concierge cage. "I told you how lethal that stuff is! Why do you do these things?"

Paolo, his dark forehead glistening with sweat from the exertion of carrying his load down six flights, grounded the suitcases gently and straightened.

"I told you upstairs, Dottore, that this is something I must do. I was a fool to accept such a task, but now that I have done it, I must finish it. This is my way, and please do not try to stop me."

"This stuff is dangerous, too dangerous, Paolo," Tom pleaded, but knowing it would be to little effect.

"That's a chance I must take."

"And the police waiting on the other side of that door?"

"I must."

He turned an earnest, anguished face to Tom.

"Look, Dottore, I am trying to find an end to this business without betrayal. Without cowardice. I must live with myself, don't you see? That is why I must deliver this stuff as promised, even if it means certain arrest."

His lips twitched with emotion, but the eyes were steady and the mouth completely determined.

"What's his problem?" Vinny asked, vaguely understanding although the nuances of the swift conversation in Italian were lost to him.

Tom turned to Vinny in the dim light of the high-ceilinged entrance way.

"He's a Communist. He stole some dynamite for the Party and promised to deliver it tonight. He's going to do it even if he blows himself up and this neighborhood too, or gets pinched by the police who are almost certainly out there waiting for him to pop his silly head through this entry."

Vinny said, nervously glancing at Paolo, "Let him do it then. What's he mean to you?"

"I think I like him. And that's his aunt upstairs, waiting for me to pull off some miracle."

"You're in enough hot water without getting involved in stolen dynamite," Vinny told him, the dispassionate diplomat again. "I hope to hell you don't have any ideas about helping him. You'd really be asking for it in the neck."

Paolo, tiring of the incomprehensible English colloquy, moved to open the door but Tom touched his arm to restrain him.

"Thanks for the good advice, Vinny," he retorted, "but it's my neck, not yours." He smiled his broadest smile of the day and added, "And besides, as for a glowing future, I'm pretty much in the same boat he's in." His hollow eyes glittered and Vinny was suddenly back in Waterstow looking at That Goddamned Linden Kid. Vinny stepped to the heavy door, pressed his back to it, and spread his arms.

"You're not going out there, Tom. I cannot permit you to help a bunch of Commies collect two suitcases of stolen dynamite for God knows what!"

He saw it wasn't enough.

"Tom, I beg you now, not as Vinny Brentwood, but as an American embassy official: don't get involved. This has absolutely nothing to do with you."

"Vinny, this kid is trying to get something off his back. If he doesn't make it, he goes down the drain one way or another. As for the dynamite; it's virtually useless to the Party. I've examined it. It's condemned stuff, deadly as hell but utterly useless."

"So call the police. Let them use the boy to round up the other Commies."

"We've been through that. The cops are undoubtedly outside now, and Paolo will never inform on anybody."

Tom stepped toward the distraught Vinny spread-eagled against the door. "Please go home. To use your own words, this has absolutely nothing to do with you."

A light clatter of leather heels and soles descending the darkened stairs froze them into momentary silence. A dapper little man, features all pointed, pattered into sight, buttoning his fly. He halted, startled at the sight of the three men at the closed door, and smiled uncertainly. Tom, remembering the activities on the third floor, asked him in a friendly tone, "It went well?"

Hearing the foreign accent, the little face lost its clouded suspicion that this might be the police, and the man made a striking motion with his fist, his face wreathed in an enthusiastic smile.

"*Perbacco!* The big blonde is a tremendous engine!" He glanced at the suitcases and the three of them.

"A little evening 'commerce'?" he asked with a raised eyebrow, and without waiting for an answer swung the heavy door open about a foot and departed swiftly into the darkness and the pelting rain.

'Vinny, we can't stand here all night. Please get out of the way."

Paolo asked Tom in Italian, "What does the *Signor Diplomatico* want?"

"To save us from ourselves."

"Please tell the *Signor Diplomatico* to get out of the way. I have a good distance to go, and I don't know whether I can make it on foot or not in this rain." Vinny moved to block him, but two men from the outside pushed in with their umbrellas, flinging the door wide open.

"Third floor?" the bigger of them asked, eyes glinting with expectation.

Tom nodded reluctantly.

"Third floor," he acknowledged. "The big blonde is a tremendous engine."

"Thanks for the recommendation," responded the second of the two, small and round, as they closed their umbrellas, shook them, and hastened to the dark stairway.

Tom turned, but Paolo had already picked up the suitcases and had pushed past Vinny into the dark, pelting street. Vinny, fists clenched, stood in the doorway.

"For the last time, Vinny, get out of my way. I know what the score is here, I want to help the boy. He can't carry that load alone."

Vinny said in exasperation, "You're dying to work off something, Tom. You're paying off on something."

Tom said tiredly, "Maybe you're right, Vin. If I hadn't stayed put thirteen years ago, things might be different today."

He pushed past Vinny who shouted at him, "You'd probably be dead!"

"Is that bad?" Tom answered over his shoulder, hunching his body as the first heavy drops splattered down on him. He spotted Paolo heading down the street with his heavy burdens toward the Ponte Sant' Angelo, dashed after him and took one of the suitcases from his hand. Paolo smiled gratefully, swung the other one onto his shoulder, and lengthened his gait. They had not taken fifty steps when an American auto squished up beside them, and the front door opened.

"Get in, goddammit!" Vinny yelled. "And quickly! I've got to shake this blasted police car on your tail!"

They hastily eased the suitcases into the back seat and crammed in front with Vinny, as he shot ahead along the deserted Tiber embankment street, windshield wipers working frantically to clear the steaming glass.

Behind Vinny's car as it roared away from the curb, Commissario De Luca in the unmarked Alfa barked to his driver, "*Avanti!* Follow that diplomatic car!"

He grabbed the mike on the dashboard and when the Questura dispatcher answered, he said, "Put the vice-questor on immediately!"

And behind them in the Fiat Topolino, Comrade Piero said to his massive driver, "After them! *Forza!* Keep him in sight but don't let the damned police in that second car see us. There's something very funny here! Comrade Paolo is making off with the stuff in a diplomatic car. If he is double-crossing us . . ."

A small squad car of the Vice Squad, staked out for the past four nights watching the arrivals and departures of the third-floor clients and the fifth-floor gambling patrons, was the only vehicle left on the rain-swept Lungotevere. The senior of its three occupants, a plainclothes *maresciallo* asked the others, "Did I see a foreign car with diplomatic plates pull away from there?"

The other two assured him that his vision was excellent. The *maresciallo*, knowing well the propensity of his Questura superior for titillation and scandals, had a sudden inspiration.

"That diplomatic car, Nino! See it? He takes a left over the Garibaldi Bridge and heads toward Sant' Andrea. Get close enough at least to read his license plate! *Porco mondo*, these diplomats are invading illegal brothels in Prati! Why don't they stay in Parioli?

By the time Vinny had gained speed and swerved onto the Tiber bridge, the number of vehicles behind him had collected to an impromptu but determined little procession.

chapter seventeen

THE CAMPO DE' FIORI, from early morning to shortly after noon, is an arena teeming with the color, babble, and haggle of the open market. At dawn, the temporary booths and pushcarts laden with produce are pushed or pulled with a rumble like tumbrils from all the cobbled side streets into the great open rectangle. The sleepy vendors arrange them in rigidly protocolled lanes, affix little canvas roofs or beach umbrellas against the Roman sun or the Roman drizzle, and head for the nearest coffee bar to drink the first of hourly espressi, syrupy black, with a brioche, or a *cognacchino* if the day is really raw. Then the shoppers arrive, formidably bosomed, piercing-eyed grandmothers or maids for the most part. They are usually in clogs and old warm coats and sweaters against the morning chill, eddying slowly through the narrow lanes of piled fruit, greens, fowl, cheese, fish and flowers. The running fight between the raucous vendors and tart-tongued customers lasts all morning long, seemingly to the point of mayhem when a melon is squeezed too critically or a thumb too noticeably apparent on the primitive tin scales. But actually it is carried on with a verve which infuses the entire tedious business of daily marketing and is secretly loved by both the merchants of the open market and their veteran clients.

By three o'clock in the afternoon, pushcarts and booths have been struck, the remaining produce carried or tucked away in antediluvian vehicles bearing some of the oldest license numbers in Italy, and the great square for a few minutes resembles an enormous and odoriferous garbage heap. Then the rubber-booted sanitary squads, with SPQR on vehicles and jackets, consolidate the garbage in huge heaps, throw it into their trucks, and cleanse the square with great gushes of their fire hoses. And the Campo de' Fiori, save for a few flower booths at one end, sinks into siesta, once again restored as a great medieval stone space flanked by ancient buildings and modest shops. It belongs to history until the following dawn.

But it is not a square like so many others, basking and smiling into the dim past. In this piazza, executions of Medieval and Renaissance Rome took place: hangings, burnings at the stake, decapitations. In the center stands a gaunt gloomy statue: the hooded figure of Giordano Bruno, freethinker and heretic, the last of the martyrs of the Campo, who was burned to death on that precise spot by order of the Holy Mother Church in 1600. During the marketing hours, the statue rears out of the noisy sea of hagglers like a forgotten island. Then the tumult and the marketing die and Giordano Bruno resumes his lonely eminence in the square of his martyrdom, staring reproachfully in the direction of the Vatican. By night, the statue is a deserted sentinel. An occasional late passerby, glancing up at him, will cross himself and hurry on.

This night, in the slashing rainstorm, the familiar statue struck Tom as a peculiarly ominous symbol when their car splashed into the cobbled square. In the dim glistening street lights, the piazza hulked like a dark implacable assassin lying in wait for them.

"What house do you seek, Paolo?" he found himself asking his companion cramped beside him.

Paolo, intently studying the faded street numbers painted on the walls, muttered, "I think it's on the other side of the piazza, Dottore, near the little fountain."

Vinny circled toward it and then glanced at his rear-vision mirror. "Good God," he groaned, "are we heading a parade, or do we have half the police in Rome on our tail?"

The others swiveled to peer through the rear window and as Vinny turned toward the other side of the square, they counted the lights of several cars, each judiciously spaced behind the other, entering the piazza from the same street they had used.

"Dottore, I want you to stop briefly, let me climb out with the suitcases and speed off. We are trapped. I do not want you or the *Signor Diplomatico* to get into any trouble."

Tom said to Vinny, "Don't stop. Go once more around the square."

Vinny shifted the car into low gear and they rolled sedately around the glistening piazza.

"How many cars are behind us?" Tom asked Paolo.

"I . . . I count four now," Paolo answered grimly. "A minute ago I thought there were only three." He licked his lips. "Now I count five."

"Wait until they bring in the tanks," Vinny said, almost proudly. "If we keep circling, we'll have the biggest midnight traffic jam in the history of Rome."

"Listen, Paolo," Tom told the young man whose body he could feel trembling beside him. "I'm going to pull an old trick. The next time around, I'm going to jump out and run across the piazza. They will certainly stop and try to catch me. My friend here will then drive on rapidly, stop long enough to let you out with the suitcases, and then go on. Deliver the suitcases, hide in an alley until it is safe, and make your way home."

He reached in his pocket and gave Paolo a large key to the front door of his apartment building. In the darkness of the vehicle, he could see only Paolo's feverishly glittering eyes.

"Why do you do this for me, Dottore?" Paolo asked.

"I do it for myself. Remember, be quick—and careful with those suitcases."

He turned to Vinny, steering intently and staring ahead through the streams of water blurring the windshield.

"When I say 'slow down,' put it in second and let me jump off. They'll all stop to chase me. This will give you time to accelerate, stop at that corner building on the other side of the piazza, drop Paolo off, and take off for home. After that, you're away free. They can't bother you with your diplomatic plates and documents."

Vinny nodded tautly, eyes straight ahead.

Tom paused and said, very close to Vinny's ear, "Linden and his gang were all wrong about you, Vinny."

"I'll remember that in front of the firing squad, when they ask me if I want a blindfold or not."

His car bumped along the cobbled surface until Tom said, "Now!"

As Vinny slowed, Tom opened the door and after a second to alert his reflexes, leaped out, holding briefly to the door as his feet touched the pavement. He slipped and fell to the wet stone surface, scrambled to his feet and was off, running swiftly across the center of the square, away from the direction of Vinny's car.

Behind him, the police Alfa predictably skidded sideways to a halt, and two of its occupants sprang out of both rear doors and ran after Tom. The vehicles behind the Alfa also filled with sounds of *"Alt! Alt!"* and cries to apprehend the running figure. A small searchlight from the police car raked the square wildly with no apparent aim or focus.

Vinny gunned his car to the designated house, stopped abruptly, and Paolo piled out with the suitcases. He disappeared into a building whose great front door was open. Vinny shifted, stepped on the gas, and sped away. Moments later, out of the huge doorway roared a small Italian car with Paolo and his two suitcases in the back and two other occupants hunched in front. With the total confusion at the other end of the Campo de' Fiori, both cars should have easily escaped by turning into the little connecting street which leads into the magnificent Piazza Farnese. But a small figure stumbled through the dark downpour directly at them: a bewildered Maresciallo Bottoni puffing along in the wrong direction in response to shouted directions by his police superiors chasing Tom. His crumpled wad of football-pool forms and tout sheets slipped out of his jacket pocket, and he stooped in the center of the street to retrieve them. Vinny saw his crouched figure in the rain-slashed glare of his lights only at the last second. In a desperate maneuver to avoid the helpless *maresciallo*, Vinny twisted his wheel violently, and his car, drifting almost sideways, struck the little plainclothesman a glancing blow which sent him flying. The speeding vehicle behind Vinny had no chance at all to avoid a collision and plowed straight into the side of Vinny's car with a resounding crash that turned on every apartment light and opened every bedroom window in the neighborhood.

Vinny, on the side of his vehicle away from the impact, shakily opened his door and stepped out, his heart like lead, to aid his victim who was already sitting up groggily on the wet pavement. Then several things happened all at once: Vice-Questor Fracassi drove up in another Alfa whose headlights lined the scene of the rammed vehicles in a garish and unreal starkness. Comrade Piero's little bug of a Fiat zipped around the police car and drove to a far corner of the square without slowing. The man behind the wheel of the car which had rammed Vinny desperately tried to pry open one of the sprung doors in the hopelessly imbedded vehicle. The Vice Squad police car roared up, and its occupants spilled out on the scene, adding to the uproar.

Tom, hearing the crash, swerved in his running course and pulled up with pounding heart and tired legs at the scene with two equally breathless uniformed pursuers at his heels. And a group of Swedish tourists, terminating a long, wine-soaked meal at the nearby Pancrazio restaurant, straggled up and weaved delightfully through the gathering mob of policemen and spectators, commenting to each other in their native tongue what a marvelous, exciting way this was to end the evening.

"You are under arrest, signore," the vice-questor announced, loping up to Tom and placing an arm on Tom's heaving shoulders. He turned to his assistant, "Commissario, arrest everybody involved in this accident! And examine the identity papers of all persons in vehicles here at this scene! *Perbacco*, for a moment back there I thought we had inadvertently gotten into a funeral procession!" Commissario De Luca shouted, "Sissignore," and rushed off to execute the orders.

"Never mind me!" Tom snapped at Fracassi. "Get those suitcases out of the second car and away from these people. They're apt to go off any . . ."

"My God, you mean the explosives are in that crash?" the vice-questor exclaimed, pointing to the twisted vehicles.

Tom nodded, and his eyes hastily scanned the square.

"There's a small fountain over there," he pleaded. "Let me give you a hand with the suitcases and we'll talk about my arrest later."

After a hard stare, the police official curtly nodded his head, and they both raced through the knots of policemen and hastily dressed neighborhood residents to the car that had smashed into Vinny. Inside, the driver was frantically tugging at his door handle. He was bleeding profusely from a cut on his forehead.

"The doors are jammed!" Tom panted to the vice-questor, "but if we pull together . . ."

With a concerted heave, they pried a rear door loose, and a wide-eyed Paolo looked up at them from his sprawled position on the floor.

"The suitcases—quick!" Tom ordered him.

Paolo, dazed, collected his senses enough to pass the suitcases one at a time through the narrow door. One valise was halfway into the right front seat, and a bulky figure slumped beneath it unconscious.

Tom passed the first to the vice-questor, grabbed the other himself, and both men moved at a trot toward the confused mass of people now surrounding the scene of the accident. One of the swaying Swedes watched them with interest and then, his befuddled mind building up to an intolerably suspicious conclusion, he shouted to his friends, "There's funny business here! Those two men are actually looting the car while its occupants are hurt! Look, they're making off with the suitcases without so much as a glance at the injured!"

"Sven's right!" a friend echoed. "After them, the rotten thieves!"

Thus, as Tom and vice-questor Fracassi half ran through the loose crowd, a phalanx of weaving shouting Swedes took after them.

"Stop them!" the Swedes shouted in their own tongue. Then, realizing that not one understood their cries, one of them remembered one of the few vital nouns in the Italian vocabulary.

"*Ladroni!*" he shouted. "Thieves!"

A nocturnal carabiniere two-man patrol, marching off duty from its guard tour at the nearby French Embassy, approached the scene and responded to the cry of "Thieves" instinctively. They unslung their short carbines and charged in the direction of the cries.

Tom, splashing heavily through the now slackening rain on the heels of the police officer, heard the cries of "Thieves" and the pounding feet behind them without relating them at all to himself and his laden companion, but when the officious shout of "*Alt! Alt!*" reached him with the warning crack of a carbine, he stopped and whirled around to look at the locus of the new action. Beyond him, Vice-Questor Fracassi also turned at the sound of the shot. That was all the time needed for the Swedish Samaritans, unsteady but game, to reach them. Within seconds the two battered valises were the center of a Laocoönian struggle, and first Tom, then the vice-questor, went down under the weight and flailing hands of the righteous Swedes. The brawling mass of men was joined by a couple of enthusiastic neighborhood youths, who commenced to kick indiscriminately at any of the figures on the pavement.

"Stop it, you silly bastards!" Tom yelled in English, supine at the bottom of the pile-up, feeling the puddle in which he was lying soak through his clothes and struggling to shift the pressure of a Scandinavian knee in his groin. Behind him, he could hear the indignant howl of the vice-questor similarly submerged. Finally, semiconscious from the fists, he felt the pressure on him slowly yielding and finally the last of the sodden Swedes atop him was pulled away and he looked up into the narrowed eyes of a squad of uniformed men: Pubblica Sicurezza, carabinieri, and a leather-jacketed nocturnal guard still holding his bicycle beside him. Vice-Questor Fracassi, his hat long knocked off and crushed, hair mussed, two welts already visible under one eye, and his blood pressure at an all-time high, was delivering a short, bitter lecture to a chastened but non-comprehending group of Swedes, who now vaguely saw that the situation had somehow become very complicated indeed.

"Take the suitcases," the vice-questor finally ordered one of his men, "and throw them into the fountain."

All police eyes turned to him with sympathy and concern; it was clear that something had shaken loose in the vice-questor's head as a result of the recent scuffle.

"Do as I say, you imbecile!" the vice-questor roared. "Hurry! There's dynamite in there that may go off at any time!"

The word "dynamite" had an effect that nothing else could have had. Within seconds, the growing crowd around them had dispersed and reassembled fearfully about fifty yards away, leaving Tom and the vice-questor alone with the suitcases. With a shrug, the latter picked up the nearest one, sauntered the remaining fifteen feet with it, and heaved it with a grunt into the shallow fountain. Tom followed, and the two pieces sank like stones to the fountain bottom.

"*Finalmente*," the police official grunted. "One less thing to worry about." He smiled with a grim conspiratorial bow at Tom. "Thank you, for your assistance." He peered at the soaked and battered Tom with some sympathy. "You are Signor Linden, no doubt, one of our dynamite conspirators."

"I am Thomas Linden, a man who two hours ago never heard of this dynamite."

The police official, himself wringing wet, pulled his crumpled raincoat smooth and pushed his glistening hair back into place, then nodded.

"Your action of a moment ago speaks in favor of what you say, but we must sort out this entire *imbroglio* down at the Questura."

Commissario De Luca loped up, horrified at the sight of his manhandled superior.

"Signore Questore!" he panted. "I was busy detaining those involved in the accident and writing down identities. What have they done to you?"

"Nothing that can't be dried, cleaned and pressed," his superior answered him, turning to watch two more police cars and a truckload of Pubblica Sicurezza men roar into the square, preceded by the two-tone siren of a city ambulance. "Commissario, load everyone involved in this affair into police cars and vans and take them all to the Questura before this square turns into a full civic demonstration. Post one of your men until the Traffic Accident unit comes to take the photographs and particulars."

"Yessir," De Luca assured him, poised to run.

"What about Maresciallo Bottoni?" the vice-questor asked anxiously. "Didn't the first of those cars hit him?"

"Just a glancing blow, Dottore," the commissario assured him. "He deserves a commendation for stopping the getaway of the cars, even if by accident. He is a little dazed but as soon as he feels all right, I'll send him home in one of our police cars."

The square rapidly filled with occupants of the neighboring houses, most of them in pajamas and house robes, standing under umbrellas in the now fading drizzle and gesticulating wildly at the wrecked cars, at the small knot of persons under guard, and at the little fountain where the two dark suitcases lay under water. Rumors started that this was the roundup of: a huge smuggling ring, a dope ring, a bunch of audacious bank robbers, international spies, a gang of *mafiosi* from Palermo. The Swedes, prodded into a police car, looked helplessly at each other.

"What did we do wrong? Why do they arrest those who catch thieves?" Sven asked the others perplexedly. They shrugged gloomily. "Who can tell who is a thief and who is not, with these rascals?" his smallest companion spoke up. But the third one only wiped away a tear of foreboding.

"Our wives," he muttered. "They'll never believe us, never. They'll think we ran off to spend the night with some signorinas."

Tom dully watched the arrests and departures as one watches a distant twinkling night shore from a passing ship. His battered and weary body cried out for sleep and he perched on the fender of the vice-questor's car under the eye of one of the vigilant policemen. The commissario, like a fussy sheep dog, loped from one point to the other, now ordering the uniformed police to keep back the considerable crowd, now coordinating the howling arrival of the Traffic unit and two engine units of the Fire Department, now supervising the body search of the shaken group from the car crash, including poor Vinny Brentwood who stood together with Paolo and with two other persons in a forlorn quartet lined up against a nearby *salsamenteria* store front. Tom also saw, out of the corner of his eye, a small Fiat make an abrupt U-turn and speed away from the crowd and the accident, and although he did not know it was Comrade Piero and his now frantic little squad, he knew that it contained persons who were most anxious for one reason or another to avoid the police control which was now spreading out to include all persons and vehicles in the square.

There was sudden animation among the police group handling the four men involved in the accident, and the vice-questor, restored now to a somewhat more normal appearance, his battered hawk face calm and confident, walked over to him with what was almost a strut.

"We pulled this from the belt of one of those four," he said to Tom in a tone of repressed excitement, nodding toward the sagging figures lined up against the store. "As an American who has served in your armed forces, do you recognize this model?"

Tom took the heavy blue automatic, turned it over carefully in his hands, and his lips tightened to a bleak line.

"It's a government-issue Colt forty-five. It holds nine rounds."

He looked up at the police official, who was startled at the intensity of the glance.

"I have already seen the holster to this very weapon today. You see these initials etched into the metal next to the safety catch— 'H.D.'? I put those initials there myself, for my wartime commander, whose pistol this was." He looked up at the police official, and his eyes narrowed with cold, demonic fury. "Where did . . ."

The vice-questor quickly reached for his cigarette box, extracted it, gave Tom an oval Egyptian cigarette and lit it for him.

"You are destroying my theory of an American Communist conspiracy," he said smiling faintly. "The man on whom this weapon was found happens to cap the crown to my months of investigation. He was the passenger in the car which rammed your diplomat friend. You see him slumped up against the wall there, the old heavy one with the twisted nose. You are looking at Spartaco Tamburri, of the Central Committee of the Communist Party, and the head of all of their Veterans of the Resistance."

"He's a murdering butcher," Tom blurted. "The fact that he has this in his possession proves it. This is the pistol of an American army major who died in an ambush. I was there; I . . ." Tom's voice rose.

"Calm yourself." The vice-questor put a hand on his arm and gently removed the pistol from his grasp. "You will have an opportunity to confront him in the Questura. Our Communist friend has many charges already against him, including possession of stolen explosives and other contraventions. Now this of the American pistol." He slipped the weapon into his raincoat pocket and exultantly rubbed his hands. "Now I have him!" he chortled. "And after him, the others!"

Two figures loomed out of the night, both with handcuffs on wrists and both supported by a policeman on either side. The vice-questor watched their approach with satisfaction, and as they were marched up to the police car against which Tom leaned, the vice-questor said with exaggerated politeness, "Signor Linden, may I introduce Comrade Spartaco Tamburri? Ah, yes, and his private secretary, Comrade Pasquale Freccia."

Tom looked straight into the small malevolent eyes of Spartaco.

"I already know him. This is the man who accepted our food, medicine, and supplies in Belinoro and reciprocated by killing his hosts and friends."

He dug into his pocket in a spasm of recollection and then held out his opened hand. In his palm lay a small metal leaf.

"Do you want it back? It's the one you stole off the collar of my superior, Major Dixon, whom you assassinated on the Belinoro road."

Spartaco stared down at the small metal object as if it were some loathsome bug, and then the small cruel eyes crept back to Tom, with slow recognition dawning in them.

"Ah, it is the American lieutenant, the one who stayed at home that night. You were the one that that traitor of a Peppino tried to warn." The mouth opened and shut like a turtle's beak. "Be glad you weren't there lying in the road with a hole in your head as well. When you ally yourselves with reactionary enemies of the true Resistance, you run great risks."

Tom swung hard, hitting Spartaco flush in the face and knocking him into the arms of his custodians. The vice-questor and a policeman immediately stepped in and vigorously but not roughly pushed Tom against the car and away from Spartaco.

"The son of a bitch!" Tom panted. *"Figlio di putana!*

Staging the whole thing so that it looked like the Germans had done it! You miserable . . ."

The vice-questor nodded a command and Tom was gently propelled away from Spartaco to another waiting car. The vice-questor pushed him in and got in beside him.

"*Avanti!*" he said to the uniformed driver, "to the Central Questura."

Vinny Brentwood was last to depart from the scene and, as befitted his diplomatic status, he was courteously ushered into a police car with the driver opening the door for him and standing at attention.

He stared through the window at the Campo de' Fiori, his wrecked car, and at the somber figure of Giordano Bruno brooding over it all, and for a moment saw the small white face of Nancy Hamill peering at him from between two pajama-clad spectators. She looked at him as a mourner peers into an open grave. Then the police motorcycle escort in front of them started up and he looked at her without so much as a wave until she disappeared from view.

Behind them, the first of the soaked suitcases was fished from the little fountain and, streaming little rivulets of water, deposited with great care at the feet of the commissario.

chapter eighteen

COMRADE PIERO PRESSED the buzzer beside the glossy veneered apartment door with a familiar sureness: two longs, two shorts, and a long. That would bring Comrade Giorgio to the door unless he were dead or unconscious. He waited impatiently, if apprehensively, with more than a suspicion as to why Giorgio was so slow, and when the double lock inside clattered and the door opened, he saw that he was right: Comrade Giorgio had shrugged on a bathrobe over his pajamas, and over his bulky shoulder, Comrade Piero saw an exaggeratedly well-developed young woman clad only in a light and filmy nightgown flitting from the bedroom of Comrade Giorgio into the bathroom. His quick eye immediately recognized her as one of the more pneumatic of the Party Mattresses, a female comrade whose ostensible job was that of head of the Party's women cultural activities, but who actually bounced up the Party ladder to a dizzying level where she was now probationary mistress of Comrade Giorgio. Comrade Giorgio of course had a wife, now in her native Viterbo, a gray little bird of a woman who had sacrificed her adult life and her highly marginal charm to Giorgio and to the Party, mostly the latter, but Comrade Giorgio, as had many other party leaders of his age, had long since tired of sleeping with dialectical materialism and required fresh talent every six months or so. Comrade Piero had checked this one out himself one time and he remembered approvingly that she was good, a bit too much flesh, but virtually untiring and no cheap conversation necessary.

Comrade Giorgio's face clearly told him: this interruption had better be worth it.

"I'm sorry," Comrade Piero said quickly, "I know it's one o'clock in the morning, but I had to tell you some bad news and ask your advice: a very serious incident had just occurred. Comrade Spartaco and his secretary have been arrested by the police in the Campo de' Fiori in the act of making off with the stolen explosives which were apparently delivered to them by Comrade Seddu right in the square. Seddu was arrested together with them, as were"—Piero could not resist rolling his eyes toward the ceiling in amazement— "two Americans, including a diplomat. They are all down at the Questura at this minute undergoing interrogation."

Giorgio carefully studied his subordinate as a deaf and dumb man seeks to read the lips of his interlocutor. His voice, when he spoke, was icily calm. He was ostensibly in complete control of himself; Piero was one of the very few who knew by the way Giorgio bit off his r's that he had reached a white heat of anger.

"Why, were you not able to gain possession of the explosives before such mischief was done?" He paused, and reached into a pajama pocket for a square box of Russian cigarettes. Piero lit it for him and was chagrined to discover that his hands, usually steady as sticks of wood, were trembling. Piero looked up, his lighter still in his hand, to see Giorgio staring at the vibrating fingers.

"I thought," Giorgio pursued, voice gentle as an old

woman's, "that you were my resourceful right hand, that I could count on you in such an emergency. Instead, you have permitted this incredible police intervention to occur." His voice sank to a rumbling leonine purr.

"We tried," Piero responded lamely, "really we did. We had shadowed Seddu for hours, from the moment that he arrived in Rome with the explosives. It's just that the damned police were blanketing the area the moment that Furbo peached to them that Seddu had the stuff. We were unable to . . . "

Giorgio held up a commanding hand.

"*Basta*, I'll hear your sad story some other time." He jabbed at Piero with the lighted Papiros. "The first thing we must do is to get Spartaco and Pasquale out of the clutches of the police," he muttered. He folded his heavy arms before him and finally smiled with that cold irresistible sureness that had drawn Piero to him in the first place. A real *pescecane*, Piero told himself with a quiver of admiration and fear, a real shark with all of his teeth. The gray eyes hooded over as they stared at the terrazzo floor in an agony of concentration and rapidly reviewed alternatives. He finally looked up again.

"Give me the telephone number of the Minister; you know, his private one."

Piero whipped out a thick black address book, riffled a page, and copied a number out of it rapidly on a blank sheet of paper which he handed to Giorgio, who glanced at it and stuffed it in his pocket.

"You want to know how it will be done, eh?" he taunted Piero. "Well, my dear comrade, it will not be easy. But I will give you a hint: even in a terrible war, two antagonists occasionally stop long enough to exchange prisoners. Do I make myself clear?"

Piero, for whom *quid pro quo* was an everyday stock of his trade, nodded eagerly, but his worried eyes resembled those of a hunting dog who has unfortunately lost the scent of the fox completely.

"I don't quite understand, Comrade Giorgio," he faltered. "We don't have any prisoners to swap."

Giorgio gave him a ponderous push on his shoulder, and flung a scornful hand in the air.

"Of course we don't, idiot. But we have something just as good." He chuckled at the blank expression of Piero and narrowed his gray eyes to a Neopolitan shrewdness.

"Don't try to understand, Piero," he hold him archly,

smoke from the Russian cigarette billowing out of his nose and mouth. "Just be ready to act when Spartaco is released. As far as that boob Pasquale is concerned, send him back to his home town up in the Brescian foothills and tell him to keep his mouth shut."

He stared down at his big square feet rammed into house slippers, as if silently rehearsing lines for a play and when his great head came up, an unholy light of triumph radiated from the heavy features.

"Out of every evil some good, dear Piero," he boomed, clapping his hand on the slender shoulder. "Here, for example, is our solution to the problem of Comrade Spartaco! The police are moving in to investigate in depth the matter of the stolen dynamite. If we can liberate Spartaco now from their custody, would it not be wiser for him to depart for a vacation abroad once he is released? For reasons of his health which, of course, has been undermined by his years of brutal sacrifices for the Party."

Piero's face lighted up in reflection of his master's.

"A trip to one of the workers' paradises," he took up the idea eagerly. "To which one?"

Comrade Giorgio thought a moment, cigarette vertical between thumb and forefinger.

"Let me see, the best one at the moment would be Czechoslovakia. We have a whole colony of Italian comrades there, including the one involved with the Dongo treasure taken from the Fascists. There is also an excellent Party school being run there for comrades and militants from Africa and Asian countries. Comrade Spartaco's vaunted underground and guerrilla experience should make him a valuable addition to the faculty there."

"Will he go?"

"He will go." Giorgio's voice was deep with finality. "I will clear the matter at the meeting of the Secretariat tomorrow. I can assure you that there will not be one voice raised against his departure. The day of the Stalinist die-hards has passed."

Comrade Giorgio was completely aroused now, and he stumped around the mottled terrazzo hallway, swinging his heavy arms as if in a victory parade.

"What do you think the rank and file will say when our good comrade departs on a vacation to recover from his arduous labors, Piero?" he asked, stopping his march in front of the little man, who was busily writing in a small black notebook. Piero looked up with surprise that such a question should be asked.

"Little or nothing. Oh, the ex-partisan comrades in the Emilia-Romagna will complain and send a few petitions to their local headquarters wishing him well and asking him to come home as soon as possible, but those in the Central Committee who looked on him to speak out bluntly against the Party's leadership and attack the new directions indicated by Comrade Khrushchev, these will see the writing on the wall."

He shut the notebook and tucked it carefully away in an inner pocket.

"Bravo," Giorgio said warmly.

"What about Comrade Seddu? No great loss, of course, but rather an innocent sheep in this business."

Giorgio made a whirling, you-handle-it gesture with his left hand.

"Wait until the whole affair blows over and explain to him the necessity of our action to preserve the good name and the position of the Party under this clerico-fascist police and government. He'll understand if it's explained correctly. And listen, if he is kept in jail for any length of time, I want him to receive anonymous gifts of food, along with Party periodicals, two or three times a week."

"*Benissimo*," Piero agreed. Then, with his hand on the door, he shot a quizzical glance at his mentor.

"Excuse, Comrade Secretary," he asked, "but assuming Spartaco *is* released, what is to prevent the police from proceeding with the investigation of the theft of dynamite anyway and exposing him as the responsible official involved with Seddu and Furbo?" He smiled knowingly. "We all know why they have been so hesitant to concern themselves with events of the wartime Resistance and the post-liberation, period, but something as recent as yesterday . . . ?"

Giorgio tapped his own massive chest with a confident thumb.

"Leave it to me," he told Piero. He dug into his pajama pocket and extracted the phone number Piero had jotted down for him.

"You see this? I think that our Spartaco will be sprung from the Questura after a phone call or two in the right place." Then, with a toss of his head in the direction of his bedroom, he smiled smugly at his lieutenant.

"And now, I shall return to finish some work I had begun and which you interrupted. Until tomorrow."

"*Buon lavoro,* Comrade," Piero said. He closed the door gently behind him. The double locks rattled shut on the other side.

The *ispettore generale,* a large fat man given to nervous gestures of enthusiasms, impatience, and irascibility, bustled into the questor's office with loosened tie and needing a shave. It was three A.M. He took a proffered seat next to the questor and bombarded the small knot of assembled police standing before him with intermittent "*Bravo . . . bravissimo . . . ottimo*" like the backfiring of a motorcycle. He wanted to hear the whole story from the very beginning and his small eyes with the huge liver patches under them reflected his professional enthusiasm at the recruitment of Franco Furbo, the Party's request for stolen dynamite and the rapidly unfolding events of this night. He cautiously asked (it bothered him more than he cared to admit) why a solid young neo-Fascist like Furbo would join the Communists at all, and he was relieved to hear that at least Franco had done so for police pay and not because he had lost any ideological convictions. Commissario De Luca pointed out dryly that Franco's sole motivation was hedonism which the police were able to satisfy with sums of money. It was good, he explained, that matters had come to a climax because Franco had become increasingly demanding. Now, of course, he would get nothing more unless he came up with new acquaintances of police interest, a rather unlikely event since he appeared to be thoroughly "burned."

The inspector general "bravo-bravo"-ed this remark as he did all the others. Then he shooed the others from the room as one drives a small flock of geese, with repetitive cries of, "*Per favore, fuori, fuori!*" leaving him alone with the questor and the vice-questor.

"Now, gentlemen," he addressed them briskly, bouncing to his feet with the verve of a much younger man and striding restlessly around the large, well-furnished office. "You have stumbled"—he looked brightly and meaningfully at each of them in turn—"onto an incident, a conspiracy, which has ramifications of which you are perhaps not aware. I do not intend to go into lengthy addresses at this indecent hour, especially when I look at your sleepy eyes and fatigued faces. I say again: Bravissimo! But"— and he held up an admonishing finger before them—"this must be handled with precision, nuance, delicacy." He made a circle of his thumb and forefinger, held up the circle horizontally on a level with his eyes, and dropped it in a straight vertical line to emphasize the precision with which he wanted the matter handled. "Thanks to your phone call, Calogero, I was able to brief very generally the Minister with whom I happened to be dining," he said, turning to the questor. "We discussed this affair at length and with a specific eye to the political ramifications . . . "

The questor, a spare giant of a man with rimless glasses, a light sweater under his old jacket, and the cold deliberateness of a prosecuting attorney, held up one tired hand protestingly.

"Now, just a minute, Giancarlo. As head of the police of Rome, I am as aware as you of 'political ramifications' in any police investigation, but I sincerely hope that you do not intend to make of this serious incident a *pasticcio* complete with parliamentary investigations, denunciations, counterdenunciations by the Reds and ink-throwing across the *aula* of the Parliament, fisticuffs, bad names . . . "

The inspector general of the police emitted a huge, booming laugh, and wagged his finger at his younger, taller colleague. "You want your pound of flesh, eh? You want to keep it a strictly criminal matter and to see everybody connected with it quietly tucked *in galera?*"

"That, yes, but more; I want a normal police prosecution and court action which will point out to every Italian that this Communist Party of ours, this so-called housebroken group of parliamentary socialists, is simply the sheep's clothing covering the same old fanged wolf which in 1946 and again in 1948 almost took this country over. The special wolf in this case is Spartaco Tamburri, Il Duro of the Party's bloodstained past, who even now does not disdain to mastermind the theft of explosives from an Italian army installation. We must remind the Italians, my dear colleague, of such activities and such people as Il Duro from time to time before they are lulled to sleep with Communist avowals that they have reformed, that Communists now are lawabiding social democrats, that we have nothing to fear— until we are awakened in our beds one morning with their knives at our throats."

Being from Calabria, the questor spoke without the use of his hands and in a quiet deadly tone. He glanced through his glasses at the long, smoothly dark features of the young vice-questor who nodded once at the end.

"Bravo, bravo! Well said, Calogero," the inspector general commended him. "But let me point out to you a couple of important factors you are brushing over here. First, there are two Americans involved, now in our custody, one of them a second secretary of embassy, no less. True, they become involved only peripherally," he added hastily, seeing the questor was ready to interrupt, "nevertheless, they are involved, and this immeasurably complicates our situation here." He bunched the fingers on one hand at them. "My God, the Ministry has already gotten a call from the American ambassador in this case."

"Dear Giancarlo!" the questor exploded. "I have already explained to you in detail that the role of the Americans in this matter, although still obscure, appears to be incidental. They were simply a couple of sentimental fools who wanted to help young Seddu, who is as much an imbecile as they. But, for God's sake, we have under interrogation at this moment Spartaco Tamburri himself, as you are well aware, a man whose hands are dipped in the blood of numbers of people, many of them innocent of anything except revulsion against the local partisan banditry after the end of the war? We caught him with two suitcases of stolen dynamite in his car and with an illegal American pistol which seems to point the finger straight at a wartime massacre . . . "

"*Silenzio!*" the inspector general roared, holding up his hand like a traffic policeman. "I've heard it all already! Do you think I am deaf, or a fool?"

He glared at them, pouched old eyes aquiver with barely restrained rage and both younger men, knowing him well, stood at what was almost attention. They were quite aware that, after almost fifty years of police career which extended in an unbroken line from the century's beginnings through the entire Fascist era to the present, the inspector general indulged himself in calculated rages when the exigencies of the moment required.

"*Va bene*, Calogero," he asked the questor after a moment of booming silence. "what would you like to do?"

The questor turned, struggled for a moment to speak, and then with a small wave of his hand, passed the initiative to the vice-questor.

"'*M beh*, you Fracassi," the old police official grunted, turning to the dark intense vice-questor, "your boss seems to have run out of words. *You* answer for him: what do you think we should do, given the complicated circumstances?"

Fracassi immediately answered, "Release the American diplomat, of course, with a reprimand. Hold all the others in Regina Coeli, including the other American, until full interrogations are completed. Then bring Tamburri and his secretary to trial under Penal Code Article 435, for conspiring to steal and to transport dynamite belonging to the Republic of Italy. Tamburri has the additional charge of being in possession of an illegal pistol. We cannot, under the previous amnesties, try him for any political crimes committed prior to 1945 but we can blacken him sufficiently in the newspapers by referring to his probable complicity in such crimes. The American we can handle by escorting him to the frontier. Furbo will get off with a suspended sentence for his co-operation. Seddu will probably get ninety days at most in jail. But I hope we can send Tamburri and his Party companion to the workhouse for at least two years."

"That's it?" grated the inspector general, "you don't want any more?"

"That will do it for now," Fracassi responded deferentially but firmly. "Then we go after the others in the Party leadership. We will show them that they must fear the law and obey it as all others do."

"How old are you, Fracassi?" The old pouched face thrust up almost close enough to touch his.

"Thirty-nine, sir."

"Thirty-nine, eh? And already vice-questor in Rome, no less! Do you know where I was at thirty-nine? In Matera, a god-forsaken hole in the heart of the Basilicata as a junior commissario, watching over a bunch of damned Reds who were put into *confino* down there. I, too, know something about making Reds obey the law, so don't stand there and talk to me as if I was learning about this problem for the first time . . . "

"Giancarlo," the questor broke in, voice sharp and angry and resisting the urge to mention the swift rise of the inspector general under Fascism and his role in the OVRA, "Fracassi is one of my best officers, one of the finest products of . . . "

"I know his breed. University laureate in law, police officers' academy, additional training abroad in America or England. Probably never missed a meal nor struck a prisoner in his life; a northerner from Milan or Turin by his accent . . ."

"Fracassi was an officer of the Arditi in the African desert," the questor continued as if he had not heard the interruption. "He was wounded twice, has the Silver Medal for Valor, was a prisoner of war of the English for three years in Kenya."

"And now he eats Communists for a living."

"Sir," said the vice-questor, " I have chosen the career

of law enforcement for a living. I pursue this career with passion and dedication. It is not an easy profession in this country, to make Italians obey the law; I know this full well. And it is very difficult for them to understand the necessity for obedience when a large group flouts the law. The Communists do so constantly. They dare us to do anything about their contraventions. That is why Tamburri must be punished. Certainly this much finds us in agreement?" His precise voice was now modulated to a plea.

The inspector general, anger completely dissipated, produced a gold-plated cigarette holder from a rumpled inner pocket, attached a cigarette to it, and lighted up. He beckoned the questor and vice-questor closer to him so that the three men huddled in a tight circle close enough to touch each other.

"Now you listen to me," he said, turning his eyes on each of them in turn, his voice sunk to a confidential growl. "Why do you think I am down here at this ungodly hour? Simply to make compliments or to engage in polemic concerning the function of the police in Italy? I come with orders, precise orders from the Minister."

He stared straight at the vice-questor.

"You will immediately release Tamburri and his secretary with instructions to remain at home at the disposition of the authorities. Since this matter has gone entirely too far to drop the case, we shall have to hold and charge young Seddu on the lesser charge of receiving stolen goods from other persons not yet identified. Furbo is to be released quietly and paid off. Nothing more."

The questor stared at him, jaw muscles working. The inspector general held up both hands protestingly.

"Orders, Calogero, orders from above! Please understand, I hated to bring them to you. But if you don't believe me, reach for that phone and dial the Minister's residence." Neither of the two police officials moved or spoke but their silence was a thundering reproach. The old man looked again at each of them in turn and he snorted with a mixture of disdain and embarrassment.

"Tomorrow afternoon," he finally said. "By that time I can assure you that Comrade Spartaco Tamburri will have departed Italy by way of Switzerland, and that it will be a long time before we ever see his likes again. He will be registered in the Ministry of Interior Frontier Control List and if he ever tries to re-enter, he will be arrested.

"Let me tell you two something I am sure you have heard

before," he continued in a more kindly tone, pacing heavily back and forth before them, his face now that of an old, weary man's. The questor recalled with a start that the inspector was over seventy. "It is true that we are the professional, objective guardians of law and order, but our governmental superiors have always been politicians, from Cavour and Giolitti to Mussolini and to the present day. Since the war, we have lived in an uneasy situation, discredited by our previous actions against anti-Fascists. All of us graybeards served some period of time under Fascism, many of us were ruthlessly purged after Fascism had been trampled in the dirt. You know of course that I was arrested and interned by the Allies in 1945?"

They nodded their heads silently.

"Well, my friends, I remember it only too well. Especially the treatment by the English who were perfectly dreadful people. Endless indignities were done to me, a professional police officer for almost forty years even then, because I had been an OVRA official for seventeen of those years. I can tell you this: for five years after I was released and rehabilitated in the Ministry of Interior, when anti-Communist activity was suggested or ordered, I did this."

He nestled his head against a simulated pillow of two clasped hands.

"I snored. It was tacit understanding: the Communists simply never attacked me in any way for my work during Fascism, and I never bothered them. When the government wanted to go into the piazzas to break up Communist demonstrators, Scelba created his fine *Nucleo Celere* with their red jeeps, truncheons, spraying of indelible red ink on the demonstrators, and the famous Scelba carrousel you have seen in which the jeeps start in roaring circles from the center of the piazza working outward until they have cleared the square of people."

"I fail to see . . ." the vice-questor began edgily.

"You will," the inspector general promised him grimly. "The Minister was telephoned no more than an hour ago as he and I sat and talked about your explosives case. The telephone call came from a high member of the Party. He was brief and to the point: he offered to exchange silence for silence. If we did nothing about Spartaco Tamburri, the Party would relinquish to us information on a scandal which would really rock the government, a scandal fully as slimy and putrid as the Montesi case." The old policeman tightened his lips. "Gentlemen, one more such Montesi scandal and the Reds could win the next election—legally."

"Who is affected by this Communist blackmail?" the questor asked, thin voice barely restraining his emotions.

"Two under-ministers and their families. We were promised full details by a courier"—he looked at his watch—"six hours from now. If the brief details he gave us are true, and enough facts were recited to indicate its validity, the present government will certainly fall."

"How are we to know that the same blackmail won't be used again and again?" the vice-questor put in angrily.

"The surprise factor would certainly be gone," the inspector general shrugged, pouched eyes shrewd. "Defenses will be ready, explanations and alibis concocted, all sorts of countering moves will be placed into effect. As it is, the Ministers will probably be quietly dropped at the next *rimpasto* of the Cabinet. And, as I told you, within twenty-four hours the head of the Stalinist faction of the Party will be gone forever. Good riddance for us and quite probably good riddance for his own dear comrades."

He clapped his hands as if a contract had been signed, sealed, and delivered.

"My friends, you have done nobly. The press will run the explosives theft story in the *Cronaca di Roma,* naming only Seddu, the Communists will undoubtedly shriek 'Fascist provocation,' and the whole affair will die down sooner than you think. And, now, how about a *cognacchino* and off to our homes and bed, eh?"

The questor looked across his desk at his young, crest-fallen subordinate. "I am truly sorry, Fracassi; I know it means your weeks of work booted away."

The vice-questor managed a very wan smile.

"'M beh, pazienza. We'll keep an eye on Tamburri until he leaves. But he shall not escape me. I have promised myself that. Some day I shall again throw him into Regina Coeli, alone or with some of his noble comrades. God willing, I want to be there personally."

The questor pulled an amber bottle out of a highly veneered cupboard and lined up three small cognac glasses which he filled.

"Chin-chin." The inspector general held up his glass to them. "To the health and continued success of the questor and vice-questor of Rome."

"Thank you. To your healths," said the questor politely.

179

"To justice," the vice-questor grated, "blind everywhere, but in Italy without even hands to hold the scales."

The questor shot his subordinate a pained and reproving glance and the inspector general looked at him without replying, making a mental note to see that this insolent *ragazzo* got a taste of Questura life in the provinces in the eventual future; perhaps Matera, or Lecce, or one of those other Meridionale posts so chilling to the hearts of those serving in Rome.

chapter nineteen

WHEN THE BLACK-JAWED Pubblica Sicurezza guard standing by the door sprang to attention, Tom Linden knew that the seemingly endless night was, in one way or another, coming to an end. Between the relays of interrogations, he had stared at the one illustration in the little waiting room that was barely more than a detention cell: a reproduction of an old lithograph of Castel Sant' Angelo as it appeared to a seventeenth-century artist. Tom had virtually memorized every feature of the massive crenellated barrel, with its sword-flourishing angel on top, and the prancing horses and strolling passersby which were always added to breathe a little life into such works. An involuntary smile creased his weary face; only in Rome could one admire Renaissance lithographs in a police headquarters while under arrest. As the pre-dawn grayness, diluting the night outside, began to filter thinly into the one barred window, clomping of distant police feet became less frequent on the stone pavement. Only occasionally could he now hear the snarl of motorcycles or police vans arriving or departing. It was the brief hour of stillness for the sleeping city.

His eyes were heavy with weariness although he was far from sleepy. He had been separated immediately from Vinny from the moment of their arrest and he had seen no one but his police interrogators since. The questioning had gone on and on and eventually started repeating itself like a stuck record. Then came the typing of the protocol, with a pompous *maresciallo* dictating his replies in bureaucratese to a slumped uniformed police steno who clacked maddeningly away on a typewriter using only one finger of each hand. Then nothing for an hour or better now, in which he sat under guard in this room looking at the Castel Sant' Angelo on the wall. The plot of *Tosca* came to mind and it amused him to imagine being led out to face the firing squad on the top rampart of that great fort and, prior to being shot, singing the final aria on tippity-toes the way the tenors always did.

What was not amusing, and here his thin smile of fantasy died, was the damage done to Vinny Brentwood. He, Tom Linden, was lost and had been for a decade, but he felt sick in his stomach for what might happen to Vinny's career. Vinny, too, had tried to work off something this night, and that this singular act of altruism might torpedo him forever was a thought that weighed on Tom like a stone.

The guard flung open the door and jerked his right hand to his visor in a splay-handed salute. Vice-Questor Fracassi strode in, his battered face and gait reflecting a fatigue equal to or greater than Tom's.

"Welcome back, Dottore," Tom said, standing. "I had thought you had forgotten about me."

The police official waved his thumb at the door wordlessly and the uniformed policeman departed, leaving them alone in the dingy whitewashed room. The vice-questor beckoned to Tom to take a chair on one side of a small rectangular table; he took the other, and for a moment the two looked at each other, each seeing the exhaustion in the other.

"We are releasing you as of now," the police official told him in a precise Italian containing a hint of his Florentine origins. "You may return to your home to remain at disposition of the questor."

"*Grazie*," Tom said. "I realize you may think I am lying but as I have repeatedly told you, I didn't know anyth—"

"I know, I know. You were brought by chance into it. You wanted to help your maid and her nephew." He smiled wanly.

"I must confess that when the trail of the explosives led to your apartment and when Dottore Brentwood showed up to take the explosives in his car, for just a few minutes we had the horrible thought that we were in the middle of the biggest conspiracy since the end of the war. You know: Communists and Americans together, like your Rosenberg case."

His mellow expression passed and he fixed a cold police stare on Tom.

"There is one other matter, signore. This involves your presence in Italy. You have been here in Rome uninterruptedly since 1945, a period of more than eleven years. Admitted, you love our country, its climate, et cetera, et cetera" —and he curved his hands briefly to form the outline of a woman's body—"but don't you ever go home? You have no real career here. Your Questura record indicates that, while you have certainly no criminal precedents and no contacts with our growing colony of foreign homosexuals, you have drifted from one temporary employment to another. You know, you have never obtained a work permit, Signor Linden, and your residence permit, last extended for one year, expired more than two months ago."

"I know," Tom said despondently. "Your men were around checking on me." His gaunt face lifted to meet the vice-questor's. "I speak to you as one man to another when I tell you that I have strong personal reasons for not returning to my homeland. There, I am in disgrace. Here I am just another foreigner, and the disgrace is known to no one."

"I understand," the police officer said slowly. "I know about the results of your court-martial."

Tom looked up sharply, and pulled a wry smile of dismay.

"Well, I guess it's getting all around the Western world."

The vice-questor shook his head emphatically.

"No. Only me. Your friend, the diplomat Brentwood, told me that. It makes your reply completely comprehensible to me." He straightened and tugged at his tie in a gesture of nobility. "A police official also understands matters of personal honor and pride, signore."

"Again, thanks," Tom said. He rose stiffly to his feet with the vice-questor.

"And what about Mr. Brentwood?" Tom asked. "In all truth, he is the really innocent one involved here . . ."

The vice-questor waved a hand.

"He was released ten minutes ago."

Tom leaned close to the somehow defeated face of the police official and a welling anger had replaced the normal timbre in his voice.

"And what about that Communist bastard, Tamburri? Do you know what he did in a place called Belinoro thirteen years ago?"

"Ah, the slaughter made to appear as a German ambush?" The vice-questor replied as if commenting on a traffic violation. "Yes, we have suspected this for many years, and this affair of the American pistol in Tamburri's possession tonight is excellent confirmatory evidence." His eyes were impenetrable, and Tom had the odd sensation that the other, despite his casual words, was in a state of contained fury more violent than his own.

"So what are you going to do with him?"

"We are releasing him, as we are releasing you," the vice-questor told him slowly and deliberately. "He will remain at his home at the disposition of the authorities." He could not repress a faint smile at the open-faced astonishment of the American.

"We are filled with mercy in Italy. You Anglo-Saxons complain about the lack of habeas corpus in Italy, the detention of prisoners in jail for months on open charges. Well, look: we are letting you go, a prime accomplice in housing and transporting stolen dynamite. And we release a top Italian Communist, a professional enemy of our government, equally involved and with a suspicion of wartime offenses. Now which system is the more humane: yours or ours?"

Tom grasped the policeman's lapels.

"You can't let him go" he shouted. "Can't you understand? Tamburri is the real reason why I am still here. He did more than kill my commander and a group of partisans: he destroyed me!"

The vice-questor gently detached Tom's hands from his jacket, but his eyes were like hot tongs as he stepped back.

"I know," he said between compressed teeth, "I *know*. Now *you* try to understand! I know and I must let him go. It is the orders of others, *capito?*"

Staring into his furious eyes, Tom knew he spoke the truth and the fire died in him.

"So both of us have been had, eh?" he said finally, his voice drained of emotion. "All right, Mr. Vice-Questor; now let me out of here."

The vice-questor marched to the door and flung it open. The policeman outside hurriedly stamped a furtive cigarette underfoot and saluted.

"It is my duty to warn you," the vice-questor said, "that you remain in Rome at our disposition until this case is completely resolved. You are a key witness, after all. Also despite my appreciation of your personal situation, after completion of this investigation your residence permit will be granted only on a normal tourist basis; you may extend it for only three months' residence at a time. Then you must come back here to extend it for another three months. And if, during this renewal period, you misbehave or incur contraventions of the law in any way, *fuori;* out of Italy." He made a rejecting gesture with his thumb.

"I understand."

The vice-questor extended his hand, and Tom shook it firmly.

"If you have suffered discomfort and distress this night, *caro signore,*" the vice-questor said. "I can assure you that I have suffered an even greater discomfort and professional defeat."

"Dottore," Tom asked him as they emerged into the bleakly lit corridor extending endlessly in both directions, "you are married; you have children?" A puzzled nod. "Parents, hopefully alive? Relatives? Friends at home? A career of honor and public service?"

Again a reluctant assent and a frown. He did not like being led on.

"Then consider yourself fortunate." Tom took the exit card from the police official's hand, held it up and said, "*Auguri.*"

"*Grazie, arrivederci,*" the vice-questor responded, his hard face for a moment open and relaxed.

"With the Questura one would rather say goodbye," Tom rejoined and slouched away down the corridor past the achingly familiar Room 37 of the Foreigners' Office. Here he had spent countless hours during the past ten years waiting in the packed room for a crook of a finger or the cocking of an eyebrow by one of the *marescialli* which signified that his annual application for renewal of the residence permit would be placed on the balance and weighed. (Two packs of American cigarettes invariably tipped the scale in his favor.) Well, there would be no more waiting. For three-month extensions, a routine rubber stamp in the ground-floor police office handling tourism would suffice. He remembered the expired passport; they were certainly not going to be ecstatic when he showed up at the American Consulate to get a new one. But they had to give him one. It was the law. Unless, of course, he was eventually sent off to jail for this night's bright little caper.

His footsteps echoed eerily as he went down the three flights of stairs to the main entrance. Inside the immense closed door, a policeman with a cape flung around him against the early morning chill accepted the exit card with a grunt and swung one half of the door sufficiently open to permit his departure. With the premonitory shiver of an animal leaving its warm burrow, he walked into the Via Genova. His hands rummaged expertly through his clothing: he didn't have a lira on him. He peered at his watch. It was four-thirty A.M. It was going to be a long quiet walk across town to the Lungotevere delle Armi. He knew The Maria would simply say nothing and prepare the coffee and the brioche.

It was awful; the whole bloody mess was awful. He turned it and turned it again in his mind, and it became worse each time. But as resolution came to him, he knew, first dimly, then with brutal clarity, what it was that he had to do. He straightened and his pace quickened. For the first time in many hundreds of mornings, he did not wish himself dead.

Vinny had a moment to view himself darkly in a glass partition and he knew just how terrible he looked. Nevertheless, moments before the questor himself announced his release, he did what he could: he combed his hair, soothed the blond mustache, tightened his tie, dusted his shoes with a handkerchief, and pulled down the waistcoat. He badly needed a shave, his trousers and jacket were masses of accordion pleats, and his body ached for a bath, but he accepted his release with an indifferent nod.

"You are, Excellency, in a rather difficult position," the questor, who looked like a particularly stern headmaster, told him. "We must now release you, of course. But we hold you quite accountable for your role in the events of this night. You remain at our disposition, you understand?"

"Yes," Vinny answered, amazed and a bit appalled at his own lack of concern. Perhaps he was in a state of shock or was simply lightheaded from lack of sleep. Certainly his detention had had an air of unreality; he had been held in one of the better-furnished offices, the kind used during the day for VIPs waiting to visit the questor himself. He had been questioned but most politely and circumspectly and had been served coffee and cognac intermittently. That all detained persons did not receive such genteel treatment had been borne out during the long night by a crashing of glass in the corridor outside, a couple of feminine screams, and groans somewhere on the same floor; others, who apparently had fallen afoul of the law, came reluctantly.

But he was in deep trouble and all the niceties of police conduct could not rub that out. His eight-year career in the Foreign Service was in serious jeopardy. Yet considering the single-mindedness with which he had pursued that career and the heartaches he had felt in the past when he had stumbled as a junior diplomat, he could not understand why his predicament wasn't bothering him more. Perhaps his mind simply had built a detour around the gaping hole of concern and the glare of morning sunshine would clear it.

He strode along with the questor on one side, the commissario on the other, and they let him out of the building with a flourish that only Italians can carry off. The questor shook his hand warmly, and said in slow, serious English, "I am terribly sorry, Mister Consul, about this business."

The commissario also shook his hand, his face reflecting nothing but a faint disapproval.

They waved a goodbye that was a half-salute and Vinny walked out of the Questura a free man again. He felt some hard objects in his pocket and remembered he had automatically taken the key chain from the ignition of his wrecked car. God, that was another headache! He wondered whether there would be a cab in the Piazza Esedra at this hour and . . .

"Hey you! Over here!" the familiar light voice called to him in English from a little bug of a Fiat parked across the street. He walked hesitantly to the window of the tiny car. Nancy Hamill looked as though she had been sitting there for some time, cramped in the narrow seat, but the auburn eyes were alert and sleepless, and the russet hair, now black in the dim light, was barely visible around the edges of a scarf.

"How's the jailbird?"

"Right this minute?" he grinned despite himself. "Couldn't be better but the room service was poor, so I checked out. And what in the name of God are you doing here?"

"Waiting for you. Oh, I knew that you were out hunting for me; in one place, Bricktop's I think, you almost found me but I saw you first and beat it to the sanctuary; the ladies' powder room." So she had been playing hide-and-seek with him!

"And why are you waiting here for me now? To knock me out of my chair again?"

"Not yet, just to give you a ride home. It's either me or nothing at this hour. Long walk to Parioli."

"You give me no choice," he said, circling the car and tiredly easing into its tiny interior. "But how did you know they were going to spring me?"

"I was at the Campo de' Fiori," she said matter-of-factly,

starting the car and pulling it away from the curb. "I saw what happened."

"I know," he said, striving for casualness himself. "I saw you looking at me from the crowd. You certainly show up at all the wrong times."

"I won't lie," she told him after a moment of silence. "I was outside Tom's house last night, waiting for you to come out and drive your damned diplomatic car away so that I could go back up to him. When you came out and picked up Tom and that boy with the suitcases in that awful rain, I didn't know what was happening but when I saw all those other cars pull away to follow you, three of them at least, I was frightened for you and decided to follow you. After the crash and that mess in the Campo, I did what you wanted me to do all day yesterday: I went home."

The little car moved up the Via Nazionale, still glistening from its nocturnal shower bath, rolling alone in the great empty street. In the center of the Piazza Esedra, the marble god wrestling with his monster marble fish seemed almost alive, now that the towering spout of water from the fish's mouth had been turned off. A squad of workmen in rubber boots sweeping clean the interior of the fountain looked up and waved at their solitary passage. One of them patted the round marble buttocks of the naiad he was scrubbing and made a cheerfully obscene gesture with the statue, a wide smile on his ugly face.

"Too bad I'm so bushed," Vinny said as if he had not heard her. "This is the time to see the city, when everybody else is asleep. Sorry we can't take in the Forum at sunrise. Some other morning, no?"

She glanced away from the road at him, taking in the exhausted profile.

"I didn't know you cared about sunrises over the Forum."

"We never got . . . friendly enough to talk about it," he responded lamely. Then, remembering, he quickly asked, "And what sort of a reception did you get when you showed up at home?"

"Just what you'd expect. Dad verbally flayed the hide off me but then he's been doing that for some years. When the phone call came through from the marine guard at the Embassy, Dad phoned the Questura and got word that you and Tom Linden had been pinched and were being held down here. I heard him make them say you would be released; so I sneaked out although he forbade me to leave the house. Here I am."

The Via Veneto in the dawn light was an old slumbering beast, disturbed only by the antlike passage of a leather-jacketed *vigile notturno* making his round of stores and shops. Up and down both broad sidewalks from the Pincian Gate to the Excelsior, the mute tables and chairs were neatly telescoped in aluminum pyramids. Here and there deep within the stores, and protected by forbidding steel curtains, an occasional night light burned lonesomely.

"Stop at Doney's," he asked wearily. "I want to get a good seat for once, without waiting."

She stopped the car without a word and they both alighted. Vinny plucked a table and two chairs from the stacked mounds, and together they sat in the middle of the yawningly empty sidewalk leaning their elbows on the cold aluminum.

"I'm sorry about knocking you out of your chair here yesterday."

"Forget it. All in a diplomat's day's work."

"The service here is horrible," she finally said, turning to watch an old taxi squish up the wet street toward the great Roman gate. "And it's so cold. Do you know what I've got under this raincoat? Just a slip. I was afraid that I'd miss you and so I hurried."

He stared at the angled, almost exotic face with the creamed skin turned up to him. The hasty smear of lipstick, the light raincoat buttoned up to the neck, and the scarf tied under the small chin, gave her the appearance of an American suburban housewife delivering her husband to the morning train.

"Nancy," he asked her with as much gentleness as his tired consciousness could summon, "what do you want? Why me? They told me they were going to release Tom. Why didn't you wait for him?"

"To tell you the truth, Vinny, I don't really know. Last night for the first time you stuck your neck out, and for no advantage for you. You helped somebody out and now you're in a jam."

She reached out, took one of his hands and brought it up to her lips and kissed it. The trembling of her fingers was like a low voltage electrical current.

"Vinny, I'm unfree, white, and twenty-four. I got damned sick a long time ago of keeping up appearances, saying just the right sweet proper thing, smiling in public at a father who cares more about his precious damned work than he ever did about his poor wife or a lonely daughter. I don't care about

188

figura or dinners where you must talk with an old bore on your left during one course and with a knee-pinching rake on your right during the next. The thing is, dammit, I don't know how to do a single wretched useful thing to get out of this terrible box of a life I lead."

Her cold fingers sank into the flesh of his palms. He sat wearily back, his hand still imprisoned, to look at her.

"What about marriage?" he said. "It isn't much, but it could spring you free of this. You don't look like anyone who would have any trouble at all finding some pliable young man."

Suddenly her grip slackened and the cords in her throat disappeared.

"No, Vinny, I'm not going to do that to any of the nice young boys I've met. I . . . I haven't got much left, but I still have the essentials of decency. I hate this damned diplomatic life, every hour of it. I'm not going to palm myself off on some embassy hotshot as something I'm not." The auburn eyes bore straight at his. "And, as you well know, I'm not the sort most potential FSO husbands would be interested in."

He peered at his watch, and looked up at the pre-sunrise sky now lightening to a pale whitish gray.

"It's about four-thirty," he said, "and I will fall asleep in the middle of the next word." He looked at her and clasped his hands together in an Italian supplication.

"Per piacere, will you take me home?"

"Only if you let me stay."

He could not restrain a tired chuckle.

"You must really be out to unhinge your dad. What if he calls up the police and they trace you to my house and I get run into the Questura again, this time for concubinage or daughter-napping?"

"He won't call!" she jeered bitterly. "Get *his* name into notoriety? Not the embassy's Mr. Hamill! He won't do a damned thing except fume, especially since I left a note saying that I was 'staying with friends' tonight." She looked past him up the great empty street. "You didn't have to chase after me yesterday, Vinny. I'm leaving, anyway. Leaving him, leaving Italy. Tomorrow, if I can."

Vinny stood up and pulled her up with him. She was slim and with her low-heeled shoes she barely reached his nose. She moved to him and his arms felt the supple young body under the trench coat; her arms slid up over his shoulders and behind his head, and in the grayness of the empty dawn

189

of the sidewalk at Doney, she kissed him with her mouth soft and loving and wandering.

They left the table and two chairs still in place in front of Doney's as mute testimony of their presence and climbed into the Fiat. Within five minutes of screeching turns through the Borghese Park spurred by the howling little rear engine, they were in front of his Parioli apartment building, and in another five they had breathlessly raced through the garishly muraled foyer and up four flights of darkened stairs. Once, on the third landing they stopped and she leaned panting and gasping with the exertion against him. Her trench coat was loosened and his hand touched her just under her heart, which pounded like a panicked rabbit's.

"Your generation just doesn't have it," he mocked her, struggling himself to force air into lungs long unaccustomed to galloping up stairs at any hour. She could only gasp in return, nod her head in smiling agreement and continue the upward flight.

Vinny reached into the dark apartment and flipped on the light switch to reveal a large, well-appointed living room with a curious but successful blending of modern Scandinavian, Persian rugs, huge hand-beaten brass trays, and a couple of Italian antique pieces. Everything reflected its owner, and Nancy stood in the middle of the room looking at the various objects with a critical eye.

"Foreign Service Rococo," she murmured finally, "but not at all bad for a bachelor."

Vinny disappeared and returned with two glasses of milk. He handed her one.

"Down the hatch. Good for what ails you. Stuffy old diplomat always drinks stuffy old glass of milk before retiring."

She freed her head of the scarf and obediently drained the glass he had given her. He carefully wiped his mustache free of a drop or two of milk, and watched her with alarm as she calmly unbuttoned the trench coat and wriggled out of it.

"Nancy, believe me when I say that I deeply appreciate your . . ."

Her body, supple as a dancer's, rose to a surprising thrust of bosom; under the sheer black slip, her breasts were like two full navel oranges. She kicked off her shoes and suddenly she was short enough to brush the top of her tight russet curls under his chin. She looked up at him, standing there with his empty milk glass, and she smiled a full sad smile as she reached up to stroke his blond stubbled chin.

"Now you're starting to look like a man instead of a Brioni model," she told him approvingly, and she moved close enough to him so that their bodies just brushed one another. She reached up with a casual gesture and loosened his tie.

"Nan," he began uncertainly, then he started over. "Dear Nan . . ."

"That's better," she encouraged, and shook her head so that her curls bounced slightly.

"No, Vinny, don't try to make an honest woman out of me now. Besides, misery loves company, and we're both in enough trouble already."

His bleary eyes were on her, incredulity written in them.

"But after our row on the Veneto yesterday . . . ?"

She reached up and her lips brushed his neck just under his ear.

"That," she answered softly, "was when you were just a stuffy errand boy for my dad. Now you're a man, Vinny, and as a man, you're damned appealing."

She moved even closer now, and her breasts touched softly through the slip at him; she was clinging as a child clings to the leg of a parent. He picked her up easily and her slim arms went around him as he marched out of the living room with her, down a dark corridor and into an even darker bedroom where he gently deposited her. The moment he had shucked his rumpled garments and slid in under the crisp sheets, she reached for him, her nude slim body cool and satiny to the touch.

He was surprised and pleased at himself and his responses despite the terrible tiredness lurking within him, and he answered eagerly and fully her every gesture and hinted wish. At the brink of climax, he trembled like a leaf, fearful and hoping it was all a dream from which he would never have to wake. He was inordinately happy, somehow, that she trembled in return. The agonizing bitter peak of love swept them up as a high wave takes flotsam, slams it on the beach, and ebbs away.

As the dawn stole through the windows of Vinny's bedroom, he turned to the soft angular young face now relaxed and totally defenseless in sleep, and he kissed it gently close to one ear. Nancy stirred but slept on.

He was no good for her, he knew, and she even less good for him. He had realized this with great clarity the moment that he had met her and she had mocked him, derided him, in a manner that had repeatedly sent him home in a dark anger. Such a person needlessly complicated one's bright,

191

orderly world, in which the norms of conduct and of daily life were clearly laid out and accepted, and the unusual was carefully avoided. She was right, just as Tom was right: he was no boat-rocker; he was a beaver eager to please, a horse's ass in Tom's brutal words.

Well, we are what we are, he thought hopelessly, and his eyes and consciousness snapped shut. Some four hours later, he opened them, peered at his watch and read the time: nine-sixteen A.M. He had missed the Big Nine O'clock Meeting, the one Addison Hamill had warned him in his crisp authoritarian tone, that he *must* attend. Well-well-well, he muttered, you are really booting this one. This one you will never get back. But it suddenly did not seem important, really not important at all. He reached out to touch and knead the curled smooth satin that was Nancy, and she turned sleepily but willingly to him.

chapter twenty

COMRADE GIORGIO LOOKED out on the gray street still glistening from the heavy shower of the night before, and the temporary absence of the Roman sun matched his mood precisely. Below, he noted sourly, his *papiros* in hand, the Forces of Order had been doubled and at some points trebled. The sidewalks opposite the Party building were filled with knots of three or four uniformed policemen, some from the Pubblica Sicurezza, some carabinieri, and out of the corner of his eye he spotted three red-painted jeeps of the *Nucleo Celere*, those head-cracking mobile goons with jack boots, truncheons, and helmets, tucked almost out of sight near the Piazza Venezia. He knew full well why the "protective guard" had been increased. It was the Authorities' way of telling the Party: you had better keep your part of the deal or you will compel us to get rough with you. And the Authorities knew that this was a moment when they could get rough with the Party and get away with it.

Well, some day the Party would be the Authority and it would not be quite so delicately Italian in its pressure on, let us say, the Christian Democrats in such an event; this he silently promised the lounging dozens of policemen below. No, indeed. But patience. The inevitable swing of time and political circumstance throughout the world was in the direction of the Left. The principal thing to do now was to shore up the Party's image, to make it attractive, reasonable, and tolerant. It was up to him and his group, on the one hand, to prevent the old-time Stalinist wreckers like Comrade Spartaco and his kind from spattering such a new image, and on the other, to keep those restive and outrageously opportunistic Socialist brethren, led by that egomaniac, Nenni, from breaking out of the Unity of Action Pact. Comrade Palmiro, *Il Migliore*, had originated this concept but he was sick, old, weary. The Party had to look to the younger, more energetic cadre headed by one like Giorgio himself, tough yet flexible, in order to dominate forcefully the entire political Left in this country which was threatening to elude the Party's control. He knew one blunt fact: the moment the Party was isolated from the Socialists, the well-wishers, and the opportunists, it would start to atrophy and die.

Comrade Giorgio punched a fist into the palm of the other hand. It was the Spartaco Tamburris who had to be rooted out of the leadership, just as they were being rooted out in Russia. And now, unexpectedly, the opportunity to rid the Party of Spartaco's presence was at hand!

He turned away from the window, his spirits already rising. When Guglielmo, his private secretary, knocked discreetly and came through the door, Comrade Giorgio was seated at his desk, a genuine exhilaration beaming on his face as he looked at the notes outlining the appointments of the day ahead.

"Comrade Passaglia, mayoress of Belinoro from the Romagna," Guglielmo intoned. "She came unannounced early this morning and begged for five minutes with you. A personal matter, she says."

"In a moment," Giorgio told him. "And bring in two *caffè neri* after she has been here ten minutes."

On the desk before him, the agenda noted that in one hour's time he would be meeting with the tight inner circle of the Party Secretariat *and* the Control Commission (four of whom, including himself, being members of both), the primary purpose of which this morning would be to place the Party stamp of approval on the departure of Comrade Spartaco Tamburri for Czechoslovakia for an indefinite period for "reasons of health." Then there was the unpleasant but necessary duty of talking to Spartaco himself at noon, and a note in Comrade Piero's precise handwriting that reservations for two persons, Spartaco and his "companion" Piero, had been confirmed for a Swissair flight leaving for Geneva (and points beyond) for four o'clock that afternoon.

He turned to the agenda. Here then, was Mayoress Passaglia from Belinoro, a woman comrade he had never met, to see him on personal matters. Guglielmo had already prepared a typewritten note, which read:

> "The Party files have the following concerning Comrade Passaglia from Belinoro. Thirty-one years old, widow, no children. Upper bourgeois origins. Cadre files indicate she joined the Party immediately after the end of the war. Sponsored by Peppino Deruta, then Party secretary of the Section encompassing Belinoro. (Deruta was later expelled on charges of collaboration with the Germans. She was not involved.) Has attended the Party cadre school in Bologna. Made an excellent impression on the instructors. 1950: made responsible for women's affairs for the Party Section of Belinoro-Altomonte. Headed Party list for municipal councillor for Belinoro in 1952. Elected Mayoress by Communist-Socialist majority 1955."

Then below, after several spaces, under the words 'strictly confidential' came another paragraph.

> "Her father was a leading bourgeois of the Belinoro region, proprietor of a pharmacy and widely known anti-Facist who became 'Guistizia e Libertà' commander of the Romagna in his area during the Resistance with American and monarchist support. Refused collaboration with patriotic forces and CLN. Father was killed with a dozen of his band in Spring 1944 under circumstances known to you. I have received telephone communications from the north in the past week that Comrade Passaglia has recently and quite unexpectedly begun a personal investigation of the tragedy. Known to have talked with Resistance comrades throughout the Po Valley from Rimini to Milano, including examination of the Resistance archives in Milano."

Guglielmo had ended the note in his own writing, a precise, tiny calligraphy. He had written at the bottom of the page, "I think she knows," and had signed it with his usual G with a circle around the letter.

Comrade Giorgio pressed the buzzer twice. The door opened and Guglielmo looked inquiringly at him. He nodded and the door was opened wider.

The woman who entered with short feminine steps was much more attractive than he would have imagined, rather short and dressed with chic in a severely tailored suit upon an excellent full body. The smoothly olive skin of her face and a generous curving mouth, all with a minimum of make-up alerted his Neapolitan instincts immediately; the overstuffed creature now enjoying his bed and board, unbridled energy and all, suddenly seemed coarse and animal-like in comparison to this fine figure of a Romagnole comrade. Only when he reached the eyes did he realize that his fantasies would have to remain just that, at least for the present. The huge eyes were steel-like and forbidding and there were severe black circles under them as if she had cried or not slept for days, or both. A realist to the core, Comrade Giorgio stifled the instinctive lust she has aroused.

He sprang agilely to his feet and reached her quickly to pump her soft but unresponsive hand. Guglielmo closed the door in his departure without a sound.

"Dear Comrade Passaglia! What a pleasure and a privilege to talk to one of our most distinguished young feminine cadres from the north! There in the Emilia-Romagna is the heart and strength of the Party, and you young comrades have made it so! Welcome to Roma and to Party headquarters!"

She closed her eyes briefly in acknowledgment of the fulsome greeting and permitted herself to be seated in one of the chairs close by the window looking out onto the Street of the Dark Shops. He took a similar seat at right angles to hers, opened the box of Russian cigarettes, and offered her one perfunctorily, knowing she would refuse. He lit one for himself.

"I thank you for giving me the opportunity of seeing you, Comrade Giorgio," she said in a low, precise voice with the up-and-down inflection of her region. "I know what an immensely busy man you are, but I have a matter which is of such great concern to me that I feel only you can give me the proper advice and reassurances."

He bowed his head in acknowledgment of his status and

his willingness to do what he could, relaxing his heavy body and looking at the tense, erect figure of the woman, his gray eyes alive with an amalgam of Latin interest and desire.

"I will be direct and blunt as is our custom. In spring of 1944, a Resistance band of which my father was head, was ambushed one rainy night a short distance outside of Belinoro by an unknown group, believed to have been Fascist thugs or an anti-partisan German unit. All were killed, including my father, my husband, and my brother who was a boy of fifteen years. An American officer was also killed. Of this you certainly must have heard."

It would be useless to play with her, to try to flood the room with false or hypocritical words, he knew instantly. But he had not realized the full extent of the disaster. Father, brother, *and husband! Porca miseria!* With this woman, one had to meet steel with steel.

"I know of it. It was truly a tragedy, a ghastly tragedy of war."

She looked at him sharply, seeking to penetrate the heavy-lidded gray eyes, but he now returned her gaze, neutrally and patiently, permitting a cloud of cigarette smoke to drift between them.

"Just one month ago," she went on, "I received . . . an indication which caused grave doubt in my mind that the Fascists had ambushed and killed my father and his group, something that had been accepted as fact all these years. When this suspicion took root, I vowed to find out the truth, no matter how long it would take."

"And just what *did* you find out, dear comrade?" Giorgio asked, his voice filled with sympathetic concern.

Her almond eyes seemed to turn a bottomless black as she turned from the huge twin portraits of Togliatti and Khrushchev to answer him.

"I started in my own area, Belinoro and Altomonte. Then I gradually worked outward, to the Romagna towns on the plain: Forlì, Forlimpòpoli, Faenza. Cesena. Then, as far as Ravenna, Bologna, Modena, and finally Milano. I have been at this task, almost continuously. Everywhere I talked to those of the Resistance, including our own Communists who led the *Garibaldini* formations, as well as the other groups. I even swallowed my pride and my hatred to interview ex-*Brigata Nera* men who were active in this zone during that period, or who knew anything about the anti-partisan operations in the region of Belinoro during the spring of 1944."

He stared at her, astonished at her tenacity and stubborn

persistence. Then he remembered what sort of people the Romagnoles were. *Teste di bue,* heads like bulls, all of them, and this female was obviously of the same breed. They made ferocious Fascists and ferocious Communists. Whatever they believed in, it was ferocious and went to extremes. He smiled carefully.

"I trust that your Party duties and your post as mayoress of Belinoro did not suffer during this period," he chided her. "Why did you not ask the Party to look into this new information concerning your family's death? You know that we at headquarters could make an inquiry throughout the entire peninsula for you in such a grave matter."

"Let's not jest," she told him, "when one suspects a murderer, one does not ask the suspect to investigate himself." The sting in her words struck a spark of anger from his eyes and he sat up stiffly in his chair.

"What kind of a provocatory answer is that! What do you mean?"

She reached into a large leather bag and came up with a sheet of folded paper which she consulted briefly.

"Just this," she said with frost on every word. "Virtually everywhere I went, Comrade Giorgio, I met with silence. But such a silence! A silence filled with meaning, with hostility, with occasional frightened glances. At every Veterans of Resistance headquarters throughout the Po, they were initially polite, as you were when I walked in, then they immediately turned cold or in many cases belligerently aggrieved that I dared to even imply any complicity of Resistance comrades in the murder of my father and his band. But the wall of silence had cracks, Comrade Giorgio." She moved her face to within a yard of his. "The cracks grew wider and I finally saw the truth on the other side."

Comrade Giorgio, his sense of equanimity now completely dissipated, sprang to his feet.

"I do not know what you are talking about so melodramatically, Comrade Passaglia," he rumbled loudly at her, "but I am astounded to hear such talk from a dedicated member of the Party cadre. What is this wall of silence you say the Party has created to keep you from learning the truth? Out with it! Immediately!"

Now that he was looking down on her, he realized that he had not noticed one of her features when she had walked in: her chin. It was set and immovably defiant now and she showed no contrition whatsoever, nor apprehension at his anger.

"Yesterday evening," she told him calmly, "I learned that a Communist group of six men, members of a small G.A.P commando, had been involved in partisan activity in the area near Belinoro when my father's band was murdered. This was the group that did the crime. At least one of them had not known that the ambush had been laid for another Resistance band; he thought that it was planned to ambush a group of Fascist irregulars raiding the villages in the area. Until he saw the dead."

Comrade Giorgio licked his lips. She *did* know, and a moment of reckoning was fast arriving between them. He stared at her with outward impassivity.

Antonella looked down at her notes.

"Of the six Gappisti, only three are alive today," she read from her notes. "One was killed on the spot that fatal night by a chance shot from one of my father's band. He was carried away and buried secretly elsewhere. Another died of wounds in a later partisan fight. A third has emigrated to South America and disappeared from sight. It was with the fourth that I spoke. It was he who told me the whole story. It was he who told me who the fifth man, the leader of the Gappisti unit, was that night at Belinoro." She took a deep breath and almost sighed. "The sixth man was Peppino Deruta, who was there but did not fire a shot.

You sit there and listen politely to this," she continued, a cutting edge of scorn in her voice. "You are pretending that you are hearing it for the first time, you contemptible hypocrite!"

Giorgio's teeth crunched the hollow paper holder of his Papiros, and great mottled hands grasped the arms of his chair for control.

"You have already trespassed into Party insubordination," he growled. "Now out with it: Who was this fifth man!"

She attempted to control herself but a twitching in her cheeks gave her away. She was barely hanging on.

"You know as well as I do. It was Spartaco Tamburri, Il Duro. It was he who created, planned, and executed the ambush, thereby eliminating one of the most determined anti-Fascist partisan groups, a group which could resist Communist control of the entire zone not only during the Resistance period but for the period *after* the Liberation."

When she stopped, the high ringing sound of her words seemed to echo in the room.

"May I ask," Comrade Giorgio said at last, deep voice

straining for normalcy, "how you acquired this information? Who told you all this?"

"Certainly. The original hint of the truth came from the lips of a dying man, Peppino himself. The full information on the ambush was finally revealed to me by one Nando Martinuzzi of Imola. Yesterday evening, he told me a dozen times with tears streaming down his face that he did not know he was killing Resistance comrades; he thought he was killing Fascist plunderers. He had lost his sanity when he realized what he had done. You may visit him whenever you like." She looked down at her notes and read quietly. "He is in the Insane Asylum of Rieti, Pavilion Four, Section D. It is not far from here, a couple of hours by train. He also cried because I was the first person outside the asylum who had visited him in a month. When I told him who I was, he collapsed temporarily but when he recovered he cursed the name of Il Duro and called him a crazy butcher."

Comrade Giorgio sat down in the adjacent chair again. The moment had come. Antonella reached in her bag and came up with a large leather object which she handed to Comrade Giorgio.

Comrade Giorgio turned it in his hand.

"Read what is on the inside of the flap," she commanded.

Comrade Giorgio bent the holster flap to read the words inside. He made out the inscription: "Major H. Dixon, U. S. Army. 0-35732."

She answered the unspoken question in his eyes as he looked up from the holster with the *U.S.* embossed on its outer surface.

"That holster was strapped to the body of the American officer killed with my father's group that night in Belinoro. Nando took it while delivering *coups de grace* to those still alive. When he rolled over the American major and my father, whom he knew well, he realized whom he had been killing. He took this with him in a state of shock and gave it and the pistol in it to Spartaco, who threw away the holster and kept the gun. Nando then retrieved the holster and when his mind gave way, he handed it, with an insignia from the American major's collar, to Peppino Deruta who was the one person to help him and visit him regularly. Nando does not know that Peppino is dead. I did not dare tell him." A chilling smile flitted across her lips. "I was bequeathed the holster as an inheritance. A gift from the grave, you might say."

Comrade Giorgio rose again and walked heavily around

the large room, great head sunk in thought. It had to be administered just so, spoken in just such a voice, the Party reason and logic limpid and understandable. Guglielmo, opening the door with the two coffees on a tray, was waved peremptorily out again before he had crossed the threshold. Giorgio walked back to her, moved his chair until it faced hers, and sat down slowly after crushing the Russian cigarette on a nearby tray.

"Did you, Comrade Passaglia, consider yourself a loyal, disciplined, and idealistic Party cadre until you heard of this information on the ambush?" She nodded slowly, keeping her eyes on him as one watches a known pocket-thief approaching.

"You believe in the Party aims and purposes still?"

"I believe in elimination of injustice of all kinds, and in this the Party plays a leading combatant role," she answered equally cautiously.

"You know of the new direction of the Party as initiated by Comrade Khrushchev in the Twentieth Communist Party Congress in January of last year?"

Again a slow nod of acquiescence.

"You know of the growing accumulation of facts now being revealed which indicate that Stalin, the great leader and propulsor of the Communist movement, was guilty of terrible, monstrous crimes and excesses in the name of Marxist-Leninism despite his known contribution to the Communist movement in Russia and abroad? In the growing aberrations of his own mental processes and the personality cult which he permitted to be built around him, he ordered executions, imprisonment, and suffering for thousands upon thousands of good, loyal Communists and fellow travelers." He looked at her with sadness. "I was one of his victims. I spent two years in a Soviet prison camp after escaping from Spain one step ahead of Franco's Moors in 1939. Only the German invasion of Russia speeded my release. Then I went to work in the Italian section of the Comintern organizing anti-Fascist propaganda and the return of experienced comrades to Italy to participate in the Resistance and the liberation from Fascism. But, during those two years in the bitterest sort of suffering in a Soviet forced labor camp, did I lose faith in Marxism-Leninism? Of course not! I knew that although I was innocent of any wrong to the Party, something had gone wrong and that one day it would be righted. And it was. Now Stalin is gone, and his excesses and certain terrible injustices are being exposed to fresh clean air. The Party was not wrong. Stalin was wrong. The Party, the movement toward elimination of the great injustices to mankind, goes ahead to new social triumphs."

She sat motionless, watching the movement of his lips. He lit up yet another *papiros* in the unbroken silence and inhaled the smoke is if it were cognac.

"What Nando, our tragic comrade in the asylum, told you is basically true," he said, knowing there was no other course with her. "The highest responsible leaders of the Party have known for years that Comrade Spartaco Tamburri organized and executed that ambush. That Spartaco did so without any specific request or permission from the top Party responsibles of the Resistance does not enter here. As a leader of the patriotic partisans, he chose in a moment of blind anger to do this terrible crime after he had been denied any arms or supplies from the band of your father and from the Americans working with your father. He completely distorted Party directives which instructed him to take steps to see that there would be no recrudescence of monarchist-fascist organizations or power in any of the areas of Resistance activity, and in doing so snuffed out the lives of over a dozen innocent persons. There are other lives of good comrades in Spain for which he must also account. These facts he and the Party have on their consciences. And for this we must all atone some day."

She swallowed, and holding the old brown leather holster in her hands, she asked, "Why did the Party not tell me of this terrible thing? Why did you permit the monstrousness of letting me enter the Party, rising in its ranks, becoming a responsible member of the regional cadre? Me, the victim and sole family survivor of a Communist massacre, now enrolled in that same Communist movement, given Party honors and distinctions! You are doing with me what the Turks did with captives: kill the parents and train the children as Janissaries!"

It was an inevitable reaction and he had been prepared for it for some minutes, but her analogy tormented him.

"I resent your accusation that the Party deliberately took you in its bosom after killing your father. I have already described to you the fact that what happened was an individual act of excess, of murderous stupidity. The Party has neither forgotten nor forgiven it. But that hardly obviates bringing in fine young women comrades like yourself to work for a better world. If we have you, we can do without the Comrade Spartacos in the future."

She looked at him in such a way that for a bad moment he thought she was going to laugh in his face. But instead she said, "I think I understand. You honestly thought that I would never learn about it. And when Peppino Deruta was expelled from the Party for threatening to expose the crime, you were certain that he would take the secret to his grave, knowing that its revelation would destroy me. Well, Peppino could not keep it to the death, even though it was he who brought me into the Party, who indoctrinated me, who breathed the idealism and the sense of purpose of the Party into me after the war. He finally got to know what the Party was like in these matters: expulsion, and the status of a leper, after all his sacrifices." Her voice rose and fell in cadences of sadness, as one would talk at the graveside.

"The party could not expose Spartaco Tamburri at that time nor can it today!" Giorgio told her with vehemence. "Surely you understand what a holiday the neo-Fascists and anti-Communists would have with the story that the great Il Duro slaughtered a Resistance group in the name of Party expediency and class struggle. With Hungary still in everyone's memory, and the falling membership of the weak and timid from Party ranks, it would harm us, and severely."

He bunched his fingers at her.

"And now, let me tell you that this very afternoon Comrade Spartaco is being banished by the Party from Italy for some time, perhaps forever. And, perhaps, in the country of his destination, we will one day hold the full hearings of his crimes and pass full punishment on him for such Stalinist excesses." He smiled.

"Rest assured, dear comrade," he said, and he patted her knee before he realized from her glance that this was a grave tactical blunder, "I want to see Comrade Spartaco punished as badly as you do. Leave it to us, to the Party's central leadership, to handle this matter and in our own good time." His voice changed to a cheery tone. "And, now that you are in Rome, I want to introduce you to others of the Party Commissions who would be only too happy to hear of your exiences as one of our very few women mayors and as one of our shining women cadre from the Romagna."

He rose, swiftly reached his desk, buzzed twice for the delayed caffè and equally quickly returned to his easy chair facing hers. She sat, seemingly inert, the holster still in her lap. Then, as the door again opened and Guglielmo entered with the cups and warmed-over *caffè nero* in the coffee maker on the tray, she quietly tucked the holster back into the woman's bag at her feet and said to him, "Then Spartaco Tamburri cannot be turned over to the Authorities for this crime?"

Giorgio watched Guglielmo adding the usual four small teaspoonsful of sugar to his cup of black liquid and shook his head at her naïve question.

"No, dear comrade, of course not. For one thing, the Party would never do this to one of its own pioneer militants. Secondly, even should he be tried, with the government amnesties on all political offenses during the 1943-45 Resistance period he would be freed immediately by any sort of good lawyer. It would simply result in disastrous notoriety for us in the reactionary press. I repeat, the Party itself will punish him in good time."

He raised his cup of *caffè nero* almost in a toast to her before sipping its black contents, but she said, not understanding, "Will the Party not publish the truth in the matter in the Party press? Can we not at least have the matter clarified, that it was Il Duro, not the Party, who did this terrible thing?" Her voice was pleading now, and her hands were held out in near-supplication.

He put down his cup carefully and his answer contained the ring of authority. He was the Party Secretary now, and he was dealing with a woman—as only an Italian male knows how to handle a woman; with initial affectionate patience and cajoling, and finally with decisiveness and masculine assertion.

"Not at this time, Comrade Passaglia. When we are ready we will print the whole story of Belinoro with all the other matters, but not now. Not at this time."

There was something in her voice now that he had not yet heard and he eyed her narrowly as she spoke, and her words came out slowly.

"I am a Communist for these ten years, but my name is Passaglia as was that of my dead father. My murdered husband's name was Fausto Cipriani and my poor brother's name was Antonio. Are they to be avenged or not?"

The question was like a pistol shot.

Comrade Giorgio squared his jaw and Guglielmo, who had been pouring the coffee, eyes opening like saucers, stood back with the aluminum coffee maker to observe his reply.

"Vendetta is a feudalistic, backward concept which I would hope is dying out," he snapped at her. "Certainly one who is a cadre in the advance guard of society, a Communist such as yourself, would forebear . . ."

He felt the hot stinging liquid in his face and eyes and reached blindly for a handkerchief.

"Signora!" Guglielmo bleated, his mouth hanging open. "What you have done to our Party Secretary!"

But as Comrade Giorgio wiped the coffee off his face, Antonella had dug into her cavernous bag and come up with a small, folded cardboard document with the hammer and sickle on its outer face. She tore it in two and tore each of the pieces again in two.

"If vendetta for one's murdered family is not permitted to Communists," she said, picking up the large handbag, "then I am no longer a Communist. My Party *tessera* is herewith returned."

She flung the bits on the floor and was out the door and gone before either of them could say a word. Guglielmo stumbled over to the table to pick up the coffee cups. Comrade Giorgio deliberately shucked off his coffee-spattered suit jacket and threw it to Guglielmo.

"Take this out and get the stains off it immediately," he said coldly. "I must attend a meeting of the Secretariat within thirty minutes and I want that jacket back without spots on it, understand, without a single spot on it!" He dabbed at his scalded cheek and chin and glared like a madman.

"*Subito!*" Guglielmo assured him, taking the garment on one arm.

"And Guglielmo!" Comrade Giorgio said, gripping his elbow as he passed.

"Oh, not a word! Not a single, blessed word, Comrade Secretary!" Guglielmo assured him, eyes gleaming at the sensation he was going to create when he told this one at the Party canteen within the hour.

chapter twenty-one

Miss Brumacher looked up as Vinny swung through the office door and her hands remained frozen over her typewriter.

"Batten down the hatches, Mr. Brentwood. Mr. Hamill wanted to see you the moment you arrived."

She gave him a fleeting glance of sympathy and, he was certain, pity. Miss Brumacher, by her own confession, was an Old Girl, an FSS with two decades of embassy and consular posts and Vinny was just another small footnote in her unwritten autobiography: the one about Eager Beaver who tripped up in Rome.

"Right now?"

"Right now," and she frowned at her keyboard as he withdrew; she had hit two keys and they were jammed inside the machine.

Vinny paused outside the office of Addison Hamill, bracing himself for the storm. He was aware that something had changed within him: it was the first time he could remember that the tiny momentary panic did not hit him in the pit of his stomach when he walked into the presence of a superior officer. Always before, it had been: how can I make myself look good on this one? That was the bad part about being a Beaver; every setback, every reprimand, no matter how minor, bothered you and even sickened you. Now he suddenly felt relaxed. It was an unusual sensation for him, and he stood there savoring it before he pushed into the large damask-walled room.

Addison Hamill was on his feet and out from behind his desk by the time Vinny had taken half a dozen steps into the room. He motioned Vinny into one of the chairs facing his desk, and he sank into the other. This was not, at least, going to be an across-the-desk official execution.

Hamill was not at the top of his form. The precise little man was dressed as faultlessly as usual but he fingered large bifocal spectacles in his hand feverishly.

"It is good to have you at work again," Hamill snapped, "even if you are four hours late."

"I'm truly sorry, sir."

Hamill opened his small bright eyes in mock surprise.

"That's all? You're truly sorry? After I specifically requested you be here at nine A.M. to handle the arrangements of the meeting between the Congressman and the Ministry of Defense officials?"

"That's really all I can say. I'm terribly sorry. I overslept."

Hamill stared at him, amazement mixing with his anger.

"Oh, you overslept.

"Of course," he added, "you had a long busy night. You were arrested by the police in the act of transporting contraband goods, you smashed up your car in the Campo de' Fiori, and you spent a few hours at the Questura before the ambassador and I secured your release. So, naturally, these off-duty relaxations absolved you from appearing this morning for work to carry out perhaps your most important assignment of this year."

"No excuse, sir," Vinny answered quietly. He had the feeling that he was in the eye of a raging storm.

Hamill himself sensed his mood and it goaded him out of his controlled sarcasm.

"Look, damn you, you're not just going to sit there like a nodding Buddha! You are in trouble, young man, deep trouble!"

Vinny sat erect in his leather chair, both feet on the ground, hands folded. "I know it, sir."

Hamill toyed with his glasses, twisting them and spinning them with greater agitation, tilting down his head as if rapt in an imaginary chess game.

"My daughter," he said in a low voice, "sneaked out of the house at two-thirty A.M. and has not reappeared." He looked up suddenly with a piercing glance. "Do you have any idea where she is?"

"She's back at your home by this time, Mr. Hamill," Vinny said, meeting his superior's gaze evenly. "She spent the night at my place."

In the long silence that followed, the hooting rumble of traffic on the Veneto filtered distantly into the room.

"*Your* place." Hamill pursed his lips as if reacting to the news of some far-off disaster, and Vinny stared at him with admiration; these old diplomatic pros really knew how to keep the lid buttoned down. But this just might unbutton it; and he hoped he had the iron in him to see it through.

"Yes, my place. She came to the Questura to drive me home and she stayed."

"Well," Hamill told him, his voice still full of authority, but in it somewhere the sound of something breaking, "I told you all about her yesterday. You can't say you weren't warned."

Vinny reached in his pocket.

"May I smoke, sir?"

Hamill nodded, and in the gesture of lighting his cigarette Vinny knew that they were now only two men concerned with one woman.

"What I say may surprise you, Mr. Hamill," he said carefully through the light haze of smoke hovering in the still air. "But I think I love your daughter. I want to be completely frank with you because it's all that's left. Whether she loves me or not, I don't know. I hope so, but only time can tell. And it may take a lot of time."

Addison Hamill put on his glasses and stared owlishly at the younger man, as if seeing him for the first time.

"A great deal seems to have happened since we last discussed my daughter."

Vinny nodded, glad that the presence of the cigarette gave him something to do with his hand.

"A good deal has, to me anyway. And that's why I would like to know what action you intend to take against me as a result of . . . last night, Mr. Hamill."

The eyebrows on the face opposite raised above the level of the lenses.

"Action against you? Why should that suddenly be of pressing concern when we are discussing Nancy?"

"Because," Vinny said doggedly, "if I stay, I want you to let *her* stay. If you're going to make me resign, why then, I won't mind if you send her back to the States, because I'll be there. Either way, I want to be near her."

Hamill peered closely at him, looking for a fleeting smirk or grimace that would give him away.

"You're serious about this?"

Vinny nodded slowly, and took the cigarette away from his lips.

"I don't want to make it sound like a matter of sink or swim but I honestly feel I need her, and I feel that she needs

207

". . . well, a lot of kindness." He blinked self-consciously. "And I need somebody who keeps telling me I'm a . . . a stuffed shirt, but in a nice way."

Hamill plucked his heavy glasses from his nose and gnawed on their frame. When he finally rose, Vinny rose with him. The two men met in the center of the space between them and Addison Hamill touched Vinny at the elbow, studying the taller man, as if rehearsing a speech in a strange language.

"Vinny," he said finally, the line of his jaw quivering, "come to my place for dinner tonight. The three of us ought to get to know each other better."

"Glad to, sir," Vinny answered automatically but politely.

The telephone burred behind Addison Hamill and he walked around to pick it up. He listened intently for a moment, said "Thank you," and replaced the instrument carefully on its cradle.

"The minister counselor is free now, Vinny," his face and tone indicated what that connoted. "We're going in to see him."

"Ready, Mr. Hamill," Vinny said, puzzled by the sudden lightness he felt and the fact that he was not gnawing at his mustache. Hamill seemed uncannily to be reading his mind.

"You really tried, didn't you? I was looking at your file this morning. You tried very hard. What kept you at it?"

There was only kindness in his voice, as the guard speaks to the prisoner on his way to the executioner, kindness and a sincere human sympathy.

"Pride, I guess," Vinny answered, with a small smile. "I always ran away from things when I was a kid, and hated myself for doing it. I didn't ever want to have to accuse myself that I ran away from this job."

He followed Addison Hamill through the great wooden door leading to the outer office and admired the little figure ahead of him, every hair on the small round head in place, the small man somehow authoritative, and confident in the great neo-Renaissance embassy corridor. Vinny took a deep breath and moved off at his side.

chapter twenty-two

FOUR MEN MARCHED into the teeming piazza like a small parade, Comrade Giorgio in the lead with his big bull head thrusting forward and eyes straight ahead at a fixed point twenty feet ahead. One pace to his left and rear strode Comrade Piero's deputy, his blue plastic raincoat buttoned to the neck despite the warm sun overhead. Two hulking aides ambled behind him, clad like their mentor in blue raincoats, one of them wearing a black beret, the other hatless.

They moved purposefully toward the center of the mellow shabbiness of the Piazza Santa Maria in Trastevere, never once looking around at the golden glory of the mosaics high on the austere church façade, ignoring a plume of water from the fountain which was caught by a teasing wind and sprayed them lightly as they clumped past.

As they entered the narrow, animated alley of the Via della Lungaretta from the open piazza, they dropped into single file as the press of traffic in the noisy street slowed their progress. Brushing aside insistent little swarms of beggars and street vendors, they turned into a gloomy cobble-stoned aisle scarcely wider than a man's outstretched hands. Comrade Giorgio glanced briefly up at the house number, turned abruptly into a doorway, and began to climb the dark stairway without a glance at the others. A cool damp smell of cat urine and decay closed in on them as they plodded steadily upward, the staircase winding in a steep spiral. Only an open grilled half-window at each spiral dispersed the dimness of the stairs. At the fifth door, on which a brass marker reading "Tamburri" was affixed, they paused, all of them breathing heavily. Comrade Giorgio looked down at Piero's goons, panting a half-dozen steps below, with an ironic sneer.

"*Compagni,* you ride in automobiles too much. Two more flights and you would have run out of fuel."

Piero's deputy said in a low voice of reproach,

"Don't worry about them. They do their work well. Ask Franco Furbo in a week's time."

Giorgio grunted, and pushed his thumb against the buzzer. After three long rings, there was a sound of movement behind the door and it finally opened a crack. A young man's face, almost pretty in its dark soft lines, appeared in the doorway, his liquid eyes narrowed with suspicion until they identified Comrade Giorgio; he immediately flung the door open.

"Welcome, comrades!" he greeted them in a reedy, lilting voice. "Comrade Spartaco has been expecting you for the past hour. Comrade Piero is already with him. Enter!"

Giorgio stepped quickly past him into a brightly illuminated corridor at the other end of which a tiny green-filled terrace could be seen, on which the sun played brightly. In contrast with the animated poverty of the streets below, the apartment was luxurious and had obviously been refurbished in excellent if rather precious taste: a genuine Venetian lantern slanted at an angle out of the wall, its concealed bulb illuminating the foyer; the corridor was paved with gleaming red ceramic tiles into which an intricate majolica design had been worked. Cheerful Dufy prints and framed water colors livened the windowless entrance hall and they stood on a modern handwoven rug of red and gold. It was apparent that Il Duro had had nothing to do with its furnishing. Other, more sensitive souls had prevailed.

"The Party's heroes live well," Giorgio commented to the nervously smiling youth after he had briefly examined the room. "And who are you?"

"I am Giordano Glorioso, private secretary to Comrade Spartaco," he answered, batting eyes with the longest lashes Giorgio had ever seen, responding boldly and unapologetically to Giorgio's hard stare. Piero's men at the door stood on the threshold looking at Giordano with unspeakable loathing.

"*Piacere,* Comrade Giordano. And now, please take me to Comrade Spartaco. My companions will wait here for me."

"Follow me, Comrade Secretary."

He moved away, his slim retreating figure swaying like a girl's, his brown leather loafers clicking almost musically as he made his way to a heavy door halfway to the terrace end.

"*Mamma mia,*" growled one of Piero's men. "*Che culo!*

I haven't seen anything better even on the Via Veneto."

"*Pazienza*," shrugged the other. "Il Duro has earned the right to a couple of little weaknesses." Giorgio turned in their direction and their chatter quickly died.

Giordano beckoned coyly from the door he had opened and as Giorgio strode toward him, a voice like a rasp called out, "Give the delegation some beer, Giordano, and be careful not to sit on their knees." This was followed by a hoarse, unpleasant laugh. Head tossed back with annoyance, Giordano stalked swiftly past him as Giorgio reached the threshold of the room. Giorgio grunted: *this* room, at least, was Il Duro's.

It was a small chamber, long and narrow, with three grimy windows facing other grimy windows in the adjacent building not ten feet away across the alley. Once a cozy study with built-in bookshelves and mahogany paneling and a large fireplace at one end, it bore signs of disinterest and decay. The shelves were bare, the paneling untended and the fireplace was boarded up. Mementoes of the Resistenza covered the dark walls: a trio of German coal-scuttle helmets forming a neat triangle, a captured flag of the Fascist Republic of Saló, and the usual photographs and drawings of partisan faces, known and unknown. Above the dead fireplace hung only one object: a large colored photograph of Stalin.

No signs of comfort or relaxation were present; no easy chairs or divans. A square conference-type table filled the near end of the room, surrounded by six massive chairs. Comrade Spartaco sat at the table's head. Behind him, a narrow rectangular frame backed in velvet hung from the wall, onto which a variety of medals had been fastened. Giorgio immediately recognized the Resistance decorations plus two Soviet ones and one from the Spanish Republic. Next to Comrade Spartaco sat Piero. Before them the table was covered with travel documents including an Italian passport, airline schedules and a pile of tourist material including a large illustrated brochure entitled "Bella Praga."

Comrade Spartaco rose slowly, almost insolently, as Giorgio walked up to him. They shook hands perfunctorily and Spartaco, with a bitter smile, indicated a chair next to him.

"It is an extremely great privilege to have the Organization Secretary of the Party, as well as the chief of our *Servizio Ordine*, together under my roof; a rare honor." His voice crackled with irony. "I had begun to think that the Party leadership no longer sought me out. As usual, I leap to serve."

Giorgio looked meaningfully at his lieutenant.

"We have been discussing the trip to Czechoslovakia," Piero assured him. "Your telephone call confirming the Secretariat's decision has been relayed to Comrade Tamburri and we were now simply discussing the mechanics of our travel: departure times, baggage, forwarding of heavy personal effects through our comrades in the Czech Embassy, et cetera."

Giorgio lowered himself into the chair at Spartaco's left and extracted a *papiros* from the pack in his jacket pocket. He lit it and leaned back. Spartaco eyed him silently and Piero, with an instinctive thrill of excitement, observed the Party's two great antagonistic forces personified before his eyes. He knew that he had instinctively picked the winner and so he turned to Spartaco Tamburri as a visitor at a zoo stares at an especially vicious tiger rendered harmless by the thick bars of his cage."

"So, my dear Party comrade of almost two decades, you are sending me away, out of Italy," Spartaco finally said to Giorgio, ignoring the presence of the little man on his right. "The tables are turned, and it is you who are on top."

"And it was *you* who ordered those two hapless ones to steal the explosives at Ardea," Giorgio replied. "All we had asked was that you assign them a Party task which would test their reliability. But no, you had to give them an assignment which inevitably landed you and them in the hands of the authorities."

"I needed those explosives," Spartaco growled unrepentantly. "You yourself will recall your interest in mounting a provocation which would bring sympathy for the Party and popular resentment against the neo-Fascists. A few harmless explosions in front of carefully selected Party offices or buildings, with dynamite traceable to the Italian military, would have been effective. Only the blundering of those two imbeciles completely ruined the play. Why didn't you tell me that Furbo was a police agent?"

A cold spark ignited in his eyes.

"Had I but suspected it, he would have died."

"We had only the most vague suspicion of him, from one of Piero's men," Giorgio retorted unruffled. "I told Piero to tell no one, not even Comrade Togliatti, until we were certain. Now, thanks to your 'brilliant' assignment, we are not only certain of his police role but we are in danger of stumbling into a first-class *pasticcio* in which the Party is suddenly revealed to be in the bomb-stealing business."

"What makes you think that my departure is going to solve your problem of the Party's damned image?" Spartaco demanded.

"How do you think I got you and Pasquale out of police hands! We have assurances, from the proper levels of the government that if you depart, this dynamite-stealing episode will be buried. We'll take care of Franco Furbo, rest assured. As for young Seddu, now in jail, he will probably be given a light sentence and released. We, of course, are publicly expelling him from the Party to wash our hands of any complicity or support of his act. Your going will clear the air completely."

Spartaco's hands rested on the table, bunched into scarred and battered fists.

"And if I don't go?"

"Comrade, the Party has spoken. You have no choice."

The eyes of the two men again locked in a silent tug of war broken only by Piero's hesitant cough.

"Perhaps Comrade Spartaco would like to finish his packing. We have but two or three hours before we drive to the airport."

Comrade Spartaco turned on him.

"Suppose, you officious little bastard, you get the hell out of here. I have something I want to discuss personally with your master."

Piero's lean cheeks darkened under the sting of the words and he shot a bitter, inquiring glance at Giorgio. The latter, with a slight movement of his head, ordered him to leave.

"My men and I will remain with you until the packing is completed, Comrade Tamburri," Piero announced as he stood to leave. "And *I* remain with you all the way to Prague." His voice clearly revealed that he did not intend to make either the departure or the long air trip a jolly one, and he slammed the heavy door behind him.

"Talking like that to a devoted Party functionary will avail you nothing, my dear Spartaco," Giorgio commented mildly. "You are hardly in a position to be your usual loving self."

"He's *your* ass-kissing lackey, not mine," Spartaco spat.

"All right, I have exactly ten minutes. What do you want to say to me in private?"

"Simply this," Spartaco began. "I know what is going on here, make no mistake of that. The explosives business is only a blind for you and your gang. My thirty-three years of struggle and sacrifice for the Party are being discarded. You're treating me like one of those village *matti*, to be shamed and hidden from sight because I am a revolutionary, a man who lives by the Marxist doctrine that we in Italy can arrive at power only as the Bolsheviks in Russia did: by force."

"You are being 'discarded' as you put it, because you *are* insane. If I may use an ugly word, Spartaco, you are a deviationist of the Right. It speaks well for the progress we have made as a Party that you can be called such and yet continue to stay alive and within the Party. You can recall the fate of deviationists in Russia, let us say, up to 1953?"

Knotted veins, purple and throbbing, stood out on Spartaco's temples and he worked his double fists in a silent agony of repression but Giorgio pretended not to notice.

"It is you, my good old comrade of Spain and Moscow and the postwar struggle here in Italy," Giorgio said in his soft mellifluous Neapolitan, "who fit precisely the category of 'dried-up dogmatism,' a group which fears changes and new things, who reject every measure for Party renewal. You are, in a word, a conservative, not a revolutionary. A political party which aspires to Marxism and must direct a vast movement among the masses cannot reduce itself to sterile slogans and formulas of the past. There on your wall, in your office, is the symbol of your sterility: Stalin. You know damned well that the socialist movement has reappraised him completely in the past year. You know that Stalin did not understand the socialist legality and thought he could resolve all problems by establishing a regime of suspicion, personality cult, and unjust repression. Well, old comrade, those of us who survived are not going to permit its return. And since you represent *him*"—and he pointed to the inscrutable Stalin —"you must go!"

Suddenly Spartaco was a weary old man whose unfolding fists again became wrinkled, mottled old hands and under the small tough jaw the soft stringy wattles sagged.

"Must it be so far? I am sixty years of age and, except for the past few years in Rome, I have never really had a home. If I promise to keep my mouth shut, could I not stay? Here I have . . ."

"Here you have your Giordano and the other little perverts, eh?" Giorgio tore at him mercilessly. "Well, no doubt our Czech comrades can supply you with another little fairy or two. No, Spartaco, you must go." His voice, at the first indication of Spartaco's crumbling resistance, grew colder and more contemptuous. Spartaco covered his eyes for a moment with his hands.

"Come now, Il Duro, the Hard Guy, getting soft? How do you think *I* felt eighteen years ago in Moscow when the Special Court sent me to a forced labor camp to what might easily have been my death? *You* testified, remember, before that court that my activities in Barcelona in '36 had been clearly deviationist and filled with ideological errors, no? That I had been in cahoots with class enemies and traitors, no? Did I cry then, Spartaco? Did I plead for mercy?"

"All right," Spartaco said finally, and his voice indicated that he had taken a new grip on himself. "I'll go. The Party is my life and has been since 1923. I walked by Gramsci's side, I have been kicked, mauled, tortured in Fascist prisons for it." He whirled and stabbed a finger at the medals arrayed in a glittering row on the red velvet cloth. "Look at those! They cost me a lifetime of blood and agony, beatings, chains, filth, pain!"

Comrade Giorgio puffed the *papiros* between thumb and forefinger. He will not give up, he thought. He is almost broken, but he will never change, or surrender.

Giorgio spoke in the mild despair of a saddened parent. "Spartaco, you have been warned a half-dozen times in the past year to shut up and stop talking blood and thunder about storming the Presidential Palace, breaching the walls of the Vatican, and so on. Each time we warned you, first by the section secretary, then by others up the rungs of the Party mechanism, you grudgingly agreed to be silent but a month later you were at it again. We are embarked on an era of peaceful coexistence with the bourgeois world for the time being. The tactics have changed if the aims have not. Do you understand that?"

Spartaco slammed his fist on the oak table surface and rose half out of his chair with the violence of his gesture.

"No, *porca miseria*, I don't understand that! Are we going to sit here like a bunch of dewy-eyed social democrats and permit the Celere to beat out our brains in the piazza because some idiot says: Coexist? I say no, damn it, no!"

"I say, yes, damn it, yes!" Giorgio's tone was dulcet as he folded his hands below his crossed knees. "That's exactly how we're going to do it here. That's how socialism will come to Italy. Then and only then will we move to climinate our enemies and to complete our fight to achieve socialism."

Comrade Spartaco seemed to swell under his sweater and jacket.

"That isn't how socialism came to Russia, or Spain, or China!" he shouted. "There you fought for it with gun in hand!"

"You never listen," Giorgio told him wagging his head. "You haven't got it through that brutal head of yours that each Party has its own way. You have heard our great Comrade Togliatti talk and write of polycentrism a dozen times and still you shout your Stalinist claptrap. We will reach Communism in Italy by our own methods, not those of the Russians and the Chinese, and here our methods are peaceful and parliamentary. By exploiting the very weaknesses and disarray of our opponents, we will conquer them. We are the worm in the apple, Spartaco, and we shall consume the apple from the inside."

A blade of iron edged his soft southern speech.

"Now sit down!" Giorgio commanded. "Before I go, I want to ask you about one small point: what about Belinoro?"

Spartaco cocked his head as if the name had been read off an Assyrian tablet.

"Eh, Belinoro? What about Belinoro?"

"The ambush of Tonio Passaglia and his partisan group in the Romagna early in 1944. Do you know that *that* stupid affair has also been exposed? And now it hangs over the Party's head like a sword of Damocles."

Spartaco's eyes were shrewd with recollection.

"The Party's orders were clear, and I gave a full account of it to the inspector sent out by Comrade Longo from Milano. The Passaglia band had organized an entire province, using vicious clerico-monarchist propaganda to attract partisan recruits. The Americans were in there with them, organizing them to become ever stronger. Despite my urgent appeals to them to join us in a united resistance and to share what they had with us, starving and weak as we were in arms and supplies after that brutal winter in the mountains, they spurned us. They even encouraged the country folk to drive us off. If this had been permitted to continue, we would have lost all of Romagna to these reactionaries, these enemies of the people. So we made our hard choice: by eliminating the Passaglia leadership, we succeeded in taking over the area." He pointed a stubby finger at Giorgio. "And we dominate it to this very day," he finished meaningfully.

Giorgio rose and stretched his arms in a mighty yawn.

Then, hands on waist, he spoke to Spartaco as a drill sergeant speaks to brand-new recruits.

"The Party, like the Church, has many supporters who serve each in his special way. You, Spartaco, are a Party butcher. In fact, you worked in a butcher shop as a lad, I am told, and a butcher you have remained. We needed you, Spartaco. You have suffered much and you have survived much and today you are a legend, Il Duro. But, comrade, that is all over and finished and you are finished. This business of the dynamite brings it to a head. But even had it not occurred, we are now faced with a terrible exposure: the daughter of Tonio Passaglia, who has been a good Party comrade for the past ten years, now knows that it was you and your Gappisti who did the killing."

Giorgio's blunt fingers instinctively touched his burnt cheek and chin and he looked down at his suit lapels with irritation that Guglielmo's cleaning experts had been unable to do much to the coffee stains blotched there.

"She is still a comrade," Spartaco growled. "She must understand why . . ."

"She tore up her Party card in pieces before my eyes and left. By this time, she is probably telling her story to one of those *stronzi* on *Momento-Sera* or *Giornale d'Italia*."

Spartaco's tough old face reflected no twinges of remorse.

"The government, the courts, they can do nothing to me. All political offenses from that period have long since been covered by amnesties."

"You forget the clamor that the reactionary press, the weeklies such as *L'Europeo* or *Settimana-Incom* or that disgusting *L'Espresso* would raise: Patriots killing other patriots; *bella cosa*, eh?"

"The Party has survived calumnies and attacks by the reactionary press before," Spartaco retorted smugly.

"And the American major, who was killed with the Passaglias? A fine *fesseria* to publicize now. Spartaco, it's one thing for Italian to kill Italian, sadly enough, but for an Italian to kill an officer of the Allies during the war? They could crucify us in print!"

"I told the Party inspector at the time and I'll tell you again. It was *not* our intention to kill the American major. I specifically sent Peppino Deruta to deliver a veiled warning to the Americans not to go out on that mission with the Passaglia demolition group. The young American, the lieutenant, didn't go and he survives. That stubborn *cretino* of a major, however, insisted on accompanying the Passaglias.

217

We were watching the lieutenant who was the leader on all of the raids, and when he did not depart, we knew he had received our warning. Only in the dark after the ambush did we discover the body of the major. It was a complete accident, I tell you."

"Try telling that to the American Embassy or to the bourgeois periodicals," Giorgio taunted, standing over him, hands still on hips. Spartaco touched the sore, puffed place just beside his nose where Tom Linden's punch had caught him the night before, shrugged.

"As for the American Embassy, who gives a damn?" He turned his small suspicious eyes on Giorgio. "Who told the Passaglia woman about Belinoro? It can't have been Peppino Deruta: he would be the last one to tell her, since he was part of the ambush himself, under my direct orders. Besides, he's discredited as a Fascist spy and she wouldn't believe him anyway. The other comrades involved? Hmm, they're either dead or migrated or . . . "

". . . or mad," Giorgio finished heavily. "And Peppino is dead also. But he gave enough information on his deathbed to arouse her suspicions. The trail has apparently led straight to you. And now she knows."

Spartaco clapped his hands in a spasm of memory, as a traveler remembers he forgot to lock the house door before departing.

"Damn! Nando Martinuzzi! I might have known someone would find him in that asylum and listen to his babblings!"

"Peppino Deruta, that craven coward!" he spat. "He cried like a baby after the ambush. Then he went into convulsive shakes, he and Martinuzzi together. I should have polished them both off then and there. They were no use to anyone after that."

"Apropos, I became very interested in this Peppino Deruta," Giorgio said in cold stiff tones. "He was expelled from the Party as a Fascist spy, eh? But I had records checked before I came here. It sounded very strange, very strange indeed."

He showed even white teeth in a mirthless smile and laid one finger beside his great nose in a Latin gesture of no-one-catches-me-napping.

"You see, my dear old comrade, I recalled that if you could testify in all sincerity in Russia two decades ago that *I* was a right-wing deviationist, you might also find unusual 'evidence' incriminating Peppino."

Spartaco folded his heavy wrinkled hands together and

hunched over the table, studying the picture book of Prague and the travel literature scattered before him.

"You don't look happy to hear about my research, dear Spartaco. You don't want me to remind you, perhaps, that this Peppino was assigned by the Party to penetrate the ranks of the Fascists and Gestapo, ostensibly as a collaborator, under the name Pietro de Franchi. Is that not so? And did not Comrade Longo himself sign a citation referring to Peppino's 'extremely dangerous and delicate work, filled with peril and personal danger.' Strangely enough, this document was never presented to the Disciplinary Commission when you instigated his dismissal on charges of Fascist collaboration. In a word, you torpedoed him when you had the right opportunity, correct?"

Spartaco said nothing, and stonily stared ahead of him. Giorgio tramped heavily behind him in an accusing prosecutor manner.

"And so, you blundered again. Instead of eliminating Peppino and Nando, which should have been a logical consequence of your stupid ambush, you permitted one to go off to a madhouse and shout the deed to the skies, and you sought to discredit the other, certain that he would be ignored even if he chose to speak out. You didn't like his reminding you what you had done, eh? The Hard One might be a little too hard even for the Communist Party to take, isn't that it?"

Giorgio had reached a point where he faced Spartaco from the other end of the long table. He flung an accusing finger at the hunched, seated figure.

"Result? Peppino hands over to the Passaglia woman the pistol holster of the dead American major, her suspicions are awakened, she hunts down Nando Martinuzzi, she learns all. Bravo, Spartaco, well done!"

He had finished and said in a normal tone,

"It's over. It is our firm determination that this mess will never emerge."

"When can I return?" Spartaco asked, small gray eyes without hope.

"When our Central Committee so informs you," Giorgio answered coldly.

A sharp rap on the door preceded Piero who marched in and announced, "The comrades with the moving van are here. Excuse, but we must get on with the job immediately."

"We are finished with our little chat," Giorgio assured him. He moved toward Spartaco, who rose like a rumpled bear. Piero looked at them both; standing together they were curiously similar in size, build, and features. And even more astonishing was the identical stamp on both of them: the ruthless seal of duress and years of Party struggle.

"*Arrivederci*, Spartaco," Giorgio said, extending his hand for a last shake.

"*Arrivederci* can last a long time, Comrade Secretary," Spartaco rasped, refusing the extended hand. He held up instead a proletarian clenched fist.

"*Salud y arriba la revoluçion.*"

"We lost the revolution in Spain," Giorgio reminded him.

"We lost it here as well," Spartaco returned.

Giorgio, nettled, stared at the grizzled head close to his. "We may have lost it your way, but we will win it by ours."

"Never!" shouted Spartaco.

Giorgio walked to the threshold of the study, his bulk almost filling the passageway.

"'*M beh*, leave it to us," he said.

He walked with a near strut of confidence down the bright ceramic corridor pavement and out the already opened door, never once looking back on his field of victory.

chapter twenty-three

IN THE TWO years and more since The Maria, completely by chance, had come grieving from the household of a dead cardinal to become his housekeeper, Tom Linden had learned infinitely less about this stoic matriarch than she had learned about him. At first, Tom had not even cared to remember her last name. He had then been under a six-month contract to teach a group of field-grade Italian army officers sufficient spoken English to permit them to go to the United States as students and eventual instructors in the esoteric lore of medium tanks, recoilless rifles, and tactical rocketry. He also drilled them in phrases specifically requested by the class, which entailed memorizing English words for the parts of the female body, conventional phrases for ritual bargaining over the price of a woman's attentions, and the names, singular and plural, for the most prized items which could be purchased at stateside PXs and stores. An artillery major from Umbria, with whom Tom had hit it off quite well, had come to Tom's shabby penthouse and had been appalled at the maidless squalor in which Tom lived. He mentioned that his batman, a Sardinian, was inquiring whether any of the wives of Italian officers needed a house servant, a veritable whale among servants, who only then had lost her employer, a cardinal, no less, by reason of death, and sought work.

Tom, indifferent and half in jest, agreed to interview the jobseeker, and the following day, the chunky, erect form, dressed in black from head to toe, appeared at the door of the rooftop flat along the Tiber. When she stepped in, she looked penetratingly around her and he was almost certain that she was prepared to swing around and depart, especially since there had been a bang-up party the night before. But something about the place must have challenged her, after the rich, precise order and calm piety of the cardinal's residence in which she was but one of eight servants, for after she had brutally commented in a baritone growl on the state of the apartment and on the sort of people who could exist in such filth, and he had nodded in complete agreement with her (much to her astonishment), she grimly announced that she would stay for two weeks to straighten things out. The two weeks had never ended.

An indefinable bond, strengthened in unpredictable ways, had given Tom some superficial insight into the woman and her real life. He saw her clean his Augean stable and prop the shabbily furnished household on its shaky feet, including her primitive but effective treatment of the refrigerator. She carefully pruned the jungle growth which threatened to proliferate over the entire terrace. He also knew that she went to pray once a day at the nearby Saint Eugenio's and that she was on familiar, if severely critical, terms with all of the parish priests there. He had accompanied her to the open market once or twice, always at a discreet distance at her specific request (it was flatly forbidden that the *padrone di casa* ever went with the house servant on purchase of the household comestibles and supplies), and he had been alternatingly appalled and tickled at the swath she cut through the raucous hawkers and the

221

servility shown her by the greens and meats merchants who threw little extra offerings of fruit or cabbage in the mesh shopping sack. He came to know that she was a personality of immense status among the Sards in Rome, that her contacts somehow extended into the shadowy upper branches of the government bureaucracy, the police, the religious hierarchy; yes, even the Black Aristocracy. The telephone in the apartment was primarily a communications means for her vast group of subjects rather than for Tom and his occasional calls.

He also learned in time that the great apparent truculence and harshly vindictive speech and manner shielded a heart so soft that it virtually required armor to protect it. He closed his eyes to the numbers of small dark people who entered, and often stayed for days, in The Maria's little room, eating from Tom's larder, if sparingly. He knew of the regal arbitration sessions over which she presided at least once weekly near the Stazione Termini, that she was a veritable female Solomon to a small world of servants, flea market salesmen, and low-rung government employees who flocked together for companionship and solidarity against the *porchi Romani* who were their masters and their antagonists.

These things he knew, and he knew about the erring Paolo, for whom The Maria had a love that was almost frightening in its tacit intensity. Otherwise, little else, except that she was exceptionally thrifty with her money and his, that she rarely had a sick day in the months she had been with him, and that she prayed in her room before an enormous crucifix in addition to her daily appearance at Saint Eugenio's. For The Maria, religion was more than a need; it was a complete way of life, as essential as bread and water. He realized this when he carelessly brought home a battered *prie-dieu* he had purchased almost as a gag at the Porta Portuese thieves' market and had presented it to her as a gift. For a moment, he feared that The Maria would kiss his hand, but she did not although she did take his hand in both of her hard calloused ones and held it for a long moment as one would cradle an egg.

Soon after her arrival, Tom brought home one of his string of steamily dispositioned females, most of whom were the married but bored variety with absent or indifferent mates and who needed periodic servicing as does any vessel or vehicle. The woman had waggled out of his flat late the following morning before the starkly horrified eyes of The Maria. But she said not one word and had gone about her chores as usual. A week later, there was another over-night guest, a tall Scandinavian female with a distressing laugh. Again, no reaction by The Maria, not a word, although she had gone straight to her room and Tom heard her pray-ing, her voice uncommonly loud in reproach to him and to God for permitting him to live such a life. She never mentioned the visitations or his fitful bouts of drinking, just as *he* never mentioned the timid dark women and children she housed in the apartment without his permission.

Early in her employment, after he had brought home the *prie-dieu*, he told her at breakfast that her polite form of address toward him was a conversational burden to him; either she would use the familiar *tu* to him as he did to her, or she was fired. After a few hesitant departures from the *lei* accompanied by what was almost a scandalized smile, she used the *tu* with vigor and it was one of the reasons that her two weeks of "temporary" employment had gone on and on.

The only real antagonism was a largely silent, unequal struggle between her and the two Siamese. The cats came with the apartment, so ruled the rather flighty female land-lord, as part of the deal, and would have to remain there to be fed and looked after by the tenant. The Maria had found them there entrenched when she arrived, and they immedi-ately resented her alien and briskly tidy ways. They were, The Maria told Tom and her friends, incarnations of evil pagan spirits and their malevolence was clearly that of the devil; you could see it in their eyes and their arrogant manner. But she fed them, she periodically scrubbed their corner of the kitchen with its old blanket and eating dishes, and apart from an occasional malediction, largely left them alone. They, in turn, while trying to trip her up by running through her legs or delighting to frighten her by pouncing out of the overhead vines through the laundry lines, acknowledged the truce; most of their arguments, howling banjo-like growls and wails, were with each other. The Conte, Tom said, had perhaps something to howl about since the Contessa had been spayed.

Thus, the oddly assorted quartet, two humans and two Siamese, had lived under the same roof more or less in equilibrium with each other, and not until yesterday had this harmony been shattered and then fragmented like a trampled mirror. Yesterday, she had as much as told her master he was a coward and had returned, first to the Church of Saint Eugenio, where she had wept and prayed for at least an hour on her knees, and then back to her room where she had done the same at her *prie-dieu* to the utter bewilderment of her nephew to whom she explained nothing. Then, when her beloved Paolo had proceeded on his insane and doomed business of delivering the suitcases of dynamite at midnight, instead of stopping him this coward of an American had deliberately shared the doomed errand and had been flung into the Questura for his trouble.

She could not recall a more terrible night in her adult life, not even those during the nightmarish months of wartime German occupation. Those times at least had not affected her directly save for the paucity of food and the general fear, the *paura*, of the Germans and their lackeys. Now, the two persons she cared for most in the world were missing, swallowed up in the night. She guessed what had happened, but she had called no one. She simply sat on her favorite canvas chair by the telephone and, with her rosary clutched in her hands, she stared at the mottled terrazzo floor and recited the fourteen prayers again and again, interlacing the recitation with purely personal passionate appeals to God and to the Virgin to watch over her hapless Paolo and the Dottore. The Siamese, usually capable of sitting directly in front of her and staring contemptuously at her, had retreated to their corner of the kitchen where she could see their eyes gleaming every now and again in the darkness.

Then, as the sky paled and the familiar forms of the apartment emerged from the darkness, she heard the tired slow clump of Tom's feet on the stairs, and she rushed to greet him. In half-sentences he spoke of his arrest with the American diplomat and her Paolo. As he unbuttoned his shirt, his fatigue-sunken eyes turned on her and he said, using the formal "you" she herself had reinstated after yesterday afternoon, "I have never asked any unusual favors of you, Maria, but I do so now." His voice was taut and bitter, and she wondered what it was that a house servant, even one such as she, could or would do for a foreign master. Without waiting for her assent, he said, "I want you to find out for me where the Communist hero, Spartaco Tamburri, also known as Il Duro, lives. I want you, through your Sardinian friends, to find him and watch him so that I may know precisely where to go and speak with him when I awaken."

He peeled off his trousers before her eyes, an act of intimacy she had never experienced with him before, and he sank to a sitting position at the edge of his low bed, lad in nothing more than his shorts. His smooth brown ody curved in a half-circle as he painstakingly untied his 1oes.

"I thought you said he was arrested with you," she asked, nd he looked up with an involuntary grin when he realized he had returned to addressing him in the old familiar *tu*. Ie was apparently forgiven.

"The police let him go, also," he said. "Two vehicles ame to fetch him at the Questura a few minutes after they eleased me and he rode home, where he now soundly leeps." His mouth tightened with bitterness. "Long live he Questura! Tamburri is released and Paolo Seddu stays in ail."

He rolled sideways onto the bed and his dark eyes looked up out of their corners at her standing massively in the grayness of the early morning. "Tamburri is not listed in the telephone book. Find him for me, Maria," he said, voice barely audible. "Find him for my sake and for Paolo's— and for an American named Dixon." In seconds he was sound asleep. She picked up and bundled his shirt and undershirt for washing, folded his trousers, and pulled a sheet and a blanket over his curled body. Then she bent over him and passed a hand along the line of his stubbled jaw so lightly that he did not even stir.

As the bright sun rose on yet another magnificent spring day in Rome, she began the task her master had asked of her.

For The Maria Seddu the job of locating Tamburri and keeping close track of his moments was simply a matter of marshaling her immense store of people, of tapping her social capital for some of the long accumulated interest due her. The methodical precision with which she went about her task would have wrung admiration from the questor himself. Sleepless as she was, she first made herself two cups of scalding black espresso and then at seven A.M. she lowered herself into the canvas chair. Nine calls and forty-five minutes later, she had located the apartment of Spartaco Tamburri in the Trastevere quarter. Four calls after that she knew a good deal about this apartment, including details on the *finocchio* named Giordano Glorioso who was truly a wife to Spartaco in every sense of the word, including the cooking, furnishings, and shrill nocturnal domestic spats. Once Spartaco's apartment had been located, other telephone calls brought a perambulating Sardinian plastic-brush salesman into the area of the alley where

Spartaco's apartment house was located. Her eyes and ears were now in place.

The Maria noiselessly scrubbed her kitchen into utter cleanliness, carefully mopped the hallway, her own room and the bathroom when another burr of the telephone (wrapped in a heavy towel to prevent its disturbing Tom) reached her ears. The plastic-brush salesman swiftly informed her in Sardinian that furniture and heavy luggage was being removed from the apartment of the Communist chief, that a Red *pezzogrosso* with an escort had arrived to confer with Spartaco, had remained half an hour, and had just departed, leaving one or two of his men behind him. The Maria merely grunted at his rambling report, told him to remain at his post until a young Sard named Tullio, with a cast in one eye, showed up to relieve him.

As the morning gave way into a brilliant cloudless noon, the telephone calls arrived, sometimes in clusters of two or three. Nothing that moved in or out of Spartaco's building escaped notice. And when Spartaco Tamburri walked out of the Trastevere alley with his escort, The Maria was ready: a city bus line conductor from her own province of Nuoro, on his day off, sat on a snorting little Lambretta. On his jump seat sat a young Sard barber for whom The Maria had found employment at one of the best shops in the city's center and who willingly was sacrificing his free hours to the task assigned. They threaded their way through the crowded streets, with Spartaco and his two walking companions rarely out of their sight for more than a few seconds. Every half-hour, following The Maria's command, they telephoned her from a public phone.

In midafternoon, The Maria shuffled into Tom's room and with great deliberation shook him into wakefulness. As he half sat up, shaking the haze of sleep from his eyes, she lowered the inevitable tray containing a hot double espresso with sugar and a sweet roll.

"If you desire to speak to Spartaco Tamburri," she announced, "you will have to move swiftly. He is now at an airlines office near the Via Veneto and will depart within an hour for the airfield. He is leaving Italy."

He gulped the coffee and the roll, ran one hand across his now heavy beard, and asked her, "Can you call a taxi to be ready below in ten minutes?"

"One already waits below," she told him. "A hot bath is ready. Your razor is ready, and fresh clothing is prepared in the bathroom."

226

He sprang from the bed and as he strode past her, he reached for her face and planted a solid kiss on the dark cheek.

"I shall find you another cardinal," he flung at her as he left the room. "You are too good for anything less."

Ten minutes later he stood in the doorway to the flat, shaven and bathed, wearing neat and pressed summer slacks and jacket and a crisp open white sports shirt. She nodded approvingly: even in the worn old clothes, he looked and walked like a *gran signore*. And in one pocket of the jacket she had placed two 500 lire notes. She wondered what it was that made him so suddenly buoyant. Before, when he had displayed such sparkle, it had been the *viski* that had done it. Now, he was cold sober and the encounter he sought was hardly a pleasant one. The Maria looked at her master more closely and she did not like what she sensed.

"What do you intend to say to this Communist, Dottore?" she asked him as he rummaged briefly in one of the drawers of the paper-crammed desk.

"Oh, I want to talk about old times," Tom said smoothly. "I want him to talk to me about the death of some friends of mine during the war." He waved at the tightly packed shelves containing the Resistance books and periodicals. "Il Duro knows many things," he added brightly.

"And what is that which you slip under your belt?" The Maria demanded.

Tom turned and the smile was still frozen to his face but his eyes glittered with something else.

"You mean this?" and he pulled a round heavy knife pointed like an ice pick, from its sheath. "This, Maria, is what they called a commando knife. I have had it since the war. With this knife one kills sentries silently, from behind."

He replaced it in its scabbard, and looked straight into the jet eyes of his servant. She knew the look: to a Sardinian it needed no further explanation.

"Why do you want to do this . . . thing now, Dottore?" she asked him in a voice as soothing as it was deep.

"Because, Zia, the law will not kill him. He is free of all punishment, by amnesties. Those who killed during the war now have been legally pardoned of all of their killings. But I am not the law. I am Thomas Linden, a foreigner, who came to Italy in the war. This man killed my commander and he killed my friends who trusted me and followed me. There is no one left to avenge my friends. So I must do it."

He patted her once on the arm as he walked by her.

"You and your people understand vendetta, no?" he flung at her as he opened the door. He glanced at his wrist watch and at the address she had given him.

"I must hurry or I will lose my opportunity." His smile at her was now warm and sincere. "Thanks for the thousand lire, Maria," he said. "You are an extraordinary woman." He paused before descending the stairs. "I am in your debt for all time, for helping me this day."

She closed the door swiftly when his swift descending footsteps no longer could be heard, and she walked in her even shuffle to the telephone. She stared down at it, loathing it, hating to reach for it. The Siamese sat on the polished stone floor and something in their unwinking glance and twitching truncated tails reminded her.

"Aha, so you have not yet been fed this day, you useless brutes!" she told them bitterly. "Well, you will have to wait another five minutes, miserable ones!"

She searched her prodigious memory for a moment and slowly dialed the desired number, standing now instead of hunching herself in her chair by the phone. To the response, she asked, "Questura? Brigadiere Anselmi? Swiftly, please; it is most important."

When the familiar soft-spoken voice of the policeman came over the wire, she cut off his greetings.

"Dear Brigadier, there is no time to lose. Tell your superiors immediately that my master, the American Dottore Linden, has just left his apartment. He goes now to kill the Communist Spartaco Tamburri with his own hand."

Ignoring the startled babble at the other end, she continued,

"Listen carefully and don't interrupt. I now give you all the details I have."

She lifted up her eyes and asked forgiveness for betraying her master in this manner. In her island village, informing the police of anything would in itself have sealed her fate. And vendetta was a sacred affair. But, after all, *she* had found Spartaco and she had seen that he was closely watched. He was a stranger to her. She did not want his blood on her hands and those of Dottore Tommaso.

And so, with the excited voice of the brigadier at police headquarters importuning her for precise facts, she most reluctantly, told him of Tom's projected act of vengeance and how it must be thwarted.

chapter twenty-four

THE FAT LITTLE travel agency clerk leaned over the counter and smiled an ingratiating and conspiratorial smile.

"The limousine to Ciampino for yourself and Comrade Tamburri will be here in about thirty minutes," he murmured into Piero's ear less than a foot away. "I suggest you take a leisurely caffè and return here then. Baggage is already at the airport."

Piero nodded curtly and turned to Spartaco whose appearance was completely altered with a slouch hat and heavy black sun glasses. He now looked like a little Neapolitan *Camorra* chief making his collection rounds, complete with brief case of soft brown rubbed leather, and he stood, passively as one waits for a long overdue streetcar.

"Half an hour. What would you like to do?" Piero asked in correct deference. Spartaco had not said a single word to him since their departure from the Trastevere apartment an hour ago after announcing abruptly that he wanted to walk all the way across the teeming city to the Via Bissolati airlines offices. He had stumped along, stopping every now and again to take in a view of a piazza, a flower stand, a dilapidated Renaissance palace, an ancient ruin sticking up like a half-buried bone in the middle of nowhere and anywhere. Piero, sensing the man's melancholy, trudged along several paces behind, with one of his men.

Once Piero's man had nudged him and furtively pointed out that they were being followed. As a matter of fact, a small police van, with four *questurini* bunched inside, quite openly chugged along behind them, the driver cursing their slow meandering progress. Piero had merely nodded his awareness and had turned down the corners of his mouth and stuck out his chin in a gesture. They were there to make sure Spartaco departed and he, Piero, was there to ensure the very same thing.

Spartaco now looked at Piero as though he had encountered a stranger.

"Eh? Half an hour wait?" The eyes, now inscrutable behind the dark lens, seemed to look away from him and finally,

"*M beh*, let's take a stroll to the Veneto for a caffè."

The Roman sun, after the downpour of the night before, was making ample amends, and the smell of a fast greening spring cut through the diesel fumes of the Via Veneto area like a siren wind, slowing the gait of those on foot to a stroll, pulling the arms of lovers around each other, bringing out a hundred thousand cats to doze in its warm allure.

Spartaco tramped ahead and Piero and his lieutenant again dropped slightly behind but all three bunched together as they reached the broad sidewalk of the once Palace of the Queen Mother of Italy and now the imposing Embassy of the United States.

"*Roma putana,*" Spartaco said to them in a grating voice as full of wonderment as anger. "Through the sweat of the people, the *cretini* of the House of Savoia built this mausoleum for one of their useless females and the moment we get rid of the Savoias, the American capitalists take it over."

He eyed with distaste the alien flag with its stripes and stars flapping at the flagstaff above a tiny and beautifully groomed green rug of a lawn, the little splashing fountains on each side of the entrance, and the erect marine guard in his tan shirt, white cap, heavy automatic on gun belt, and razor-creased blue dress trousers standing at parade rest beside the great open gate. Then he turned with a crooked grin to Piero.

"I have kept my eye on this place for years," he said. "It will make a much more convenient Party headquarters than the Quirinal, don't you think?"

Piero, glad to have his truculent companion break his silence with a few ironies, responded with a tight little smile.

"Speaking as a Milanese," he said, "I was hoping we would move the Party headquarters to the north and make a Party rest hotel out of this place."

The two men, trailed by Piero's assistant, walked slowly up the Veneto, feeling the warmth of the early afternoon sunshine and looking ahead to the vari-colored umbrellas of the outdoor cafés, gay and saucy up both sides of the street as far as the terminal bulk of the Pincian Gate.

The three blocks of the Via Veneto were landlocked

beaches, sprinkled here and there with fully clothed sun-bathers immobile in their chairs. At this hour of the noonday meal and the beginning of the siesta, the tempo of traffic and animation ebbed as usual. Only the regulars were still slouched in the café chairs; many of them sat from late morning to late evening, with a half-finished caffè nero or *vermut* giving them squatters' rights which the waiters deplored but did little to protest. They hunched behind their black sun glasses, unmoving as lizards yet taking in every bearded hitchhiker, every painted whore now appearing to snare the evening's customer, every American female of indeterminate age in her morning mink stole, every slim-bodied nylon drip-dry American teen-ager, fresh eyes like saucers at the indolence and the wicked aimlessness of it all. The Veneto had only one purpose: to see and be seen, and it fulfilled this in a measure that approached a way of life.

The three men sank into chairs at Doney midway up its great street front, and a waiter rushed to adjust the blue and white umbrella to a proper angle of shade. Spartaco sat down with a grunt and removed his slouch hat placing it carefully on top of the brief case on an empty chair beside him. Without the hat, he blended with the other clients of Doney; a gray heavy old man sitting in the sun.

All three sat almost side by side facing the street and with a view of the twin red rivers of geraniums coursing in their potted beds down either side of the Veneto. They stared in silence at the sluggish stream of vehicles struggling against invisible traffic tides. A trio of young broad-hipped girls, virtually identically clad in rump-clinging slacks, fluffy shapeless sweaters, with streaming straight hair and eyes like blotches of soot, shuffled languidly by in their flat sandals.

"*Roma putana,*" Spartaco repeated. "Look at them! Scarcely women and already parading around like prostitutes. I'll bet not one of them ever did an honest day's work in the office, the factory, the fields. *Vitellone!* For this we fought and bled."

The white-jacketed Doney waiter again materialized and bowed before them.

"The gentlemen desire . . . ?"

Piero looked inquiringly at Spartaco.

"Cognac," Spartaco ordered. "A double cognac."

"A cognac for me also," Piero said. "And another for my friend here," he turned his head to his assistant; they exchanged fleeting glances. So far, so good. It was all going much more smoothly than they had dared to hope. Spartaco,

Comrade Giorgio had warned them, might prove to be a very difficult customer at the wrong moment because he had flatly stated he was leaving only under Party duress. But he had supervised the packing of his effects, the departure of the furniture, the travel briefing, the answering of several questions posed by the comrades from the Czech Embassy, without any tantrums albeit sullenly. The only sticky moment had been his parting from the long-lashed Comrade Glorioso. For that, Piero had tactfully left them alone. If an air of sadness hung over Spartaco, it was completely understandable.

Spartaco raised his well-filled cognac glass to the others.

"Well, my guardian angels, shall we drink to my triumphal departure?" he asked them.

"To our safe trip and to your health," Piero responded prudently. Spartaco merely grunted again and drank heavily.

"They say," Piero's man Gianni spoke up, "that if one sits here on the Veneto long enough, sooner or later he will see everyone he knows pass by."

"There are many I would never care to see again," Spartaco grunted, looking out at the street and the spring-daubed sunshine playing among the tassels and flaps of a hundred umbrellas.

Piero finished his cognac in a gulp and glanced at his watch. The warmth of the fiery liquid soothed his tightly wound sense of vigilance and responsibility, but he was genuinely glad that they were only a few minutes away from the ride to the airfield and the plane ride northward. It had been a tense and unpleasant past three days, all in all, and still ahead was the brutal going-over they would give ex-Comrade Furbo as payment for his treachery the moment he reappeared at his usual haunts after his stay at the Questura. Piero reflected that he would resume with pleasure the inspection of the Puglia region for Comrade Giorgio upon his return from Prague. There was a Party comrade in Lecce, a young wife of an ancient shoemaker, who would be waiting with considerable impatience for resumption of his suddenly interrupted Party labors in that area. And he would return in two days from this little escort trip abroad with his party reputation and status considerably enhanced, not only because he was Comrade Giorgio's man and, as head of the *Servizio Ordine*, someone to be feared, but because he had fielded this rather nasty little situation with aplomb and a sureness that would be most appreciated by the leadership.

He leaned toward Gianni.

"Eyes open, now," he said to him in a barely audible undertone. "I'm going inside to ring up Comrade Giorgio to report that all is going well. Two minutes." Gianni nodded and immediately turned his eyes on Spartaco. Piero said, "*Scusi un momento*" to Spartaco and slipped out of his chair, disappearing immediately into the shadowy interior of Doney. Spartaco seemed not to have seen him go. He stared at the little flag on its staff in the precise center of the circular table, peered at it over his dark glasses, and suddenly burst into a brief croaking laugh.

"*Mannaggia!*" he commented to no one at all, reaching to examine the little banner. "Comrade Piero is most thorough! A Czech flag!" And indeed it was. "Drink," Spartaco commanded, "Drink, Gianni, to the flag of the People's Republic of Czechoslovakia! Drink to my new home!" His bitter mouth and tone brooked no rejoinders and Gianni dutifully raised his glass and drained it together with Spartaco.

Across the street, near the huge mushroom of a newspaper stand, Vice-Questor Fracassi, his long serious face half concealed behind dark glasses, hurried up to his plainclothes assistant, Commissario De Luca, who stood reading a newspaper facing the traffic and the splendid frontage of Doney across the wide street. The commissario looked up at him with blank surprise, and lowered his newspaper.

"Dottore!" he began, "Why do you . . .?"

Fracassi gripped his elbow.

"Listen!" he told him, speaking with a swift staccato, "do you have any extra men?"

"Two in reserve around the corner, in front of the Hotel Savoia. Why do you ask?"

"Get one of them to take your place here to watch the departing Hero of the Resistance," Fracassi told him, his words vibrating with tension. "You remember the American we arrested and released last night? The one named Linden?"

De Luca nodded, puzzlement knotting his blunt face.

"We just got a telephone call at the Questura from his maid," Fracassi said, eyes already scanning up and down the sidewalk on the other side. "She said he was coming down here to kill Spartaco Tamburri. The American has learned Tamburri is here at Doney and seeks revenge for the wartime murder of his major." He noted the tightening of the heavy-muscled jaw of De Luca and added caustically, "The crime which can no longer be considered a crime because of the amnesties."

"I would be glad to give the American the loaded pistol

233

we took from Tamburri, if I knew he would use it well," the commissario murmured, his own eyes also moving to the street above and below the Doney chairs.

"I did not hear that, De Luca," his superior snapped. "We are here to prevent new crimes, not to permit private vengeance of old ones."

"Yes, and we Italians have also developed wings and halos and we will, all of us, fly to heaven," De Luca said, permitting himself a full ironic smile. "Well, Dottore, since you and I are the only ones here who could recognize the American by sight, I move to obey. I will get one of the reserve men to watch our Communist and his two comrades from here, and I shall move to the corner of the Excelsior and watch for the American there."

"Good," Fracassi agreed. "I'll take position at the entrance of the Doney bar. We will get him from either direction." He waved impatiently.

"Forza! Sbrigatevi!"

The vice-questor reached his corner and, with his short-cut jacket, dark glasses, cuffless trousers, and pointed highly glossed shoes, he blended in with two similarly dressed hangers-on eternally lounging on the curb at Doney. He glanced down the broad sloping sidewalk, noted with satisfaction that De Luca had already reached his post on the double, and reached for a cigarette with a sigh of relief. Spartaco Tamburri sat with one of his two comrades half facing him and the vice-questor stared at the bulky arrogant Party hierarch with a hatred that made him double his fists. The irony of the moment was enough to make one laugh or cry. He took a vicious long drag on his cigarette and put a deliberate iron clamp of professional discipline on himself: he was, after all, a sworn guardian of the public order. He had to do his duty no matter how he felt. His orders were clear. Since this *simpatico* American Linden had apparently made up his mind to kill Spartaco, there was only one course open: to prevent the attempt from succeeding.

It was a comparatively easy job, given the thin siesta crowd, to pick out the rotund figure of Maresciallo Bottoni seated four tables away from Spartaco. That Bottoni! Simply by slipping and falling down last night, he had brought about the arrest of Tamburri and the two Americans and the stolen dynamite recovered. What incredible luck for such an inept and stupid policeman, happy with his fantastic obsession for football-pool gambling, while he, Vice-Questor

Fracassi, who had nurtured and guided the entire investigation of Spartaco Tamburri for months with skill and delicacy, now had to eat the bitter herb of defeat and watch his prey go free and sit there in a chair at Doney having himself a leisurely cognac!

He carefully touched the welts under one eye, mementi of the mauling he had taken the night before, and turned to look up the Via Veneto . . . just in time. Half a block away, Tom Linden strode rapidly toward him and Fracassi knew the information in the telephone call had been right. This man had the unseeing concentration of a man out to kill. The vice-questor raised one hand briefly in a signal to the commissario, beckoning him to come join him, then briskly threw his cigarette away and crossed the narrow Via Sicilia to meet his man. Precisely at the entrance to the Bricktop night club, he deliberately walked straight at Tom who, spotting his quarry, was about to break into a run. The near-collision brought both of them to an abrupt halt, their bodies inches from each other, and the vice-questor clamped a restraining hand on Tom's forearm as the other sought to move around him with an irritated apology.

"No, Signor Linden," the vice-questor said, and Tom's face tightened with angry recognition.

"Take your hand off me. You have no reason to detain me. I am free as long as I stay here in Rome and report to you when you want me, no? Then why are you bothering me now?"

The commissario hurried up to join them in the middle of the sidewalk and he and Fracassi moved Tom quickly into the open doorway that led to the cellar that was Bricktop's. There in the cool corridor, the two police officials swiftly and methodically patted Tom from shoulders to knees. The commissario extracted the commando knife from Tom's belt and touched its pin-point tip with an appraising finger.

"You are accustomed to carrying knives such as this one around with you, signore?" he asked Tom with careful courtesy, hefting the heavy, murderous dirk in one hand. "Perhaps you are going out after more dynamite?"

Tom said nothing, breathing deeply from his rapid walk, the swift move from the sidewalk, and his deepening frustration. The vice-questor, watching him intently, said softly, almost pleadingly, "*Caro signore,* I can understand your motives far more than you may think. May I say that I even share them. But we cannot let you do it. Tamburri must be left alone. He departs from Italy within an hour or so. We will probably never see him again. Let it be so. Let him go."

"He has blood on his hands, blood of my friends. And he ruined me, you know that. All that's left to me is to kill him."

The vice-questor shook his head.

"No, signore. You are not going to kill him. You are going to remain in my personal custody for the next two hours until I am certain his plane has left Ciampino. Nobody is going to kill Spartaco Tamburri, understand?"

On the sidewalk at Doney, Comrade Gianni, a short tub of a man, stared with pleasure at the variety of women sauntering up or down the sidewalk, some of them close enough to mutter a ribald compliment to, or even suggest a closer acquaintanceship. Damn it that he was on this escort detail with Comrade Piero! It was rare enough that he got up here to where the big shots and the foreigners came to sit and drink and to watch all of these elegant *donnacce* move by. He caught one out of the corner of his eye; she looked like the same one who had walked slowly by the travel office on the Via Bissolati a few minutes before. A real chunk of a woman she was; despite the tailored suit she was wearing, he could tell by an expert glance just how firm and ripe those breasts were underneath, just how ample the hips, the proper fullness to the belly. The woman passed the pretentious entrance to the Excelsior Hotel and walked with a slow deliberate undulance up the sidewalk into the gauntlet of Doney's sidewalk tables and chairs.

Che donnina! Gianni thought, and looked around to see if Spartaco was aware of what he was enjoying. But no, Spartaco appeared lost in thought. His seamed gray chin was sunk into his collar and he appeared entranced by the little Czech flag now rippling out, stirred by a slight afternoon zephyr. Gianni remembered; this old bastard liked boys, not girls. He was probably thinking of that wet-lipped Glorioso he had left behind. Well, the Party had put up with a lot of guff from this old warhorse and now, *finito*. In an hour or two he, Gianni, would be free to go about sitting in outdoor cafés and ogle the girls to his heart's content. There was that dark one down at Federation headquarters, who had given him the eye and who . . .

The woman in the tailored suit and carrying a large leather pocketbook approached with a slow feminine rhythm, and her large eyes turned on Gianni and Spartaco with a kindling of near-recognition. As Gianni goggled appreciatively, she halted directly in front of him and her shadow fell lightly across his face.

"Excuse me," she addressed herself with a soft-spoken courtesy to Gianni, "but would your companion be Spartaco Tamburri?"

Gianni looked up into the soft-molded face and large eyes with soaring appreciation. Probably one of those vapid females who intended to ask Spartaco for his autograph as so many of these women did at Party rallies and congresses, but Madonna, what a creature! Before he had the opportunity to open his mouth, Spartaco turned his glance from the other direction, listed his head at her from his chair and stared intently at her through the black glasses.

"Yes, I am Spartaco Tamburri," he told her coldly, still seated and making no effort to rise. "What do you want?"

"You are Il Duro of the Resistance?" she asked, eyes moving from Gianni's moon face to his. Spartaco nodded slowly, grimly.

"Would you know who I am?" she asked him, her voice keyed to a courteous request.

Spartaco looked long into the face of the young woman; then he pushed his sun glasses up on his forehead and stared intently, the pupils of his cruel little eyes dilating to pinpoints in the sudden glare.

"Yes," he said after a long moment, his voice harsh and dry. "By your speech you are of Romagna. By the chin and eyes, you are a Passaglia." His old stubby fingers gripped the table's edge. "You are the daughter of old Tonio Passaglia of Belinoro, not so?"

She nodded with deliberation.

"I am she. Did Comrade Giorgio speak with you of our meeting today?"

Spartaco stared at her as if mesmerized, and his hands slowly became tense fists at the table's edge.

"Giorgio spoke of you, yes," he said. Gianni turned his puzzled head to each of them in turn like a fan following a tennis volley.

"Only by accident did I see you in the airlines office a few minutes ago," Antonella said, standing placidly before him as would a casual passing neighbor. "But I have been looking for you, Signor Tamburri, for hours. I went to your apartment, but they told me you have moved out. Imagine, I was about to take a *corriera* back to Belinoro without having seen you. And here you are, drinking a cognac at Doney, just as if you were waiting for me all the time." She smiled faintly. "Strange, I never thought to find you here. But then at Doney one truly meets all kinds."

Spartaco made no move to stand or to invite her to sit, and Gianni turned to stare at him angrily for this lapse of basic Italian courtesy. But Spartaco paid no attention. He sat, hands gripping the table and he finally said almost in apology. "Being here is not my idea. I had a few minutes to kill before departing for the airfield." He readjusted the sun glasses over his eyes and added, "I am leaving this country— for a long time."

"Oh, indeed?" she rejoined, voice bearing a semblance of regret. "For a long time? Then can I ask you one very brief question? It means very much to me."

The gray lips parted in a humorless smile.

"You mean, about Peppino Deruta?"

"Yes, Peppino," she said swiftly as if anxious to run for a departing bus. "Was he . . . actually a German collaborator as was stated. Did he betray his comrades?"

He studied the soft handsome face for long seconds as if they were alone in a deserted park.

"You are no longer a comrade," he reminded her contemptuously. "You tore up your *tessera* this morning. Why should I tell you anything?"

"So that I may know whether to spit on his grave or weep over it. Nothing more."

Spartaco ran his tongue quickly over his lips once, looked away from her at the little Czech flag on his table, and finally said, without meeting her eyes,

"Weep, then."

She stood before him in the pale sunshine, her body shielding Spartaco's face from mild April sun.

"Spartaco Tamburri," she said, and the words dropped clearly and flatly from her tongue, "I came to repay you in full. For my father. My husband. My poor brother. All the other innocents. And for Peppino Deruta whom you betrayed." Her voice was impartial, her words deliberate, as a judge pronouncing sentence.

Antonella Passaglia took a large blue-black automatic from her bag and holding it in both hands, pointed it at arm's length down at Spartaco, less than a yard away. He studied the black circle of the weapon's muzzle, expressionless, absolutely motionless.

Piero, returning from his telephone call, stood transfixed in the open entrance of Doney, his horrified eyes taking in the full meaning of the tableau a split second before hurling himself at the raised gun ten paces away. He might easily have reached her and batted the gun from her outstretched hand had not Maresciallo Bottoni chosen that moment to lift his bruised and aching body from the chair. The maresciallo had seen nothing out of the ordinary, only a handsome young woman passerby whose back was toward him and who was idly chatting with Il Duro. He had risen from his chair simply to stretch his protesting muscles and to find a football-pool tout sheet somewhere in his trouser pocket, and as he stepped clumsily out into the free space of the sidewalk, a desperate and unseeing Piero crashed into him. The two men sprawled in a crash of overturned chairs, tables, coffee cups and seltzer bottles. Every eye in the Doney block swung around to look at them, as Antonella fired the first shot.

The cracking explosions followed one another in precise rapid sequence like so many dry barks of a distant dog in the night, curiously muffled by the roar of a pair of noisy diesel buses laboring uphill past the scene. Gianni, his fat mouth babbling incoherent words, finally buried his face in his hands. Spartaco Tamburri gripped the arms of his chair and with a convulsive gesture stood up, toppling the tiny table with its cognac glasses and the little flag. He extended a hand toward Antonella as if to shake hers but she held the gun toward him with the gesture of a lion tamer using a chair to fend off his snarling beasts. The shots seemed to have no effect on him at all. But as the shouting vice-questor, with Tom and the commissario at his heels, rushed up behind her to wrest the gun from her unresisting hands, Spartaco spun slowly around and he fell backward without a sound, the upper half of his body landing in the geranium flower bed where the gay little red flowers matched almost perfectly the spreading stain on his shirt under the opened jacket and the slight rivulet coursing down his face. His sun glasses flew off and his battered face pointed straight up at the incandescent blue sky. Only then did a woman sitting at the next table scream, a high uneven little scream that swiveled all eyes from the sprawled Bottoni and Piero to the pinioned Antonella and the fallen body in the flower bed in front of Doney's. Then, after a second of almost prayerful silence, everyone raced to the spot as if a giant magnet had suddenly been activated where Spartaco fell.

chapter twenty-five

FOR THE ITALIAN and some of the foreign press, the killing of Spartaco Tamburri was a springtime journalistic festival, although it of course depended very much on the political coloration of the newspaper or magazine involved on how the story was played. All except the Communist periodicals (whose *Paese Sera* was more shrill in its sorrow than any of its blood brothers) were more or less agreed that Spartaco Tamburri, with all of his career as a party warrior, richly deserved being killed, although much lip service was paid to the fact that it was unfortunate that a Resistance hero and an anti-Fascist of such prominence had to die in such a violent manner at such a time.

The Communists naturally mourned him as a great Party hero and pioneer. They duly resurrected and printed the stiff group photos of the early 1920s complete with arrows identifying Tamburri and the great Gramsci standing together with the studious youthful Togliatti and the other eventual greats of the Italian Communist Party. Only the barest mention was made by any of the Communist sheets concerning Antonella's Party affiliations, although this delicacy was shared by no one else. The Party press gave a large play to the impressive official Party funeral they held for Il Duro with the massed Resistance battle flags, red bandannas around five thousand aging partisan throats, and they printed every word of the solemn, if overlong, eulogy delivered over his bier by Il Migliore himself, before relegating the story and its ensuing painful revelations at the trial to stiff little stories in the back pages.

But no such hesitancy stayed the pen or presses of anyone else. The right-wing and neo-Fascist papers were beside themselves with joy at the opportunity to regurgitate all of the old wartime partisan excesses, as well as a full serialized account by a survivor of the International Brigade in Spain which delineated the executioner role of Il Duro during the Civil War there. Antonella was piously described as the long avenging hand of God, the Bolt from Heaven, the Warning to the Godless. *Il Borghese,* in a brilliantly mordant piece, dwelt at length on the symbolism of Il Duro's death at the precise spot in Rome where gathered and lounged all of the depraved, corrupt, parasitic drones of a society whom Spartaco Tamburri had fought all of his tough life. The author took the shade of Il Duro sternly to task for not having had the foresight or the decency to die where he was needed: crushing the Fascist counterrevolutionaries in Budapest, for example. An especially tasteless front-page cartoon in the neo-Fascist paper of Naples depicted the ghost of a bullet-ridden Stalin swooping down on the Veneto to pick up the ghost of Spartaco with the caption, HA DA VENI BAFFONE!: "Big Mustache is Coming!"

Even the generally moderate and non-political dailies and weeklies went into exhaustive if morbid details, especially on the second and third day after the killing when the police statement of the circumstances and the autopsy results were announced. There was a universal incredulity that, irony of ironies, the very murder weapon, was a wartime gift to Antonella's father by the poor devil of the American major murdered thirteen years ago by the band of Il Duro. One paper, in a moment of great inspiration, called in a staff psychiatrist from the Policlinico to explain the coolness of the Signora Passaglia, widow Cipriani, which enabled her to empty the entire magazine of the pistol in rapid fire, all nine slugs of which struck the hapless Tamburri: four in the chest and stomach, three in the arms and shoulders, one through the right cheek and one through his left temple, the last killing him instantly. (Would that, the preface to the learned opinion went, soldiers of the armed forces could fire as effectively.) This was hardly the act of a demented wild woman and much more indicative of a highly organized well-coordinated human mechanism simply bent on an act of cold implacable revenge. He cited the Dottoressa Passaglia's statement to the police that she had taken the trouble to learn to operate the weapon perfectly, that she knew it was a nine-shot affair, eight bullets in the clip and one in the chamber, that she knew how to clean and strip the weapon. *Giorno* devoted a full-page photo close-up of the holster Antonella had thrown on the body and a close-up of the name of the late Major Dixon and his army serial number

241

inside its flap. *Rotosei* went one better and printed a full page of poignant cemetery photos: first one of Major Dixon's grave in the U. S. Military Cemetery of Florence, and the others of the tombs and crypts in the cemetery of Belinoro.

As is always the case, however, there was substantial disagreement as to just what happened in front of Doney's at the moment of the killing. One scandal-mongering weekly described the Communist leader as dying stoically and instantly, without even having the brief necessary moment to form the word "Mamma" on his lips before expiring. Another indignantly insisted that Tamburri had indeed said something, that he had faced the horrid maw of the gun of his death with the snarling curse, "*Figlia di p—.*" Still another paper wearily insisted that the others were wrong, quite hysterically wrong; that an eyewitness, telling his story exclusively to the editors, recalled that Il Duro had recognized his assassin, had held out a hand to her and whispered, "*Et tu, Antonella,*" before he fell. Everyone agreed that it was magnificently ironic that the little flag of the Czechoslovak People's Republic, a simple rectangle of red and white cloth with a blue triangle wedged in it, should have fallen from the sidewalk table at Tamburri's feet. Later photographs of the recumbent corpse lying there indicated that the flag had mysteriously moved to a point where his dead fingers were touching it, but this troubled no one.

For several weeks it became virtually impossible to get a seat at Doney's, especially at the approximate spot of the killing, and groups of gap-mouthed countrymen and city folk alike knotted around the slight indentation in the dirt of the flower bed where Spartaco had fallen, to the intense annoyance and anger of the Doney waiters and their clientele. The tourist buses made it a point to slow down at the café and all eyes within goggled at the crowded confusion as the guides rattled a tinny narrative of the murder in a dozen tongues.

With the trial, which did not even begin until summer, the story, which had died down after the first few days, burst into incandescence again. Every moment of the life of the poor Signora Antonella was chronicled on RAI-TV, Italian cinema news, and in the press. A wave of revulsion against the late Il Duro and the Communists welled up as the testimony encompassed details of the massacre of the Passaglia partisans performed by the Communists in their drive for political power over that still occupied zone of 1944. A Greek journalist weighed in with firsthand accounts of similar post-war Communist slaughters of anti-Communists patriots in the same sordid fight for supremacy all over shattered Hellas. A survivor of the anti-Communist Ossovani Partisan Brigade in the Udinese was dredged up to tell *his* tragic story of Communist revenge and politically motivated suppression. It was a foregone conclusion that Antonella would be gently handled by the court, although the entire Communist press now bitterly protested that the whole affair was clearly a brutal clerico-fascist assassination plot using the pathetic woman as a blind tool to bring death to a great anti-Fascist patriot and to heap discredit on the Italian Resistance movement.

The hot summer wore on, and the court proceedings dragged. The story of Antonella and her revenge receded grudgingly into the inside pages and to occasional features by the weeklies, with photos of a patient and calmly dignified Antonella managing to look attractive even in her wretched prison dress, being escorted to and from Mantellate Women's Prison or sitting in the defendant's cage in the usually packed courtroom with hands in lap as if she were a mildly interested spectator instead of the defendant. Her lawyer, a bright bald young man from the Abruzzi, played with unerring instinct on the one jangling open nerve which no Italian, judge or otherwise, can resist: the fact that this handsome young woman had in one terrible moment been made an orphan, robbed of her only brother, and made a widow without even a child to rear as solace. The chilling word *trucidato*, "slaughtered," was repeated a dozen times or more at each session to describe the fate of the Passaglia group leaders. The young lawyer (secretly fascinated with his icily calm, almost phlegmatic client) nursed this central theme straight through the more factual wall of the none too forceful public prosecutor's charge of premeditated murder. For years, the defense pointed out, the Communist Party had callously misled this decent and idealistic young woman of *famiglia per bene*, of good family stock, by concealing from her the true facts of her family's death and had enrolled her in its ranks. How would any one in this courtroom react, he asked in ringing and vibrantly emotional tones, if he found out one brutal morning that his own trusted friends and comrades had murdered his own parent and husband and brother? Was this murder, he asked, or was it purely the complete natural cry of the poor dead crying out to be avenged? The public prosecutor, try as he might, could not dim this terrible theme, even aided by detailed and horrendously fascinating medical testimony to the precise effect that the nine bullets had wreaked on the body of Spartaco Tamburri.

As was to be expected, side issues developed, like brush fires on either side of a forest conflagration. One of the neo-Fascist papers printed the now famous 1945 photo of Mussolini, Petacci, and the other hierarchs hanging bullet-ridden by their heels in the gasoline station at Piazzale Loreto in Milan, and next to it the photograph of the equally bullet-ridden body of Spartaco with the caption, FINALLY, REVENGE. This raised a tremendous furor which became the focus for an angry political polemic for months afterward. Then when the name of the late Major Dixon was raised in testimony, the Communist press went to work on the theme that the monarchist-clerico-fascists of that wartime period, battening in the liberated south of Italy while their comrades died for freedom in the north, had brought on the entire tragic denouement by inducing the misinformed Americans to send the ill-fated major and his small mission to disrupt anti-Fascist unity behind the German lines. This touched off a series of angry blasts by the Monarchists of Italy, the Repubblicani, the veterans of the Giustizia e Libertà and Fiamma Verde formations, as well as the Christian Democrats, which continued unabated long after the trial of Antonella Passaglia had faded from the public's memory.

As the public prosecutor later wryly admitted to the defense counsel, if the late Tamburri had only left one presentable next of kin—a pathetic widow, a sad-eyed child or two—their appearance in court dressed in black and tears could have countered somewhat the emotional impact of Antonella's overwhelming family loss. But Il Duro unfortunately left no one except a pair of rather dazed middle-aged brothers, both simple peasants from the Rovigo area, who briefly appeared at one of the court sessions and then immediately returned to their fields. And the defense attorney maliciously and unsuccessfuly dared the prosecutor, during a brief recess over a caffè, to put Comrade Giordano Glorioso and the other *finocchi* of the late Party hero on the stand to testify as to *their* bereavement.

The court sentence made front-page news again throughout the peninsula: the accused Dottoressa Passaglia was formally found guilty of involuntary homicide with grossly extenuating circumstances. The court followed (in addition to its heart) the thesis that if the late Spartaco Tamburri could not now be tried for political crimes committed during the Resistance period in the light of subsequent general amnesties granted for such offenses, neither could legitimate revenge for such non-punishable "political crimes" be exorbitantly punished. She was sentenced to two years in jail, sentence suspended. The accused was also found guilty of illegal possession and use of firearms and for this offense was sentenced to six months and six days in jail, all of which had already been served by the defendant in the Mantellate during the lengthy investigation and trial. And so Antonella Passaglia, widow of Cipriani, was photographed by a large noisy swarm of photographers, first as she walked out of the prison door in the ancient Trastevere section of Rome, and finally as she stood on the threshold of the ancient Farmacia Passaglia in her little home town of Belinoro which she had left half a year before to seek her revenge. That was all. The story had been played vigorously and well, journalists of all political colorations agreed to that. But a series of new drug scandals involving young Roman *gioventù bruciata* in the Parioli area, as well as an equally noisome affair involving teen-age free-lance prostitution by a ring of girls from some of the best families in Milano, now occupied the avid public attention, and the Passaglia affair receded into the background, raising only provincial and regional political tempers at municipal and national elections.

Only the most devoted readers of the Rome press would have taken the effort and time to plow through the half-columns set in pica type which are devoted to petty crimes and to read there (printed in almost identical words by the two major dailies of the capital about five days after the murder of Spartaco Tamburri) the brief paragraph which announced that one Paolo Seddu, aged twenty-four, notary's assistant, had been found in illegal possession of explosives in contravention of Articles 678 and 679 of the Penal Code, fined forty thousand lire and given a suspended sentence of six months. An equally careful reader, with good eyesight to make out the tiny print used for such reportage, would have read, about two days afterwards, another three-line item reporting that one Franco Furbo of Torpignattara suburb had been set upon late last night near his home by unknown malefactors and had been beaten to such a degree that he had been hospitalized at the Santo Spirito hospital, declared curable in thirty days.

Assiduous and dedicated readers of that achingly boring daily, the Communist *L'Unità*, might also have noted in the drowsy Ferragosto period a very modest item concerning the transfer of Comrade Piero Bronzini from special duties with the Central Committee to a new assignment in western Sicily as chief of Party agitation and propaganda activity. All faithful *L'Unità* readers knew well the flintiness of Sicilian soil in terms of Party roots because of the malevolent and unremitting opposition to it by the Mafia and the Church, and Comrade Piero (his Party friends commented to each other with wry smiles) would really be on the front lines of the Party struggle. Piero's base of activity would be Trapani, the little news story announced, without describing that port or its questionable charms.

As autumn arrived, a short paragraph printed only in the "Lend Me Your Ears" column of the English language newspaper in Rome, announced the marriage of Mr. T. Vincennes Brentwood III in quiet civil ceremony in New York to Miss Nancy Hamill, daughter of the first secretary of embassy, Mr. Addison Hamill. Mr. Brentwood, the paragraph read, had been second secretary in Rome until his resignation from the Foreign Service the previous June, and the couple was moving to Waterstow, Massachusetts, where the groom was taking a position in his family's firm there.

And finally, two of the Rome dailies, in very small type, briefly but warmly congratulated Maresciallo Bottoni, a veteran official of the Rome police force, for his promotion to *maresciallo-maggiore*, an honor well deserved after his service of thirty years to his corps and to his country.

chapter twenty-six

THE MARIA SAT erectly in her usual place of honor in the Caffè Cagliari. At the head of four little aluminum tables pushed together in a reserved corner of the crowded coffee bar, she surveyed the dozen dark, chattering women of all ages and sizes crammed around her, listening and occasionally responding in a slow and dignified manner. A dozen cups of black-syrupy espresso littered the tables and they nibbled sugar-coated brioches, licking their fingers and gesticulating wildly with the exaggerated hand movements of those who simply cannot talk fast enough to friends, while their coffees cooled.

Looking straight ahead through the beaded entrance of the bar, she could see the pullulating life of the central railroad station across the way: peasants bent under the weight of cheap cardboard suitcases and bundles, taxis arriving and departing to the accompaniment of verbal skirmishes over the fare, perambulating hawkers and pimps and whores, all of the daily frenzied animation and movement of the Stazione Termini punctuated by the clang of trams and the roar of the heavy diesel buses. Her severe glance moved from face to face around the impromptu festive board which was also a judicial bench. Only the glistening of the jet eyes and a slight movement of her black dress adorned only with a little gold pin hinted at the depth of her emotion. She was at home here, among her own, respected and loved, listening to the news of the city through the eyes and ears of a dozen intuitively inquisitive household and office servants who would very soon depart on the various Thursday afternoon outings, to be replaced one by one by other Sardinians celebrating their half-day of freedom from drudgery. This was their tacitly agreed rendezvous point; here, with the endless caffès and chatter, she heard the pleas for assistance and advice, and handed down her personal ukases and judgments (usually accepted, if after vigorous objections and clarifications). Then finally she would move on to the Trattoria Tanaunella where, surrounded by still more of her flock, she would partake of her beloved Sardinian cuisine: the *gnocchi alla sarda*, then the tender little goat's meat, the *capretto*, cooked as only those of Deciomannu know how. All washed down with the amber wine of Oristano, the *Verdaccia*, topped off with fruit and sweet little hard Sardinian cakes, and inevitably more coffee and conversation far into the evening.

The proprietor of Trattoria Tanaunella would welcome her as one greets manna from heaven, for, in addition to the group who inevitably came to join her in eating there, she had elevated his establishment to a status as the *only* place in the capital where real Sardinian wedding repasts and first communion dinners could be cheaply and fully celebrated, complete with a young guitarist from Sassari who sang the weird Arab-tinged folk songs of the island and who also owed his modest rise to fame through The Maria's personal seal of endorsement.

The cheerily noisy babble reached her in little fragments, all of which had meaning for her. She was keenly aware of the pitying undertones expressed in the glances and the occasional brief whispers behind the ostentatiously shielding hands: the growing murmur of jokes and sarcastic expressions referring to her long employment with the now departed American bachelor. Although these had been restrained of late by her new-lustered position in the home of an American *professore* and his family arrived on a Fulbright Fellowship, she knew full well the ugly implications of a new nickname for her which had been recently circulating among her fellow Sards in the city: *L'Americana*. She looked at them and, knowing what was in store for them all, she smiled wryly, picked up her caffè nero cup and drained it.

Her glance rolled slowly along until it stopped at a dark, blooming girl, with hair as soft and fluffy as a black lamb's, a girl with breasts and flowing ample lines, with an open laughing face and olive skin like dark cream, never once sullied by cosmetics. She had planned to speak with this girl for two weeks and the opportunity was at hand.

"You, Margherita, how goes your job at the central post office? Are you content?"

The fluffy head dipped rapidly twice.

"Yes, and many thanks to you, Signora Maria, but there are many of these foul-mouthed youths who come in and make the most outrageous remarks instead of buying the post cards and stamps."

A sympathetic murmur of outrage and sympathy welled from each of her listeners. The Maria, who had already completed full discreet inquiries into this young fresh girl from Olbia, including her kitchen skills, instinct for thrift, and her attendance at Sunday Mass, said in a low thrumming purr,

"I know what these imbeciles say. I would like to talk with you privately for a moment later, dear girl, and give you some good counsel."

In the revival of the normal hubbub and scraping of chairs, The Maria heard with a tiny almost invisible grin of satisfaction the loud whisper from Margherita's neighbor into her ear which turned the smooth olive cheeks to a spreading brick-red,

"You, little Olbianese, are the chosen one. Speak nicely to

your future aunt, for the fiancée of Paolo Seddu has just been selected. And what a handsome one he is!"

The Maria pointed a psuedo-accusing, work-stained finger at the portiere's irrepressible wife who had made the remark. "You cackle like an empty-headed goose, Elena, do you know that?"

But the eyes of four other little dark-faced maids present reflected their envy and their congratulations as Margherita moved slowly to the end of the table where The Maria sat heavily and regally. Before she reached her, however, a monstrously swollen woman, swaying proudly with the weight and visibility of her pregnancy, brushed through the beads of the Caffè Cagliari, and greeted them all in the broad shout of her native dialect.

"*Ecco,* The Maria is still here, thanks to God!" she called, moving to where The Maria raised a hand in greeting. The others drifted in behind her and formed a semicircular screen of bodies and they pressed in with curiosity to hear anything to be said.

"You see me, cara Maria, full of child!" The pregnant woman in a thin and non-concealing colored dress patted her belly as if no one otherwise would have noticed its jutting protrusion. "My man told me, 'Luisa, you must go to The Maria and ask for a name. The Maria has hands and heart of gold, and she must touch you and give the name of the child.' And so, here I am. Put your hand here and give me the name for the child."

The little knot of broad dark faces was silent as The Maria reached out and her heavy blunt fingers rested lightly on the great distended belly of the woman, touching the stretched flesh for a brief instant. She look up straight into the face of the woman and then she permitted the lids to fall over her own eyes as if concentrating in a prayer. Finally she said, in a voice that was muffled and strained to the wall of women around her,

"Name the child Tommaso if it is a boy, Antonella if it is a girl. These are good names and the child will surely be blessed and grow up strong, obedient, and loved."

As the group broke into a delighted applause and Margherita shyly and expectantly moved closer to hear more of Paolo Seddu, The Maria picked up a paper napkin before her and, looking straight ahead, wiped away a tentative tear that would never fail to appear whenever the name or the image of Dottore Tommaso came to mind.

She glanced up again to study the entrance to the café.

The portiere's wife, a thin bony woman with black eyes extremely close together, lifted her head in an interrogatory gesture.

"For whom do you look? Our Sardinian compatriot, the Minister Segni, perhaps?"

"I am waiting," The Maria said slowly and meaningfully, knowing that every ear at the table was attuned to her words, "for a certain Pinetta of Iglesias, a compatriot of ours whom many of you certainly know."

A hush settled on the group momentarily as if a name of one recently dead had been mentioned.

"Eh, you all sit there so silently?" she challenged them. "She has sold you all the American cigarettes and canned goods and items of clothing cheaply, has she not? She considers herself one of the local glories of our island in Rome, no? Why, then, *zitta-zitta?* Has she caught the cholera?"

A broad-faced wet nurse from Porto Torres with two bulbous mounds of breasts welling under her cheap silken blouse as valid advertisement of her livelihood, rasped at The Maria, after looking at all of the others who said nothing,

"Aha, you haven't heard! The police stopped her this morning as she left the house of her employer, the American diplomat, on her free afternoon out. In her bag, under some soiled linen, they found cartons of cigarettes, two bottles of the American whisky, and many valuable items from the wardrobe of her master. They have taken her to the police commissariat of the Flaminio district. Have you not heard?"

And she stared at The Maria increduously; that The Maria should not have received such tidings indicated a scandalous breakdown in their city-wide communications system. A low babbling murmur of commiseration mingled with disdain for the ill-starred Pinetta followed her words, and The Maria smiled darkly as she tilted another tiny cup with its black liquid to her lips.

"I knew of it within half an hour of her arrival at the district police station on the Via Flaminia," she told them matter-of-factly savoring the moment with inner delight before she added, "and that is why I await her. She will be freed, and I wait for her now."

Their dark liquid eyes flashed at each other as they turned to each other and exchanged fearful glances. It was one thing for The Maria to find them jobs or to slip them inconspicuously in and out of the Anagrafe after normal hours to register them (quite illegally) as residents of Rome, or to arrange priority for free medical out-patient treatment for them at

250

the Policlinico. But to spring someone loose from the clutches of the dread police within an hour! This was black magic!

Because she knew The Maria longest and because she was known as a woman of brutal frankness, it was the portiere's wife who finally expressed the incredulous thought of all of them.

"Did you have your big-shot friends do this for the Pinetta? First of all, I find it almost impossible to believe, and if it is true, why did you do so? Do you know how this woman has slandered you? She has a *lingua sporca* when she speaks of you, my friend. She hints of many things she knows about you. She alluded much evil to your status with your former employer, the American bachelor. I cannot understand . . ."

The Maria raised an imperious hand and her heavy slablike face turned to the café entrance, this time with a great flash of the jet eyes.

"Ah, la Pinetta!" she boomed. "Enter! Come over here and sit with your *campaesani* for a few moments!" And she heaved her great bulk to her feet and waited. Pinetta, olive complexion now pale and sickly, walked as if she were pulling a great dead weight behind her, but she neared the table as a moth moves toward the flame. The gabble of the circle of women was now absolutely stilled, amplifying the cries and the roar from the railroad station traffic outside.

"*Com'è sta usted?*" The Maria greeted her formally in Sardinian. Pinetta Vitale of Iglesias still wore the white cotton summer dress and shoes with which she had left her employer's home that morning and her crackling black hair was restrained by a gay colored band. But there were deep stains of sweat under the arms of the dress and down the back, and her face, usually bold as a Cossack's, bore the stamp of someone who has been shaken to the very marrow.

"Are you well?" The Maria demanded, half in compassion, half to impel her to speak. She waggled a finger at one of the younger women who immediately picked up her light aluminum chair and brought it around to The Maria's side. Pinetta said nothing and the two women stood facing each other as if alone.

"*Ebbeh,*" The Maria said. "Since you will not speak, *I* will. The last time we met, you and your father had brutal things to say about my former *padrone*, Dottore Linden. A coward, you called him, and I a servant of such a *disgraziato*. You have said much about me, my personal conduct, unspecified crimes in my past. Well then, here I am to hear them and to make my *mea culpa* here before our friends and countrymen." Her voice was like the sound of a brass trumpet. "Now, speak. Tell of my evil-doings! Tell of my cowardly master! Here is your chance!"

The full lips of Pinetta quivered, and she bit them to hold back her crumbling emotions. Then slowly, deliberately, she sank to her knees on the soiled café floor and she leaned her head against the black dress of The Maria.

"Perdonatemi!" she croaked in what was a loud whisper. "Forgive me. The maresciallo at the Commissariato Flamino was a countryman from Nola. He told me that I would surely have gone to jail for months and then received a *foglio di via obbligatoria* compelling me to return to Iglesias for the rest of my life, except for you. He said that he was much beholden to you and that he was releasing me only when you called him pleading that I be let off with an official warning."

She encircled the knees of The Maria and the words chattered from her lips like little bits of ice. "I beg of you to forgive every word we have said about you and your master in the past; all of the ugly lies . . ."

The Maria looked impassively down at the pleading eyes rolled upward.

"Lies, did you say?"

The kinky black head pumped up and down.

"Lies. I will confess them all at my parish church on Sunday."

With a discreet tug of her powerful hand, The Maria pulled the woman to her feet in a slow deliberate gesture, she smothered her in a giant embrace. The Sard women at the table shrieked with joy and pleasure at the unexpected spectacle of debasement and forgiveness; it would be something to fill their swift-flying tongues for years. The proprietor of the café, busy with the espresso machine in his white apron behind the garish aluminum-sheathed bar, looked up in startled surprise at the sudden uproar.

"What's with you noisy hens?" he asked them with a puzzled smile. "Has someone hit the Lotto for a packet?"

"Carpano!" The Maria called to him. "A glass of Carpano for everyone from Maria Seddu who, with God's help, looks after her own."

And when all of them stood up with glasses in hand and the gabble of their appreciation died down for a moment, The Maria held up her glass and said, looking straight into the eyes of Pinetta,

"May God forgive us all our sins, yours and mine."

They, defying them all, she held her glass a bit higher and said loudly,

"To the Americans!"

They knew precisely what she meant, and they loudly and dutifully repeated, *"Agli americani!"*

They clinked glasses and gulped the strong bittersweet liquid down, but the mind of The Maria was already far beyond them, planning the marriage of her Paolo and the buxom Margherita where they would live in the capital, and what name they would give to their first-born.

chapter twenty-seven

THE NOISY CHATTER of the other passengers on the crowded local *corriera* was momentarily stilled as the driver, at Tom's request, pulled over to the shoulder of the Emilian Way and Tom slowly descended, easing the plaid canvas suitcase before him down through the bus door. A wave of the hand to the driver and the door closed. The bus moved slowly on, groaning carefully onto the macadam surface again, and the tough, sunburned peasant faces on the side nearest him looked down on him through the open windows with interested stares. Few *stranieri* ever rode these local buses and almost never did they ask to be let out at a deserted stretch where only a small Agipgas filling station marked the juncture of a lonely provincial road with the Nazionale.

The noon heat of the Po Valley hit him with a directness that almost buckled his kness, and he was thankful that he had left the other larger suitcase in the baggage section of the train station at Rimini. He looked past the deep ditch between the road shoulder and the fields beyond and narrowed his eyes against the October sun to survey the familiar fruit orchards stretching away to the horizon on one side and the billowing rise of the Apennine foothills on the other. The silence of the day was broken only by the occasional approaching hum—louder, louder, snarling past him with a whoosh—of speeding vehicles boring through the shimmering heat up or down the arrow-straight Via Emilia, in this direction to Rimini, in that to Bologna.

He hurried across the highway with his burden and, without stopping at the filling station whose overalled attendant could be seen snoozing inside his little glass hut, he moved slowly into the hard-packed provincial dirt road leading up into the mounting green hills beyond. A metal sign announced: ALTOMONTE DI ROMAGNA — 8 and underneath, BELINORO — 5.

He stopped, stripped off his jacket and jammed it into the already full suitcase and, placing the suitcase on one shoulder, he stepped off slowly through the heat, keeping to the road edge almost by instinct, feeling the pull of the road as it commenced its gradual climb into the highlands. Walking here now in the autumn, with the plucked fields and trees all around him, a momentary tranquillity settled on him that matched the ageless calm of the landscape. The gnarled twisted olive trees and the stubbled rows, long past their brief hour of fruition, seemed a hundred times brighter than he could ever recall, and the familiar yet strange scene almost blinded the pale image of the same fields of thirteen years before.

Then he remembered, and it explained the brilliance of this scene. Not once in that experience of a dozen years ago had he been able to walk in broad daylight up that wide dirt and gravel country road to Belinoro. Then, he and Henning Dixon and the radio operator had lived the lives of moles, shrinking from the light, from strange shadows and unfamiliar, ever ominous sounds. Only at night did they freely emerge in the open to breathe deeply of the fresh night hillside air, shucking their clothes and splashing in the black and cold stinging waters of a hillside stream to wash off the grime of days of unwashed vigilance and the accumulated sweat of fear and anticipation. He had walked this way only at night under a full, and then a waning moon, and its shining pallor had given the shadowy silence of the fields and the gray, unpainted stone houses a quality of unreality as if a mirage had floated the landscape into his vision. Even at night, one usually walked in silence, alertly poised, jump-booted feet moving carefully to avoid a noisy stumble. Even at night, there had been danger, there were always eyes that might see, ears than could hear an alien English word, and lips to betray them to the nearest German command.

But now the silence under the relentless sun was a drowsy thing, not to be feared, twittered by birds and rustled by an occasional slough of a hot wind from the Po Valley slowly dropping below him. And he could hear nothing from the dotted farmhouses still far above him. He walked slowly and steadily, shifting the suitcase from shoulder to shoulder. At one brief halt, he turned to look back at the orange-yellow dirt track sloping behind him which was Belinoro's link with Romagna and the plain and the Via Emilia and Italy. He glimpsed Cesena's church towers and the Malatesta castle tiny and infinitely far away, and the yellow-brown pancake of the Po Plain blended and disappeared in the haze of blue which wiped out horizon and the distinction between sky and earth.

The dirt road bent back on itself twice in tight, climbing turns. Perspiration now soaked his back and underarms, but he did not slacken his deliberate stride along the right edge of the road whose verges sloped into shallow, rocky rain ditches. A snarling sputter of a motor-scooter engine laboring upward reached his ears and he stopped, lowered his burden, and turned to watch a little gray Vespa shoot by, occupant's head almost invisible behind a dark orange plastic face shield which covered forehead, eyes, nose, and mouth. Tom instinctively waved and the face atop a stocky heavy body turned to stare at him briefly and a gloved hand lifted from one of the handlebars and waved perfunctorily in return. Although the scooter contained a jump seat on which a passenger could sit sideways and grasp the waist of the scooter driver, the visored figure made no move to stop or to give him a lift, and disappeared in a lazy swirl of dust which blew back into Tom's eyes, covering his face and shoes with a fine yellow film.

Tom shrugged his shoulders and continued his uphill pace. You could never depend on the reception of the Romagnoli, a people of extremes, violent extremes, and one did not have to look far for good examples. Mussolini, for instance, born in Predappio about two hills over there on the right. Hardly an open-hearted moderate, with that jaw of supreme stubbornness and overweening will. Or the Malatestas, whose concept of living was immortalized in fraternal murder and incest. The Red Belt of Italy, they now called this zone, with the Communist vote now running well over half the electorate. Once the bloody center of Italian anarchism and nihilism, it had turned into a stronghold of strutting arrogant Fascist *squadristi*, then from Blackshirt to reddest Red. What

255

was it that flung these dark, proud people to the ends of the political and social spectrum? Was it the air? The water? Some Teutonic fierceness brought into the area by Theodoric's Gothic legions a millennium and a half ago and fanning the Latin smoulder into an intransigent physical and political bullheadedness? He had heard enough about Romagna in the long nights of a dozen years ago to peer into the flinty souls of its people, but the explanations did not entirely answer the question of why Romagna had more of a chip on its shoulder than, say, Piedmont or Tuscany or Lazio. He would have to leave that to the anthropologists and the social scientists and to the ghost of the late Benito for more definitive probing. Perhaps a field study of Predappio and the Mussolini family tree would come up with something.

He had been climbing the spiraling road well over an hour, lost in thought, when the way leveled and ahead, where the road cut through a deep defile, an old prewar metal sign reared out of the weeds; BELINORO, the letters spelled out in little raised, glass reflector discs. In the upper left-hand corner of the metal sign were three deadly and now rusted bullet perforations, one almost vertically under the other, with a dot of blue sky showing through each hole, for this was the site of the ambush.

Tom slowed, turned off the road, dropped his burden and came to rest half leaning, half sitting on a crumbling stone wall behind which an olive orchard extended thickly up the rise. Belinoro village lay half a mile around the bend and there was not much to see on this dirt road empty in the lazy heavy silence of the siesta. He pulled out a handkerchief and, inserting it under his shirt collar, slowly wiped the streams of perspiration.

That night they must have proceeded as always: Fausto *Il Seghela*—The Cicada—Antonella's bridegroom, a nerveless, stolid man with an orsine roll to his gait, in his advance-scout position perhaps seventy-five yards in front of the main body, mouth ready to give the danger-and-dispersal signal that was like a loud cicada chirp, hand clenched around the captured Mauser, moving cautiously and silently in the blackness, peering and sniffing his familiar heath in all directions. Antonino, Antonella's brother and barely old enough to shave the dark, proud fuzz of manhood, who was forbidden to go out but disobeyed and went along anyway, his sten gun with full clip ready to spray, his square serious young face masking fear and concern and responsibility in the utter gloom. And on that long-ago wet black night Henning Dixon had marched at the head of one of the files, opposite old Tonio himself; Henning, .45 holster flap open, occupying with Tonio the command position Tom himself should have held.

He recalled, eyes closed with the pain of remembering, how he found them after staggering through the wet treacherous night down the tomblike main street of Belinoro in the direction of the terrible sounds and explosions. With Antonella racing like a man beside him, they had first come upon Nino Passaglia together with the bodies of the two rear guards, lying on his right side, boy's eyes slitted and staring and his adapted army tunic tufted with holes torn by a half-dozen slugs. Then the others, twelve of them, in little heaps and mounds sprawled all across the sunken road and its edges, some lying in the tall wet grass. Two Belinoro men, ordnance non-coms recently returned from a demobilized Italian regiment who had marched near the head of the alternate file, were literally in shreds. Bullets must have struck and exploded the hand grenades they were carrying in sacks at their waists. And in the middle of the road, the dead German lay, face up, eyes glassy under the muddy *landser* hat.

He and Antonella had barely stopped, stumbling unbelievingly past the others to where a heavy body lay, hands clenched like claws as if waiting to come to grips with his assassins. Only there had Antonella spoken for the first time; she whispered to him as if it were not polite to speak aloud.

"There lies Fausto, my husband."

She left him alone and he swayed along, knees buckling with rising panic and nausea as the nightmare gradually closed in on him. She went to Fausto, rolled the massive riddled body on its back and, cradling the unshaven head, kissed the dead lips and eased the blunt head back to the willing earth. They had walked back slowly and unsteadily to where the band lay together in death and Antonella had said calmly,

"The ambushers took the dynamite and detonators and the submachine guns. They left only the old carbines."

Then she pointed.

"Look, my father and your major."

And indeed the two bodies appeared to have been arm in arm where they fell. Closing Henning Dixon's eyes must have sapped his last energies because he remembered no more about that night than Antonella's white face staring around her as he sank to the road beside the body of his superior and the howling and keening of the arriving villagers began.

And now as he looked at the ambush site in the heat of the early October afternoon, he shielded his eyes against the brightness of the day to calculate the precise spot in the road where he had rolled over the body of Major Henning Dixon. He remembered that the gold leaves of Dixon's rank pinned on the shoulders of his field jacket under the parka were discolored with Dixon's life blood. Strange, he had not noticed then or afterward that Dixon's shoulder holster and pistol and one of his insignia were missing. It was incredible that the weapon had appeared in the hand of an Italian police official in Rome a dozen years later. But there were many strange things that had happened then and afterwards. He remembered closing Henning's eyes and looking down on the long serious face and sobbing, "Get up, you bastard! Get up! Please!" But Dixon had never moved and Tom had wiped a tiny rivulet of blood from a corner of the sagging mouth. And now the road lay flat and innocent and mindless of the deed committed there.

Tom eased awkwardly from his perch on the stone wall and continued his march into Belinoro, feeling the suitcase bite into his aching shoulders no matter how he shifted it. The road, now turning slightly, was flanked on its right side by a high whitewashed stucco wall, behind which the dead of Belinoro for the past two hundred years had been laid away in graves varying from crypts filed like safe drawers atop each other to marble mausoleums each almost the size of a peasant hut. Tom did not slacken his gait as he passed the iron-grilled gate, although he knew that from the entrance one could see the roof of the tomb in which the Passaglia family lay.

Elsewhere in the little cemetery, he knew, were all the others, the two young courier girls included. He, wrapped in an anonymous heavy peasant cape in the shelter of a nearby tomb, had witnessed the mass funeral and services celebrated among the tombs. Enough tears were shed and shrieks of mourning that day alone to last the cemetery its lifetime. Henning Dixon was not in there although Henning had been the recipient of the tears and the prayers along with all the others slain. He had even briefly rested with them there, but a Graves Registration unit had passed that way within a month after Ghurka brigade liberated the village, and

Henning now lay in the very green landscaped military cemetery on a hillside south of Florence with the flag flying over him that Henning had always called "The Old Girl."

Belinoro lay around the bend, a great cluster of houses drowsing in the heat of the siesta hour with its main cobblestoned street yawning empty, as Tom strode along, trying to conjure up a mental overlay which would reveal how much of the wartime Belinoro remained and how much was new. Despite the silence of the deserted streets, he had the uncomfortable, not unfamiliar feeling that several pairs of eyes were watching his slow, burdened march. In Italy, no matter what time of day, whether in the heart of Rome or on the most remote cliff of the Dolomites, invisible and curious eyes were inevitably watching. One simply had to accept the fact that in Italy one was rarely ever alone and unobserved. Belinoro was no exception, and he wondered uneasily why this fact should trouble him now.

Just before he reached the slightly sloping open rectangle that was the main piazza of the village, with the *farmacia* of Old Tonio Passaglia in one corner, he realized all at once that the invisible eyes were not merely curious; the silence was oppressive, the very air hostile and sullen. As he stepped onto the stone stoop of the pharmacy door, he turned to look at the empty little square with its shuttered windows, its obelisk to the war dead, and its handful of struggling shade trees. A rustle of movement caught his eye. On the far side, almost obscured by the obelisk, two small Fiats huddled against a building front, together with the little scooter, now on its stand. Beside the scooter stood its flashy driver, the man who had passed Tom in the dust, his orange dust visor now pushed up over his forehead. He was pointing at Tom and speaking to a little fair-haired man with a snub nose and a nondescript suit with tieless shirt unbuttoned. A large red-lettered sign above the heads of the two men advertised the nature of the premises directly behind them: "PARTITO COMUNISTA ITALIANO," it read, and in smaller letters, "Sezione di Belinoro-Altomonte." *That* had not been there in 1944.

He was almost certain that the pharmacy door would be locked during the siesta hour, and it was almost with a sense of shock that he leaned against it and it swung open. He stepped in and felt for the well-remembered steps leading into the dimness of the store, nose assailed by a hundred obscure and venerable herb and medicine smells.

Antonella's dark head was bent over a medical catalogue spread open on the counter and, at the clang of the bells on the door, she looked up seeking to identify the silhouetted figure. Tom lowered his suitcase and carried it slowly down the three stone steps, the cool air of the pharmacy a balm to his sweat-beaded face. Now that he was here, a tightness grasped him at the chest and throat. He had come here again because it had seemed such a natural and necessary thing to do after all that had happened. But facing her again here in the dim pharmacy with its smells and its memories, his body trembled involuntarily as if in a sudden chill.

In the half-year that had passed, Antonella had thinned considerably and the once full face had hollowed, stamping the high soft cheekbones and the great eyes with a near-gauntness and projecting the straight long nose to an uncompromising prominence. Under the firm, cleft Passaglia chin, the hint of chubbiness had vanished, and the remnants of a prison pallor were reflected in the unnatural whiteness of her features. It was immediately clear to him that if the long months had been unkind for him, they had been brutal for her.

"You!" she breathed, involuntarily using the familiar *tu*. He remembered that a dozen years ago she had used only the *tu*.

"Yes," he answered, feeling lumpish and gauche. "You would not see me before or during the trial and when you were released you departed from Rome without even a telephone call. So I had to come and see you."

"You!" She stared at him across the counter as at a ghost. Then she flew around the counter at him, and for a split second he thought she was going to hurl herself at him with fists and curses. He reached out almost defensively with both his grimy hands. She grasped them and shook them with both of hers, and then she pulled him to her and kissed him warmly on each cheek as the enormous eyes welled with silent tears that coursed down her cheeks.

Tom held her briefly to him and felt her soft hair against his lips, knowing it was a moment and a caress that had to be savored. Then they both slowly moved away and he said, looking at her,

"They do not feed one well in Roman prisons."

She shook her head before answering.

"No, I cannot complain about the prison or the food. They were actually very kind to me, prisoners and guards alike. It was just that I could not eat." Her eyes dropped to the floor. "When one kills another human being, and the memory of him lying dead at one's feet glows like an illuminated photograph before one's eyes night and day, there is not much room for appetite. There is no room for anything, and that is why I could not bear to see you or talk to you or to anyone while I was in Mantellate."

"I wanted to kill him myself."

She nodded, and a smile appeared hesitantly, as if she had almost forgotten how.

"I know this. They told me you tried. I am glad you failed. It would have gone more harshly for you had you accomplished it, and besides it was I who had to repay him." In a much lower voice, she added, "They all know, the judges, that the real punishment is the one I carry around with me until the day I die: the sin of taking the life of another."

"He was a swine!" Tom burst out. "A butcher. He lived like one and he died like one!"

She looked up at him with haunted eyes.

"Yes, caro, he was perhaps that. But he was also a living person. I know what it is to kill a human being. Do you?"

Their eyes locked and his finally lowered.

"No. I have done many things but I have not ever killed a man."

She squeezed one of his hands.

"I am glad for you, Tommaso." Then, noting the drying sweat on his forehead and cheeks and the deep stains under the arms and on the front of his shirt, she clapped her hands in apology like a forgetful schoolgirl.

"How stupid of me!" she exclaimed. "You have been walking in this heat and with that heavy suitcase! Please sit down and rest; let me get you a glass of wine. You will certainly stay for supper. What are your plans? Where . . ."

He smiled at the sudden rush of proprieties and hospitality with which the Italian seeks to drown the visitor.

"*Piano piano*, Dottoressa. I simply came up here to see how you were, and to finish our conversation of seven months ago."

The great eyes peered inquiringly at him, and he nodded at her as if she had actually asked the question.

"Yes, when you left on the train to Rieti, I said 'Ciao.' Now I come to say 'Addio.' The nightmare is over, for me at least. The dead have been avenged." The pharmacy was still as a tomb.

"I am glad for you, Tommaso," she said.

"And you?" His face hardened with the recollection of the hostile men standing across the square under the hammer and sickle. "Where do you stand with this Party of yours now?"

"I tore up my Party card in Rome and left the pieces in the

Party headquarters on the Botteghe Oscure," she answered matter-of-factly. "When I returned here three weeks ago, I resigned my post as mayoress. Now I am pharmacist in the Farmacia Passaglia as my father and grandfather were before me." She paused and the hurt glittered in her eyes. "The Party tried to cancel my pharmacist's license but the authorities would not permit it. Now the Party here does to me what we did to poor Peppino Deruta before he died: it ignores me. None of them speaks to me. They pass me on the street and they do not see me. When I stop in the market place, those farmers and tradespeople who were old comrades simply turn their backs on me. They say I betrayed them and that I should not have killed Il Duro."

She gave a short bitter laugh.

"You know, Tommaso, at the end of the war the non-Communists here scorned me because I, a Passaglia, betrayed the old way, renouncing the Christian traditions of my family by joining the Communists. They would pass me in silence or make the horn sign with their fingers to ward off my evil eye. Then I didn't care, because I had the warmth and friendship of my Party comrades."

The wide mouth curled in a bitter caricature of a smile.

"Now *both* groups, Communist and anti-Communist, pass me by." Her slightly staring eyes looked up at him, brimming but defiant. "And so, I live most of the time in a world of silence, surely the worst of hells for an Italian."

Were it not for a certain vibrato in her voice, she might have been relating an amusing story from the past.

"Why do you stay here? Why don't you move elsewhere: Bologna, Rimini, Rome? A licensed pharmacist can always find work anywhere."

Her eyes widened even larger with genuine surprise.

"Leave Belinoro? My home? Of course not! Let them erect their wall of silence. I have many things to do. I have an orphange at Altomonte to worry about. Two old maiden aunts in Forlì need my visits there once a week. I own a fruit orchard and grazing land just off the Via Emilia which I look after together with a tenant family." And the faintest of self-conscious grins rippled the somber face. "Every month my defense lawyer drives up from Ancona and takes lunch with me. He says I am *formidabile*. So you see, the wall of silence has holes in it after all."

He listened to her, his eyes reflecting his admiration.

"And you are willing to do this—alone? Without anyone?"

"I had a husband once," she murmured. "You remember

262

him well: my Fausto, a good one, a sweet rock of a man. It was only for a short time but it will have to last." Up came the straight nose and the Passaglia chin. "There have been a good number in the past few years who wanted to marry the widowed daughter of Tonio Passaglia but they were either terribly old, or quite ugly, or they coveted the Passaglia pharmacy or the Passaglia land. As for the others, they brought pity, not love. I cannot take either pity or greed to bed with me. Not after Fausto. Better alone."

There was nothing he could add to that. He looked slowly around him.

"I had pictured this place a hundred times in my mind since I left here," he spoke half to himself. "Very little has changed. A dozen times I passed this area along the Via Emilia, looking up in this direction but never could I bring myself to turn off and come back here. I left here in a brutal moment and I could never return. I had to wipe it away. Then with Spartaco dead, I had to come back and stand here again. Do you understand?"

"I understand," Antonella said.

He looked into the pitying eyes and he knew what she saw: the frayed, sweat-drenched shirt, his stubbling beard powdered with the dust of the Belinoro road, his haggard face and eyes and graying temples. But he had come too far and had waited too long to turn and walk away now, without saying what lay on his tongue like lead.

"It will mean nothing to the dead," he said in his soft, American-tinged Italian, "but it must be said. Your Peppino Deruta flatly warned me not to accompany the Passaglia band because, as he said, he had definite knowledge that a German ambush was being prepared in the area. If it had been anyone but Peppino, I would have paid little attention, because we received such warnings all the time. With Peppino it was different. So I met immediately with your father and Major Dixon and told them that we must cancel the mission for that night."

She held his eyes steadily and nodded.

"I remember," she said. "You met in the back room behind the pharmacy. There was a loud argument."

"A very bitter argument," Tom agreed, looking at her as one survivor of a shipwreck stares at another. "Major Dixon would not cancel the mission. He said it was essential to the winning of the war, that he had received a message from Allied Headquarters in Caserta to do everything to cut German communications and supply lines to the south where a great battle was raging. I tried to make him understand that the information concerning a German ambush was so reliable that it would be almost suicide to go out that night to destroy the bridge."

"What did my father say?" Antonella asked him, almost timidly.

"He said nothing; just sat there smoking his pipe and listening. Finally, my major said to me, 'I order you to accompany the Passaglia group tonight and see that the bridge gets blown,' and I lost my head completely. I turned to your father and told him not to go out, to cancel the mission for that night. The major was beside himself with rage. He called in the radio operator, whom you remember, Sergeant di Tullio, and pointed to me, saying, 'Sergeant, I want you to testify at any court-martial that I am placing Lieutenant Linden under arrest for disobeying a direct order of his commanding officer and for misconduct in the face of the enemy.' " Tom's lips held a lopsided grin for a moment.

"Di Tullio didn't forget a word at the court-martial."

Her white face glowed in the dimly-lit pharmacy like a wraith's. Apart from the inquiring eyes focused steadily on his, she was motionless.

"When your Peppino came to warn me of the ambush," Tom went on in a spent voice, "I had told him that I would certainly not permit your father and his group to go on the mission that night. But the Passaglias did go out, and Major Dixon with them, and Peppino had to watch the murder of his friends. When the hour of the mission's departure from Belinoro arrived, I decided to join them anyway. But Sergeant di Tullio sat there with his gun trained on me and told me he had orders from Major Dixon to blow my head off if I moved. So I sat there until we heard the sound of the ambush . . ." His voice broke and he covered his bowed head with his hands.

Antonella placed her hands gently atop his.

"They are all dead, Tommaso, all of them. My family, the Belinoro partisans, Peppino, and now Spartaco. They are all dead and buried, and it is useless to keep plunging the knife into one's own heart."

"But why did he ignore such a warning?" Tom railed, inconsolable. "Why did your father listen to him?"

"Because he was a Passaglia, Tommaso. We are a stubborn, proud lot, and I could not imagine that he would show the same reasonable fear you did, or think of disappointing the Major Dixon he so admired."

Something of the knotted sorrow faded from his face and he stood in the pharmacy holding her fingers as if deriving warmth from them.

"What about Peppino Deruta?" he asked, at last. "Do you forgive him?"

"The question is, Tommaso: Will he ever forgive me?"

"We would have made quite a pair, Peppino and I," he said. "Each of us smelled very bad to those whom we cared about at all."

"It is useless," she again insisted gently. "You may have made a mistake and paid dearly. So did the major and my father; they and all who were with them paid. I made my mistakes and I am paying for mine, no?" It was the saddest smile he had ever seen.

She pointed to a spot high on the pharmacy wall where a rough oval hole had been chipped open in the masonry.

"Do you remember a little Madonna who used to be affixed up there, with a tiny electric light burning always?"

He followed her pointed finger and nodded.

"What happened to it?"

"The Party made me take it down over a year ago as a test of my Communist discipline. I obeyed them. But now I am having it reinstalled. One of Padre Tiberio's little men has installed the wiring. The Madonna and the light bulb will be ready this evening, and then Don Tiberio will bless it. It is the least I can do for him."

She shook her head admiringly.

"You have no idea how that old priest has struggled for my soul!"

A little vein near Tom's right eye flickered spasmodically like a live thing under the skin, and he wiped his hands on his trouser legs nervously. The gesture did not escape her.

"What is it, Tommaso? Are you well?"

"Yes," he told her hurriedly. "I am well. But I really must go."

"Go where?" she asked in surprise.

"I really don't know," he said rapidly, "but I suddenly feel that I cannot stay here. I see you standing here, cast out by your own, a stranger in your own village. This is something else that I have brought about, an additional misery which started with me thirteen years ago."

"You have the Anglo-Saxon bad conscience about everything," she said with her thin face diffused in a sad humor. "Let me assure you that it was as much Padre Tiberio and the words of Peppino Deruta on his deathbed that brought

265

me to where I am this moment as anything you did. Otherwise, I would still be Comrade Antonella, the busy Communist mayoress of Belinoro, and the truth would have remained buried forever."

"I must go," he said, his voice revealing the pain.

"To Rome?"

"No, not Rome. Rome and I are tired of each other after so many years, like a bad marriage. I lived a foolish life there. *Basta.*"

"Where, then?"

"Until I came here, I did not know. Now I think I do. If *you* can do what you did, I can try to do as well. I shall return to my birthplace which I left in youth and honor fourteen years ago and to which I shall return a graying scoundrel."

"Is it so hard to return, Tommaso? Do they place you in *confino?* Are you persecuted by the authorities because you were degraded by a court-martial?"

"No, *cara,* they do not touch the body. One is free, one can earn a living, one can marry, beget children, buy a home, own a car. But it is always there. Once dishonored by decision of an American court, one lives a kind of half-life. Whenever you fill out a questionnaire form for employment, whenever you seek government employment, whenever you desire to hold the humblest public post in the community, the record of dishonor rises like a specter to haunt you. Mine will be a life somewhat like yours: shunned, but in a subtle insidious way. It rubs off on your family, your children, your friends."

"Then why return? Why not stay in Europe, in Italy . . . here?"

She was almost touching him now, standing very close, smelling his man's sweat and looking up at his eyes which were dark and determined.

"Because I know something now that I did not know before, and for this I thank you. What you did, your present sacrifice, can only be repaid by an act similar in intent if not in courage. And so I shall repay you in that manner. I will be what your Padre Tiberio used to call an act of expiation." He looked at his watch, and turned for his suitcase, but she grasped his arm.

"He would call it an act of faith. But there is no reason to leave today, is there?" she asked pleadingly.

"None, except that I have nothing more here to say or do, except to visit the cemetery before I leave."

He was looking away from her but she turned his head back toward her with one gentle hand, and there for a brief moment was the girl-wife, painfully coveted, that was once Antonella Cipriani, Fausto's bride.

"You loved me once, Tommaso, in that brutal moment of the war, and you kissed me in Rome just before I . . . found Spartaco. Do I mean nothing to you now, Tommaso?"

"You mean very much to me now, more than I can tell you."

"Then why don't you stay, until tomorrow at least. Padre Tiberio would very much want to see you. He loves to talk about the war. So would a few others who would remember you and who are still my friends."

He did not resist her touching hands but he looked somberly into her clear brown eyes, no longer tense or staring now; his glance wandered to the straight, slightly overlong nose, to the slight lines that now crinkled at the edges of the eyes, and he reminded her,

"You said in Rome that you would not bed with pity. I can't even remain in the same house with it."

"And if I told you it was kindness and from the heart, and not pity?"

The two bells on the pharmacy door jangled violently as a round plump old figure pushed spryly through it. Father Tiberio took off his beret and slapped the dust from it vigorously against the side of his equally dusty cassock.

"*Buona sera*, Dottoressa!" he called in his thin, reedy voice. "I was pedaling through the piazza and saw nothing but black frowns from Little Lenin over there and his minuscule demons. Anything that can dishearten that group of the Damned means certain good news for me, and I stopped to . . ."

Tom turned to face him with a strained and embarrassed smile.

"Tenente Tommaso, after all these years!" the old priest exclaimed after a long moment of squinting surprise, and he clumped down the stairs in his heavy boots with the cautious speed of the very old. He embraced Tom in a restrained bear hug, and stepped back to look at him.

"*Santo Cielo*, how *sciupato* you are!" he grumbled. "Thin, dusty, sweaty, tired!"

He turned indignantly to Antonella.

"Is this the way a Passaglia treats a guest, and especially one such as Tenente Tommaso! He looks as though he had been dragged through the dust all the way from Milano!"

"He came only briefly. He desires to leave," Antonella answered him, a tremolo of anxiety betraying her calm reply.

"Leave? Without even seeing his benefactor, Don Tiberio, a servant of Christ who had to sit and listen to this Protestant puppy yap about the Albigensian heresy and the sins of the Inquisition for weeks on end in the cellar of my own church? Impossible! Impossible, I tell you! He must stay at least overnight! I insist! As my guest in the rectory."

He turned brightly to Antonella and to Tom and back again and the broad flat nose seemed to have an antenna quality as it probed the emotional intensity of the room.

"Where is your car, Tenente Tommaso? We shall drive to my quarters with your bags."

His energetic confidence that all Americans had automobiles nudged an involuntary grin out of Tom.

"I am sorry, Padre Tiberio, but I have no car. I walked up here from the National Highway. And I really must go, after I stop off at the cemetery for a moment."

Father Tiberio whirled to look at Antonella. The rheumy old eyes peered at her intently for a long moment and then he turned his grizzled head to Tom and his voice dropped to a throaty imploring note.

"Dear Lieutenant Tommaso," he said in words of flat incontrovertibility, "we have so much to talk about, I must insist that you stay with me for the night."

Tom grasped the heavy black cassock where the tough old shoulders sloped into still strong if stringy arms, as if he were about to embrace him.

"Padre Tiberio, I will tell you without mincing words, as the Romagnoles like to speak, that I am no longer a lieutenant; I am a *poveraccio*, a disgraced American who has not had the courage to return to his country, a man without a future."

The old priest met his level glance quizzically.

"You tell me little that is new, Tenente," he finally said in a voice that was a soft singing lilt of the region. "Antonella has told me about you and your life in Rome." He reached up to give the taller young man a benevolent whack on the shoulder. "Your soul is sick. A few days up here in the wholesome hills with sun and fresh air will do you a world of good."

He turned to clamber up the short flight of stairs leading to the street level and as he passed Antonella, he did something he had not done for twelve years; he nipped her cheek gently with his thumb and forefinger.

"In an hour, a horse-drawn *carozza* will arrive to fetch your valise to my house. Be ready," he said in a statement that was a command.

A thought struck him like an unexpected arrow, and he whirled around halfway up the stairs, to stare at the small hole in the pharmacy wall.

"Hasn't that *cretino* Adolfo installed the little electric lamp for the Madonna on that wall yet? Lazy pagans, our Romagnoles; Communists all of them, even the Christians! I'll pedal by his shop and give him a few ecclesiastical words, be assured of that!"

At the top of the stairs, he cut the air with a lightning sign of the cross and looked down on them for a moment.

"*Ebbeh,* quite a pair, you two," he said in a curiously reflective voice. "But while neither of you runs any risk of beatification, much can be done." He rubbed his old hands briefly and departed with a jangle of the door bells. As he pulled his bicycle away from the wall of the Passaglia house, he lifted his eyes to the bright rim of autumn sky and gave brief silent thanks to God who again had moved in His inscrutable way to bring this wretched bruised young man, barely a *cristiano,* back to this place and who would help him, Don Tiberio, to bring God back into the heart of Antonella Passaglia. His old heart pounded with elation. God and love could save Antonella; God and love. He pedaled slowly past the Communist quartet slouched in their straw-bottomed chairs in the shade of the modest *galleria* on the other side of the piazza and chuckled aloud at their hostile stare.

"*Disgraziati!*" he hurled at them at the last possible moment to cut off the inevitable uncomplimentary retort, as he rounded the corner, hunched forward and low over the handles like a racer, out of their sight.

Antonella shook her head with an embarrassed smile as the doorbells clanged with the old priest's departure.

"I'm afraid he misunderstands your presence, Tommaso, just as he persistently misunderstands me. That old optimist now thinks he can somehow play the role of matchmaker and save two souls instead of one. What a stubborn one-track mind he has!"

A dozen images flashed through Tom's mind as he opened his mouth to respond: the kiss and embrace from The Maria which was nothing less than the farewell of mother to son; the yawning jagged void of the years since he had held this woman briefly in his arms, this woman then a weeping, half-crazed girl made widow, with flesh and arms and resisting-yielding lips that remained etched in his memory despite the countless encounters with other flesh and arms and lips since then. His hand involuntarily touched the shirt pocket in which a small crumpled envelope with a Waterstow postmark contained a wedding announcement from a foolishly wise Nancy and from a once foolishly prudent Vinny. To think that two such wildly disparate people should somehow be saved for each other! Somewhere, a law of compensation must be operating overtime.

The great soft almond eyes watched him closely and he could not but be amused at her irked perspicacity of the priest's intentions before he replied, his own glance lifting to meet the challenge of hers.

"A dozen years ago, Don Tiberio would have been right: the souls he wanted to save and bring together needed each other. You know that full well. Now, we would only bring added difficulties for each other. In Belinoro I leave a large torn fragment of my life. In Belinoro there will always be Antonella, and all the memories. But to stay here would be too easy—and too sad." He looked about the cool pharmacy, the crowded shelves of medicines and tablets, the ornate diplomas of other Passaglias, and the little oval hole high in the ceiling waiting for the Madonna to return, and he said almost to himself,

"To take you away from here would be almost as tragic as my staying."

Antonella said, visibly moved,

"Of course you are right. I have my little war to fight here in Belinoro and I must win it with my own Belinorese. And your little war lies with your own people in your own land. There I could not help you at all."

He took one of the small acid-stained hands and he kissed it with warmth and affection.

"But please stay today," Antonella asked almost timidly, her great eyes searching his face, beseeching assent. "I want you to stay as much as does Don Tiberio."

He shrugged in surrender.

"My crowded schedule will, of course, have to be somewhat adjusted. But given the overwhelmingly popular demand, and fearing the fury of Romagnole hospitality scorned, I cannot refuse. Do not envy my stay at the rectory tonight, however, when Don Tiberio finally understands that I didn't come back to Belinoro for purposes of lust or matrimony, or both."

They laughed quietly together and for the first time since he had entered the pharmacy, her soft suffering face relaxed and glowed. Someone again had hurdled the barrier of hostile silence to reach her and Tom was suddenly glad he had been virtually compelled to stay.

She held out a guiding hand, half shy, as a child leads a new acquaintance into his playroom.

"Come," she said, "wash off the sweat and dirt of the journey. Then after a plate of pasta and a glass of wine, we shall walk down to the cemetery and visit . . . for a few moments."

He moved to follow Antonella behind the well-remembered patent medicine counter to the little doorway which led back to the family area of the Passaglias, and a great wave of relief and suffused expectancy rolled over him as he looked down at his feet and realized, as does every outbound passenger at a certain point in his journey, that each step he was taking from this moment was a step at last homeward.